AN UNOFFICIAL GRAPHIC NOVEL FOR MINECRAFTERS

The BATTLE for the DRAGON'S TEMPLE

CARA J. STEVENS

ART BY DAVID NORGREN

SKY PONY PRESS
NEW YORK

To Mom and Dad,
for giving me roots and wings

Copyright © 2016 by Hollan Publishing, Inc.

All rights reserved. No part of this book may be reproduced in any manner without
the express written consent of the publisher, except in the case of brief excerpts in
critical reviews or articles. All inquiries should be addressed to Sky Pony Press, 307
West 36th Street, 11th Floor, New York, NY 10018.

Sky Pony Press books may be purchased in bulk at special discounts for sales
promotion, corporate gifts, fund-raising, or educational purposes. Special editions
can also be created to specifications. For details, contact the Special Sales
Department, Sky Pony Press, 307 West 36th Street, 11th Floor, New York, NY
10018 or info@skyhorsepublishing.com.

Sky Pony® is a registered trademark of Skyhorse Publishing, Inc.®, a Delaware
corporation.

Visit our website at www.skyponypress.com.

10 9 8 7 6 5 4 3 2

Library of Congress Cataloging-in-Publication Data is available on file.

Special thanks to Cara J. Stevens, David Norgren, and Elias Norgren

Cover design by Brian Peterson
Cover illustration credit David Norgren

Print ISBN: 978-1-5107-1798-5
Ebook ISBN: 978-1-5107-1802-9

Printed in China

Editor: Rachel Stark
Designer and Production Manager: Joshua Barnaby

INTRODUCTION

If you have played Minecraft, then you know all about Minecraft worlds. They're made of blocks you can mine: coal, dirt, and sand. In the game, you'll find many different creatures, lands, and villages inhabited by strange villagers with bald heads. The villagers who live there have their own special, magical worlds that are protected by a string of border worlds to stop outsiders from finding them.

When we last left off on the small border world of Xenos, Phoenix had just discovered her true parents were dragon slayers who died in their quest to kill the Ender Dragon.

Our story resumes as Phoenix enjoys quiet time back at home. But her stay is far from peaceful. The elders are not happy about Phoenix's presence in the village, and, unable to stop thinking about her parents' failed quest to kill the dragon, Phoenix wonders whether she should remain at home or set out to finish the deed her parents began long ago.

CHAPTER 1

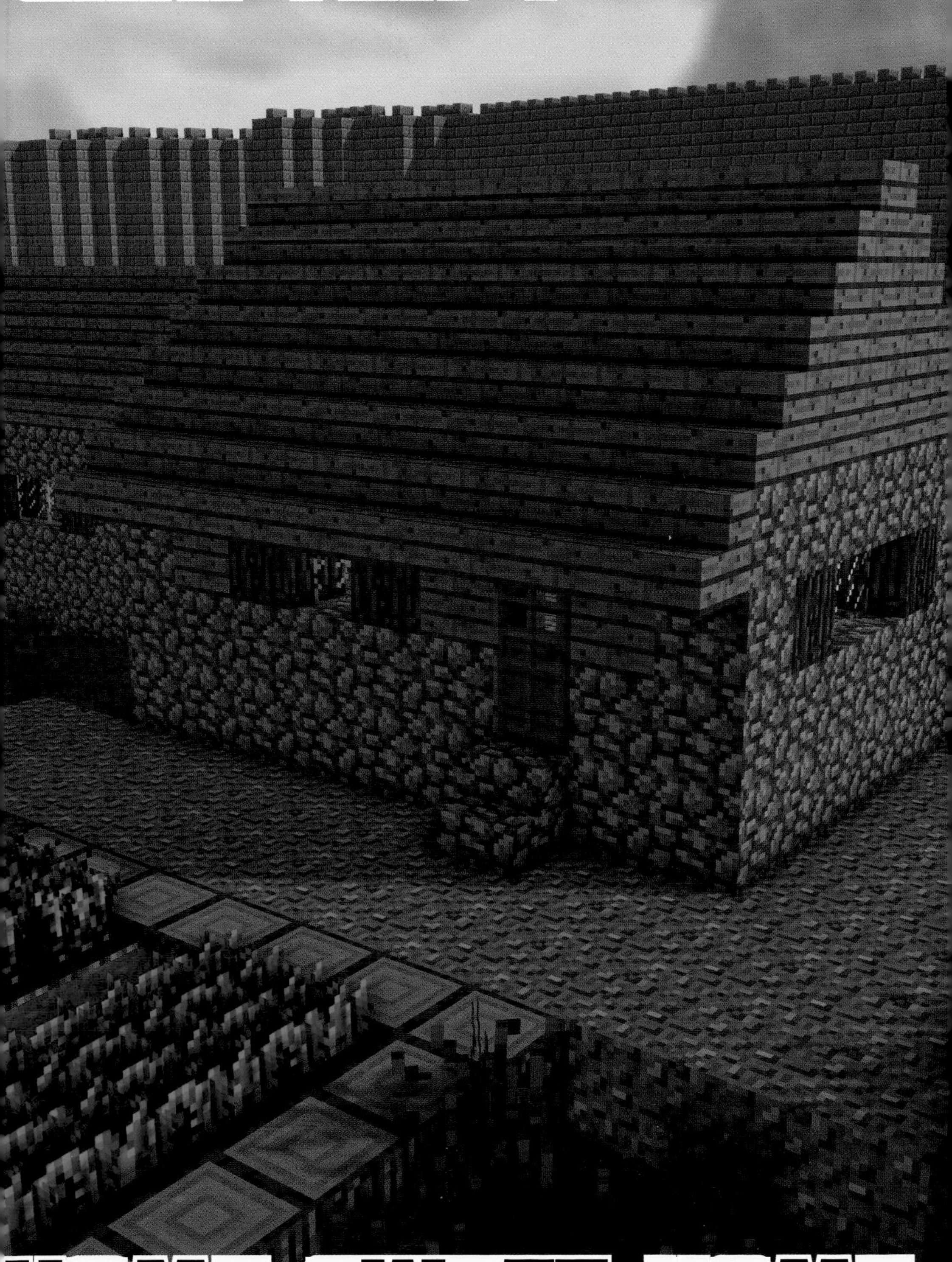

HOME SWEET HOME

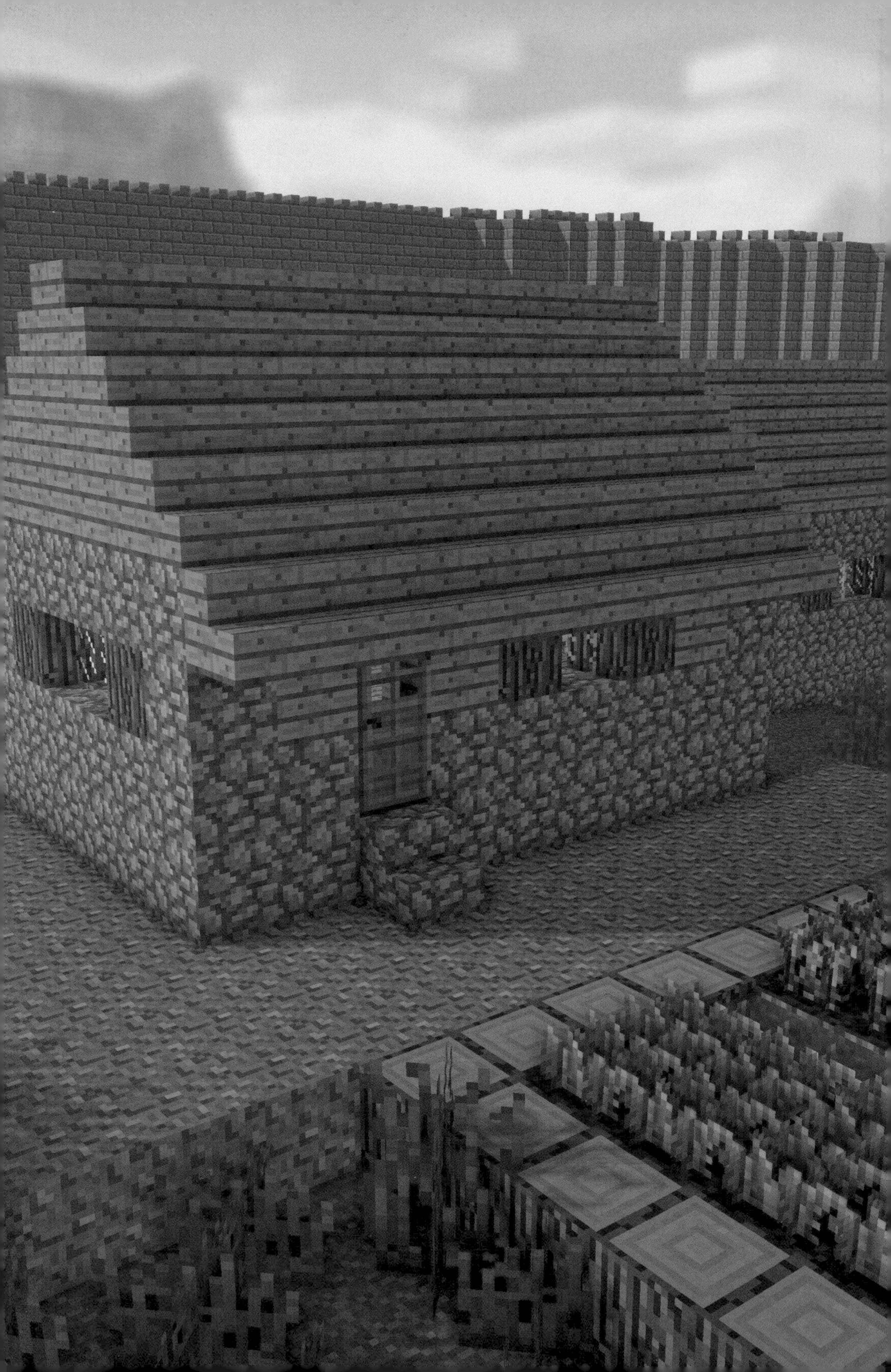

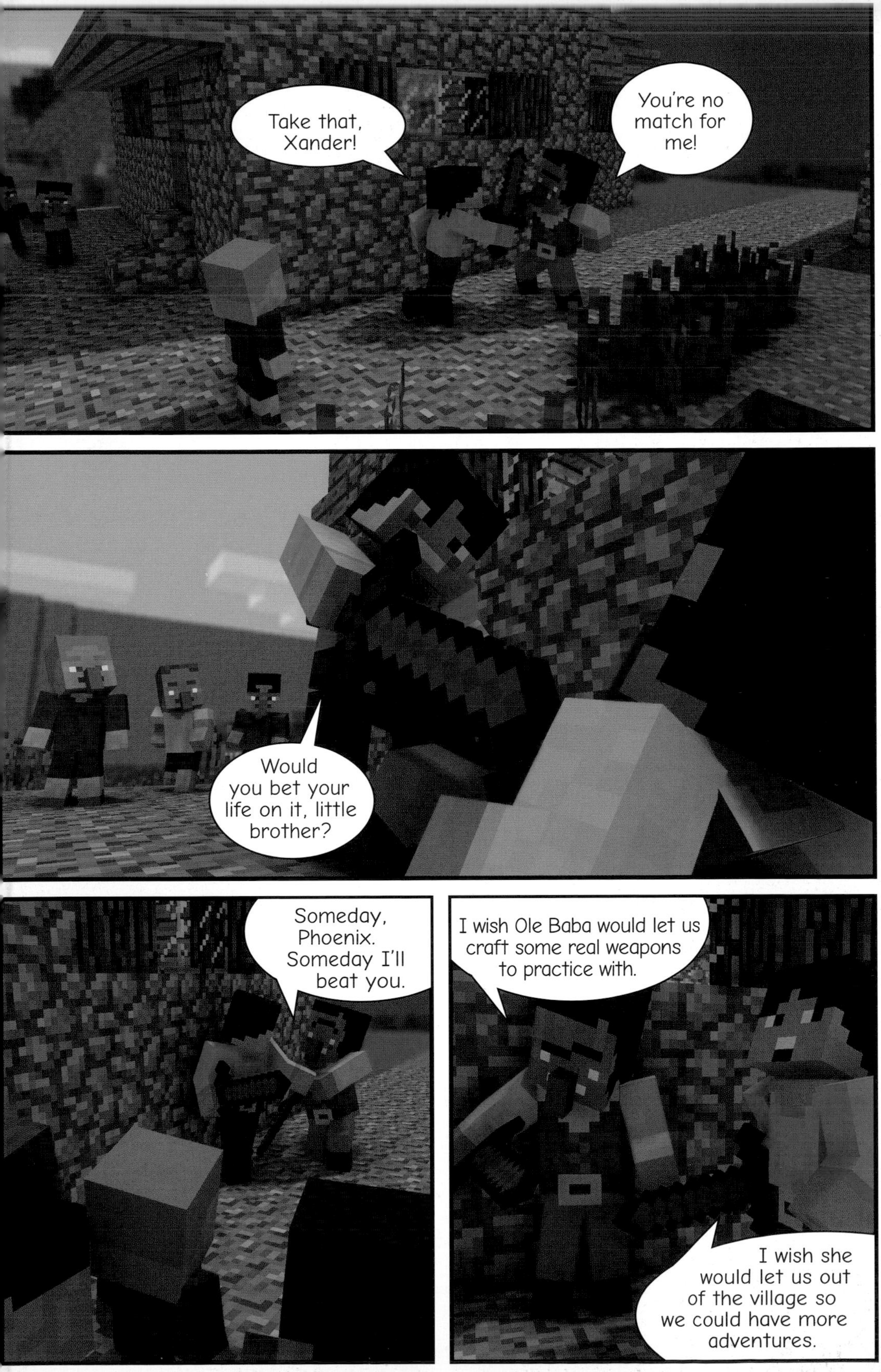
Take that, Xander!
You're no match for me!
Would you bet your life on it, little brother?
Someday, Phoenix. Someday I'll beat you.
I wish Ole Baba would let us craft some real weapons to practice with.
I wish she would let us out of the village so we could have more adventures.

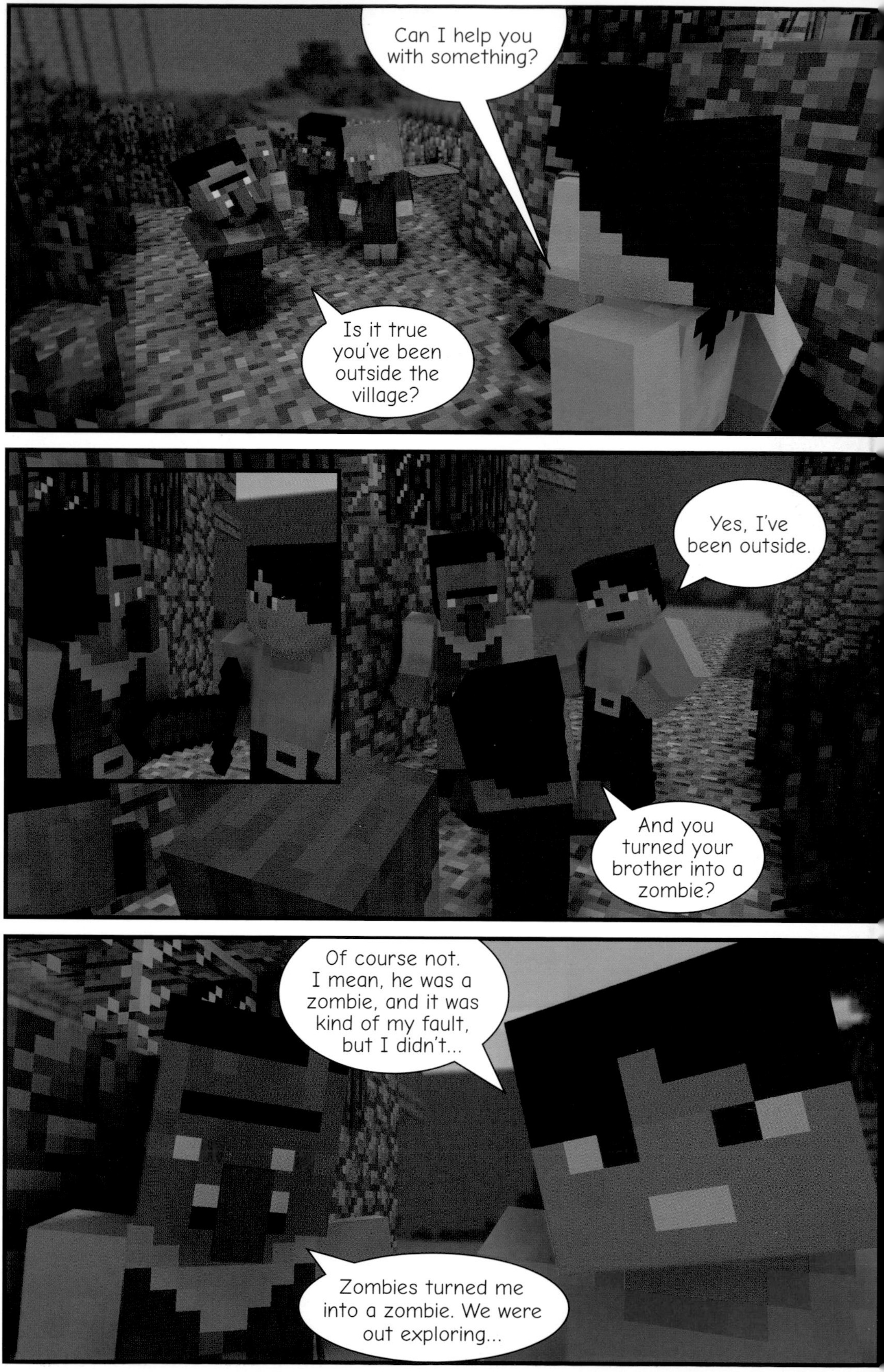
Can I help you with something?
Is it true you've been outside the village?
Yes, I've been outside.
And you turned your brother into a zombie?
Of course not. I mean, he was a zombie, and it was kind of my fault, but I didn't...
Zombies turned me into a zombie. We were out exploring...

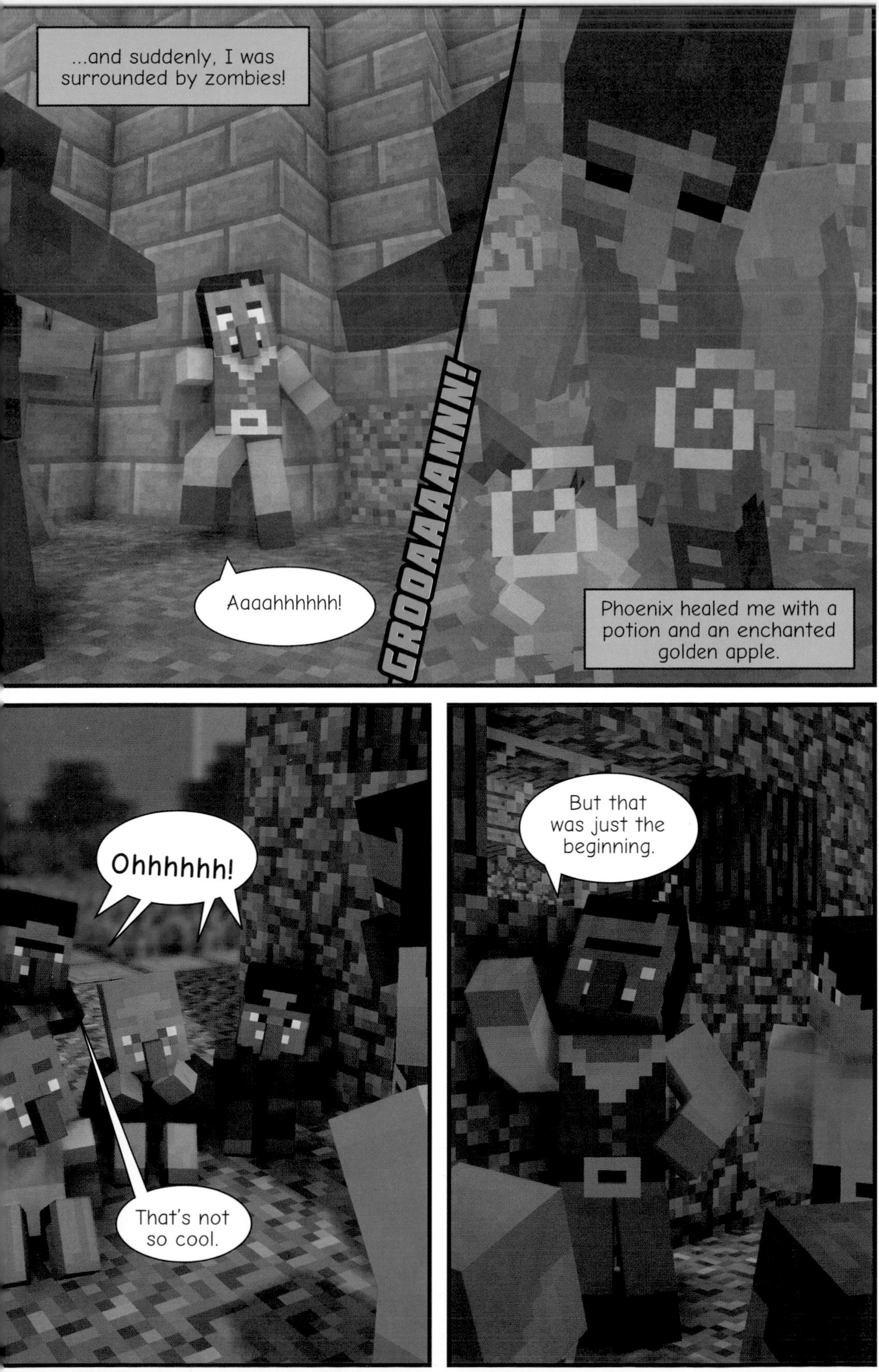
...and suddenly, I was surrounded by zombies!
Aaaahhhhhh!
GROOAAAANN!
Phoenix healed me with a potion and an enchanted golden apple.
Ohhhhhh!
That's not so cool.
But that was just the beginning.

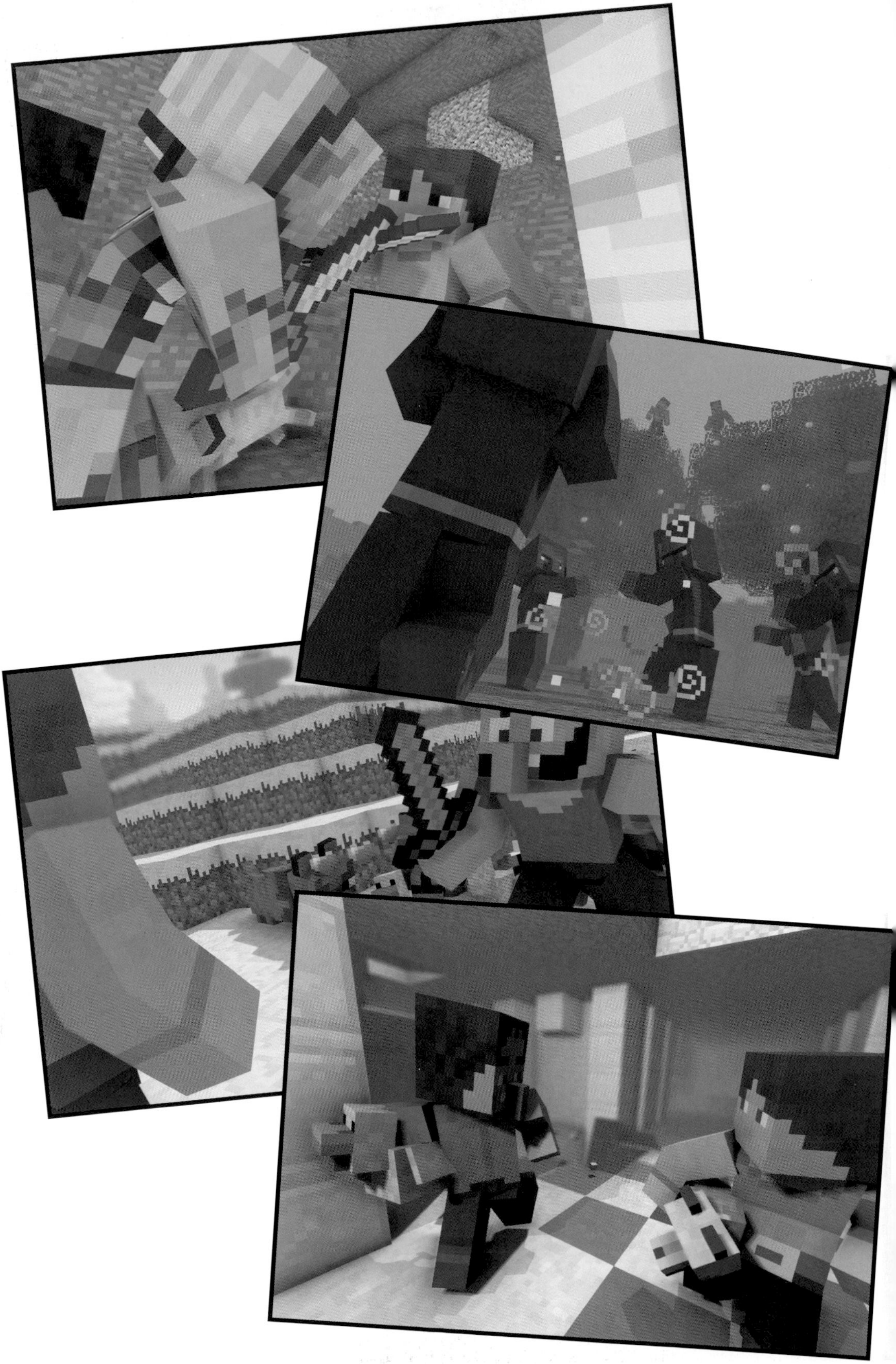

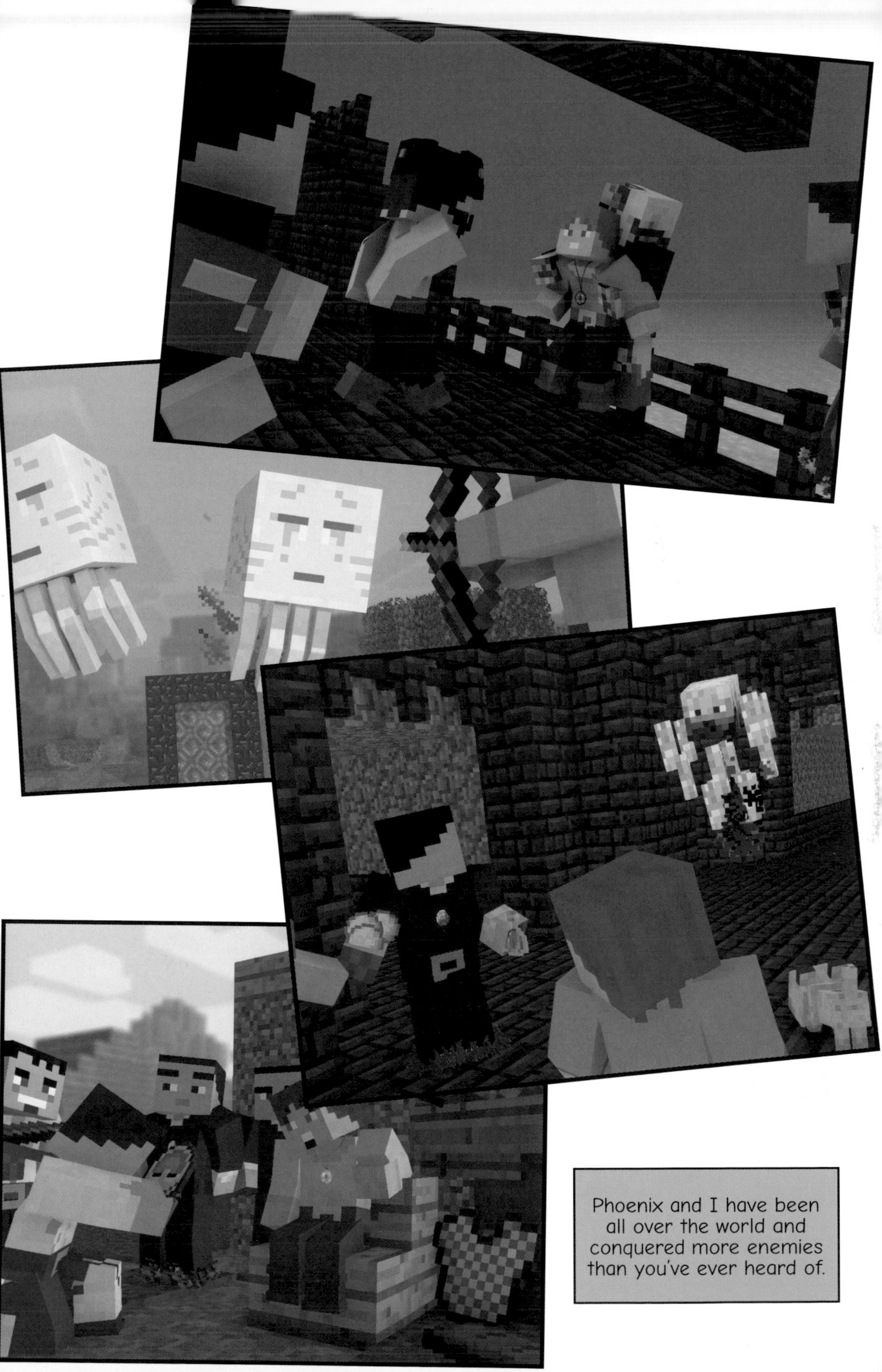
Phoenix and I have been all over the world and conquered more enemies than you've ever heard of.

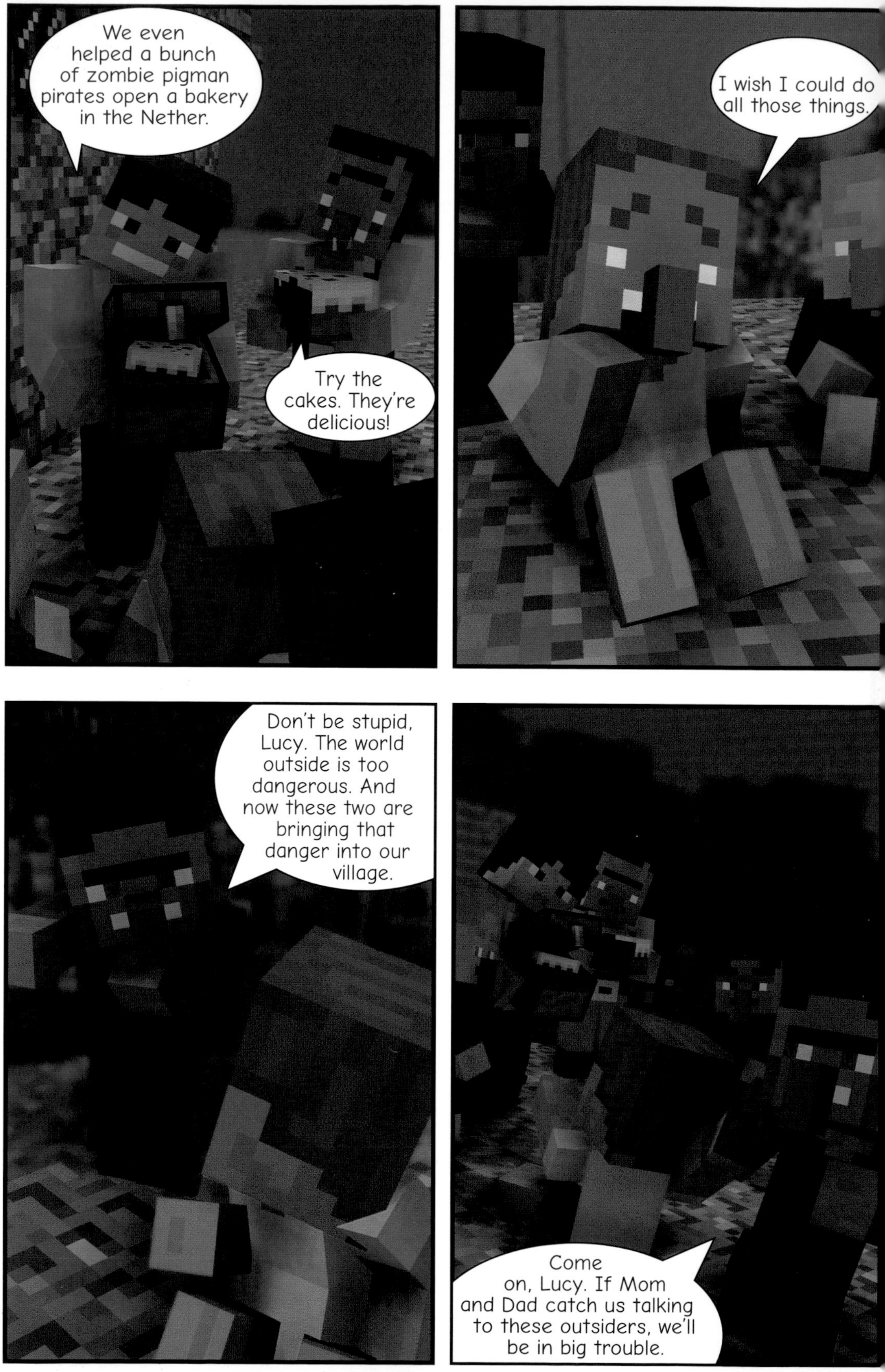
We even helped a bunch of zombie pigman pirates open a bakery in the Nether.
Try the cakes. They're delicious!
I wish I could do all those things.
Don't be stupid, Lucy. The world outside is too dangerous. And now these two are bringing that danger into our village.
Come on, Lucy. If Mom and Dad catch us talking to these outsiders, we'll be in big trouble.

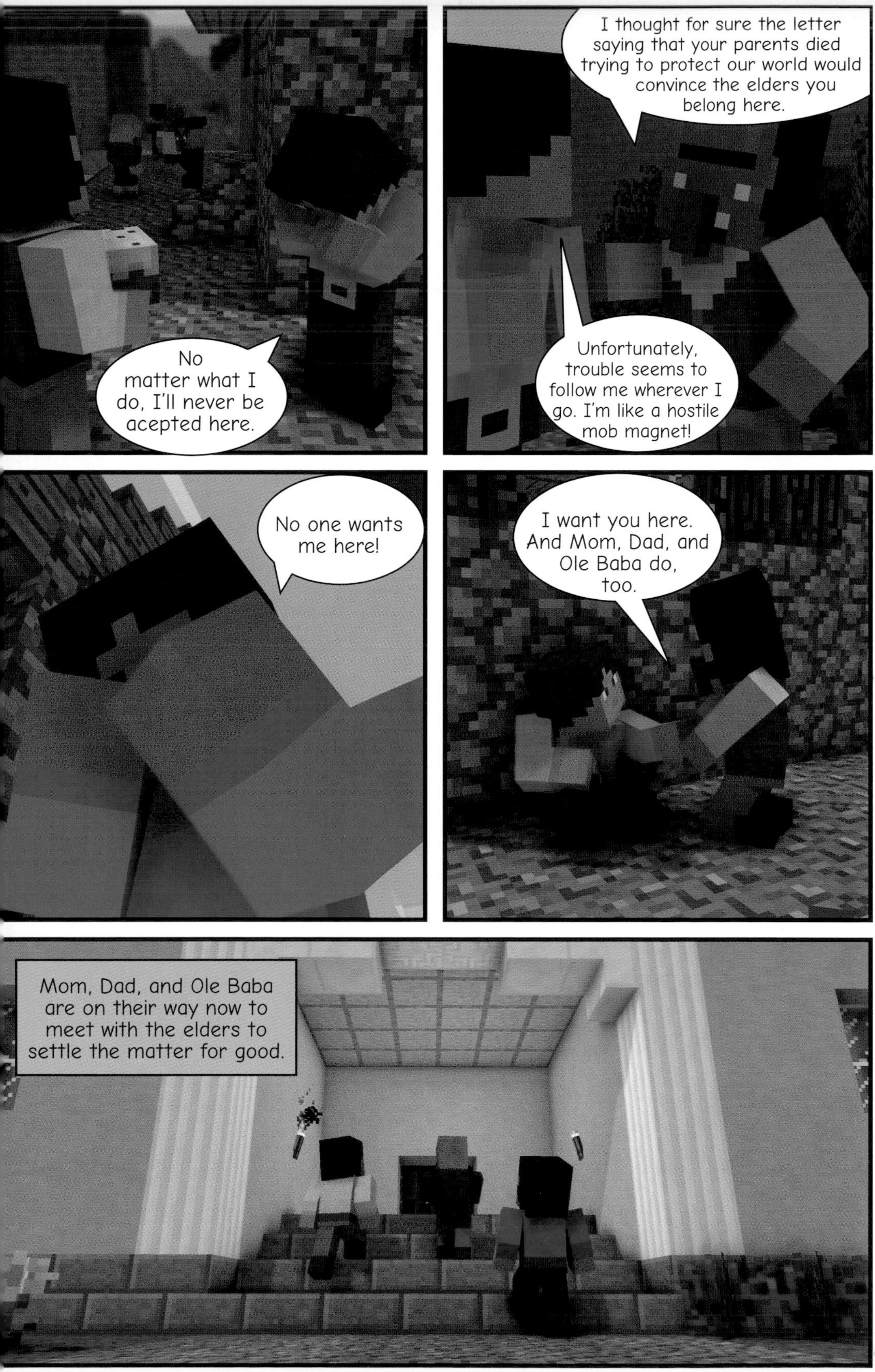
No matter what I do, I'll never be acepted here.
I thought for sure the letter saying that your parents died trying to protect our world would convince the elders you belong here.
Unfortunately, trouble seems to follow me wherever I go. I'm like a hostile mob magnet!
No one wants me here!
I want you here. And Mom, Dad, and Ole Baba do, too.
Mom, Dad, and Ole Baba are on their way now to meet with the elders to settle the matter for good.

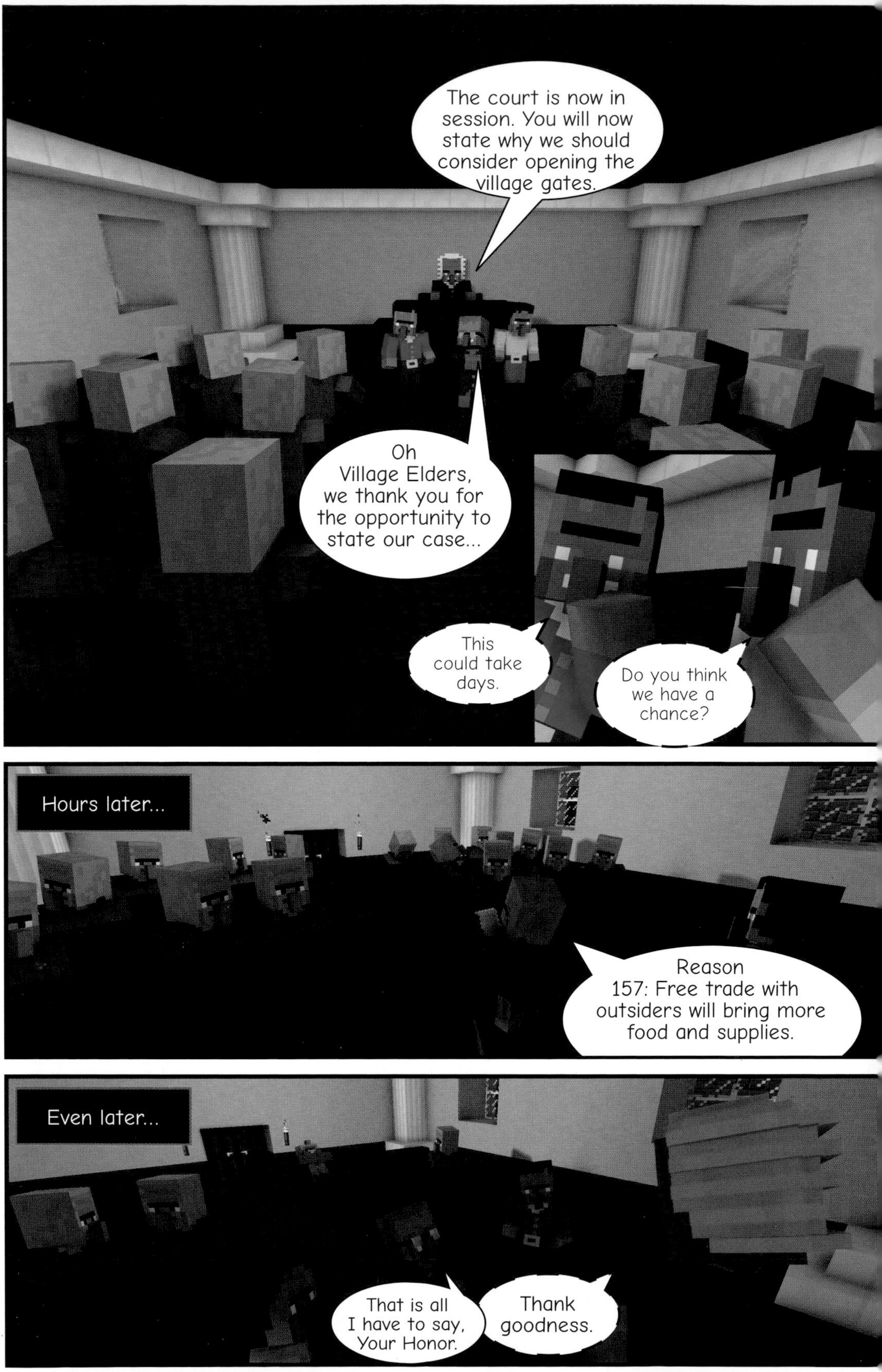
The court is now in session. You will now state why we should consider opening the village gates.
Oh Village Elders, we thank you for the opportunity to state our case...
This could take days.
Do you think we have a chance?
Hours later...
Reason 157: Free trade with outsiders will bring more food and supplies.
Even later...
That is all I have to say, Your Honor.
Thank goodness.

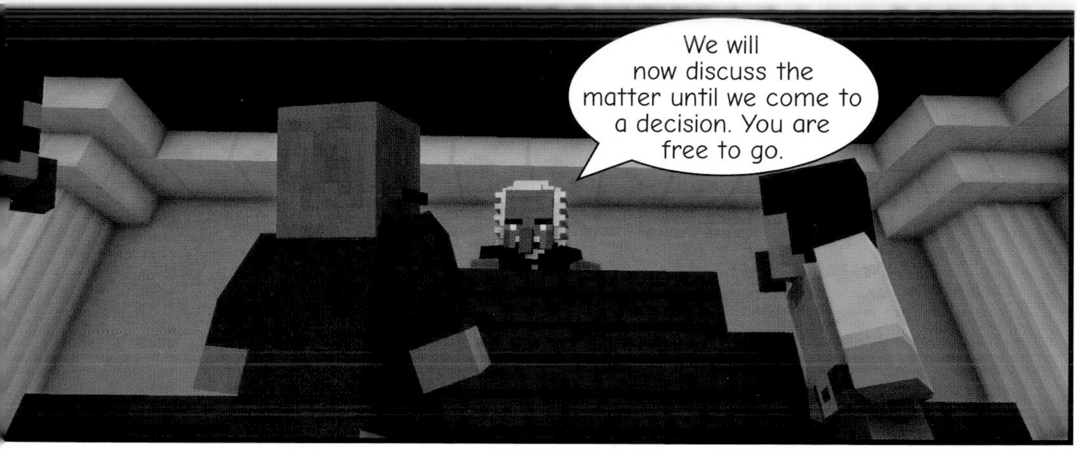
We will now discuss the matter until we come to a decision. You are free to go.

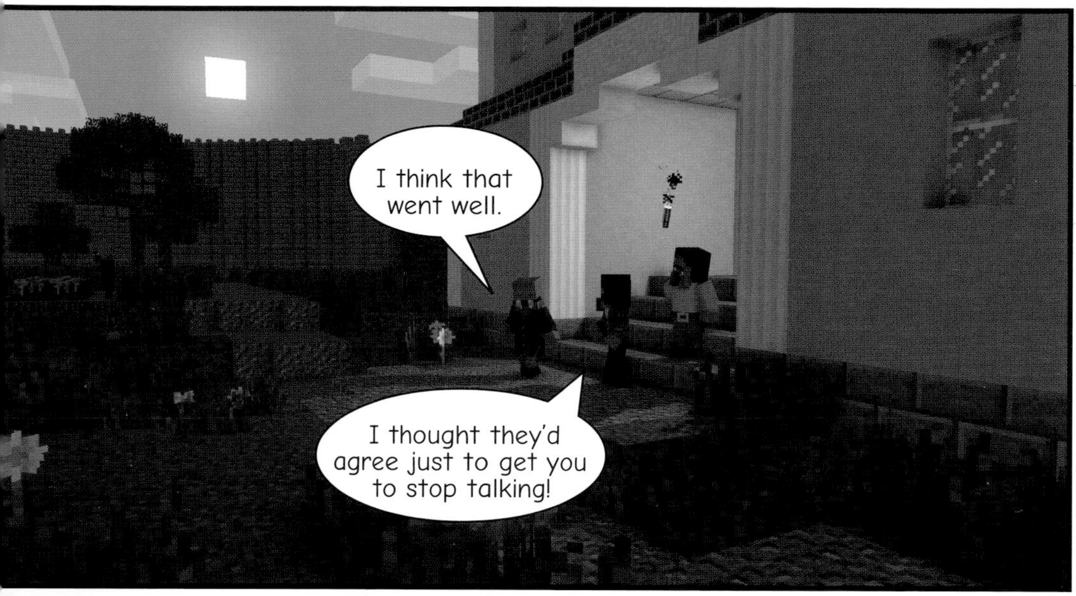
I think that went well.
I thought they'd agree just to get you to stop talking!

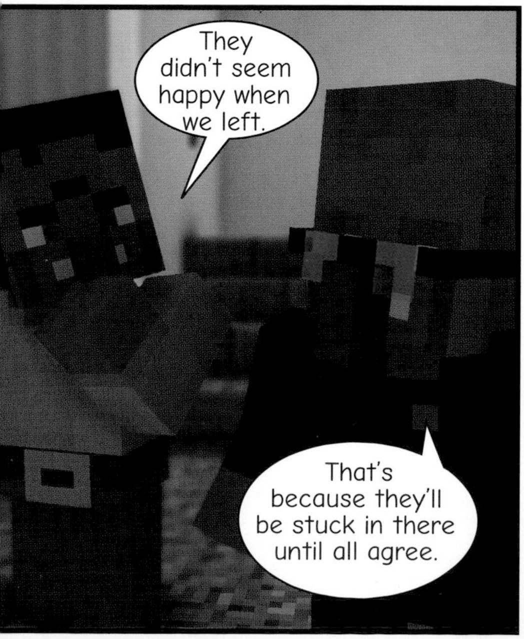
They didn't seem happy when we left.
That's because they'll be stuck in there until all agree.

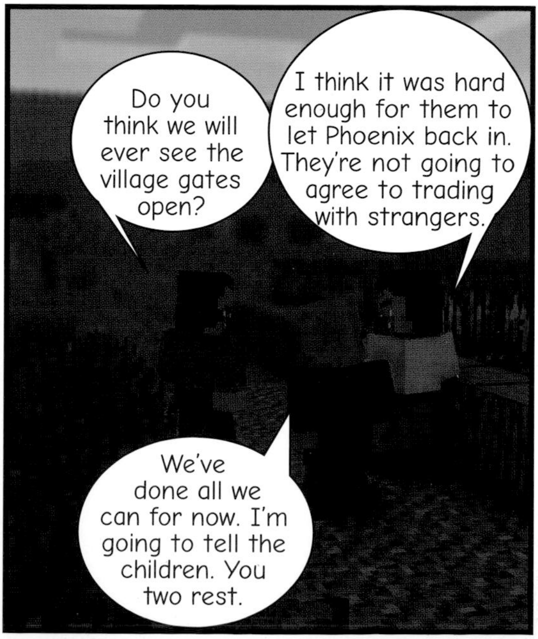
Do you think we will ever see the village gates open?
I think it was hard enough for them to let Phoenix back in. They're not going to agree to trading with strangers.
We've done all we can for now. I'm going to tell the children. You two rest.

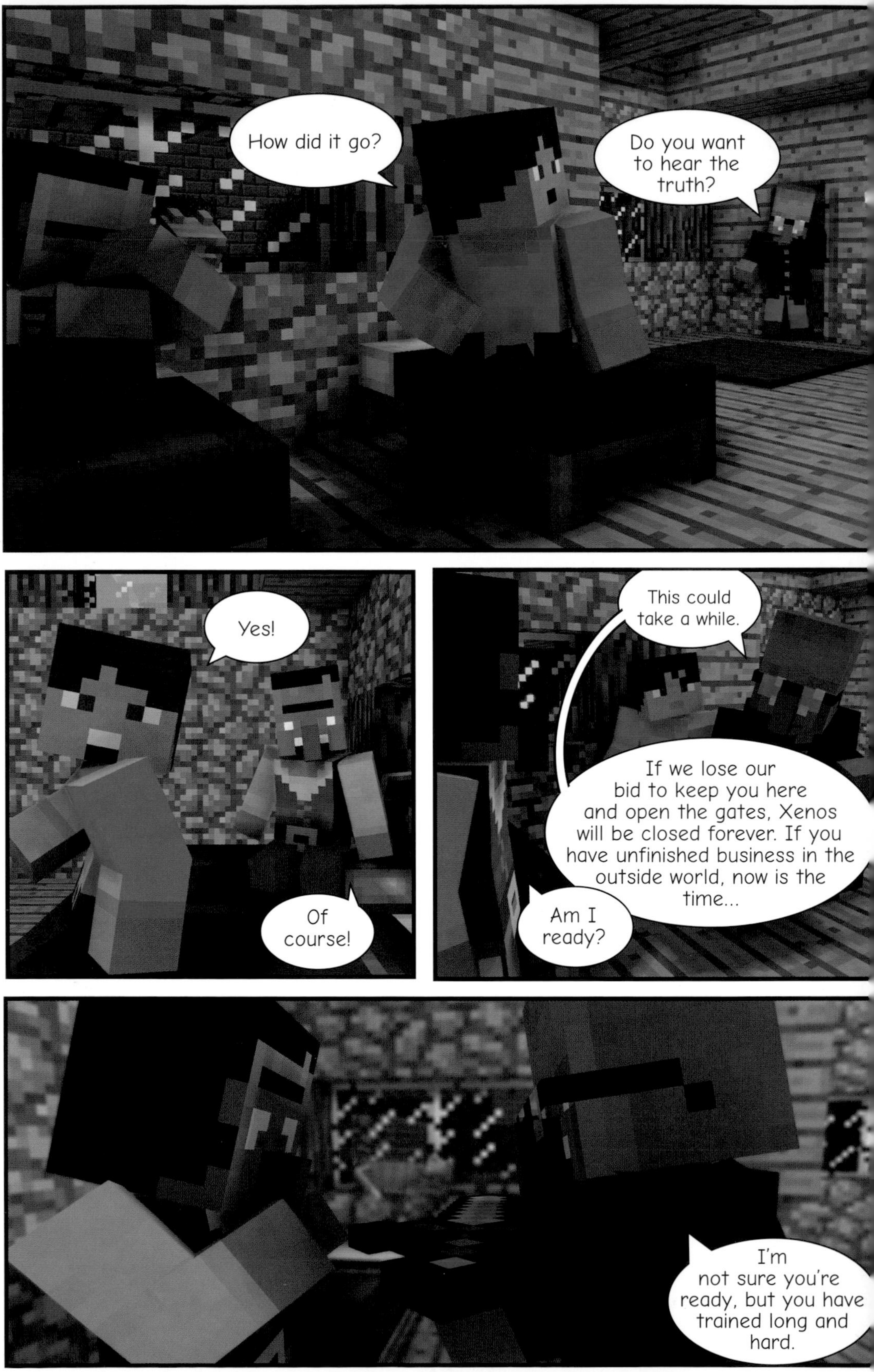
How did it go?
Do you want to hear the truth?
Yes!
Of course!
This could take a while.
If we lose our bid to keep you here and open the gates, Xenos will be closed forever. If you have unfinished business in the outside world, now is the time...
Am I ready?
I'm not sure you're ready, but you have trained long and hard.

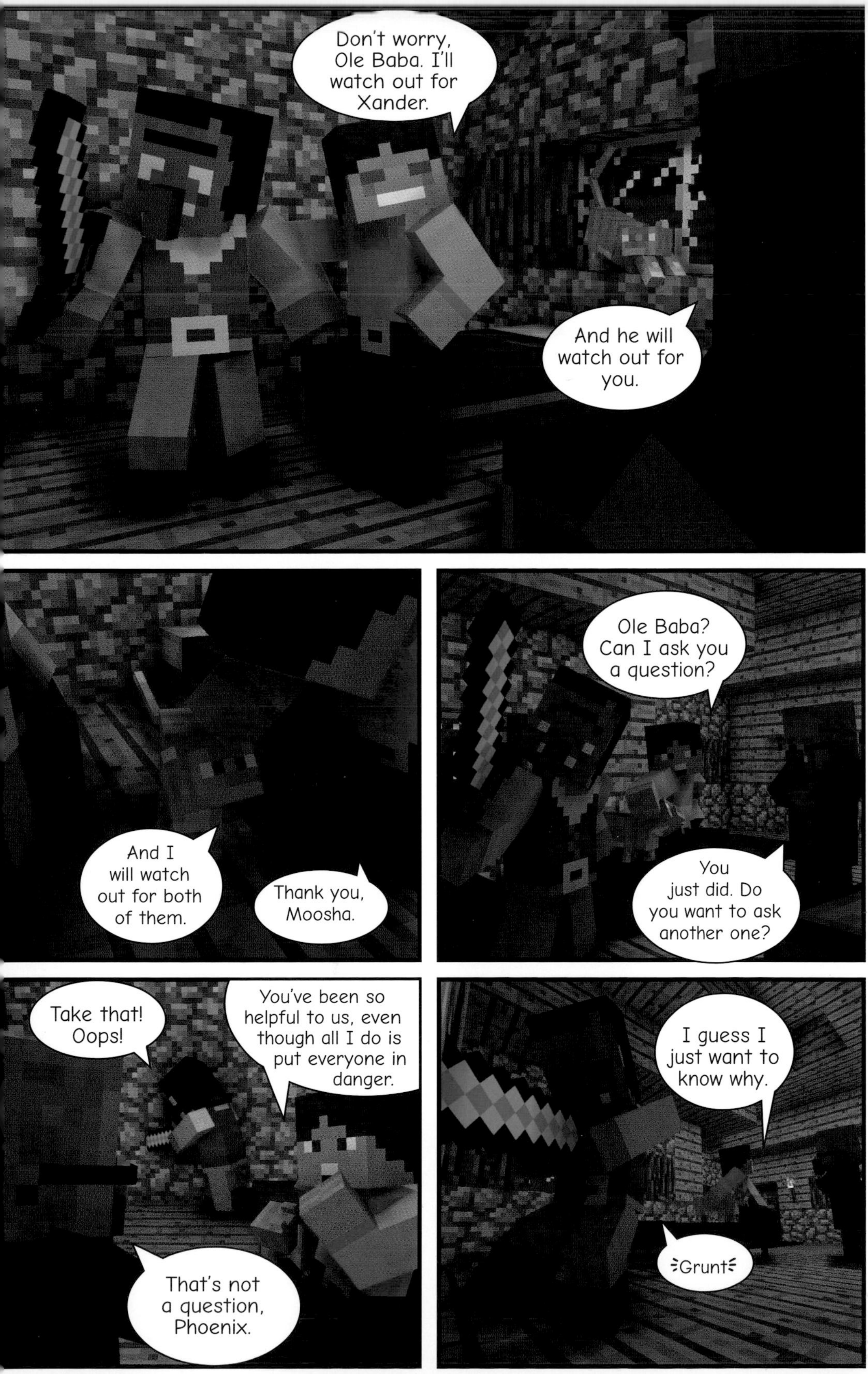
Don't worry, Ole Baba. I'll watch out for Xander.
And he will watch out for you.
And I will watch out for both of them.
Thank you, Moosha.
Ole Baba? Can I ask you a question?
You just did. Do you want to ask another one?
Take that! Oops!
You've been so helpful to us, even though all I do is put everyone in danger.
That's not a question, Phoenix.
I guess I just want to know why.
Grunt

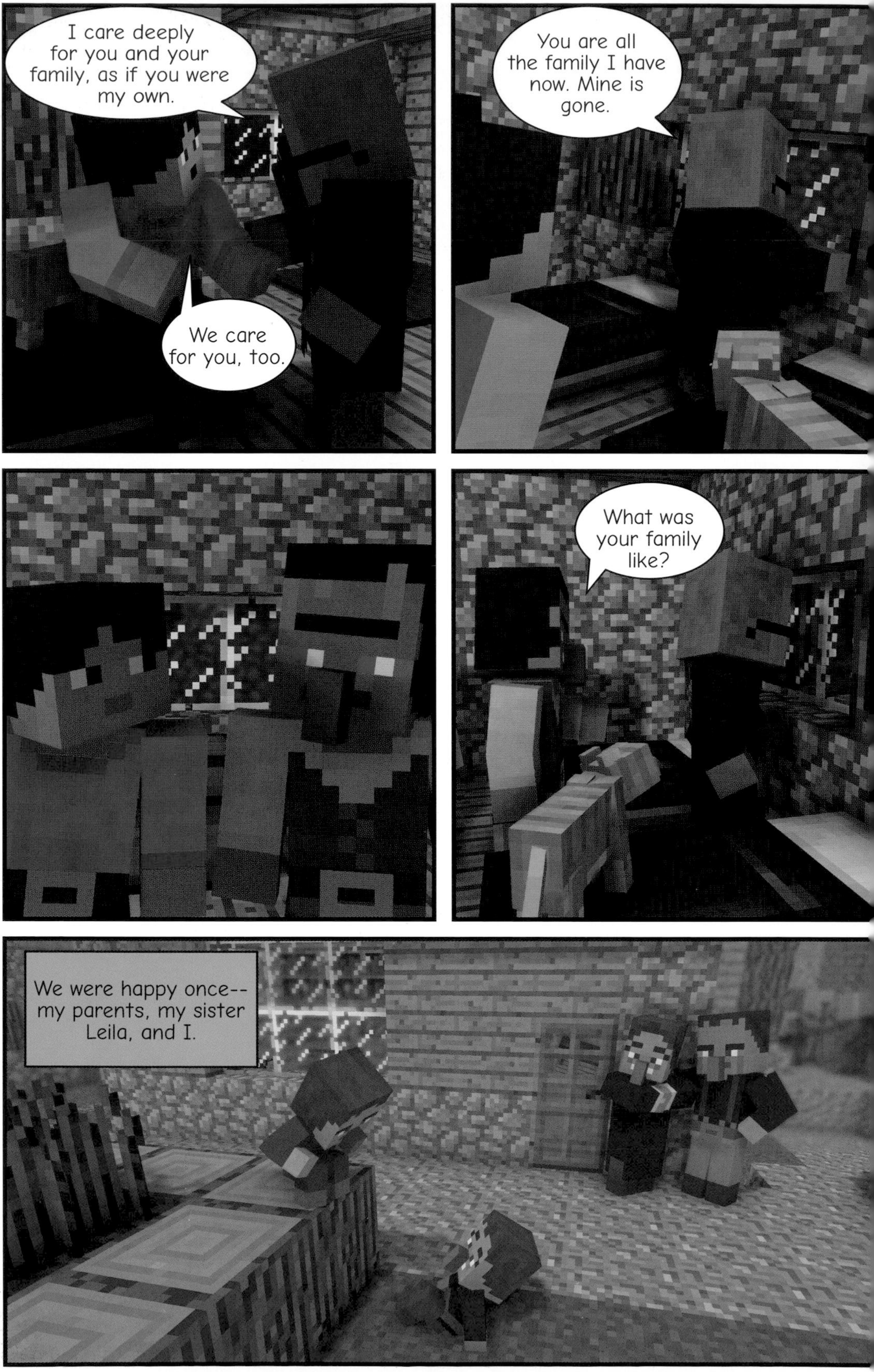
I care deeply for you and your family, as if you were my own.
We care for you, too.
You are all the family I have now. Mine is gone.
What was your family like?
We were happy once-- my parents, my sister Leila, and I.

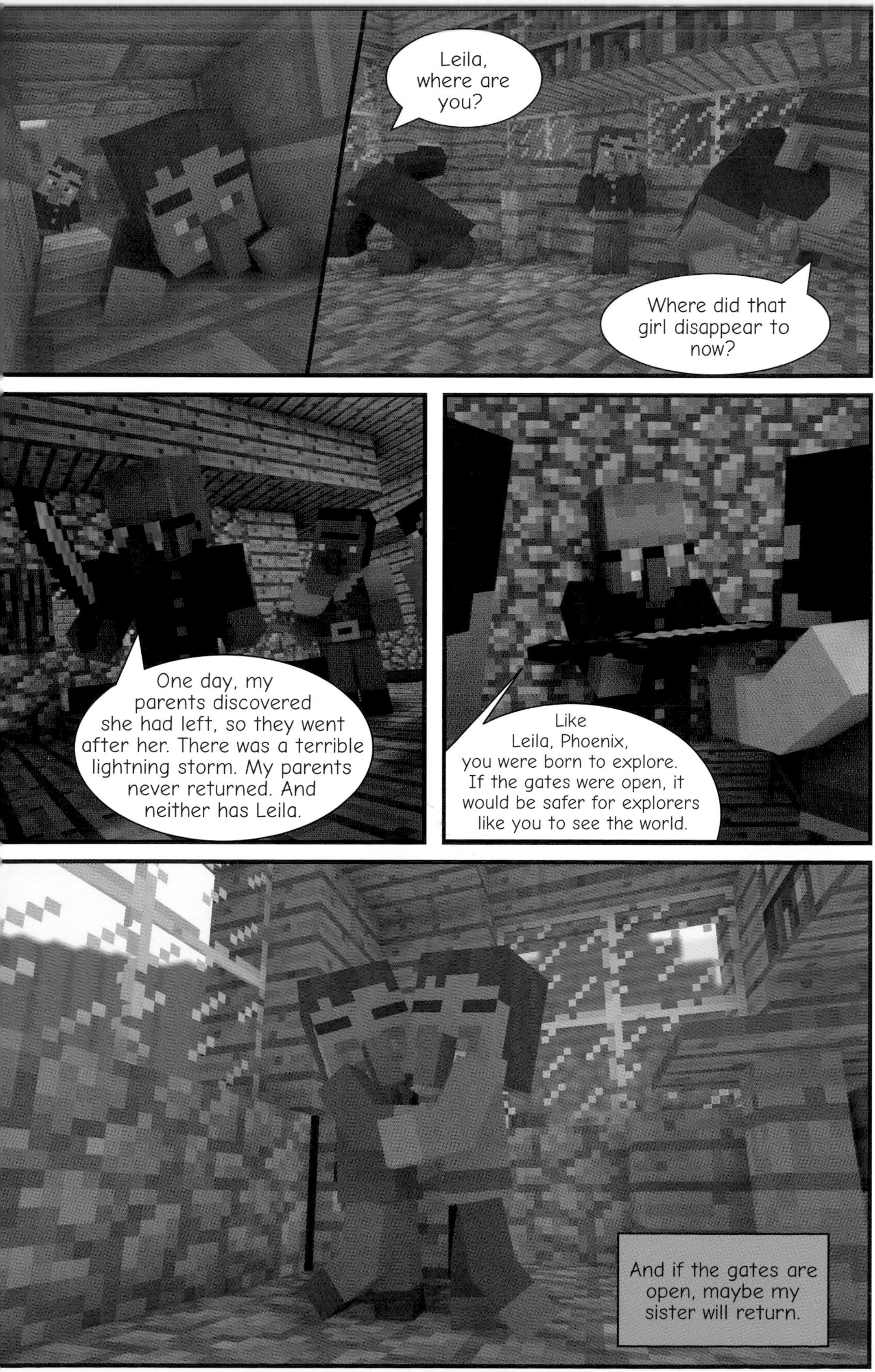

Leila, where are you?
Where did that girl disappear to now?
One day, my parents discovered she had left, so they went after her. There was a terrible lightning storm. My parents never returned. And neither has Leila.
Like Leila, Phoenix, you were born to explore. If the gates were open, it would be safer for explorers like you to see the world.
And if the gates are open, maybe my sister will return.

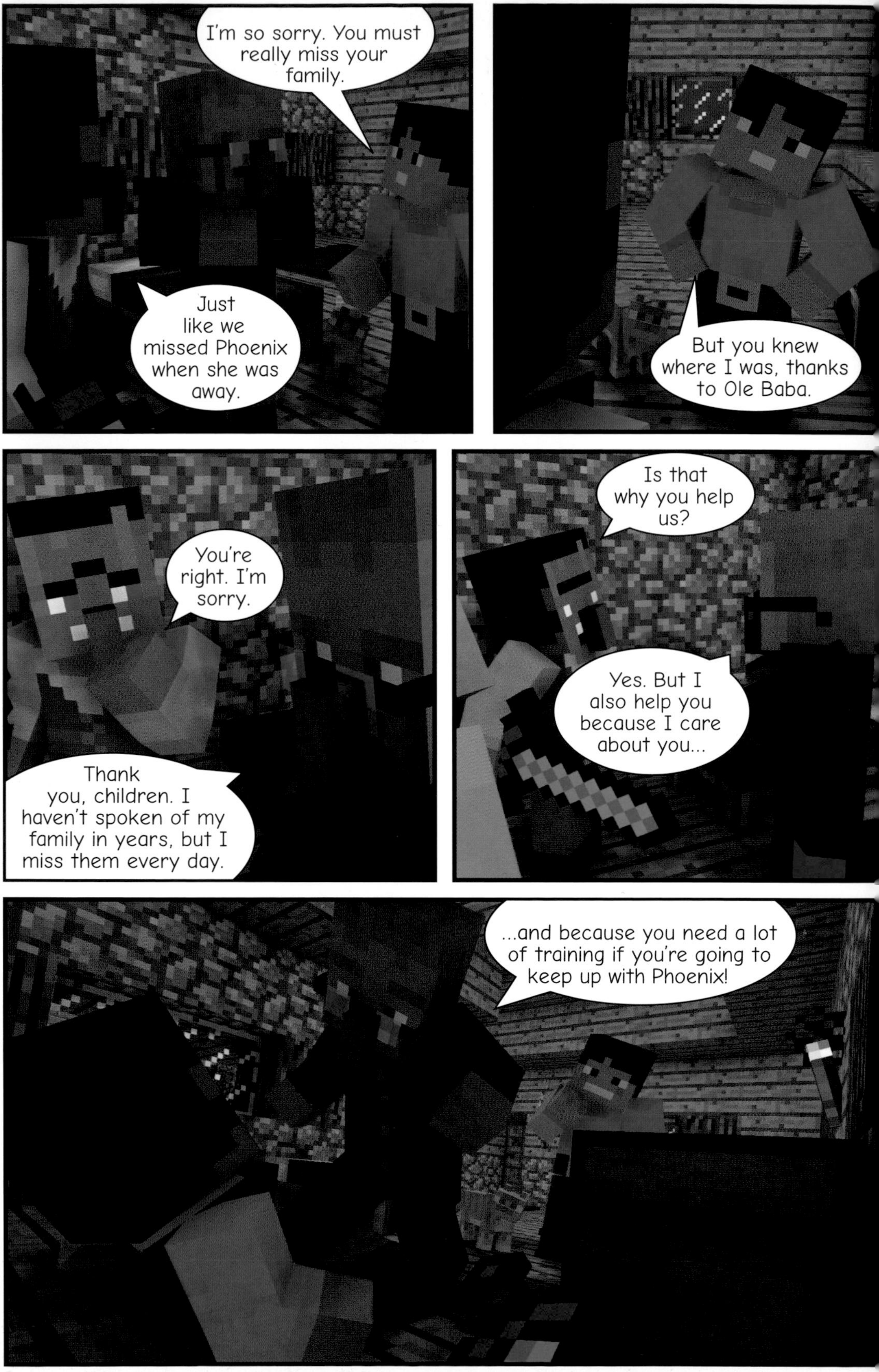
I'm so sorry. You must really miss your family.
Just like we missed Phoenix when she was away.
But you knew where I was, thanks to Ole Baba.
You're right. I'm sorry.
Thank you, children. I haven't spoken of my family in years, but I miss them every day.
Is that why you help us?
Yes. But I also help you because I care about you...
...and because you need a lot of training if you're going to keep up with Phoenix!

CHAPTER 2

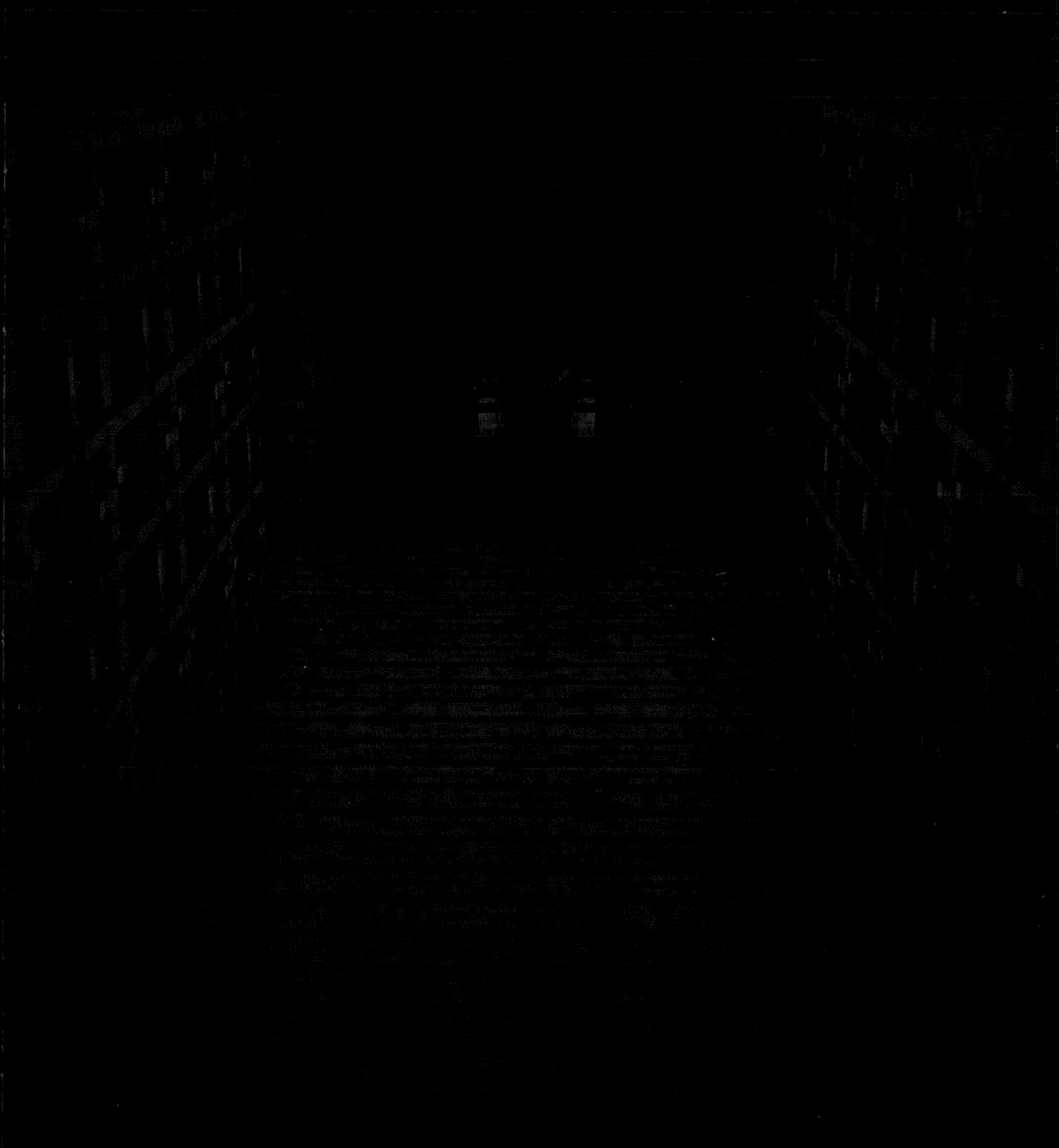

SECRETS

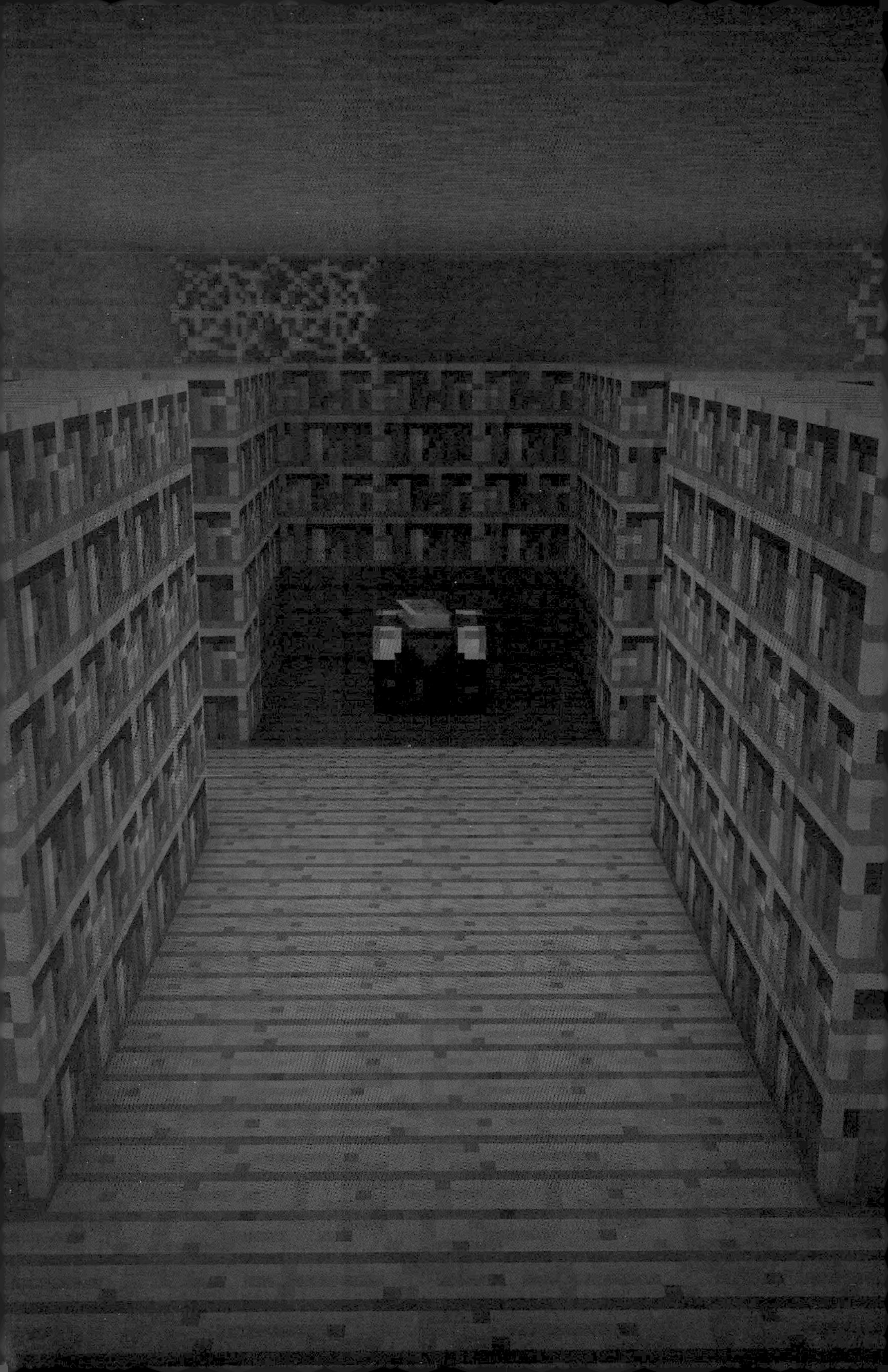

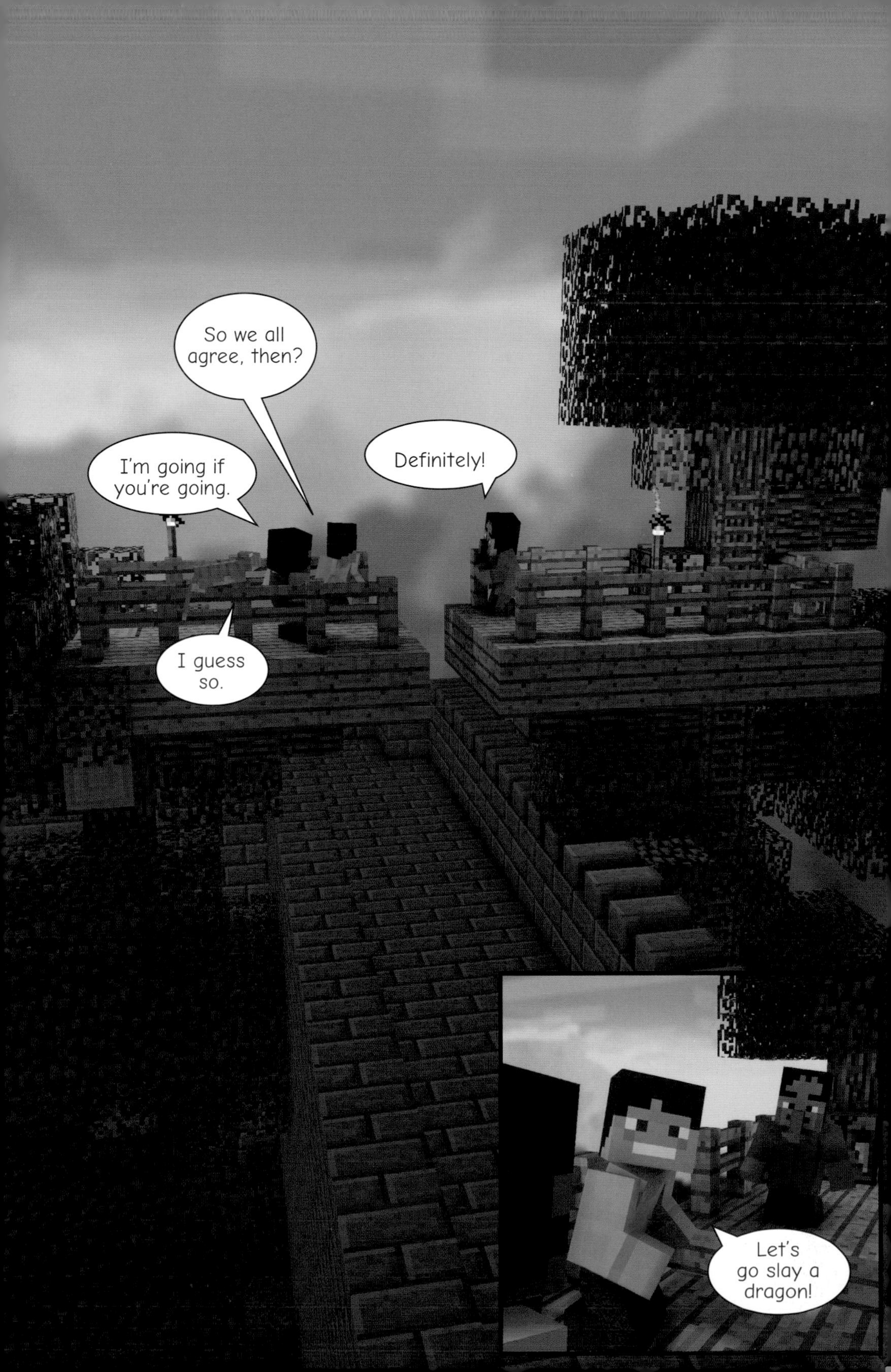
So we all agree, then?
I'm going if you're going.
Definitely!
I guess so.
Let's go slay a dragon!

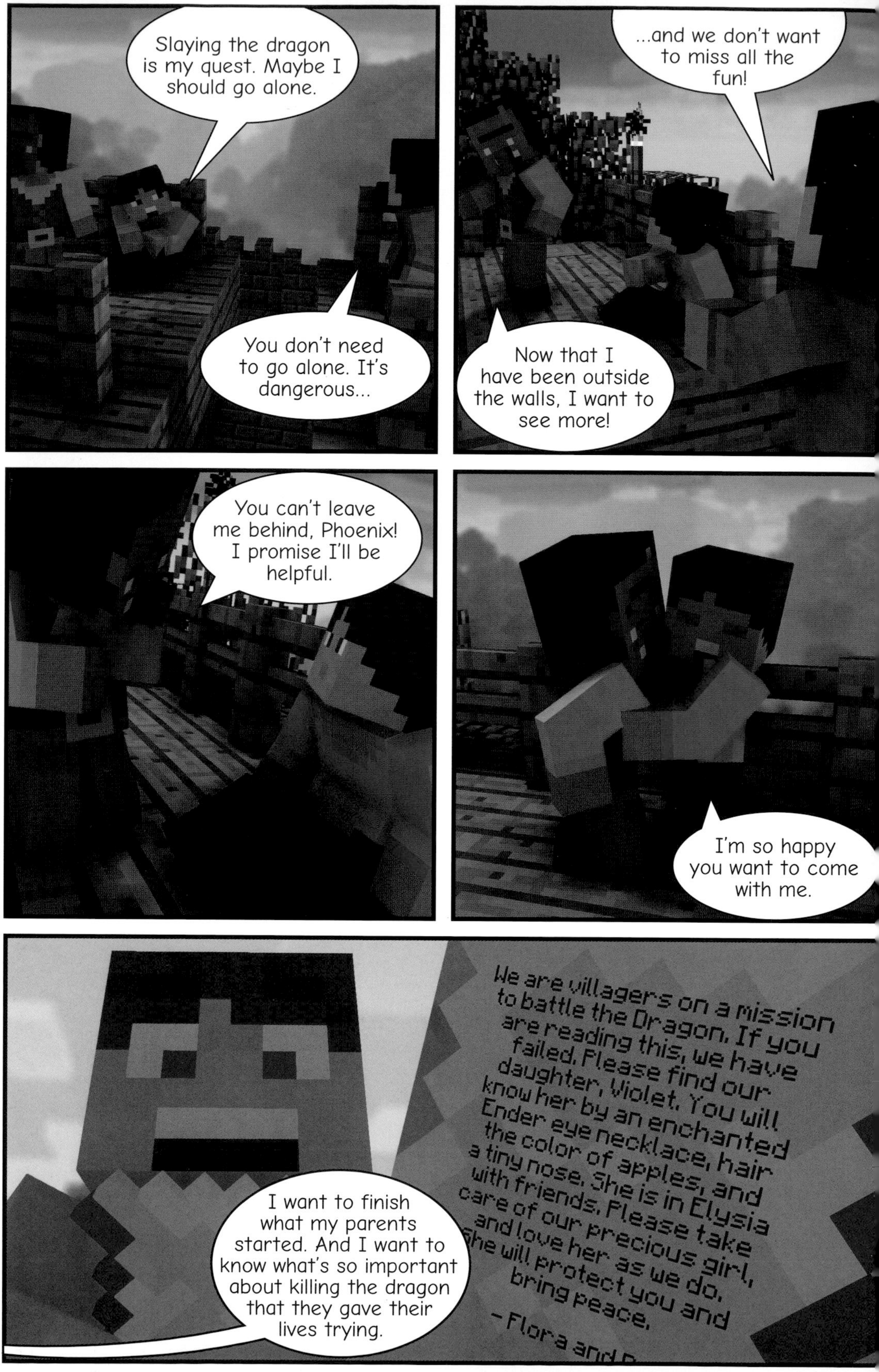
Slaying the dragon is my quest. Maybe I should go alone.
You don't need to go alone. It's dangerous...
...and we don't want to miss all the fun!
Now that I have been outside the walls, I want to see more!
You can't leave me behind, Phoenix! I promise I'll be helpful.
I'm so happy you want to come with me.
We are villagers on a mission to battle the Dragon. If you are reading this, we have failed. Please find our daughter, Violet. You will know her by an enchanted Ender eye necklace, hair the color of apples, and a tiny nose. She is in Elysia with friends. Please take care of our precious girl, and love her as we do. She will protect you and bring peace.
- Flora and
I want to finish what my parents started. And I want to know what's so important about killing the dragon that they gave their lives trying.

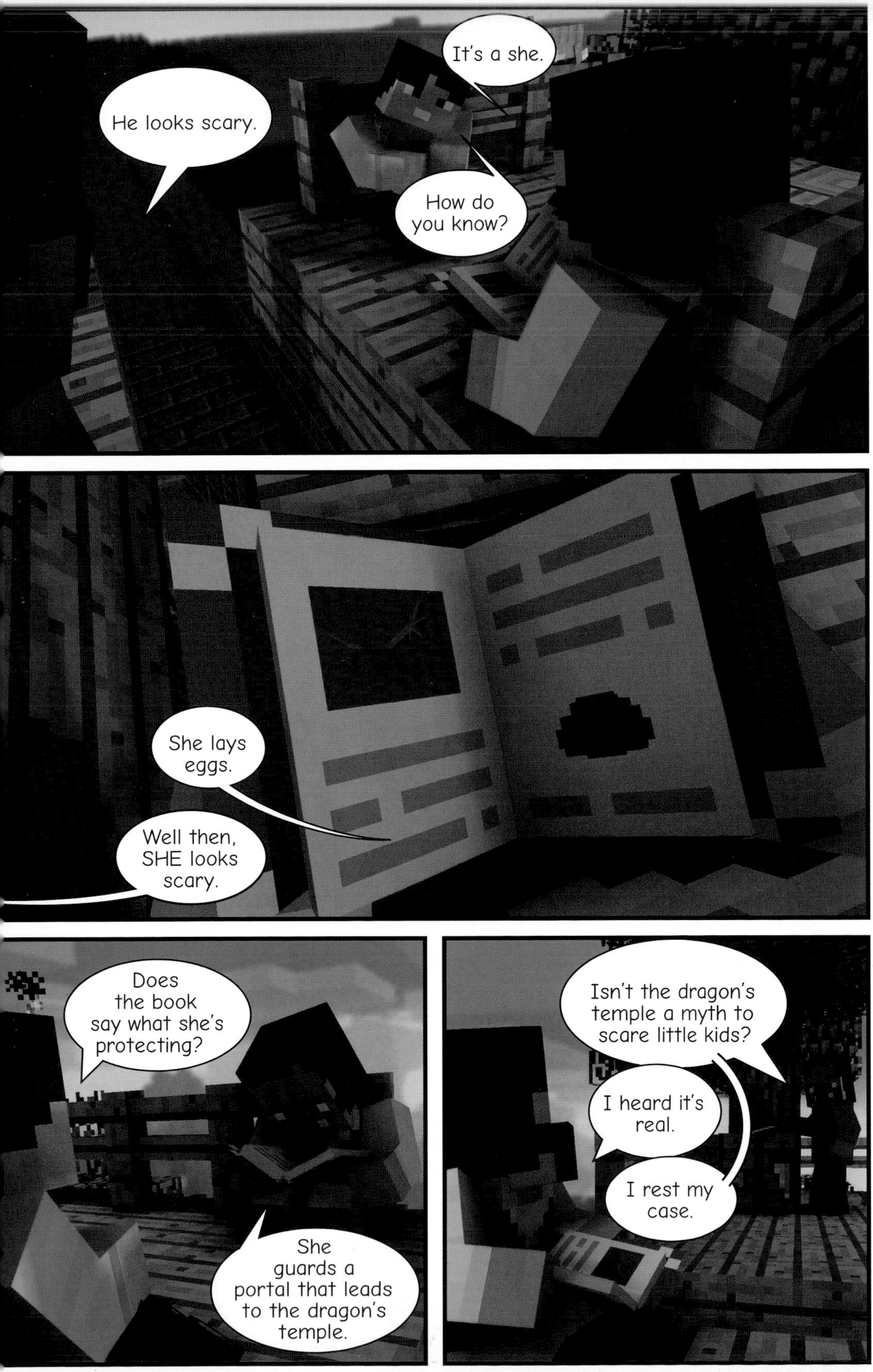
He looks scary.
It's a she.
How do you know?
She lays eggs.
Well then, SHE looks scary.
Does the book say what she's protecting?
She guards a portal that leads to the dragon's temple.
Isn't the dragon's temple a myth to scare little kids?
I heard it's real.
I rest my case.

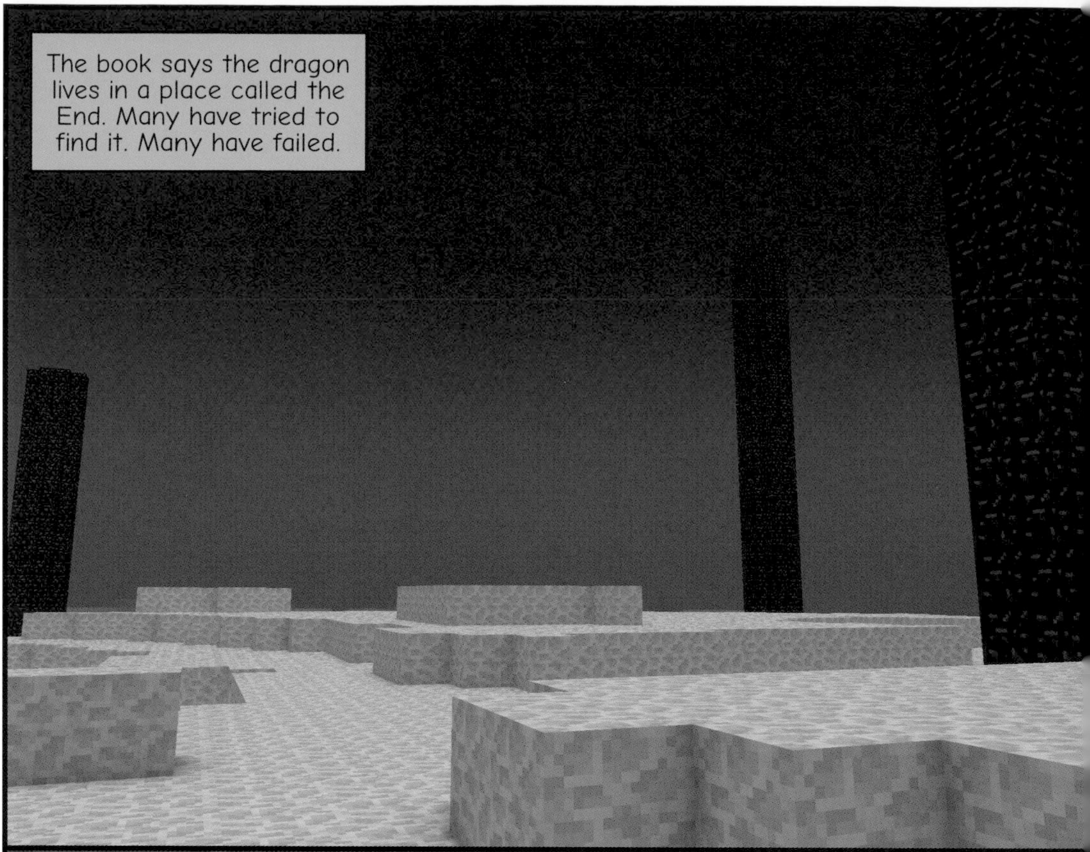
The book says the dragon lives in a place called the End. Many have tried to find it. Many have failed.

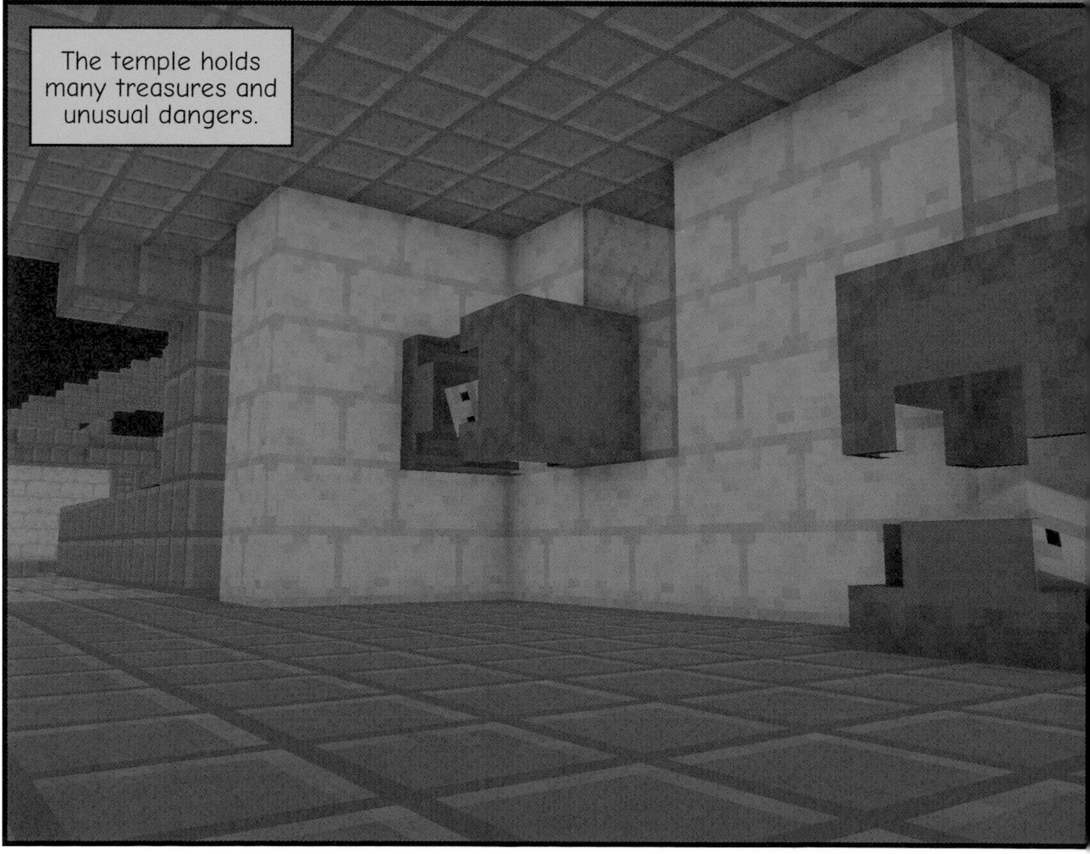
The temple holds many treasures and unusual dangers.

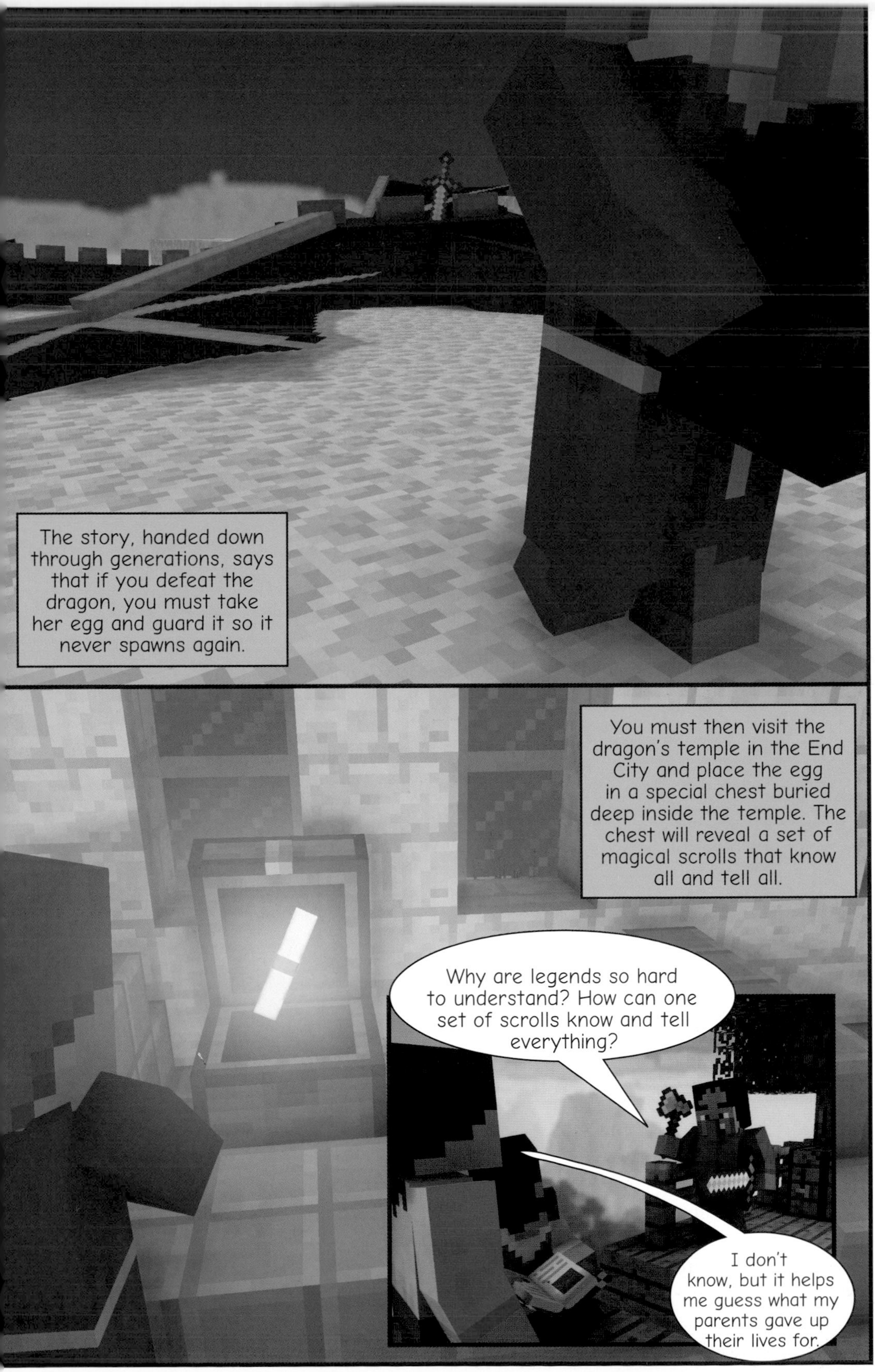
The story, handed down through generations, says that if you defeat the dragon, you must take her egg and guard it so it never spawns again.
You must then visit the dragon's temple in the End City and place the egg in a special chest buried deep inside the temple. The chest will reveal a set of magical scrolls that know all and tell all.
Why are legends so hard to understand? How can one set of scrolls know and tell everything?
I don't know, but it helps me guess what my parents gave up their lives for.

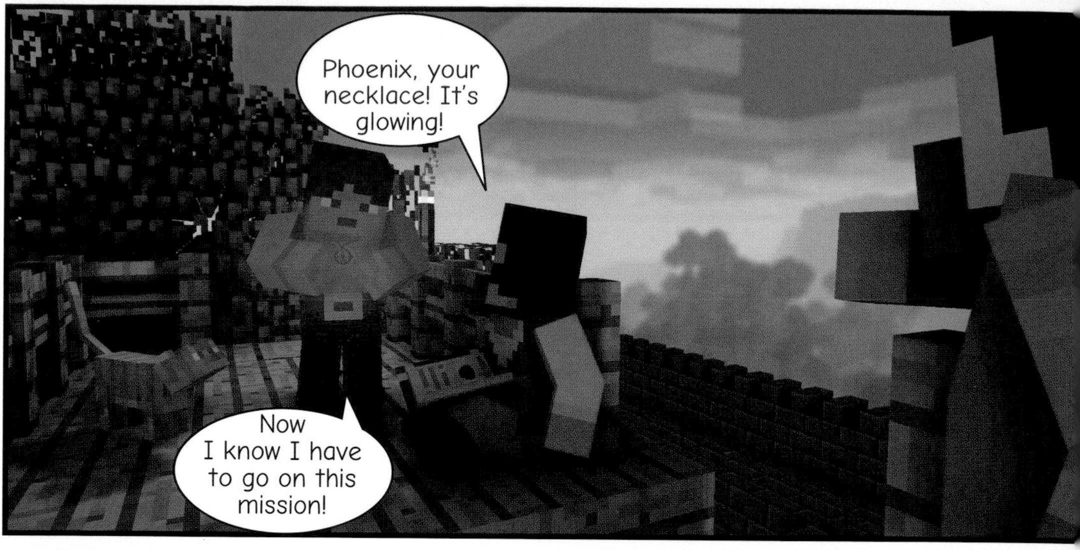
Phoenix, your necklace! It's glowing!
Now I know I have to go on this mission!
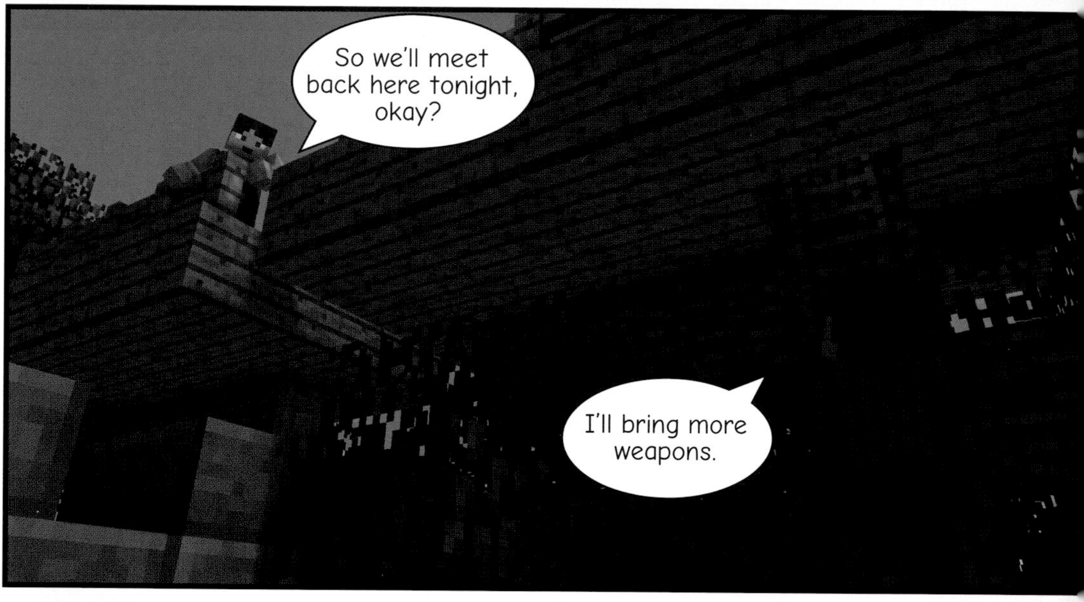
So we'll meet back here tonight, okay?
I'll bring more weapons.
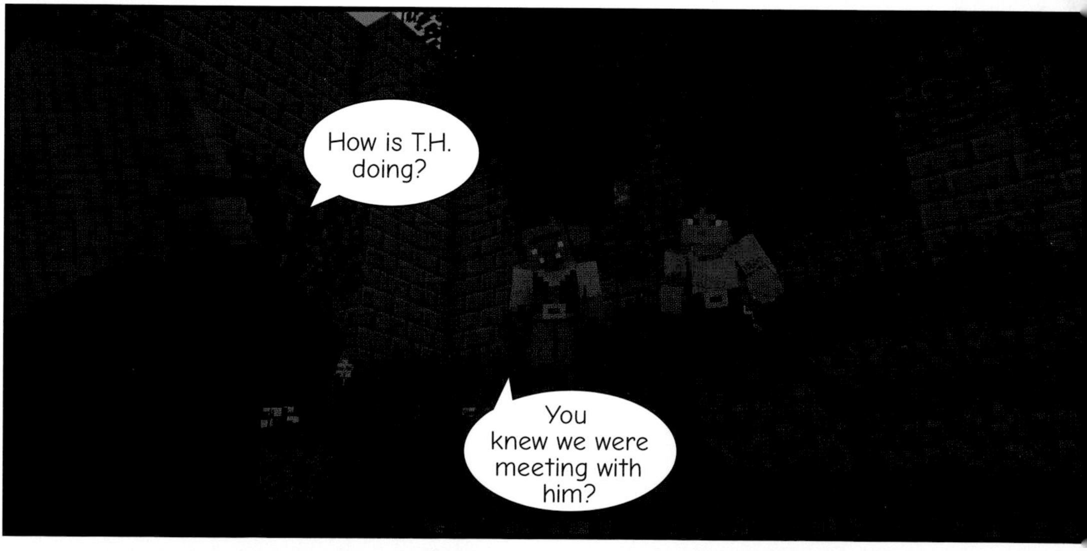
How is T.H. doing?
You knew we were meeting with him?

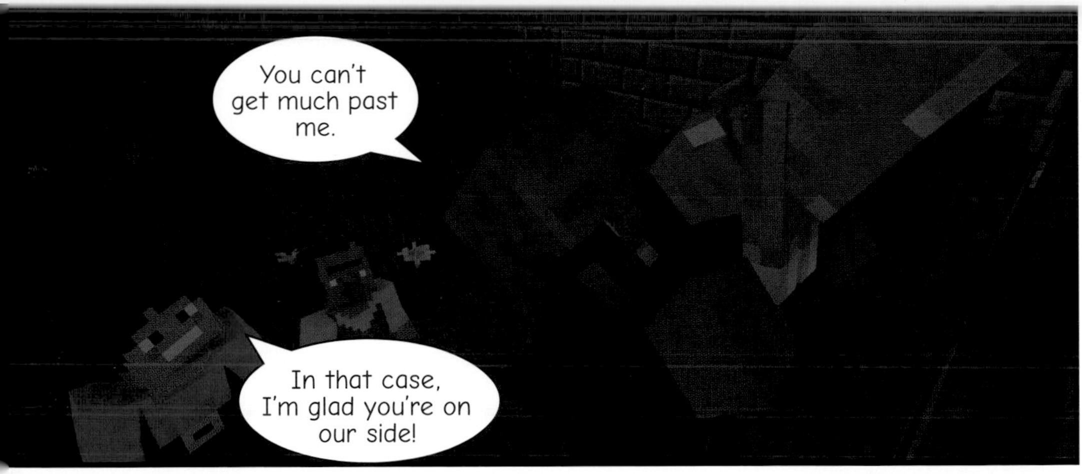
You can't get much past me.
In that case, I'm glad you're on our side!

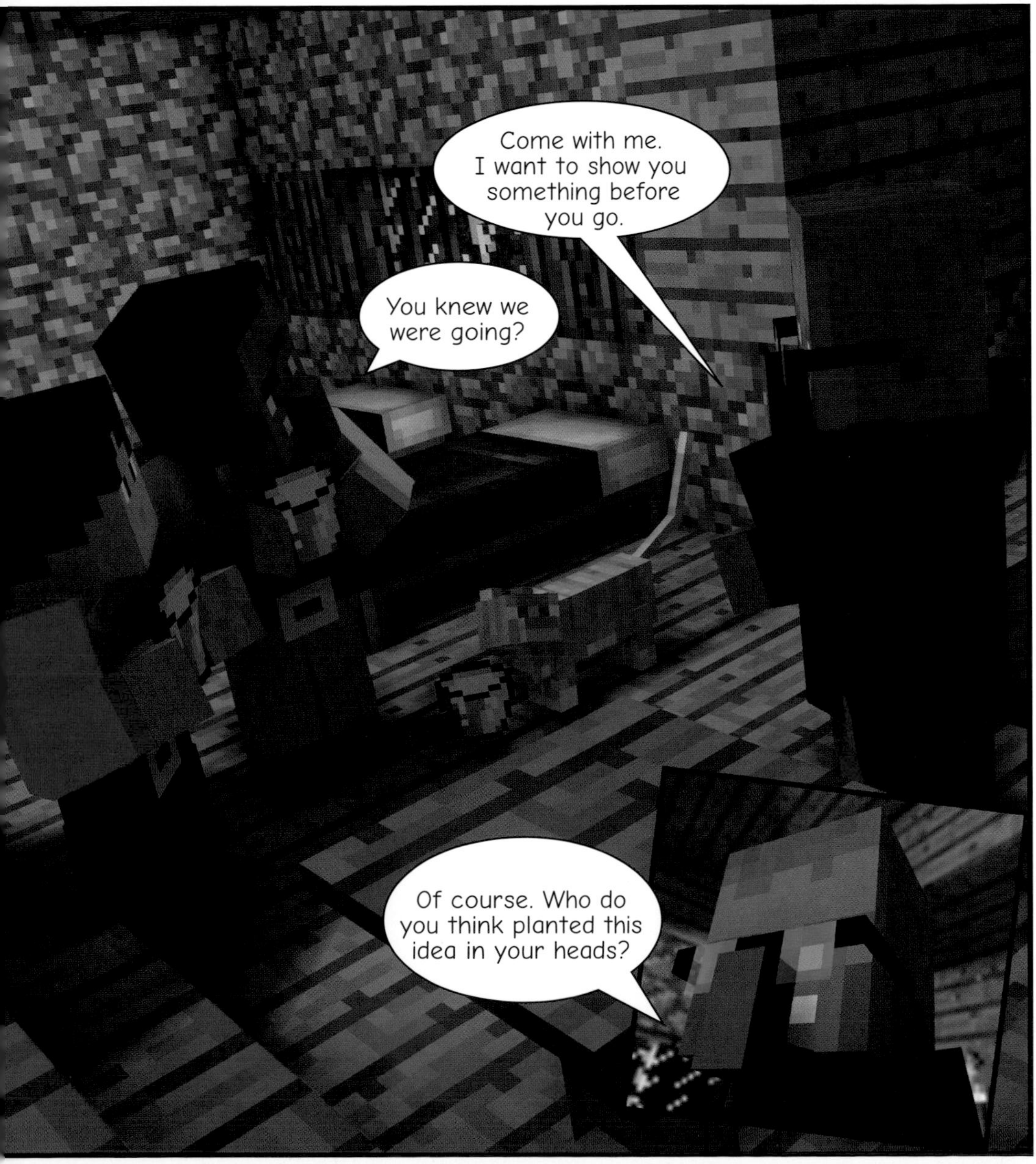
Come with me. I want to show you something before you go.
You knew we were going?
Of course. Who do you think planted this idea in your heads?

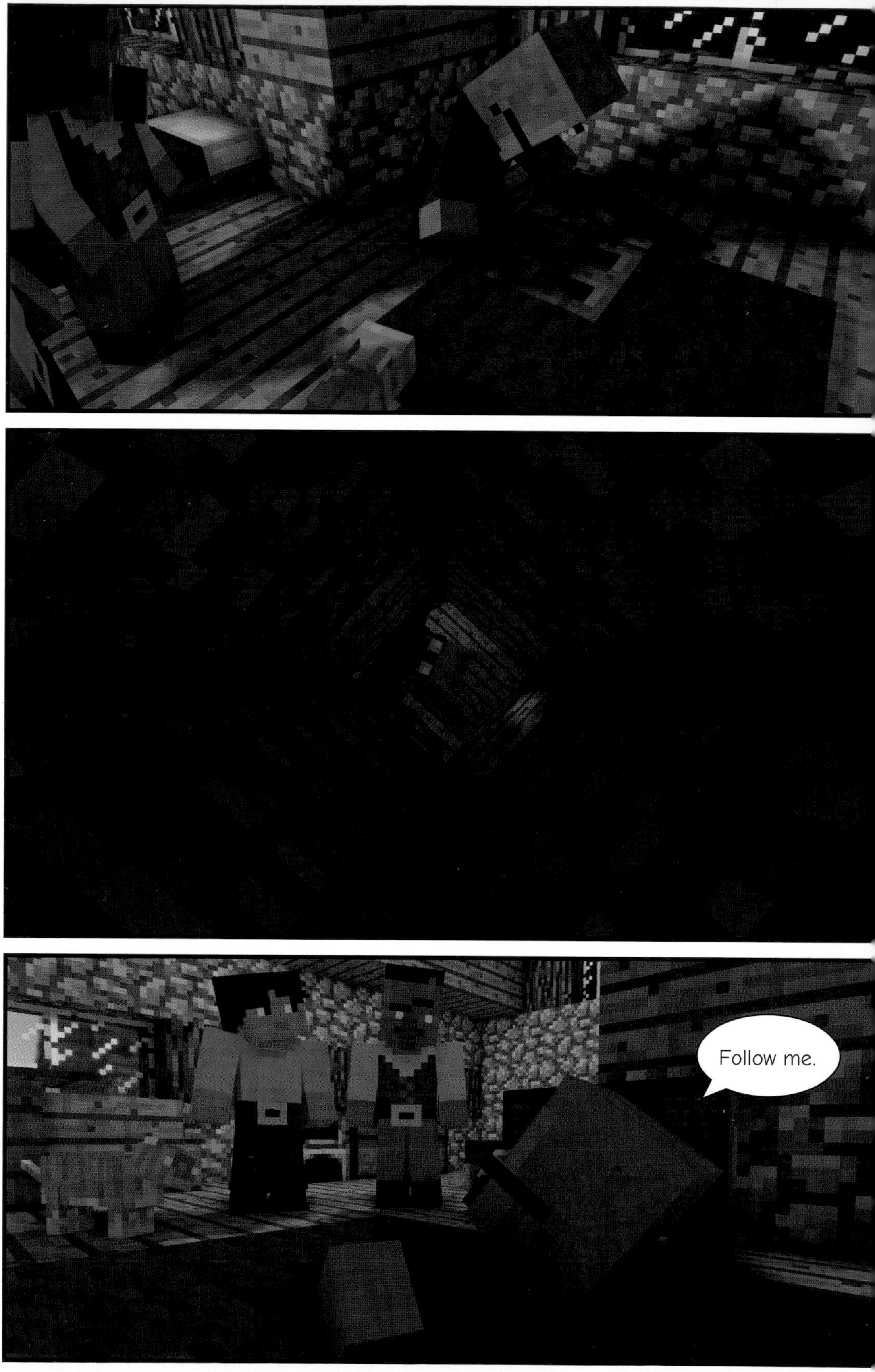
Follow me.

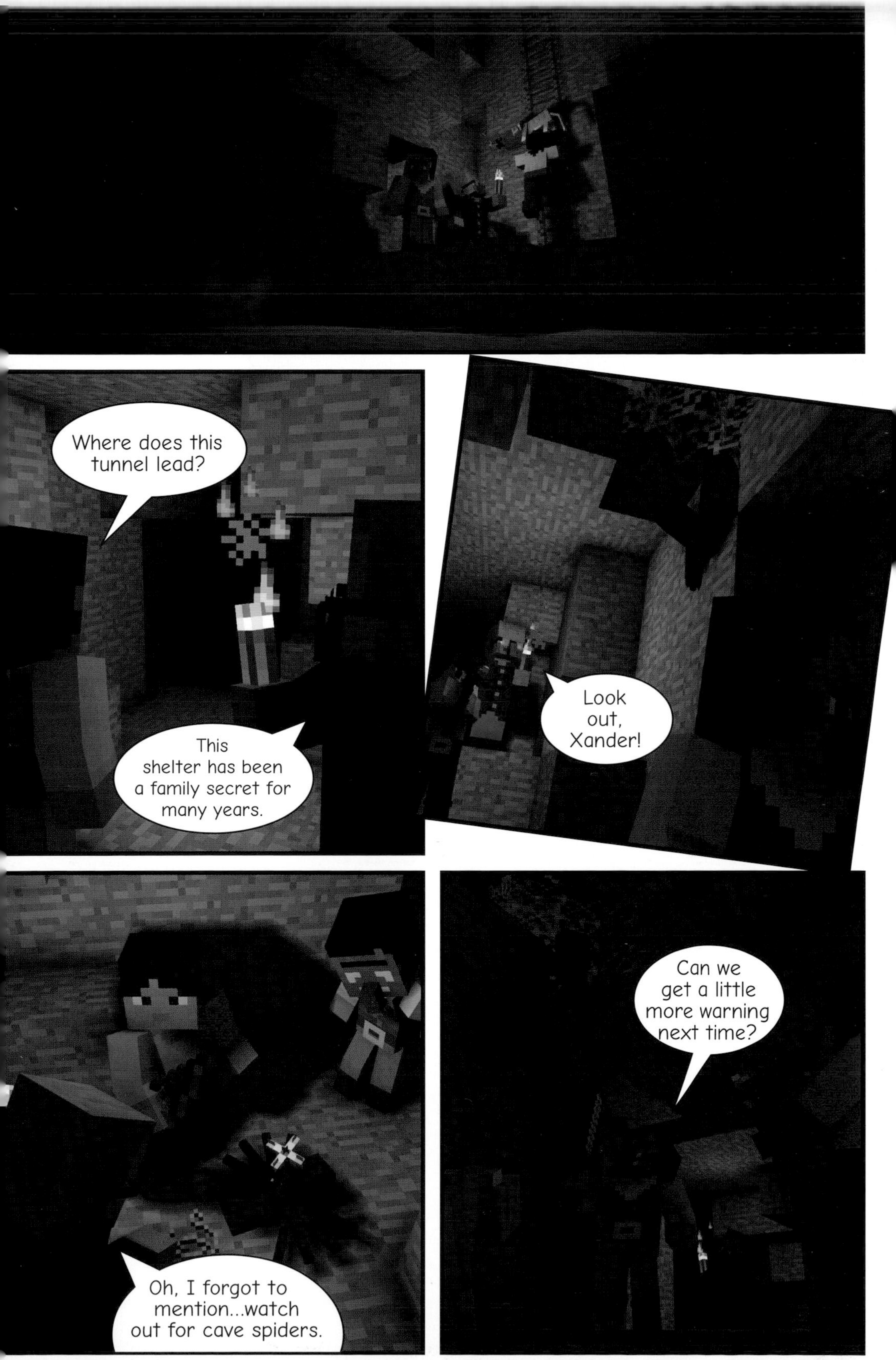
Where does this tunnel lead?
This shelter has been a family secret for many years.
Look out, Xander!
Oh, I forgot to mention...watch out for cave spiders.
Can we get a little more warning next time?

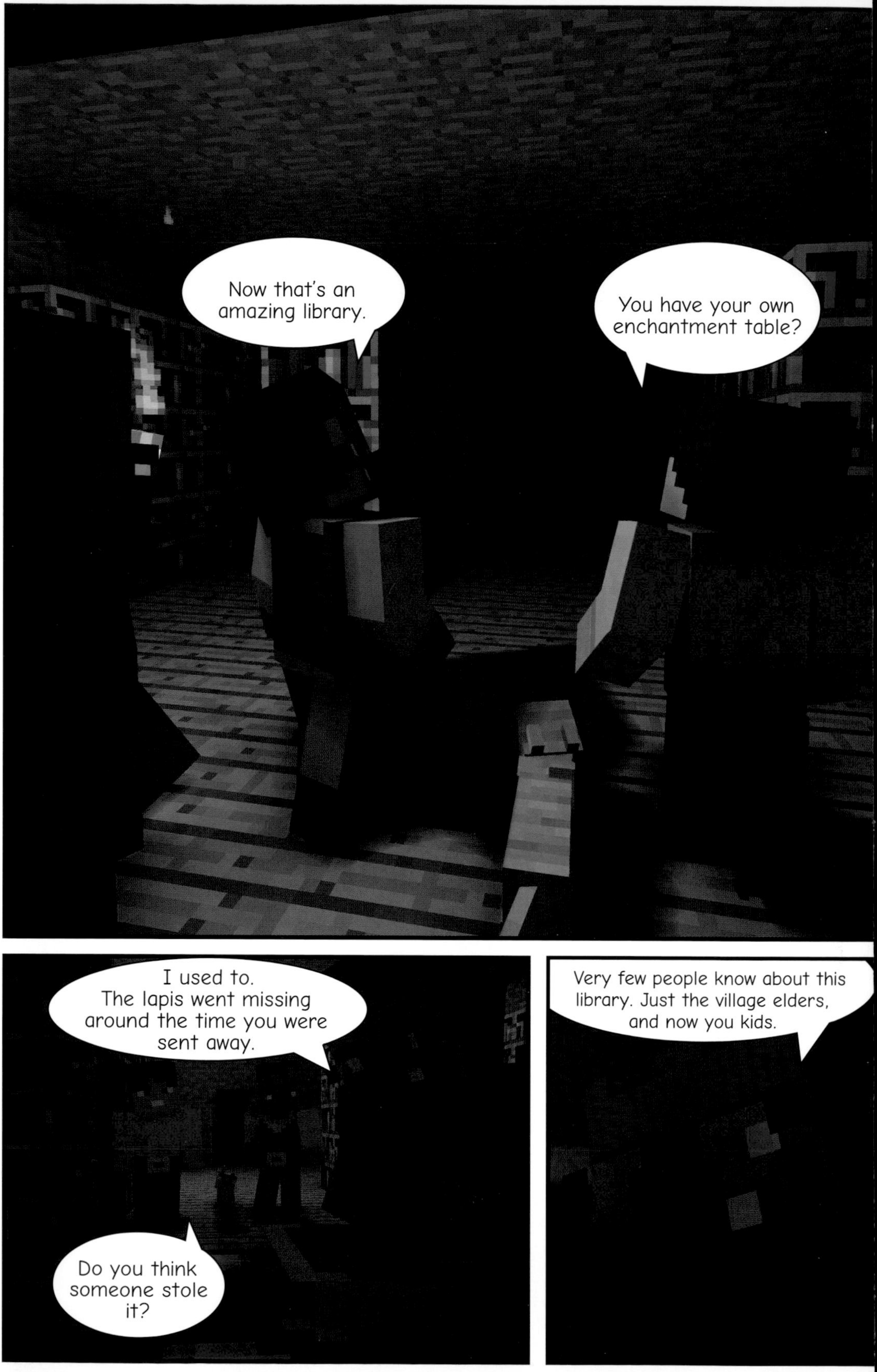
Now that's an amazing library.
You have your own enchantment table?
I used to. The lapis went missing around the time you were sent away.
Do you think someone stole it?
Very few people know about this library. Just the village elders, and now you kids.

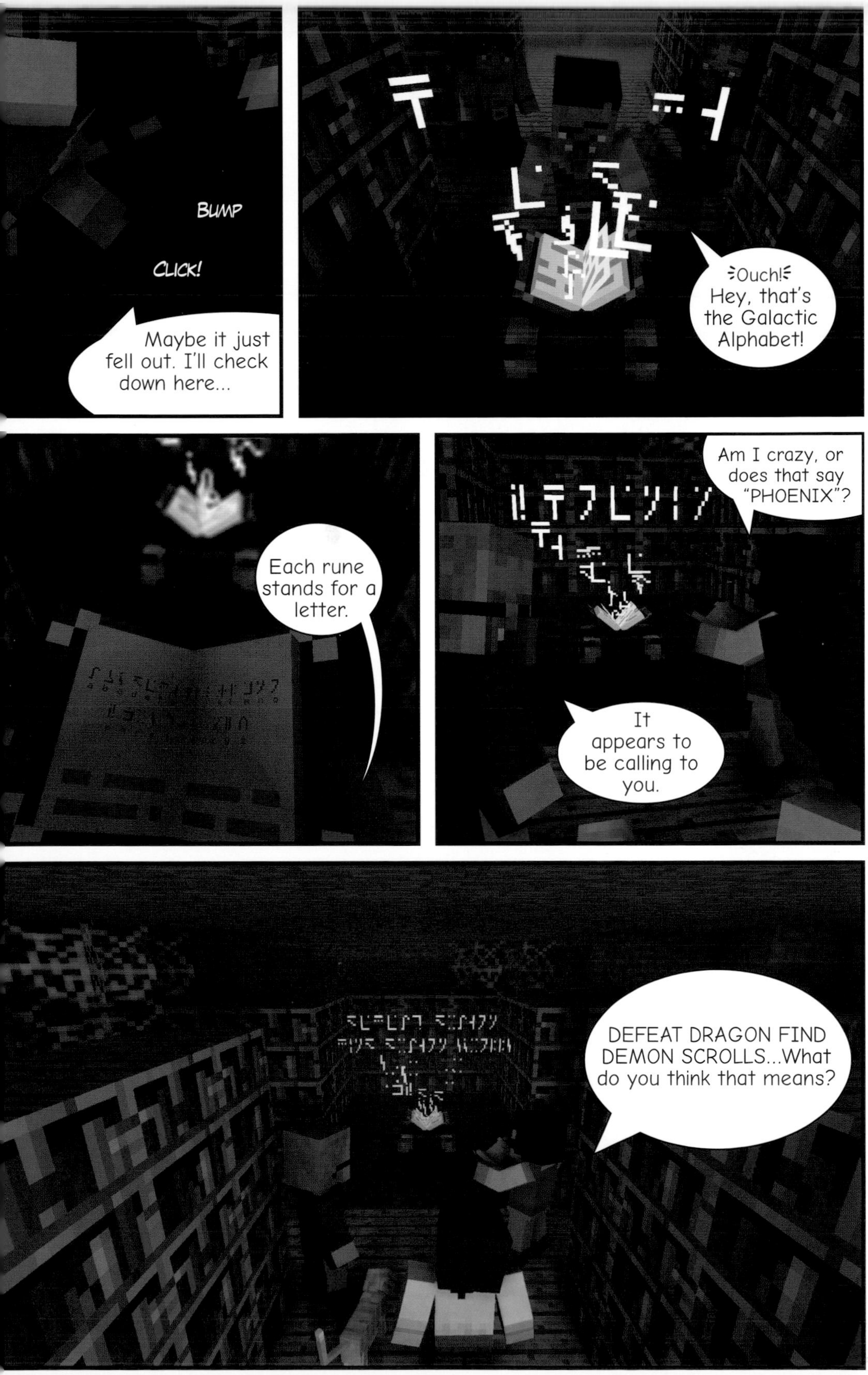
BUMP
CLICK!
Maybe it just fell out. I'll check down here...
Ouch! Hey, that's the Galactic Alphabet!
Each rune stands for a letter.
Am I crazy, or does that say "PHOENIX"?
It appears to be calling to you.
DEFEAT DRAGON FIND DEMON SCROLLS...What do you think that means?

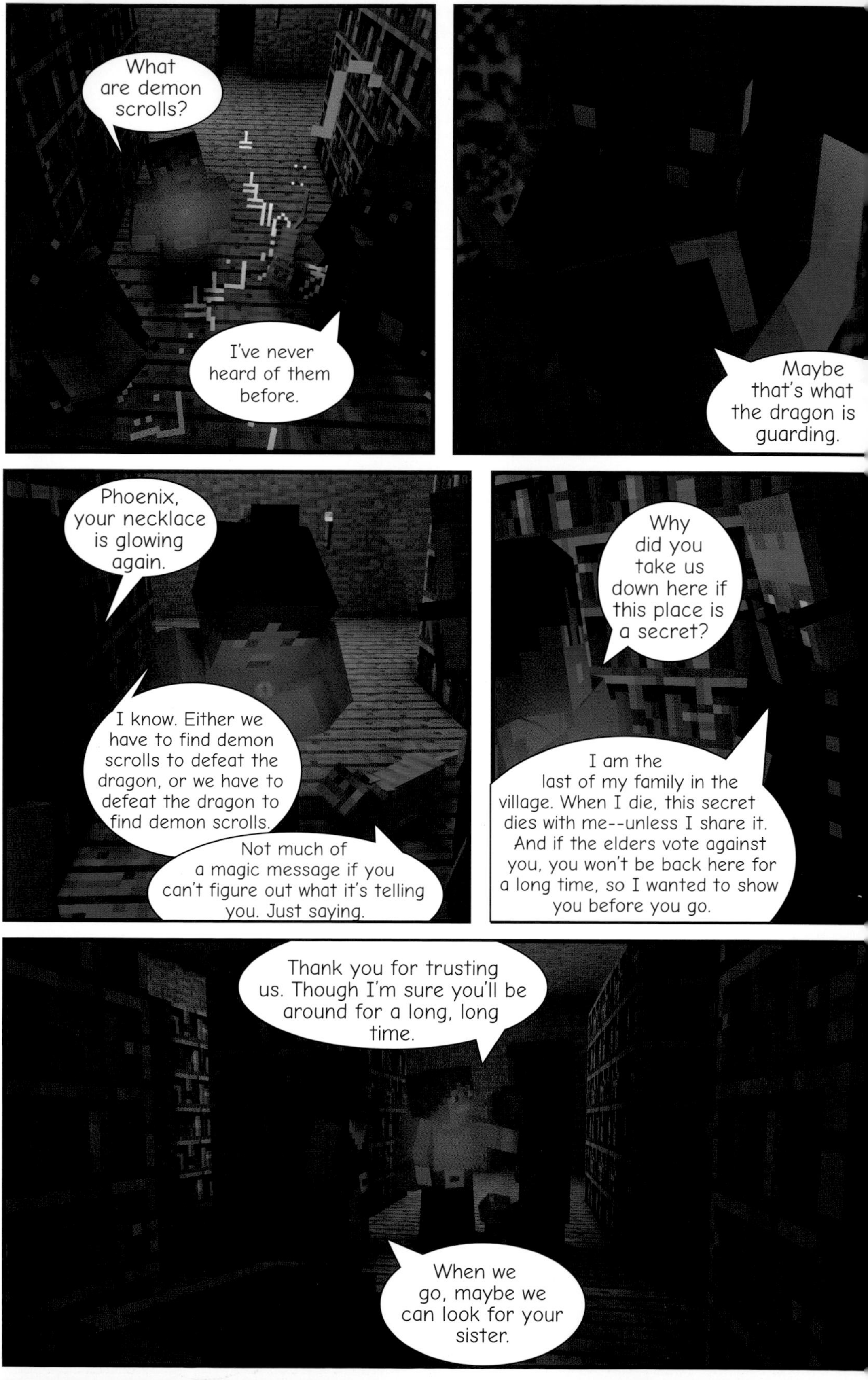
What are demon scrolls?
I've never heard of them before.
Maybe that's what the dragon is guarding.
Phoenix, your necklace is glowing again.
I know. Either we have to find demon scrolls to defeat the dragon, or we have to defeat the dragon to find demon scrolls.
Not much of a magic message if you can't figure out what it's telling you. Just saying.
Why did you take us down here if this place is a secret?
I am the last of my family in the village. When I die, this secret dies with me--unless I share it. And if the elders vote against you, you won't be back here for a long time, so I wanted to show you before you go.
Thank you for trusting us. Though I'm sure you'll be around for a long, long time.
When we go, maybe we can look for your sister.

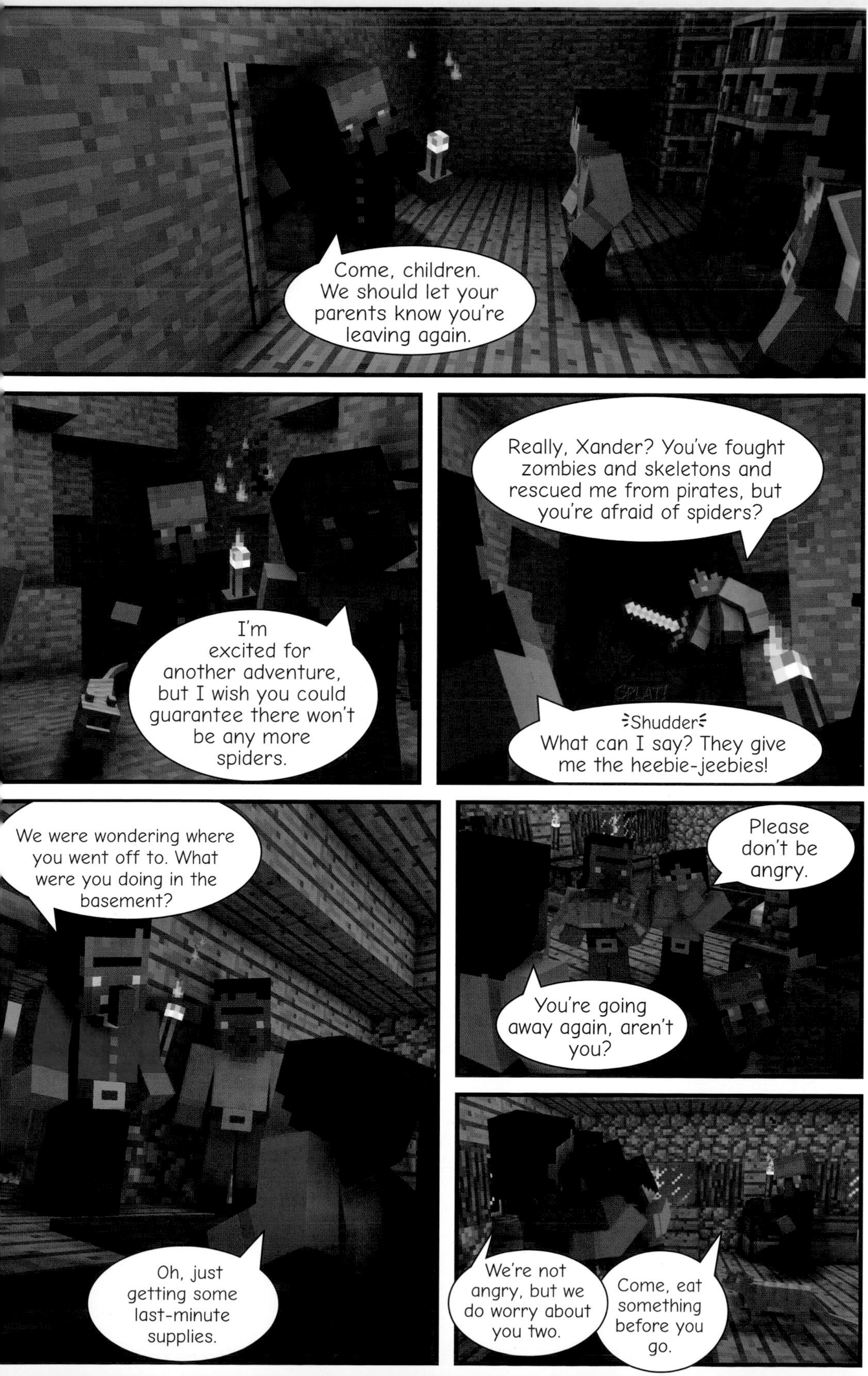
Come, children. We should let your parents know you're leaving again.
I'm excited for another adventure, but I wish you could guarantee there won't be any more spiders.
Really, Xander? You've fought zombies and skeletons and rescued me from pirates, but you're afraid of spiders?
SPLAT!
Shudder
What can I say? They give me the heebie-jeebies!
We were wondering where you went off to. What were you doing in the basement?
Oh, just getting some last-minute supplies.
Please don't be angry.
You're going away again, aren't you?
We're not angry, but we do worry about you two.
Come, eat something before you go.

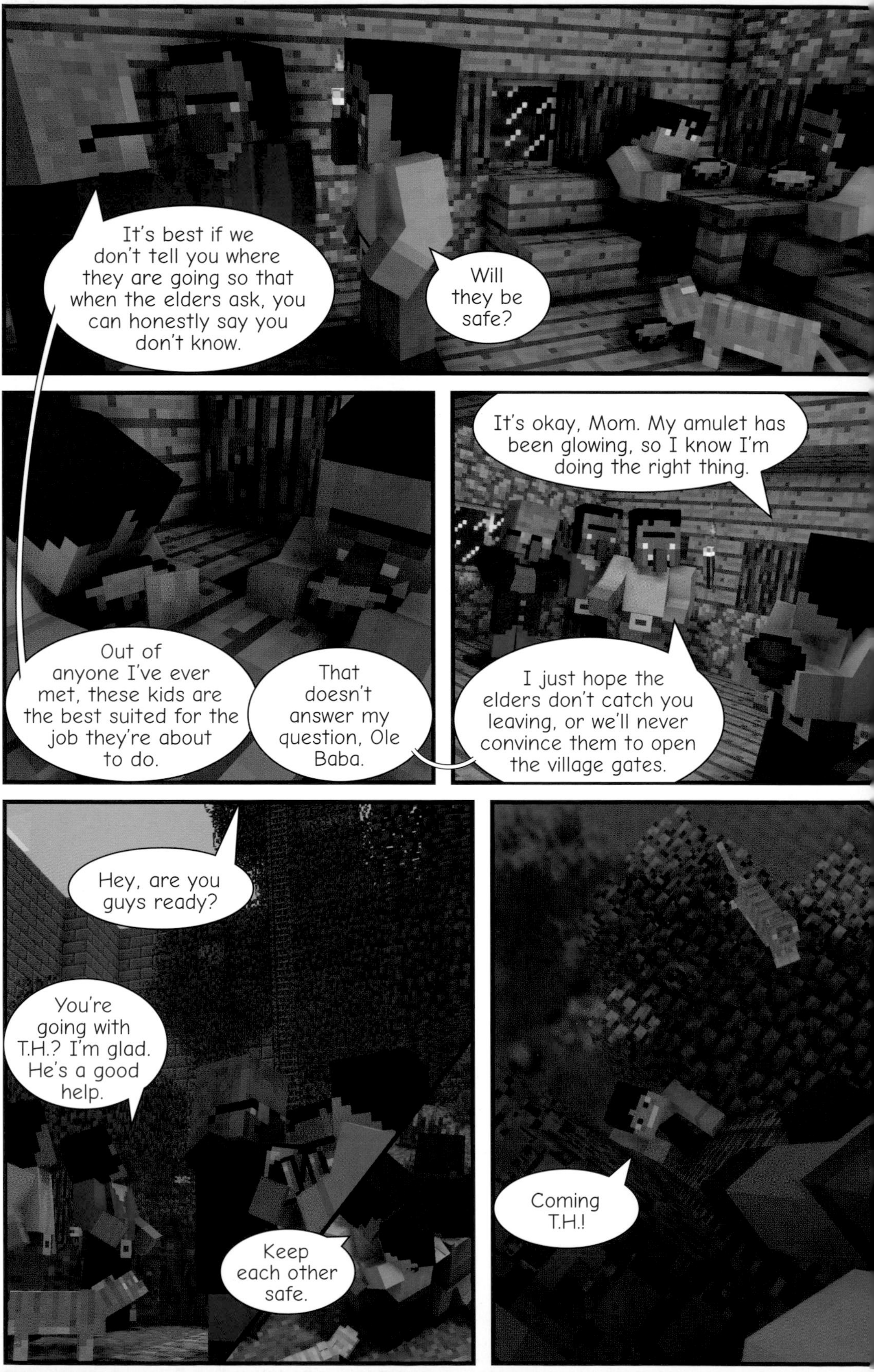
It's best if we don't tell you where they are going so that when the elders ask, you can honestly say you don't know.
Will they be safe?
Out of anyone I've ever met, these kids are the best suited for the job they're about to do.
That doesn't answer my question, Ole Baba.
It's okay, Mom. My amulet has been glowing, so I know I'm doing the right thing.
I just hope the elders don't catch you leaving, or we'll never convince them to open the village gates.
Hey, are you guys ready?
You're going with T.H.? I'm glad. He's a good help.
Keep each other safe.
Coming T.H.!

CHAPTER 3

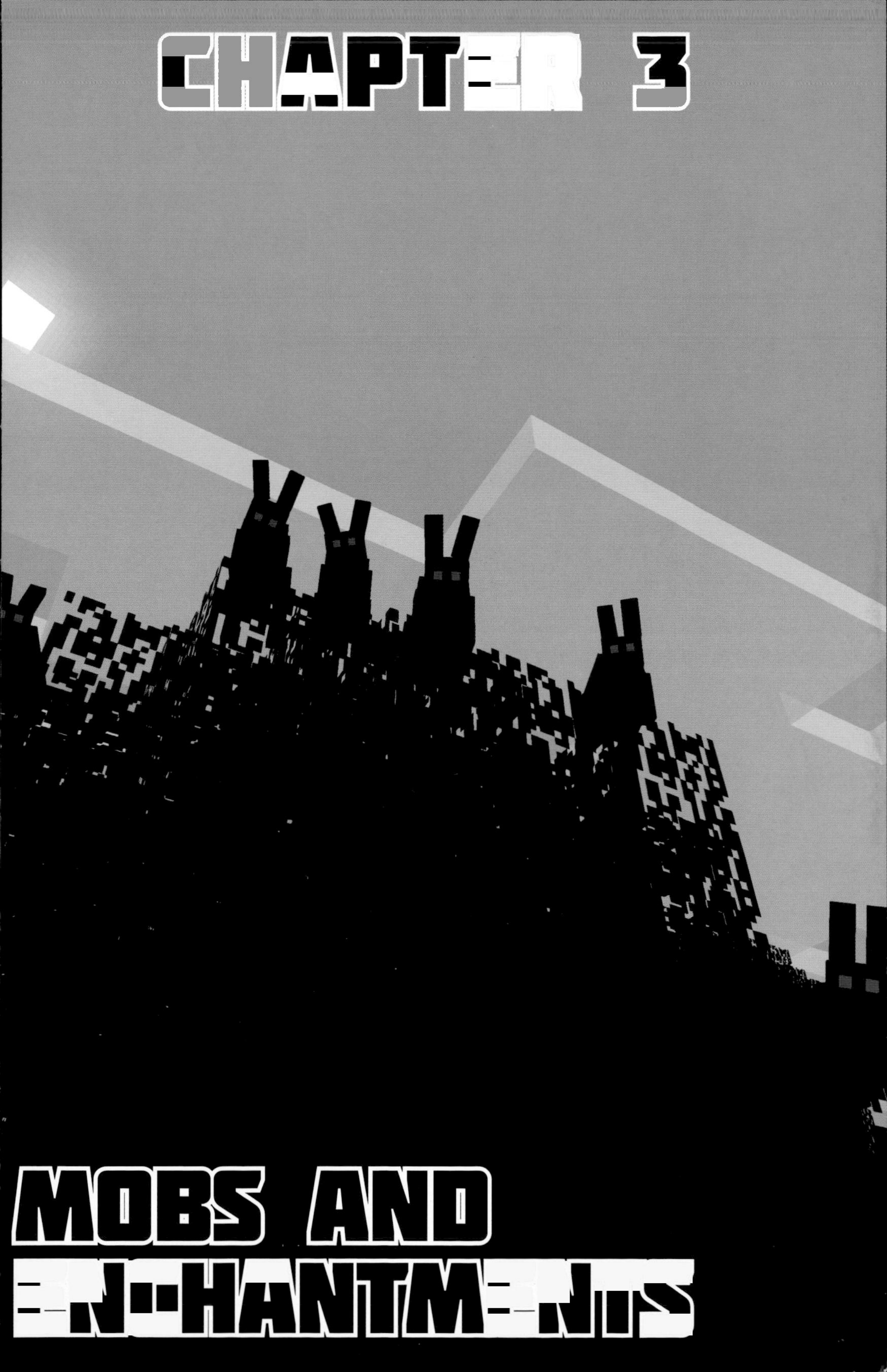

MOBS AND ENCHANTMENTS

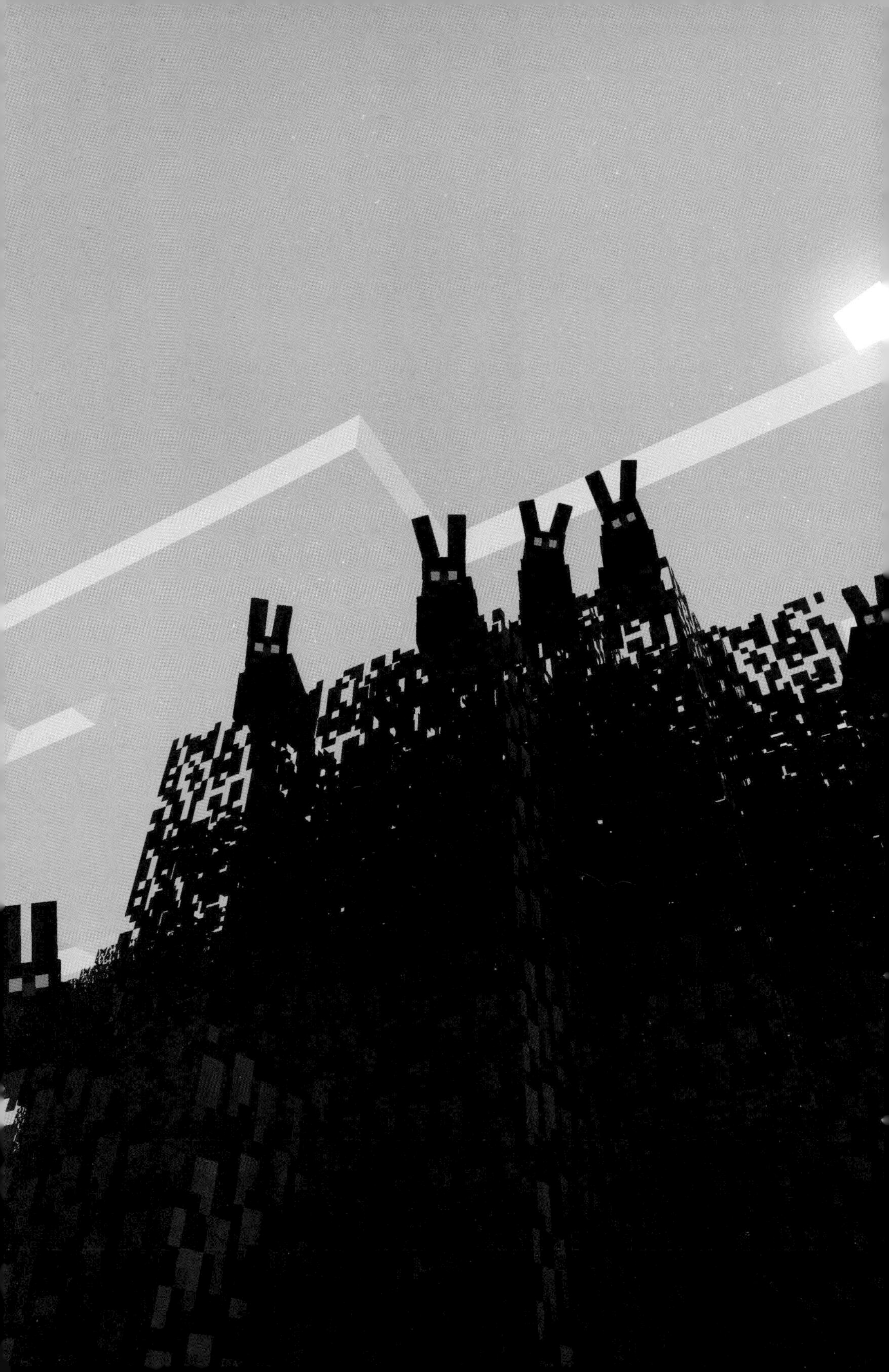

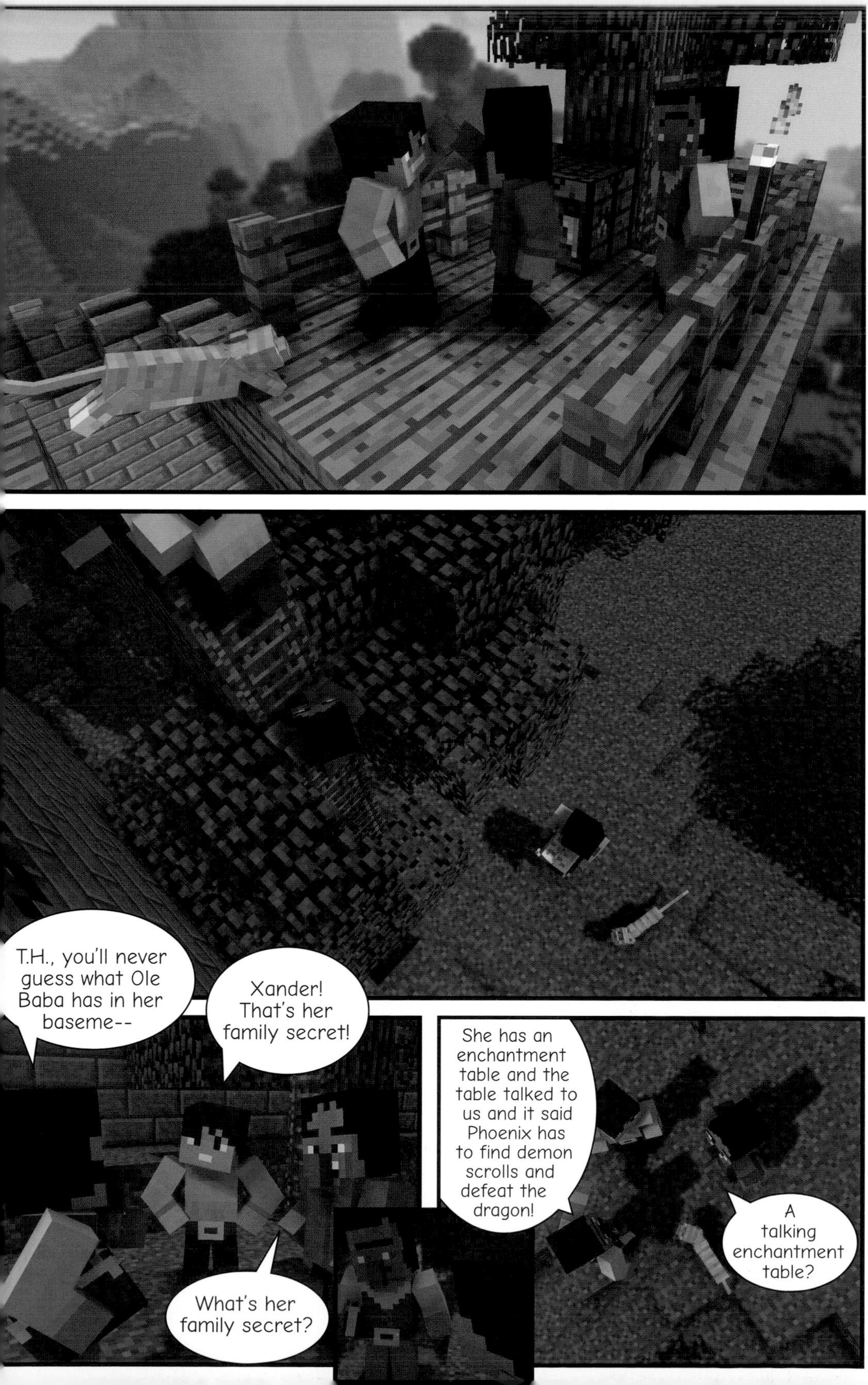
T.H., you'll never guess what Ole Baba has in her baseme--
Xander! That's her family secret!
What's her family secret?
She has an enchantment table and the table talked to us and it said Phoenix has to find demon scrolls and defeat the dragon!
A talking enchantment table?

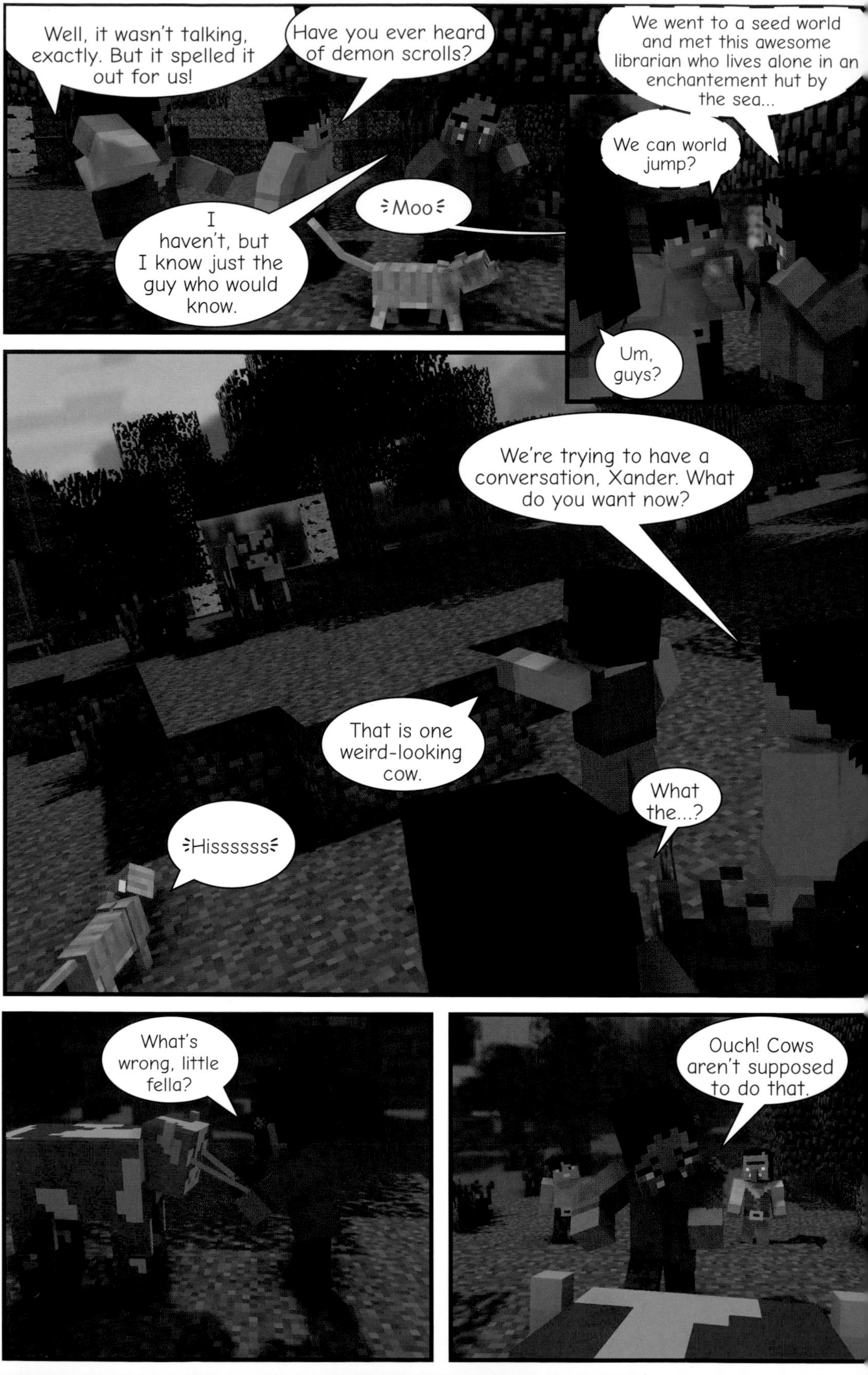
Well, it wasn't talking, exactly. But it spelled it out for us!
Have you ever heard of demon scrolls?
I haven't, but I know just the guy who would know.
Moo
We went to a seed world and met this awesome librarian who lives alone in an enchantement hut by the sea...
We can world jump?
Um, guys?
We're trying to have a conversation, Xander. What do you want now?
That is one weird-looking cow.
What the...?
Hissssss
What's wrong, little fella?
Ouch! Cows aren't supposed to do that.

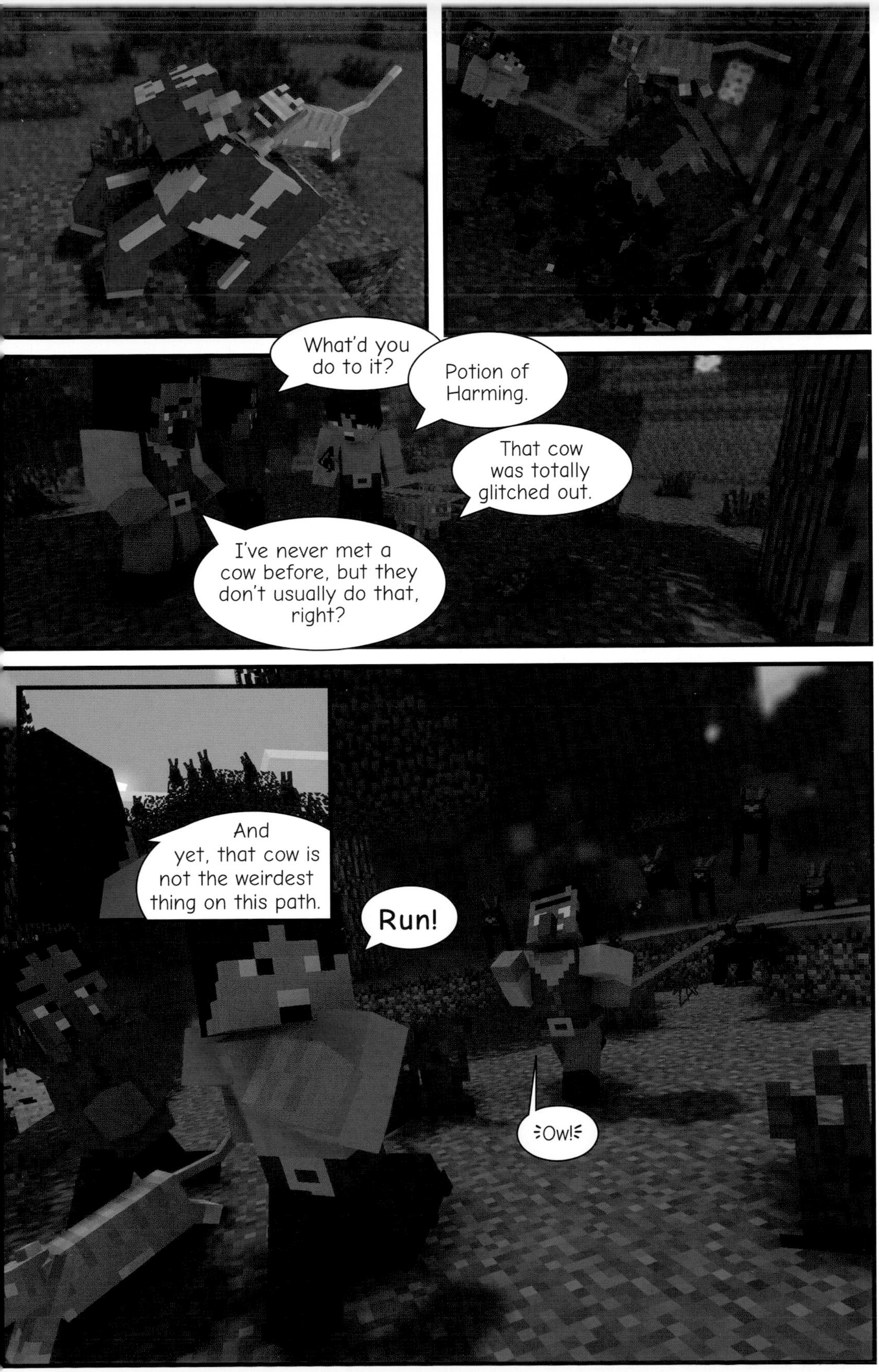
What'd you do to it?
Potion of Harming.
That cow was totally glitched out.
I've never met a cow before, but they don't usually do that, right?
And yet, that cow is not the weirdest thing on this path.
Run!
Ow!

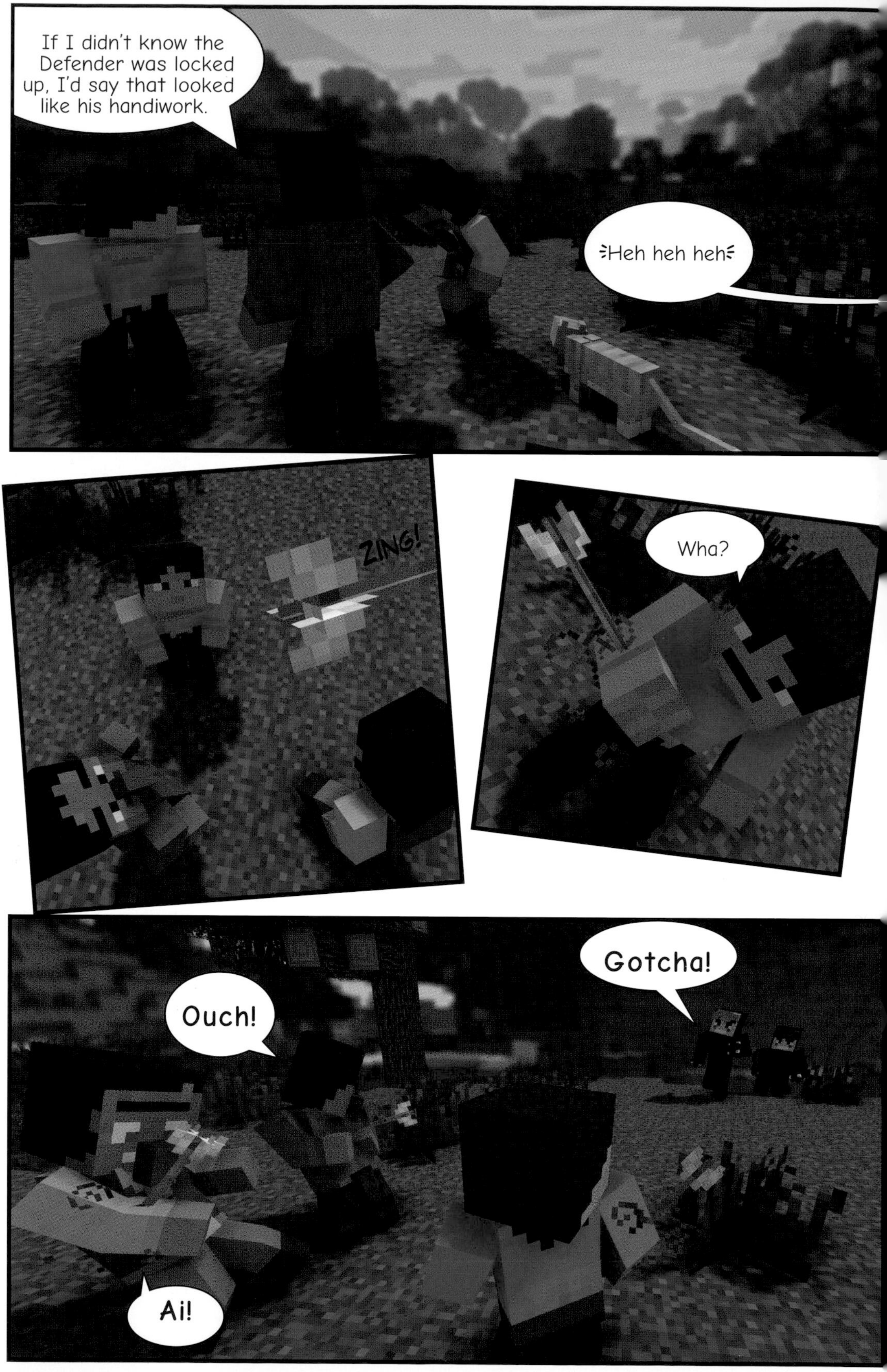
If I didn't know the Defender was locked up, I'd say that looked like his handiwork.
Heh heh heh
ZING!
Wha?
Gotcha!
Ouch!
Ai!

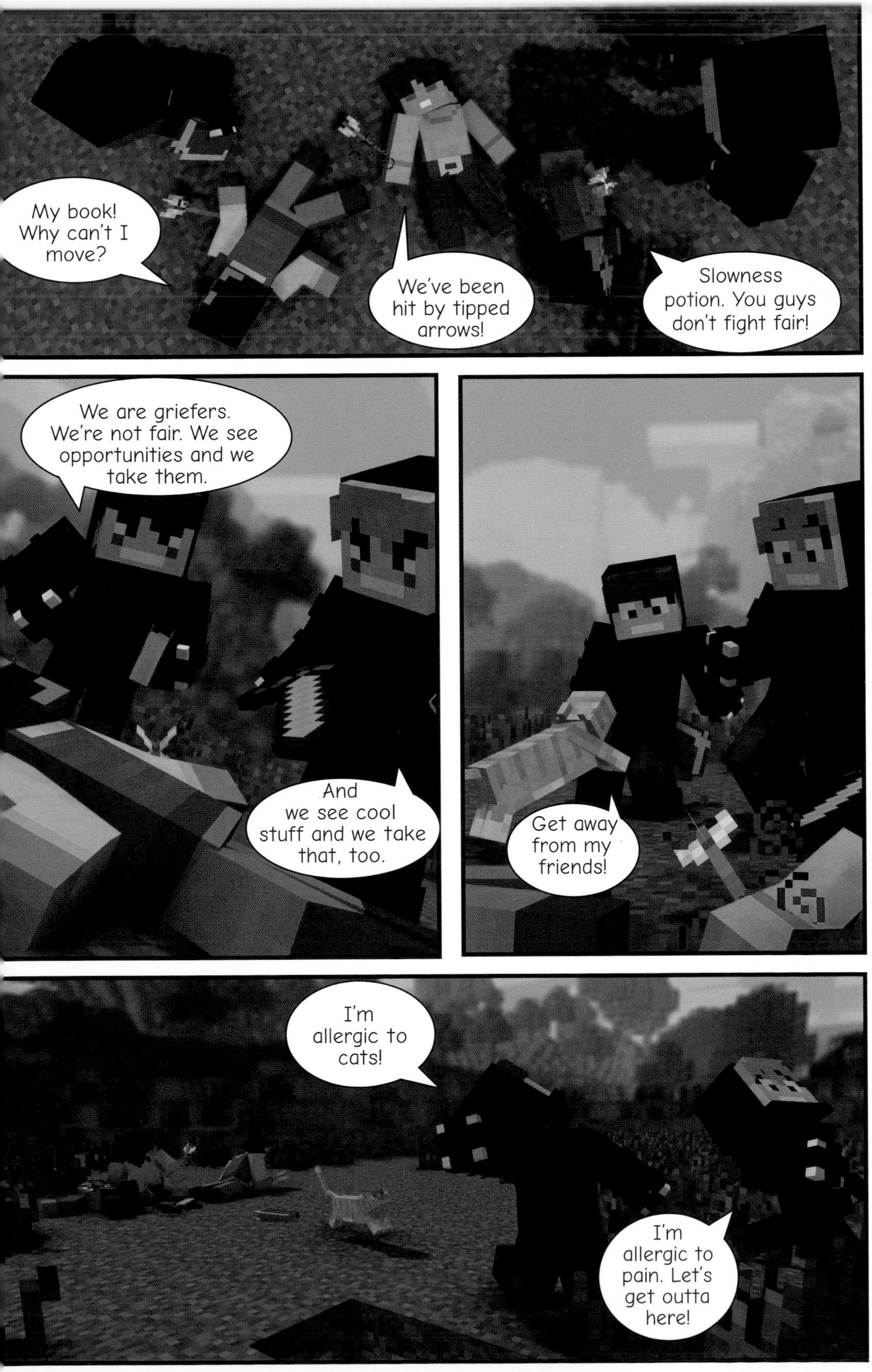
My book! Why can't I move?
We've been hit by tipped arrows!
Slowness potion. You guys don't fight fair!
We are griefers. We're not fair. We see opportunities and we take them.
And we see cool stuff and we take that, too.
Get away from my friends!
I'm allergic to cats!
I'm allergic to pain. Let's get outta here!

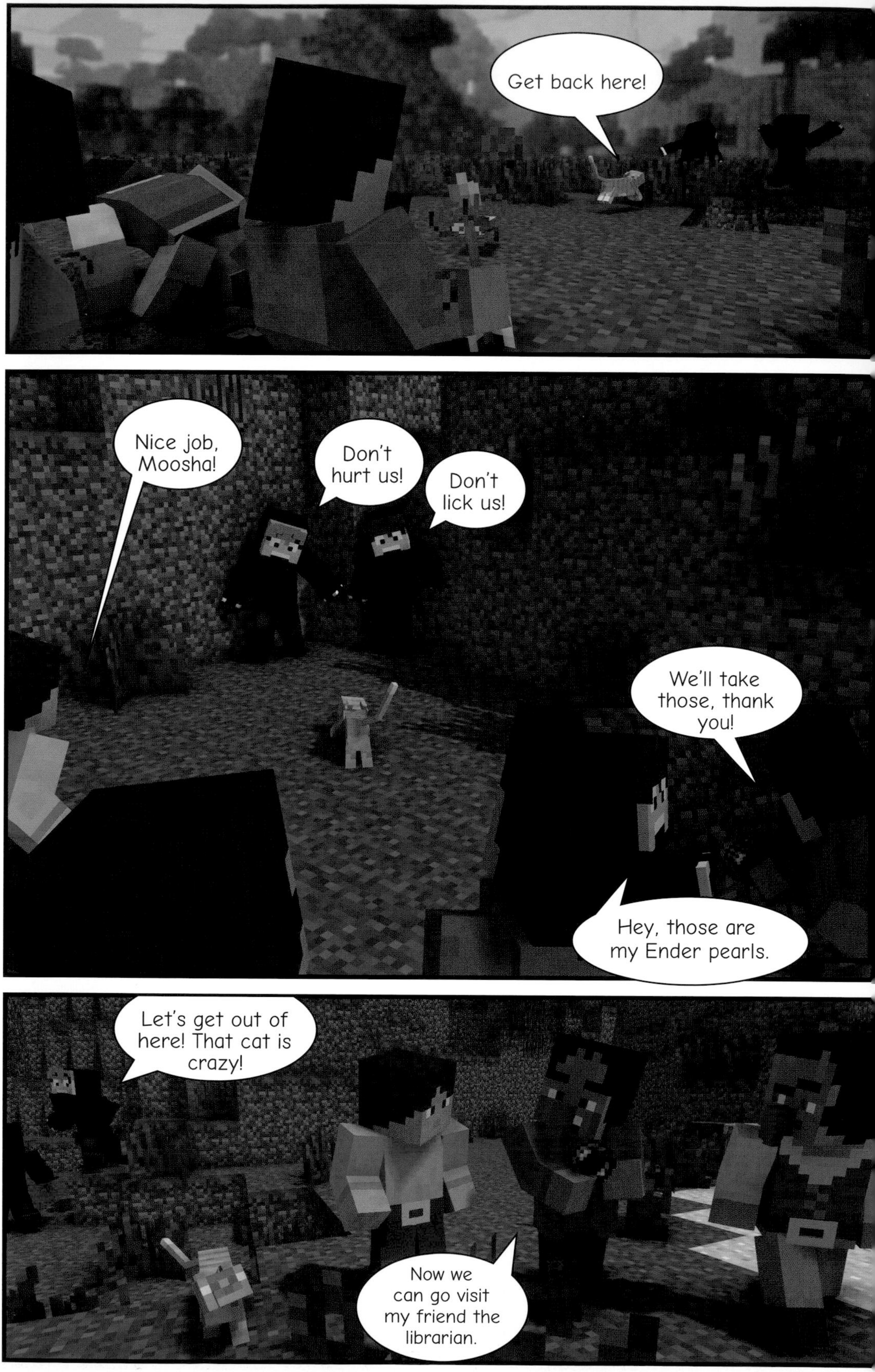
Get back here!
Nice job, Moosha!
Don't hurt us!
Don't lick us!
We'll take those, thank you!
Hey, those are my Ender pearls.
Let's get out of here! That cat is crazy!
Now we can go visit my friend the librarian.

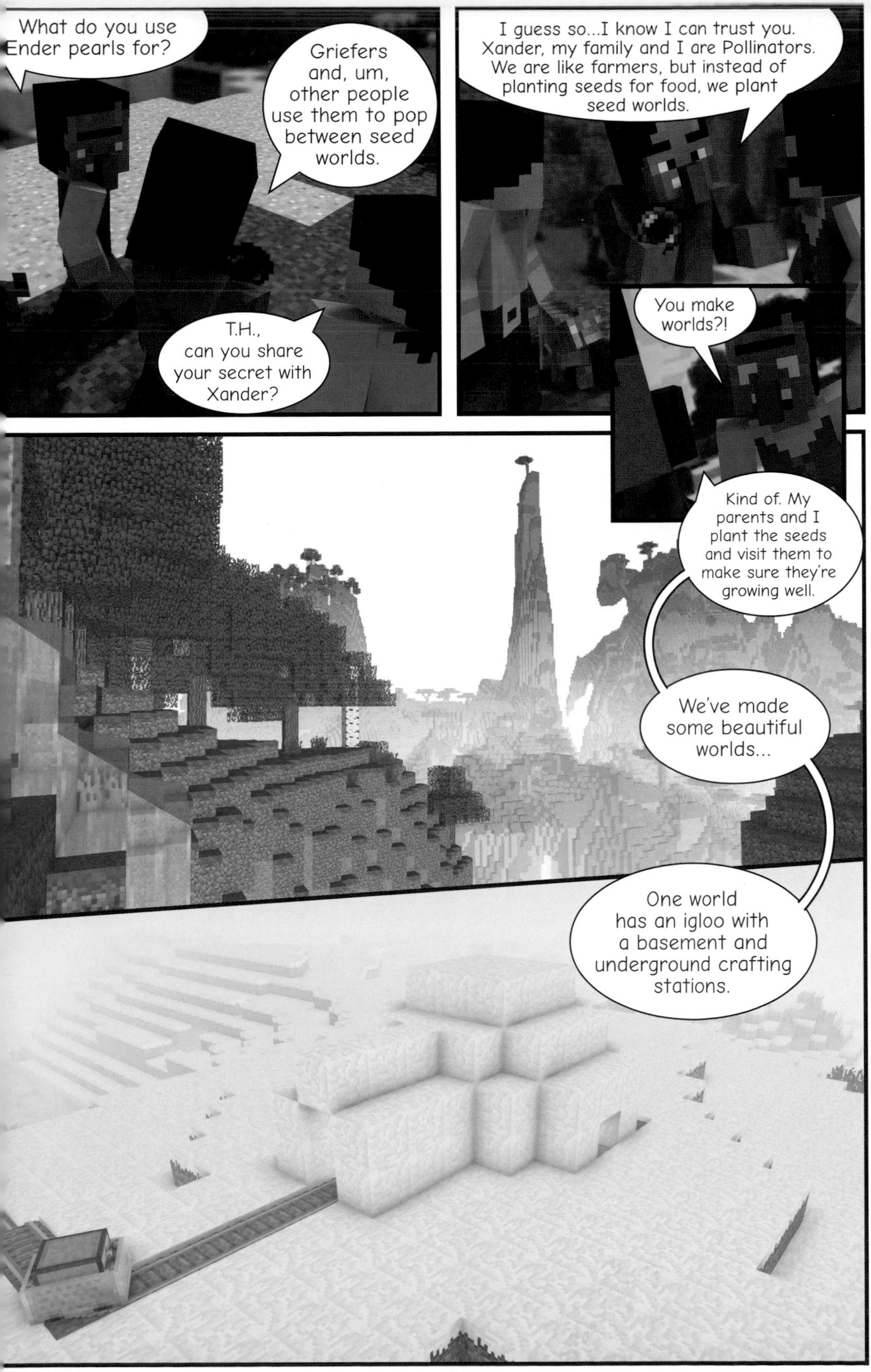
What do you use Ender pearls for?
Griefers and, um, other people use them to pop between seed worlds.
T.H., can you share your secret with Xander?
I guess so...I know I can trust you. Xander, my family and I are Pollinators. We are like farmers, but instead of planting seeds for food, we plant seed worlds.
You make worlds?!
Kind of. My parents and I plant the seeds and visit them to make sure they're growing well.
We've made some beautiful worlds...
One world has an igloo with a basement and underground crafting stations.

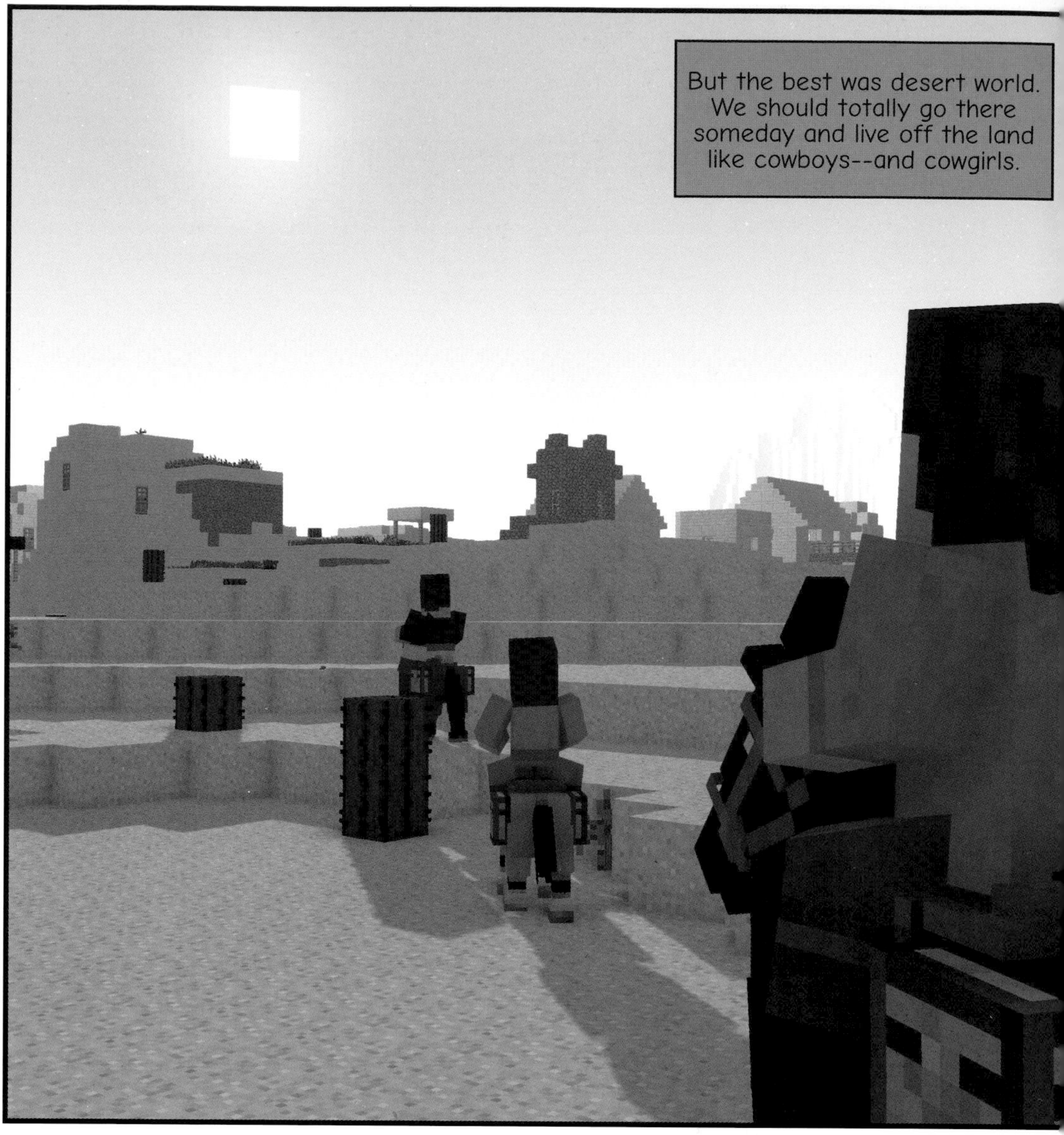
But the best was desert world. We should totally go there someday and live off the land like cowboys--and cowgirls.

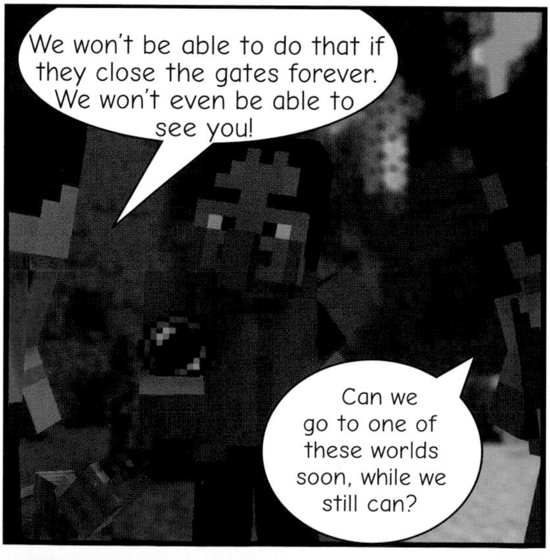
We won't be able to do that if they close the gates forever. We won't even be able to see you!
Can we go to one of these worlds soon, while we still can?

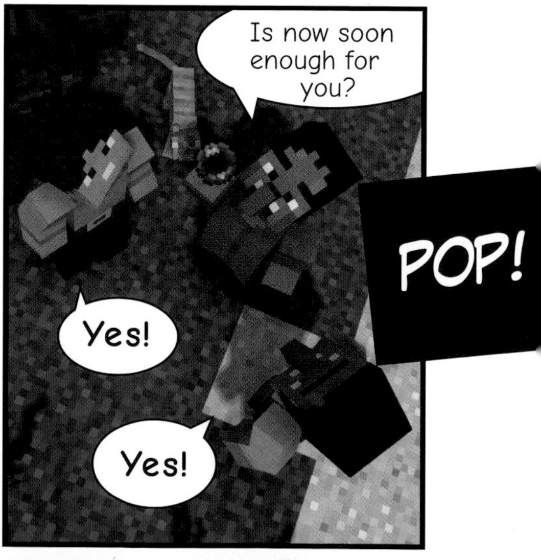
Is now soon enough for you?
POP!
Yes!
Yes!

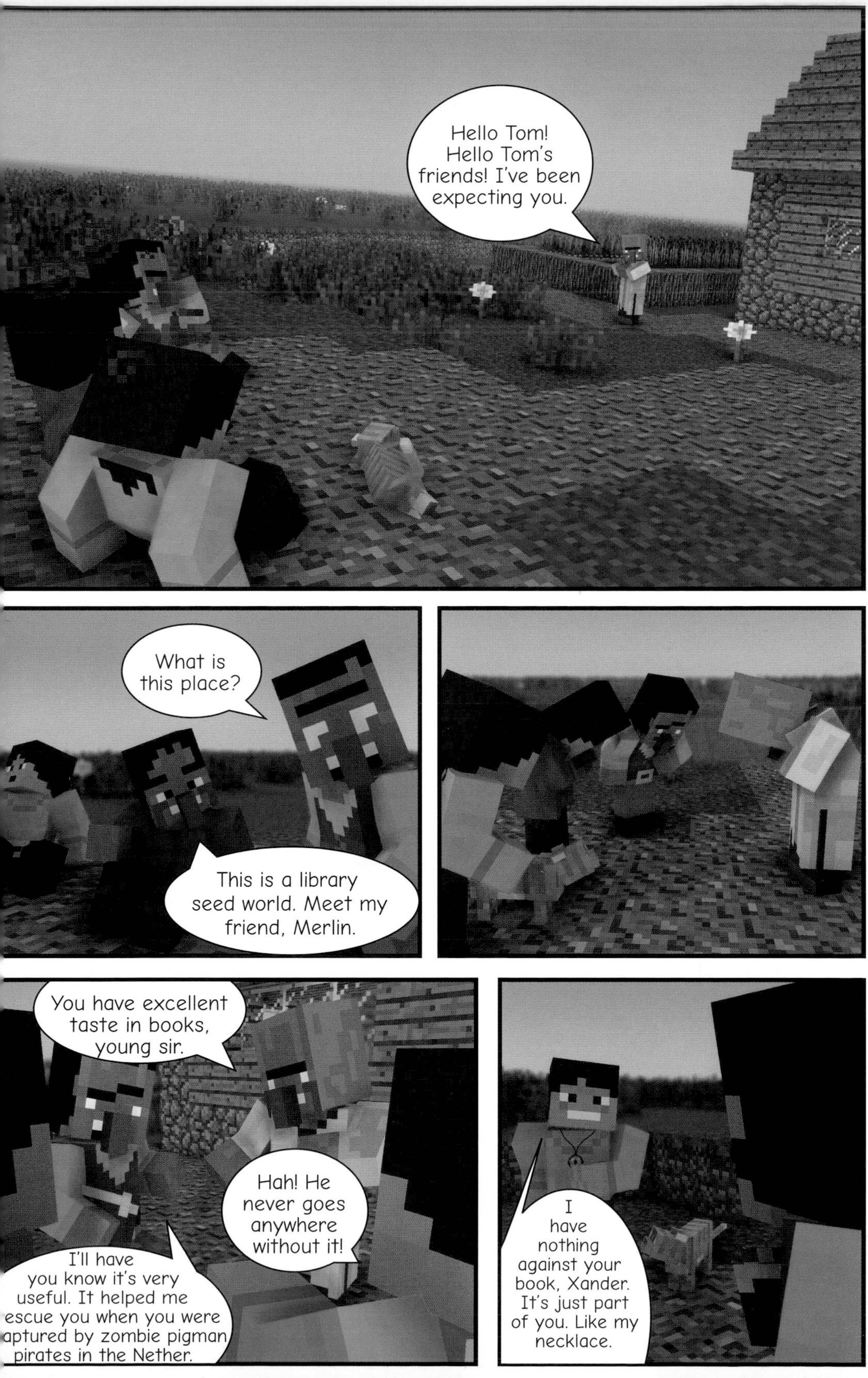
Hello Tom! Hello Tom's friends! I've been expecting you.
What is this place?
This is a library seed world. Meet my friend, Merlin.
You have excellent taste in books, young sir.
I'll have you know it's very useful. It helped me escue you when you were aptured by zombie pigman pirates in the Nether.
Hah! He never goes anywhere without it!
I have nothing against your book, Xander. It's just part of you. Like my necklace.

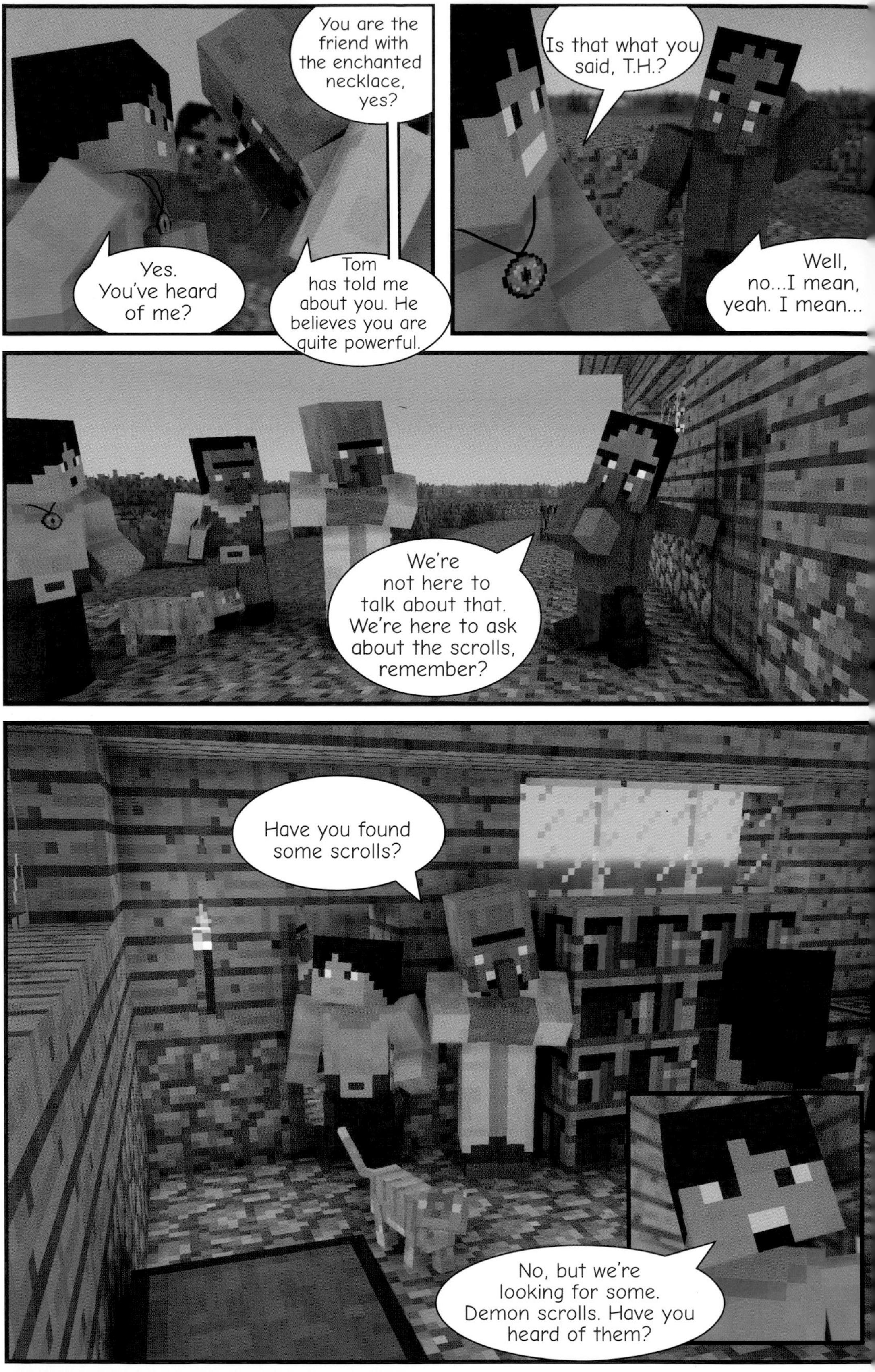
You are the friend with the enchanted necklace, yes?
Yes. You've heard of me?
Tom has told me about you. He believes you are quite powerful.
Is that what you said, T.H.?
Well, no...I mean, yeah. I mean...
We're not here to talk about that. We're here to ask about the scrolls, remember?
Have you found some scrolls?
No, but we're looking for some. Demon scrolls. Have you heard of them?

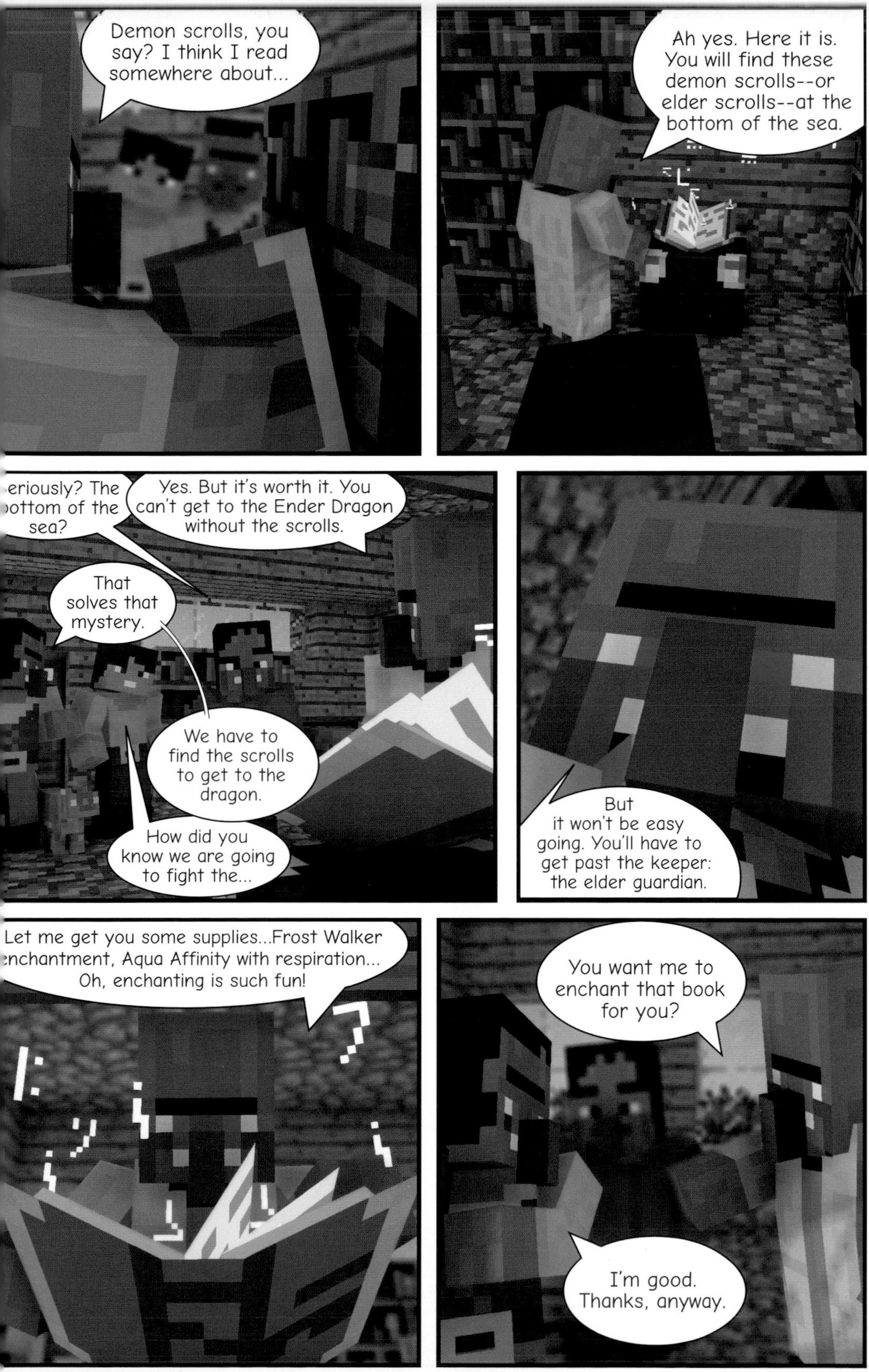
Demon scrolls, you say? I think I read somewhere about...
Ah yes. Here it is. You will find these demon scrolls--or elder scrolls--at the bottom of the sea.
eriously? The ottom of the sea?
Yes. But it's worth it. You can't get to the Ender Dragon without the scrolls.
That solves that mystery.
We have to find the scrolls to get to the dragon.
How did you know we are going to fight the...
But it won't be easy going. You'll have to get past the keeper: the elder guardian.
Let me get you some supplies...Frost Walker enchantment, Aqua Affinity with respiration... Oh, enchanting is such fun!
You want me to enchant that book for you?
I'm good. Thanks, anyway.

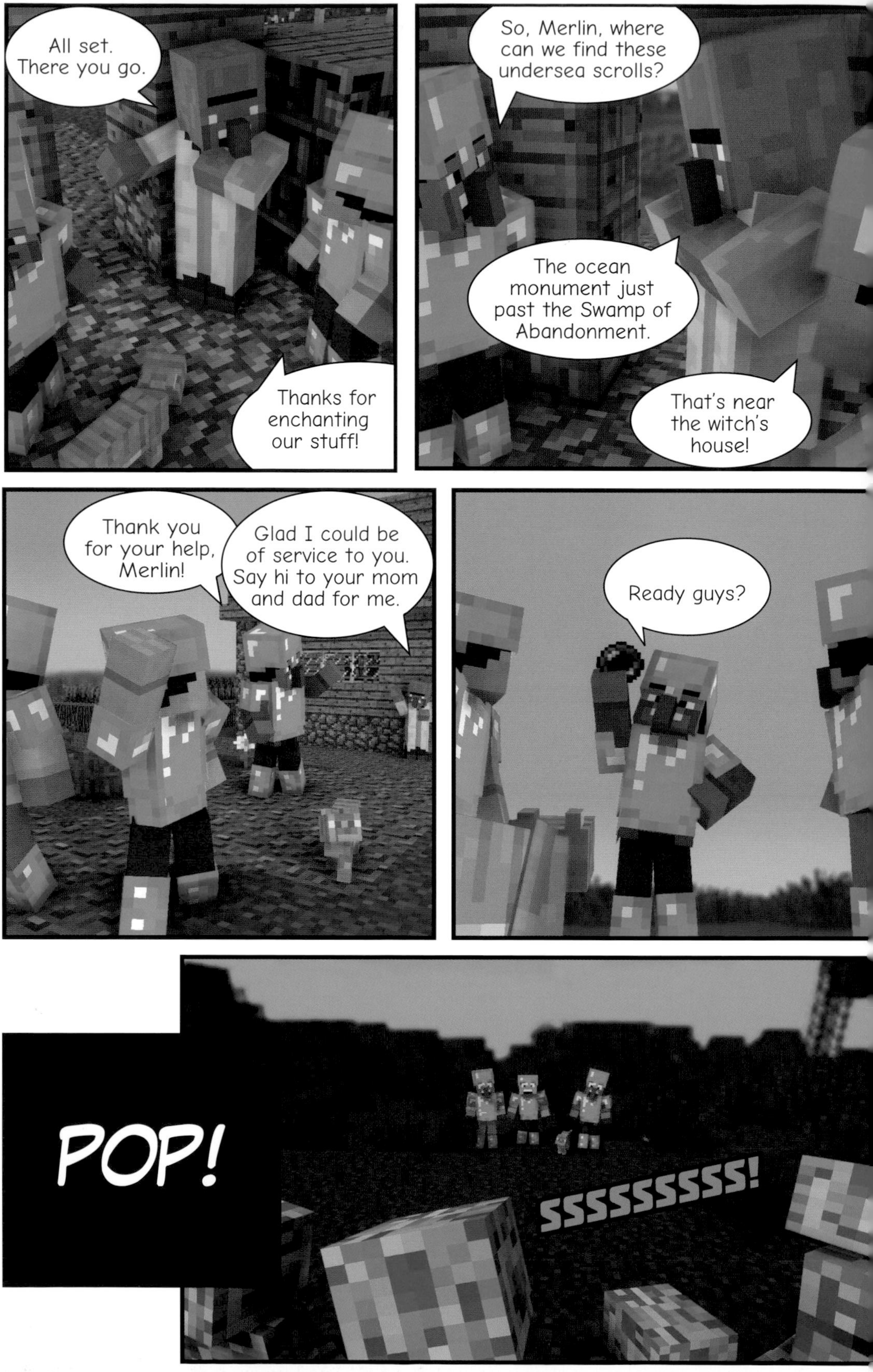
All set. There you go.
Thanks for enchanting our stuff!
So, Merlin, where can we find these undersea scrolls?
The ocean monument just past the Swamp of Abandonment.
That's near the witch's house!
Thank you for your help, Merlin!
Glad I could be of service to you. Say hi to your mom and dad for me.
Ready guys?
POP!
SSSSSSSSS!

CHAPTER 4

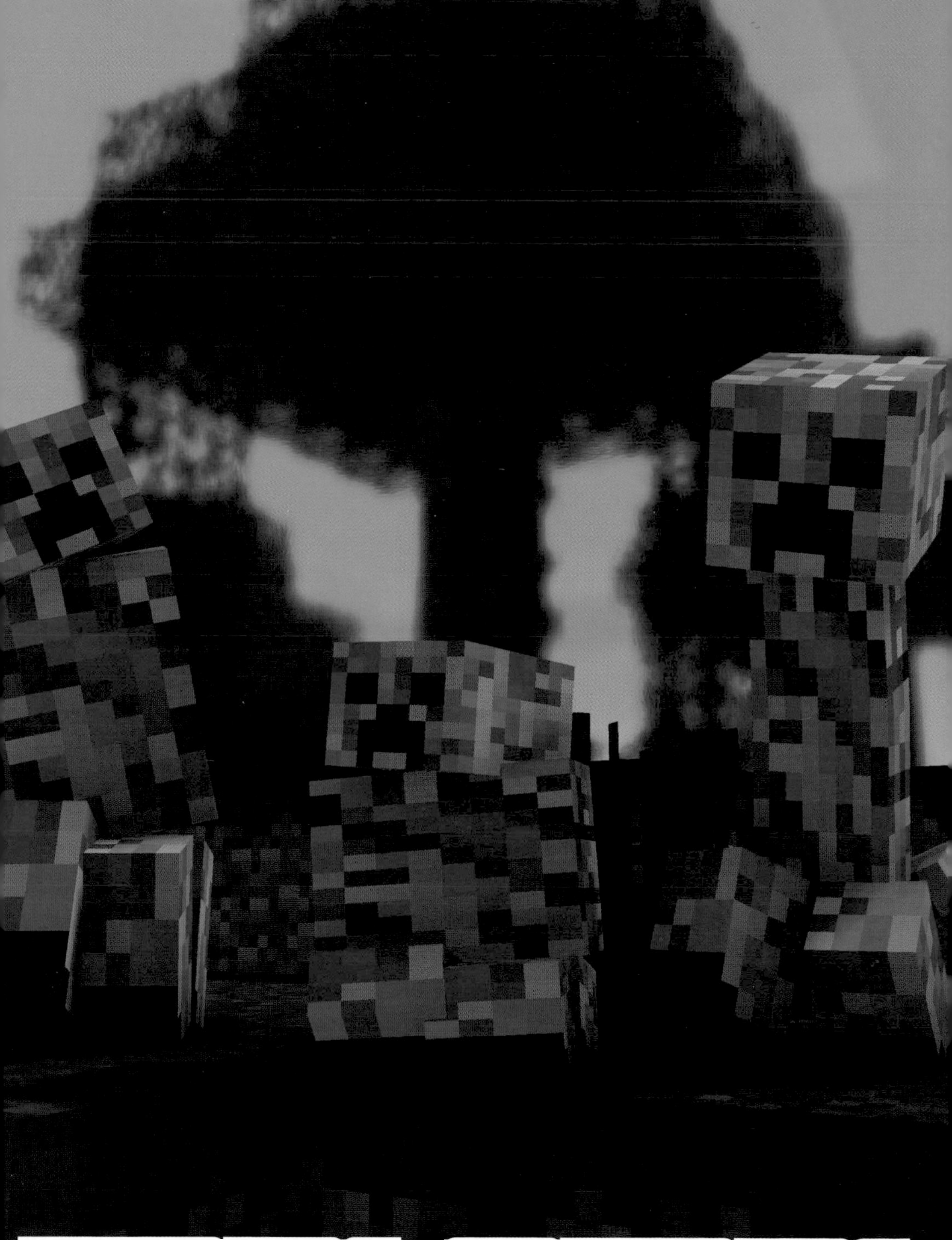

JEEPERS CREEPERS

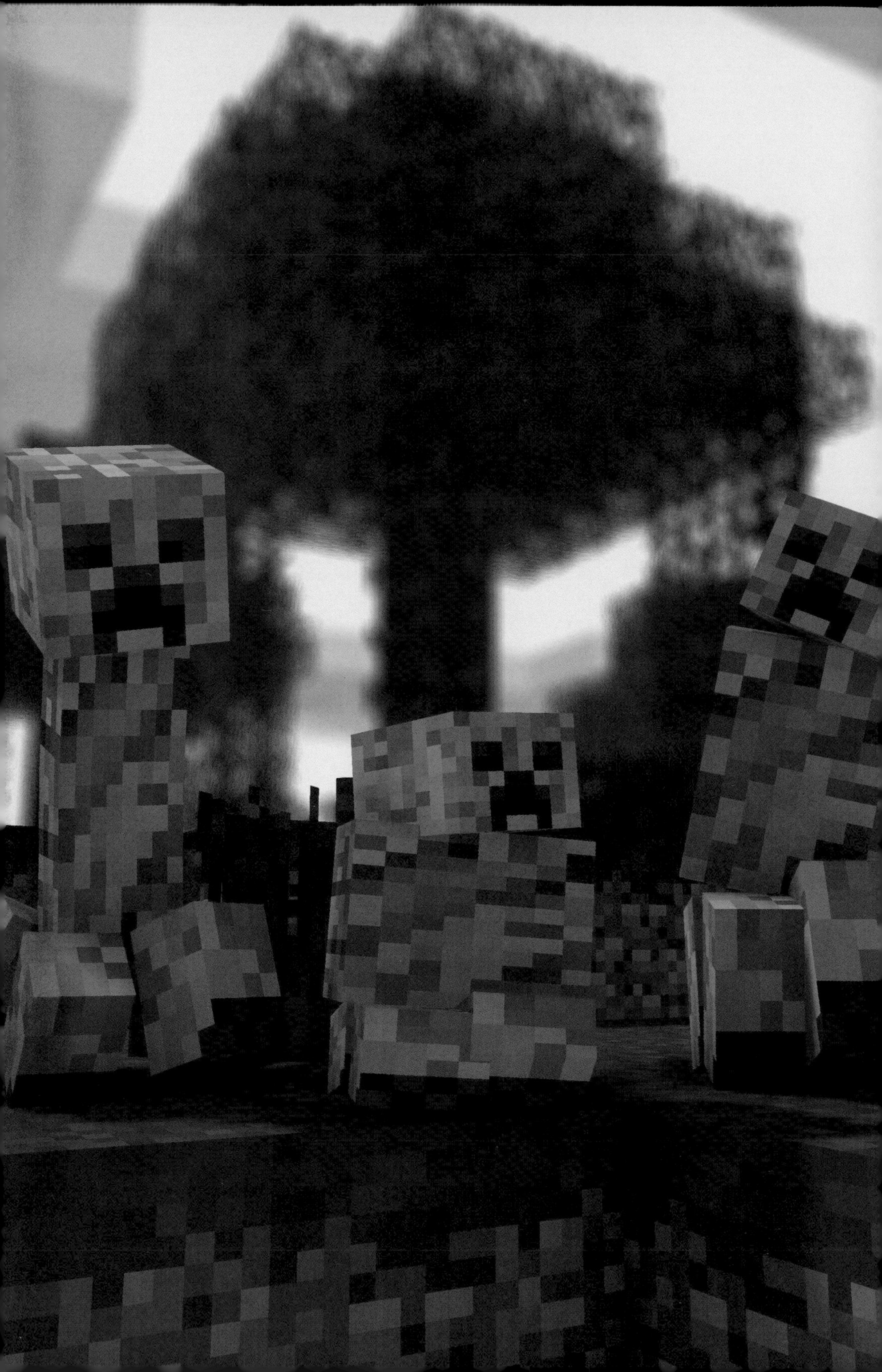

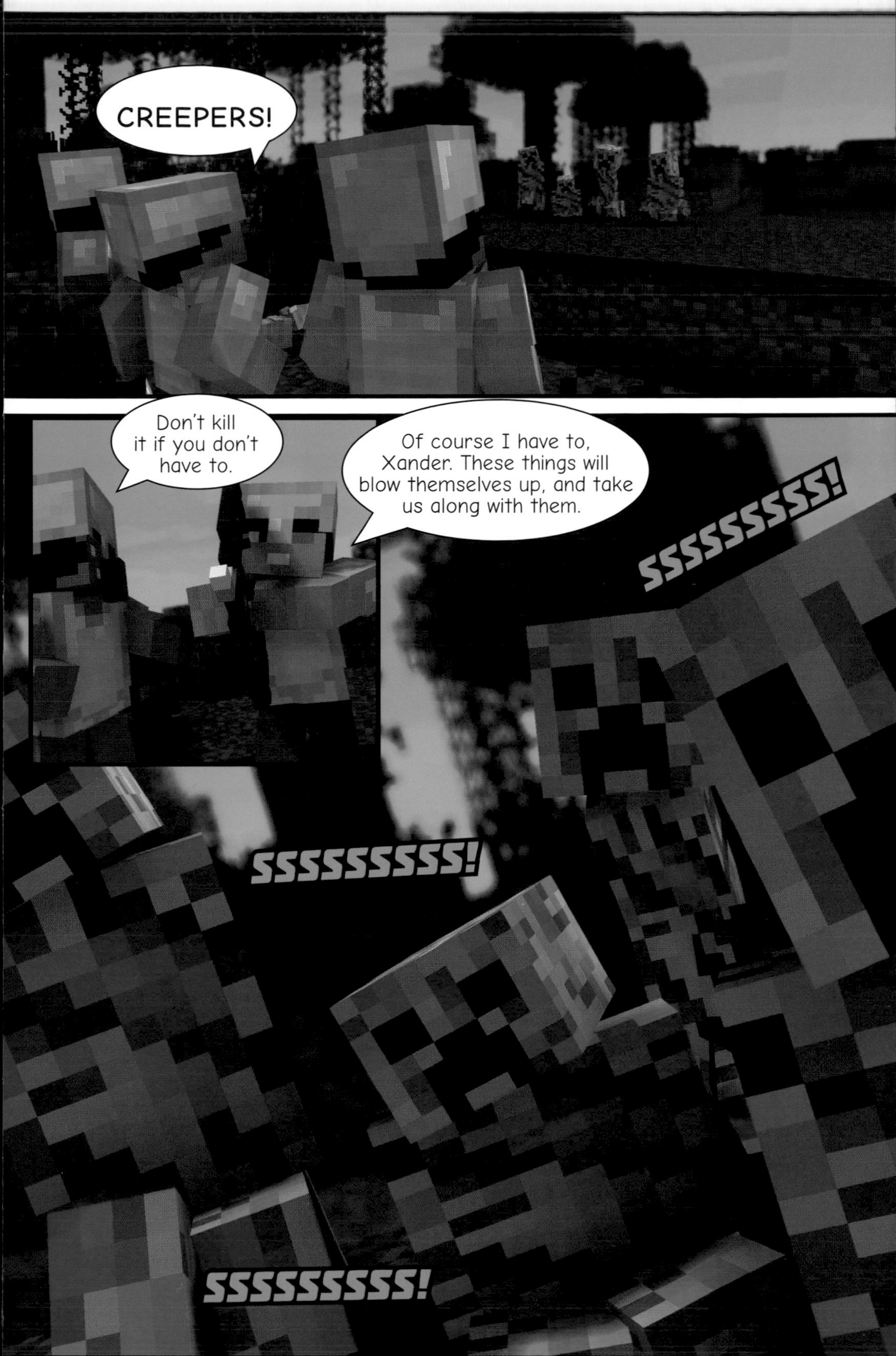
CREEPERS!
Don't kill it if you don't have to.
Of course I have to, Xander. These things will blow themselves up, and take us along with them.
SSSSSSSSS!
SSSSSSSSS!
SSSSSSSSS!

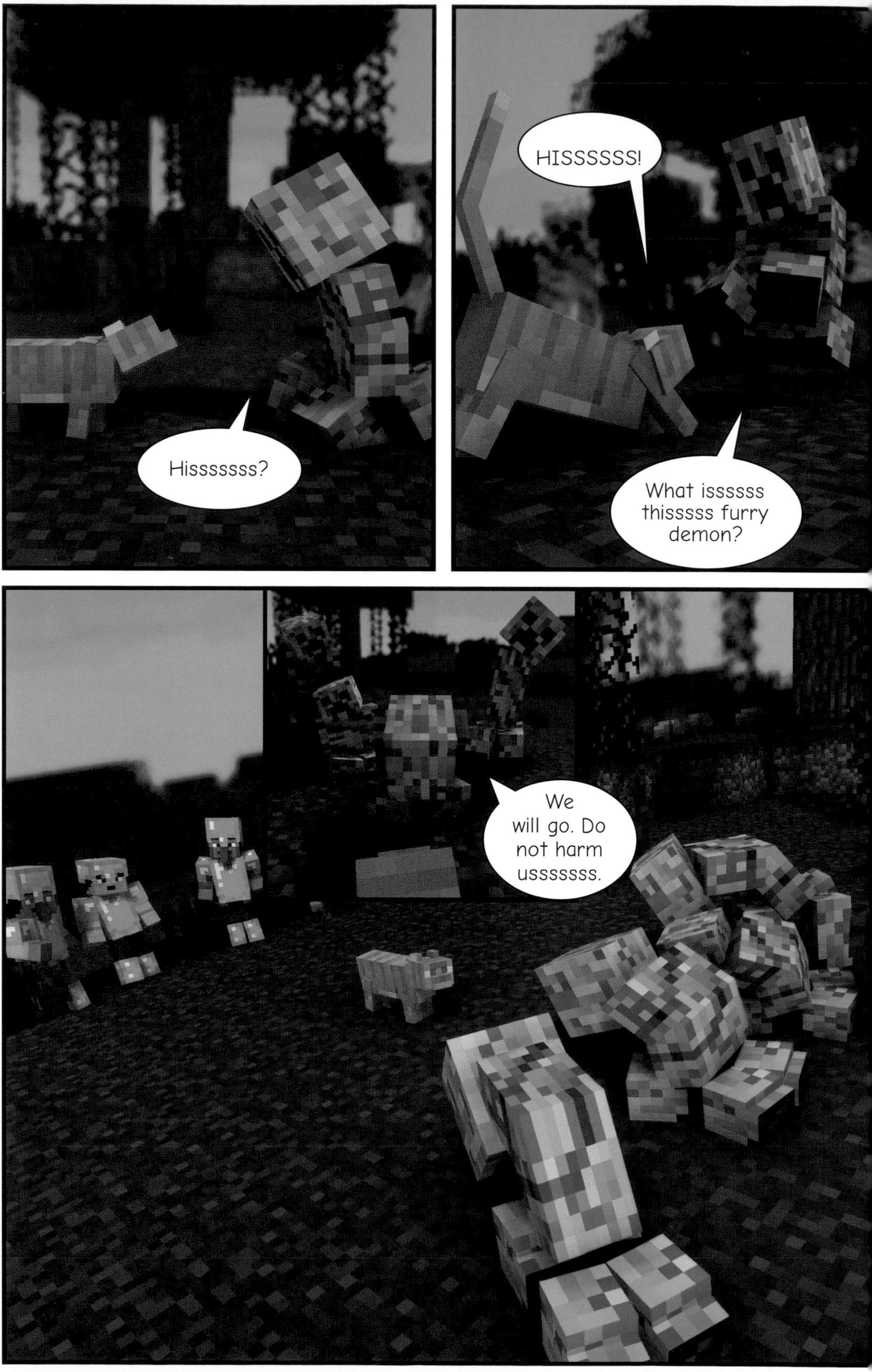
Hissssssss?
HISSSSSS!
What issssss thissssss furry demon?
We will go. Do not harm usssssss.

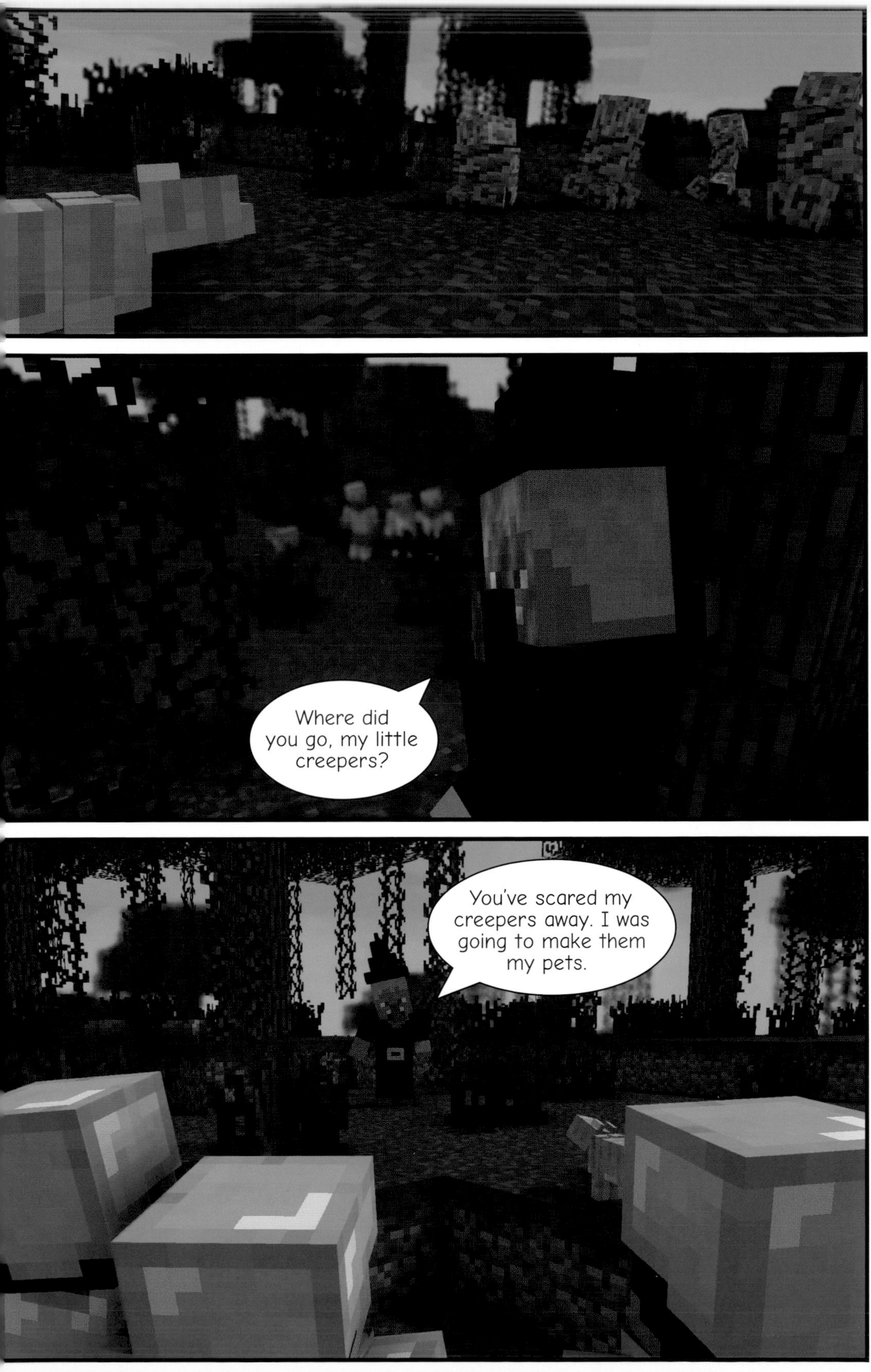
Where did you go, my little creepers?
You've scared my creepers away. I was going to make them my pets.

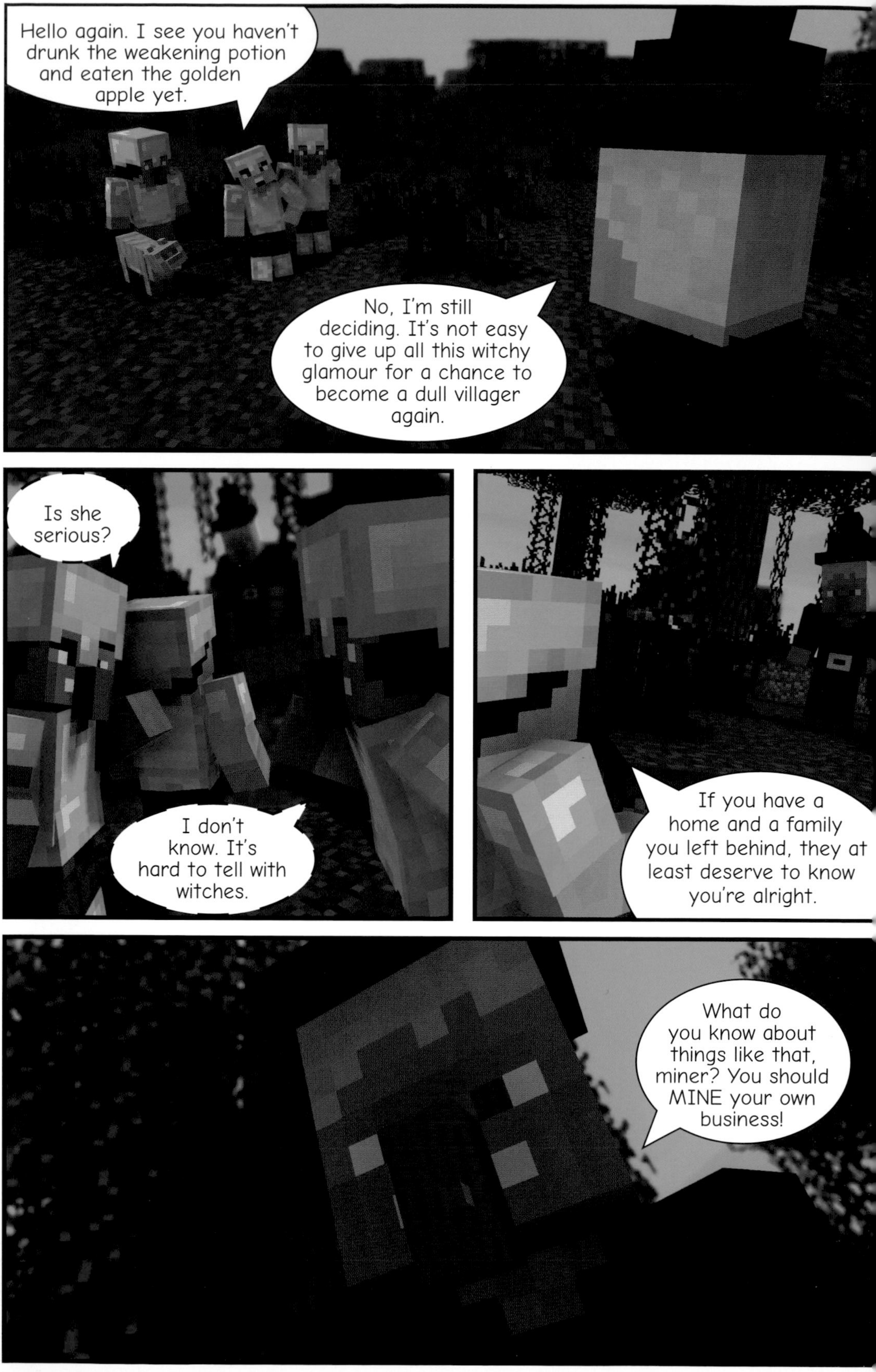
Hello again. I see you haven't drunk the weakening potion and eaten the golden apple yet.
No, I'm still deciding. It's not easy to give up all this witchy glamour for a chance to become a dull villager again.
Is she serious?
I don't know. It's hard to tell with witches.
If you have a home and a family you left behind, they at least deserve to know you're alright.
What do you know about things like that, miner? You should MINE your own business!

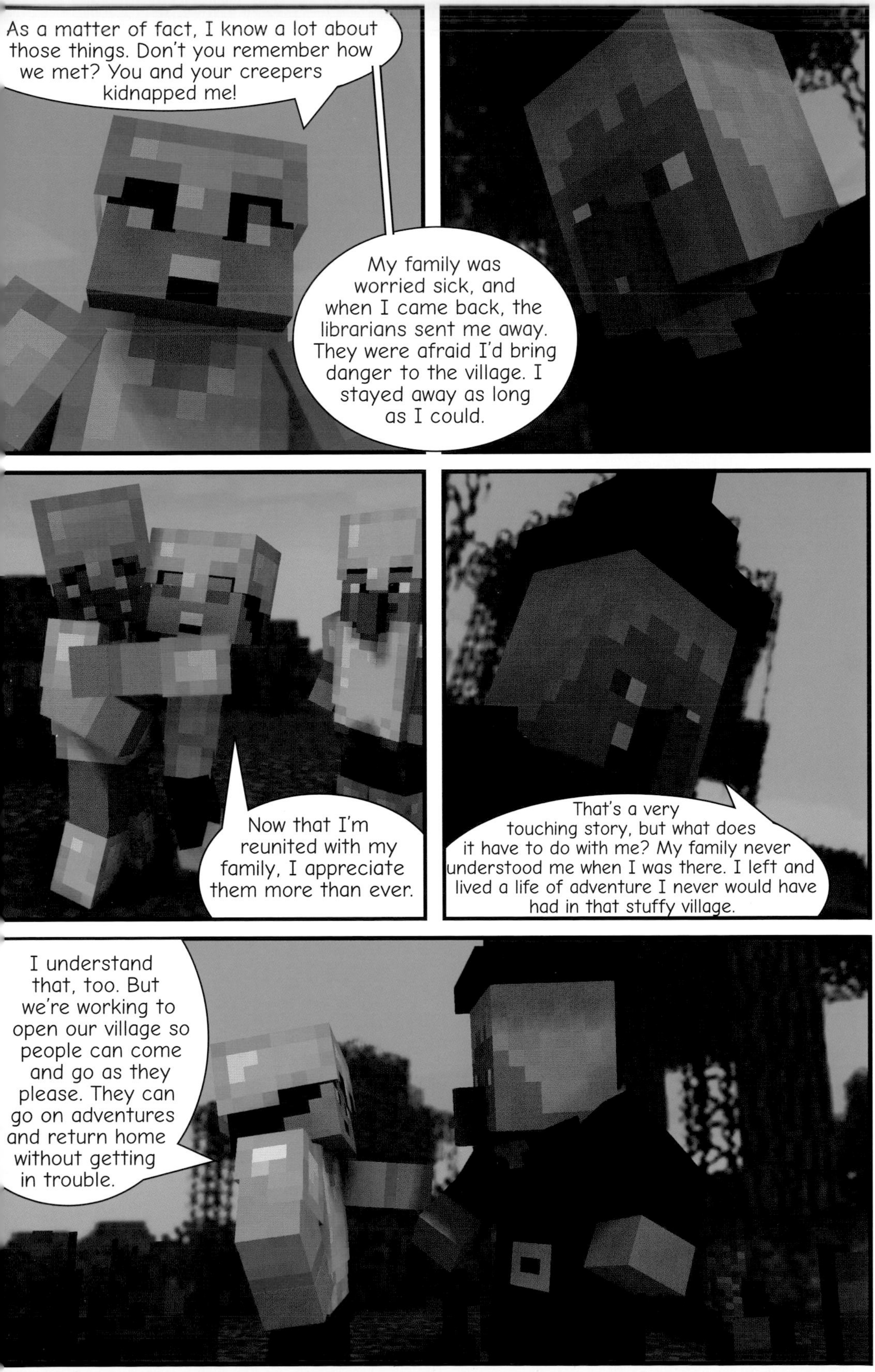
As a matter of fact, I know a lot about those things. Don't you remember how we met? You and your creepers kidnapped me!
My family was worried sick, and when I came back, the librarians sent me away. They were afraid I'd bring danger to the village. I stayed away as long as I could.
Now that I'm reunited with my family, I appreciate them more than ever.
That's a very touching story, but what does it have to do with me? My family never understood me when I was there. I left and lived a life of adventure I never would have had in that stuffy village.
I understand that, too. But we're working to open our village so people can come and go as they please. They can go on adventures and return home without getting in trouble.

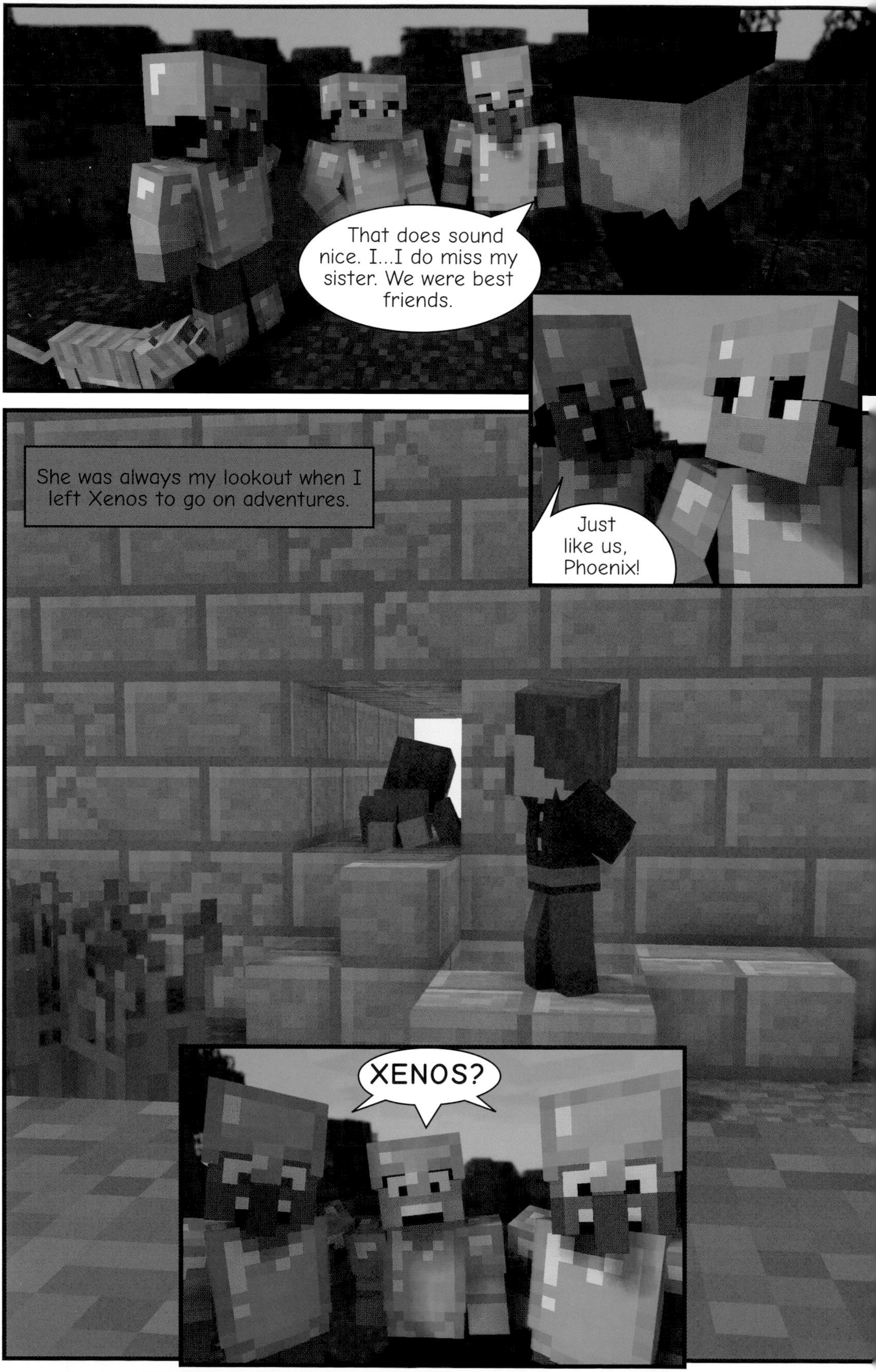
That does sound nice. I...I do miss my sister. We were best friends.
Just like us, Phoenix!
She was always my lookout when I left Xenos to go on adventures.
XENOS?

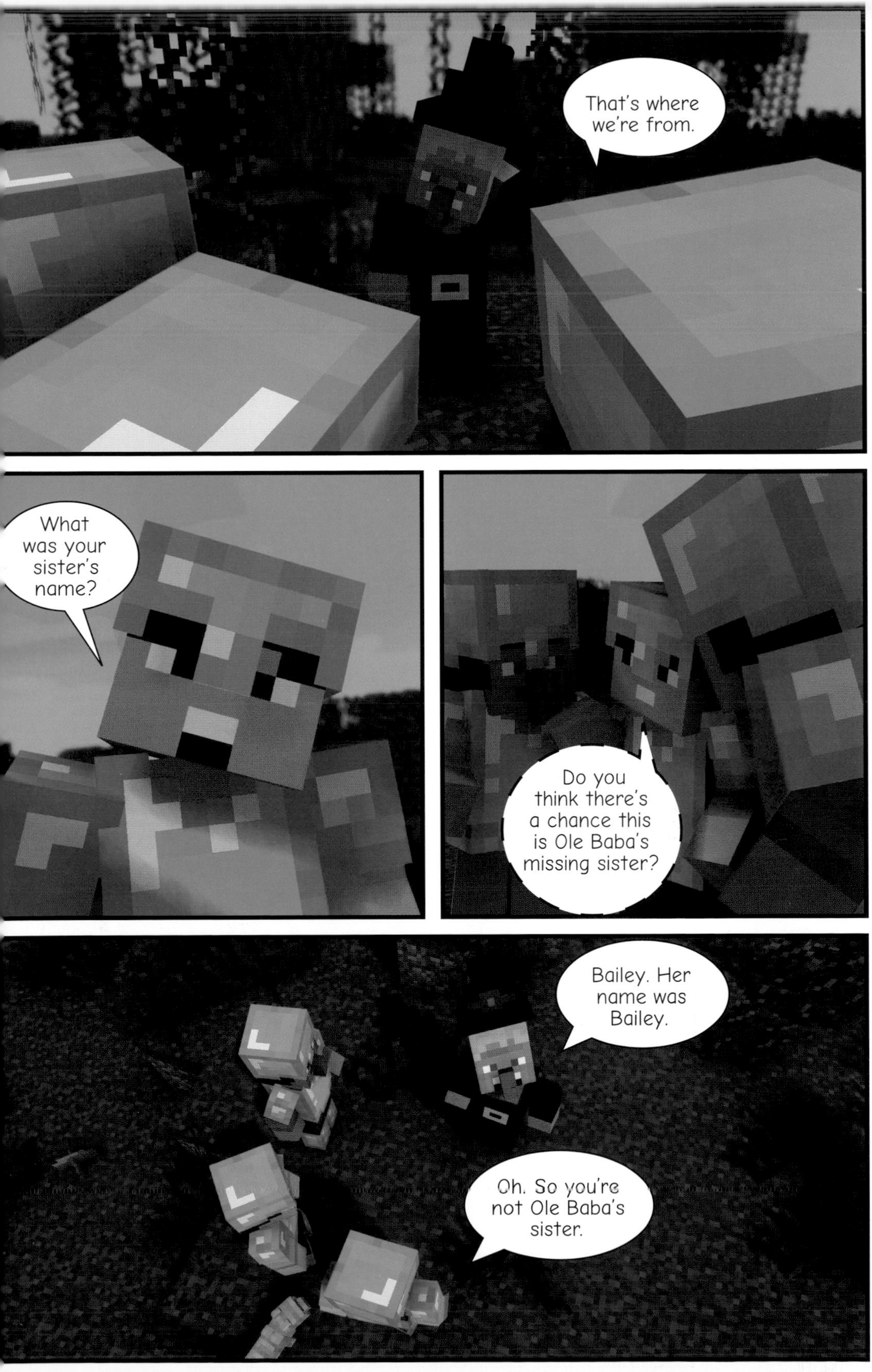
That's where we're from.
What was your sister's name?
Do you think there's a chance this is Ole Baba's missing sister?
Bailey. Her name was Bailey.
Oh. So you're not Ole Baba's sister.

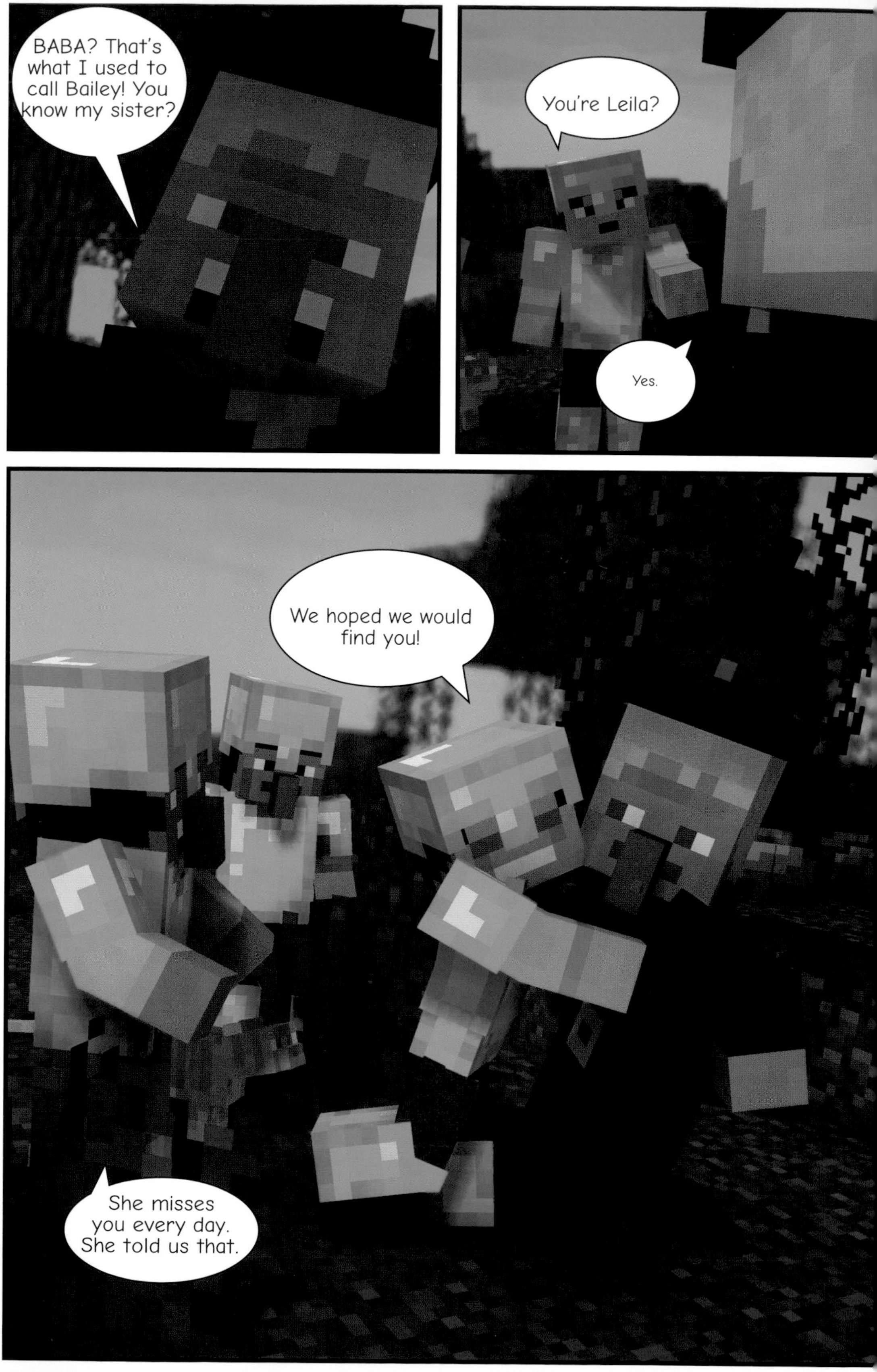
BABA? That's what I used to call Bailey! You know my sister?
You're Leila?
Yes.
We hoped we would find you!
She misses you every day. She told us that.

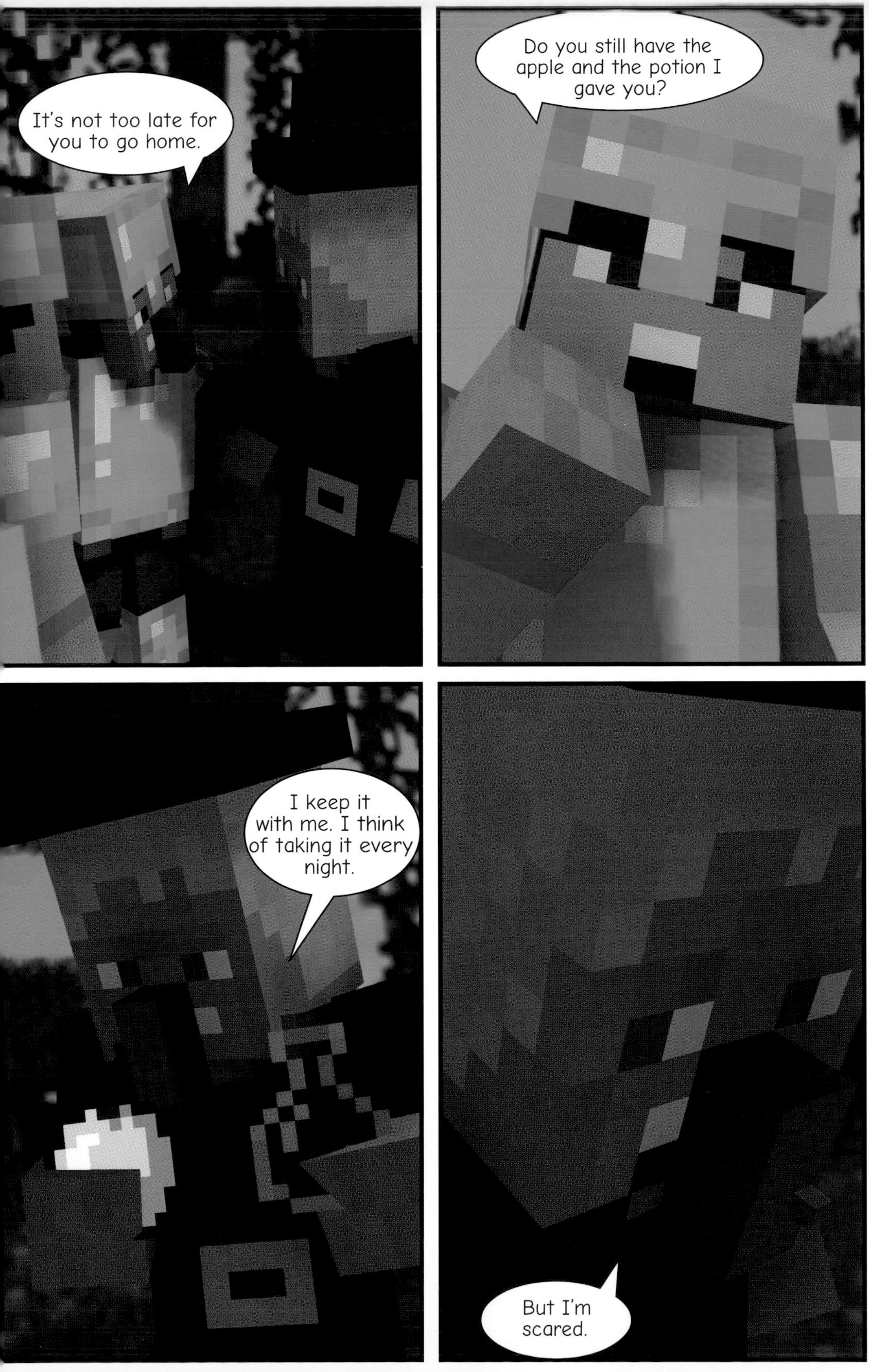
It's not too late for you to go home.
Do you still have the apple and the potion I gave you?
I keep it with me. I think of taking it every night.
But I'm scared.

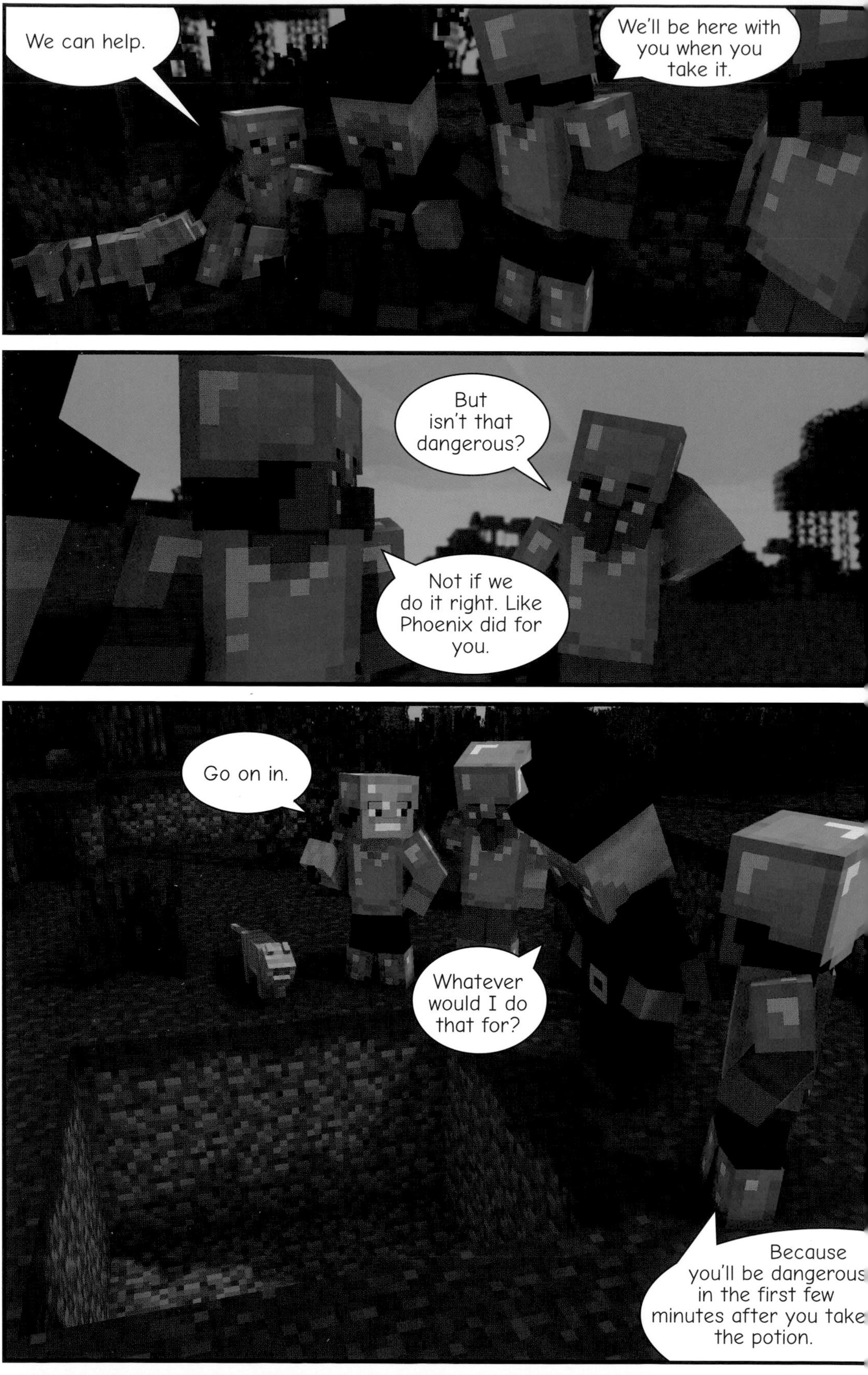
We can help.
We'll be here with you when you take it.
But isn't that dangerous?
Not if we do it right. Like Phoenix did for you.
Go on in.
Whatever would I do that for?
Because you'll be dangerous in the first few minutes after you take the potion.

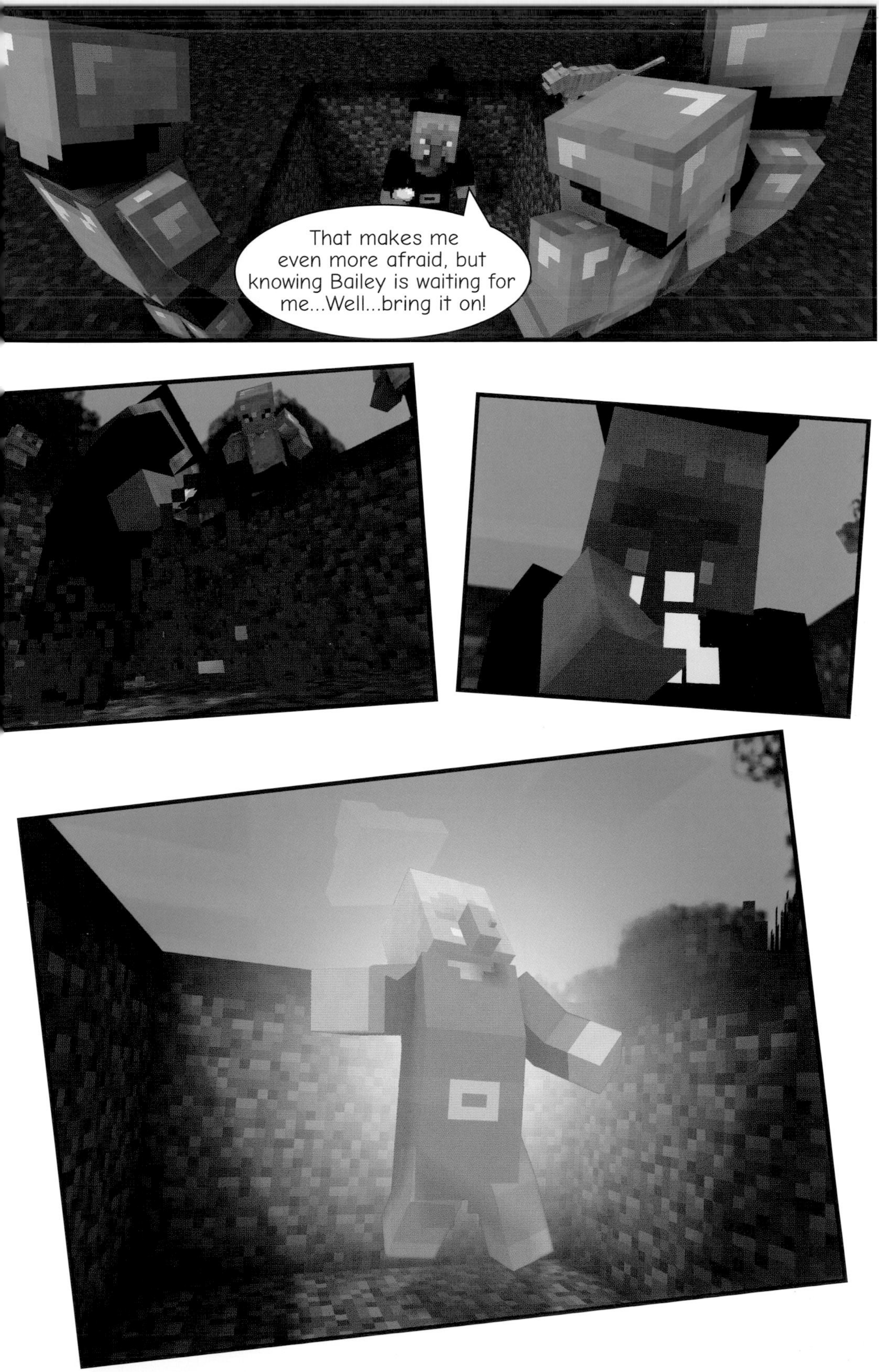
That makes me even more afraid, but knowing Bailey is waiting for me...Well...bring it on!

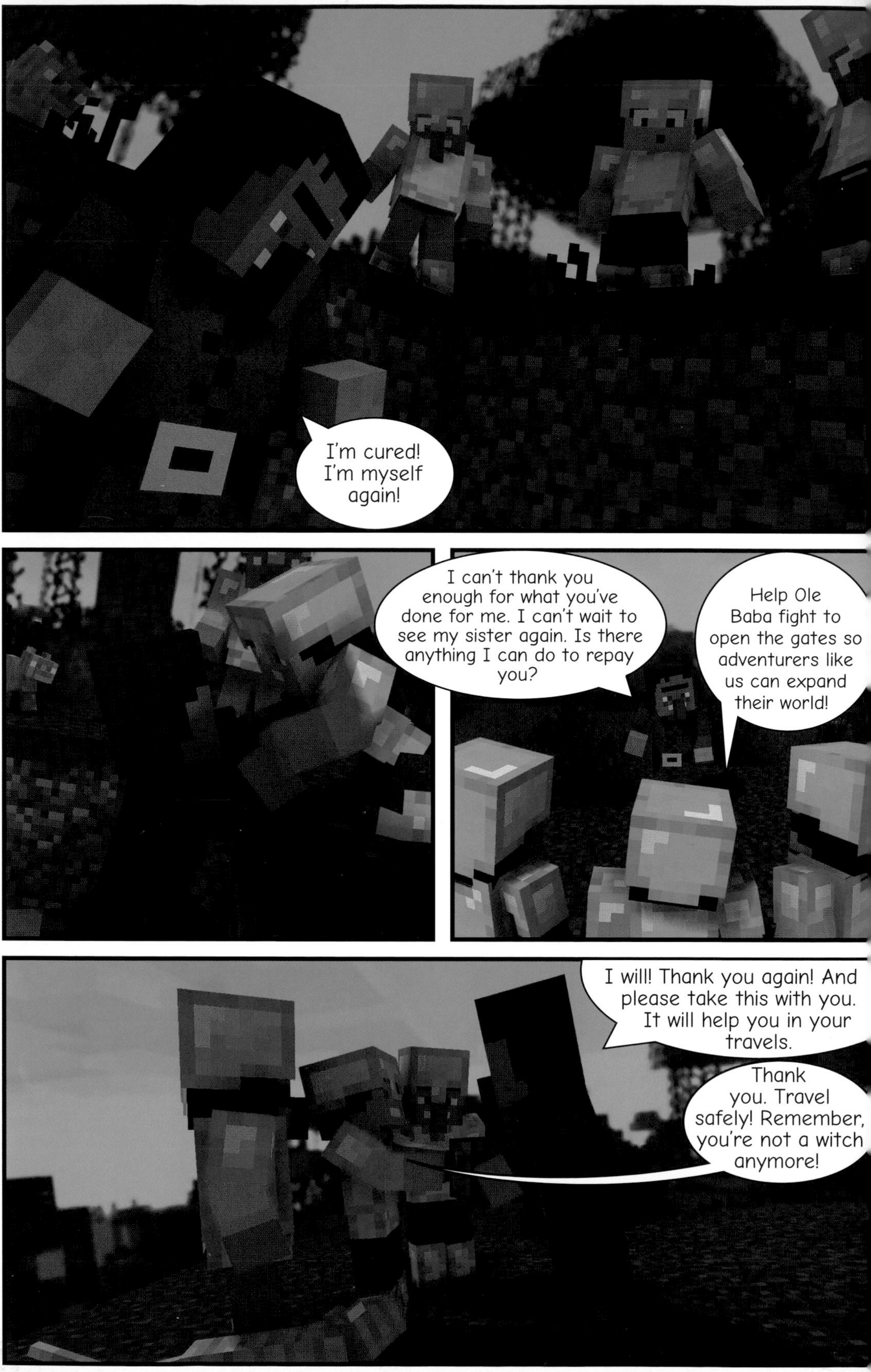
I'm cured! I'm myself again!
I can't thank you enough for what you've done for me. I can't wait to see my sister again. Is there anything I can do to repay you?
Help Ole Baba fight to open the gates so adventurers like us can expand their world!
I will! Thank you again! And please take this with you. It will help you in your travels.
Thank you. Travel safely! Remember, you're not a witch anymore!

CHAPTER 5

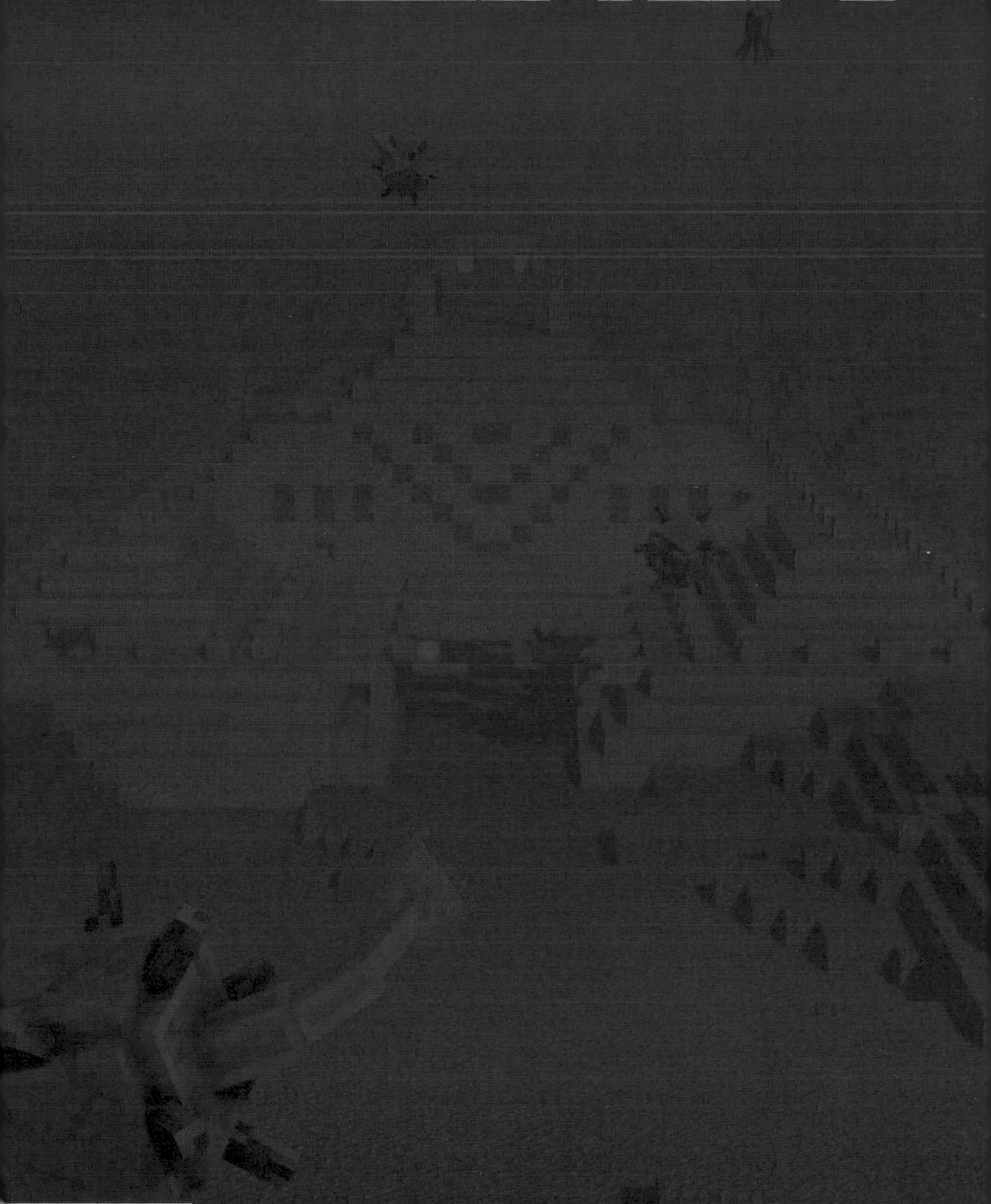

THE GUARDIAN BATTLE

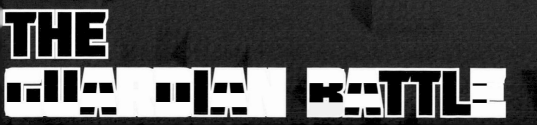

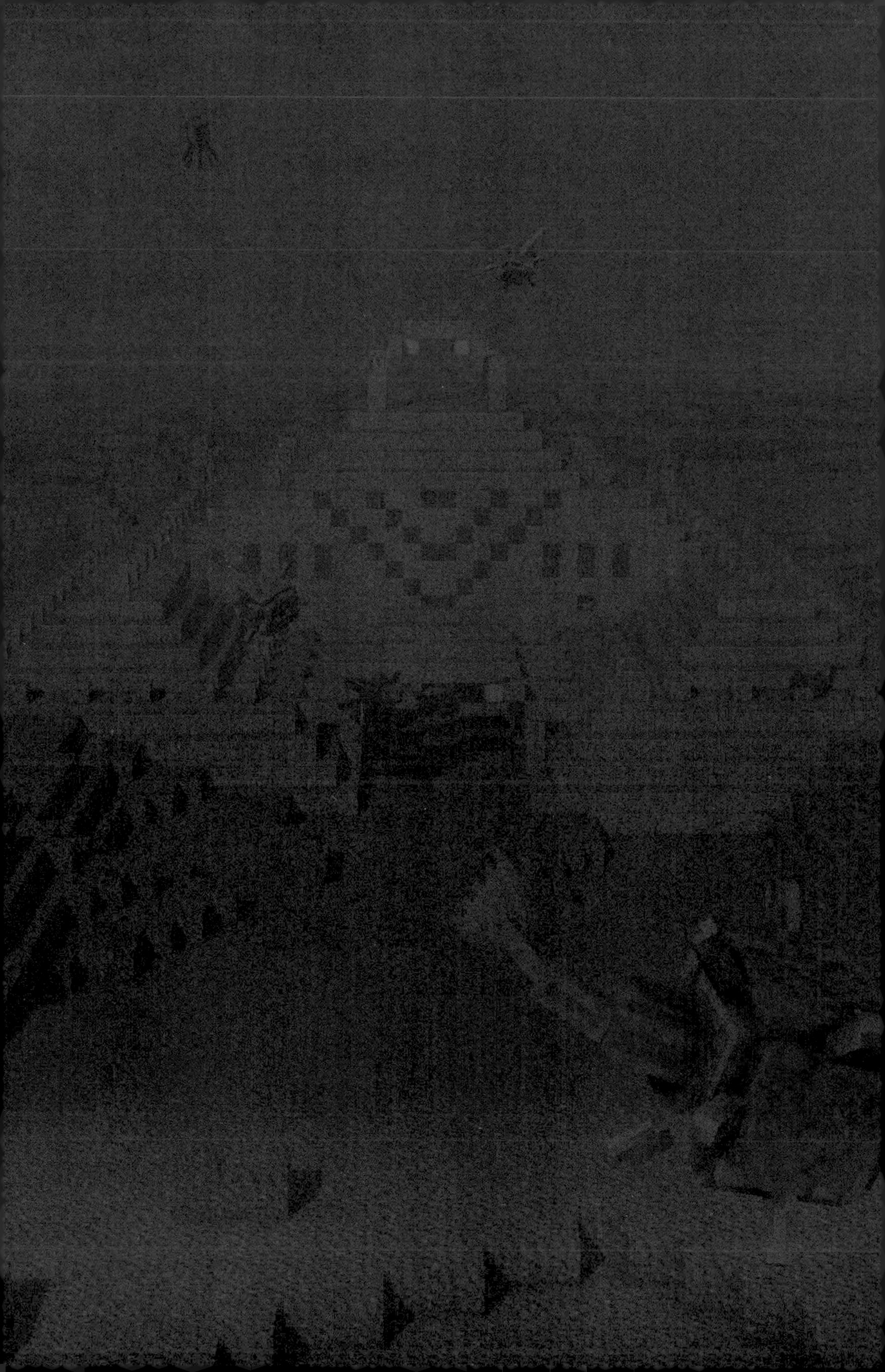

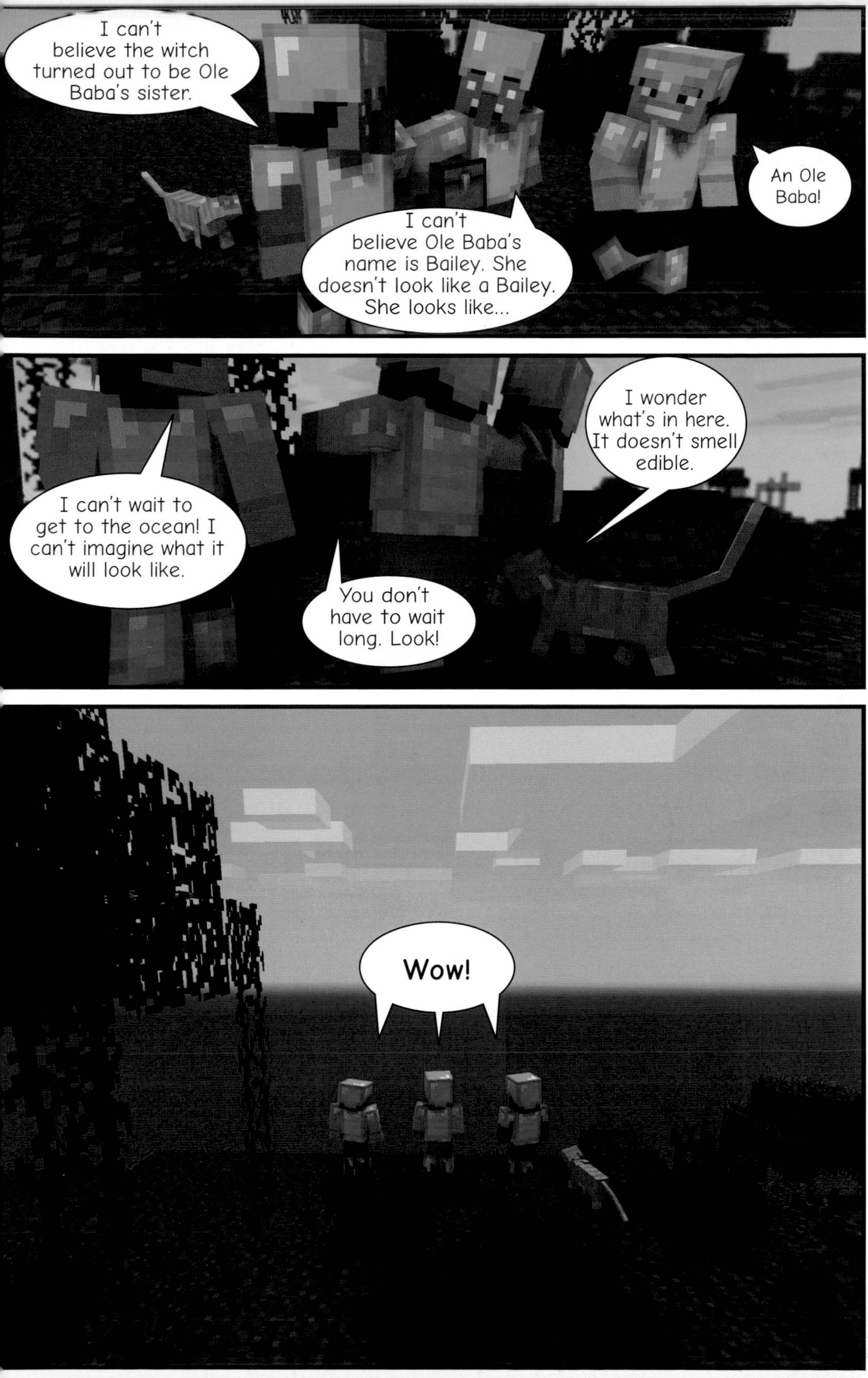
I can't believe the witch turned out to be Ole Baba's sister.
An Ole Baba!
I can't believe Ole Baba's name is Bailey. She doesn't look like a Bailey. She looks like...
I can't wait to get to the ocean! I can't imagine what it will look like.
I wonder what's in here. It doesn't smell edible.
You don't have to wait long. Look!
Wow!

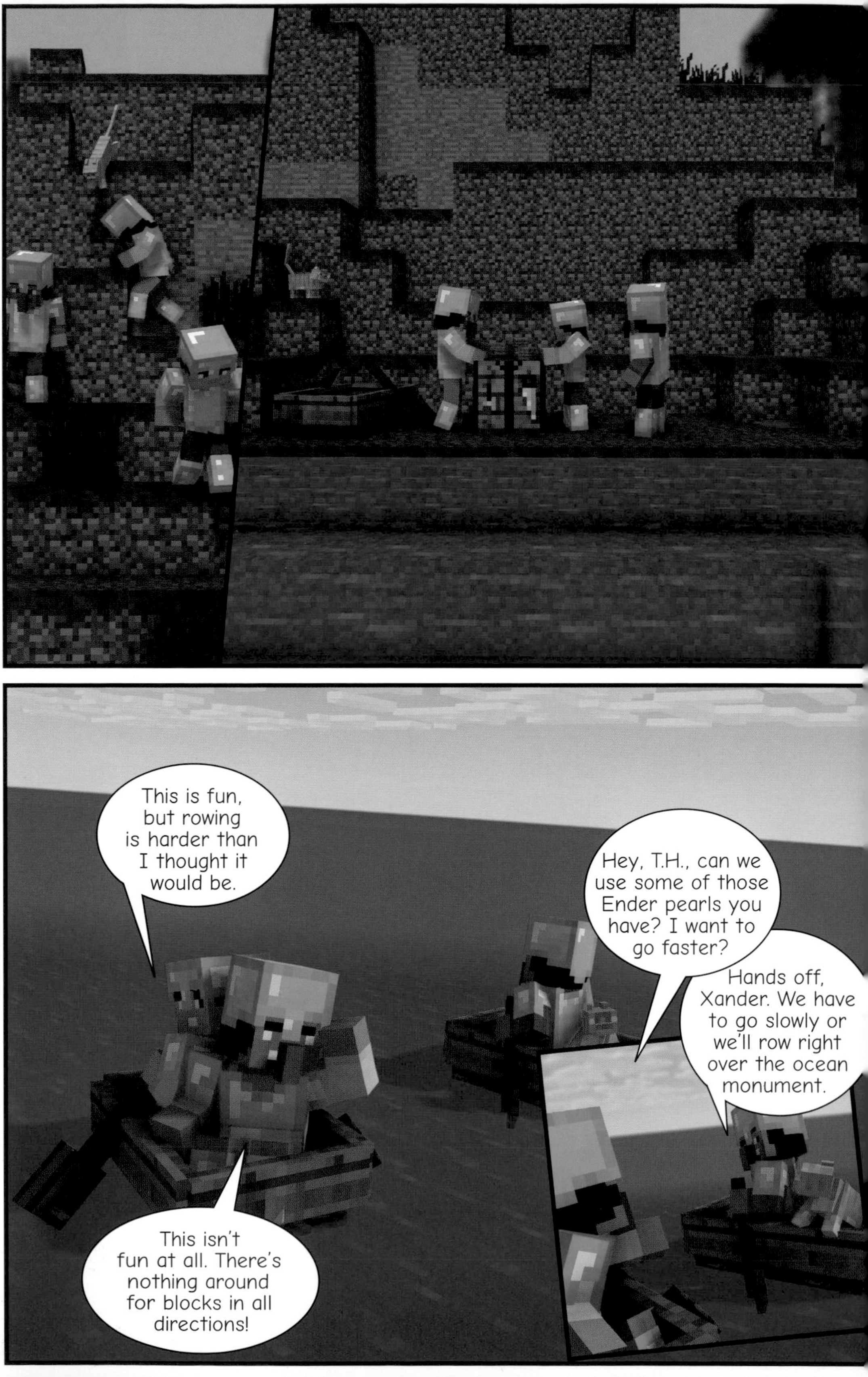
This is fun, but rowing is harder than I thought it would be.
This isn't fun at all. There's nothing around for blocks in all directions!
Hey, T.H., can we use some of those Ender pearls you have? I want to go faster?
Hands off, Xander. We have to go slowly or we'll row right over the ocean monument.

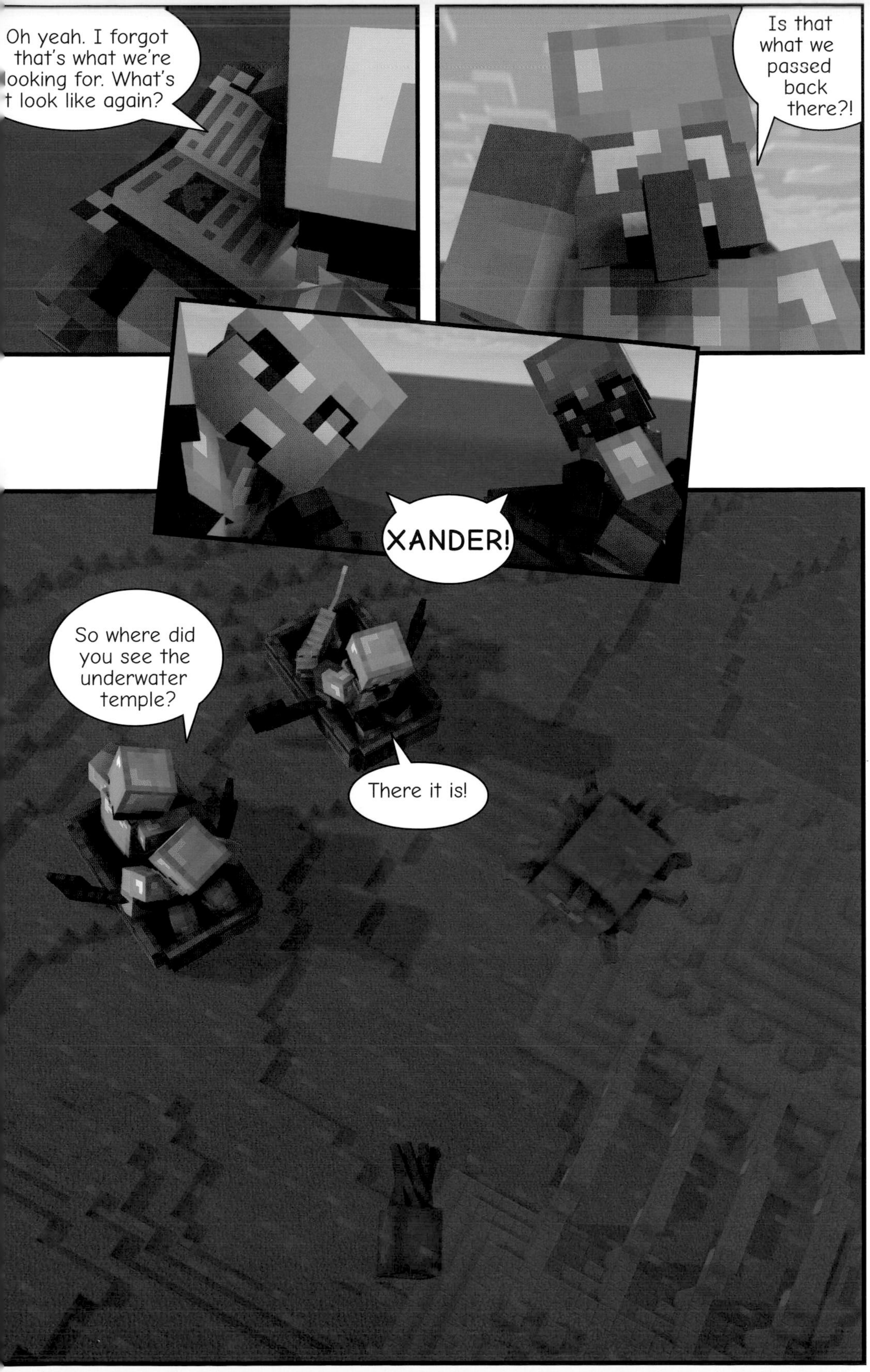
Oh yeah. I forgot that's what we're looking for. What's it look like again?
Is that what we passed back there?!
XANDER!
So where did you see the underwater temple?
There it is!

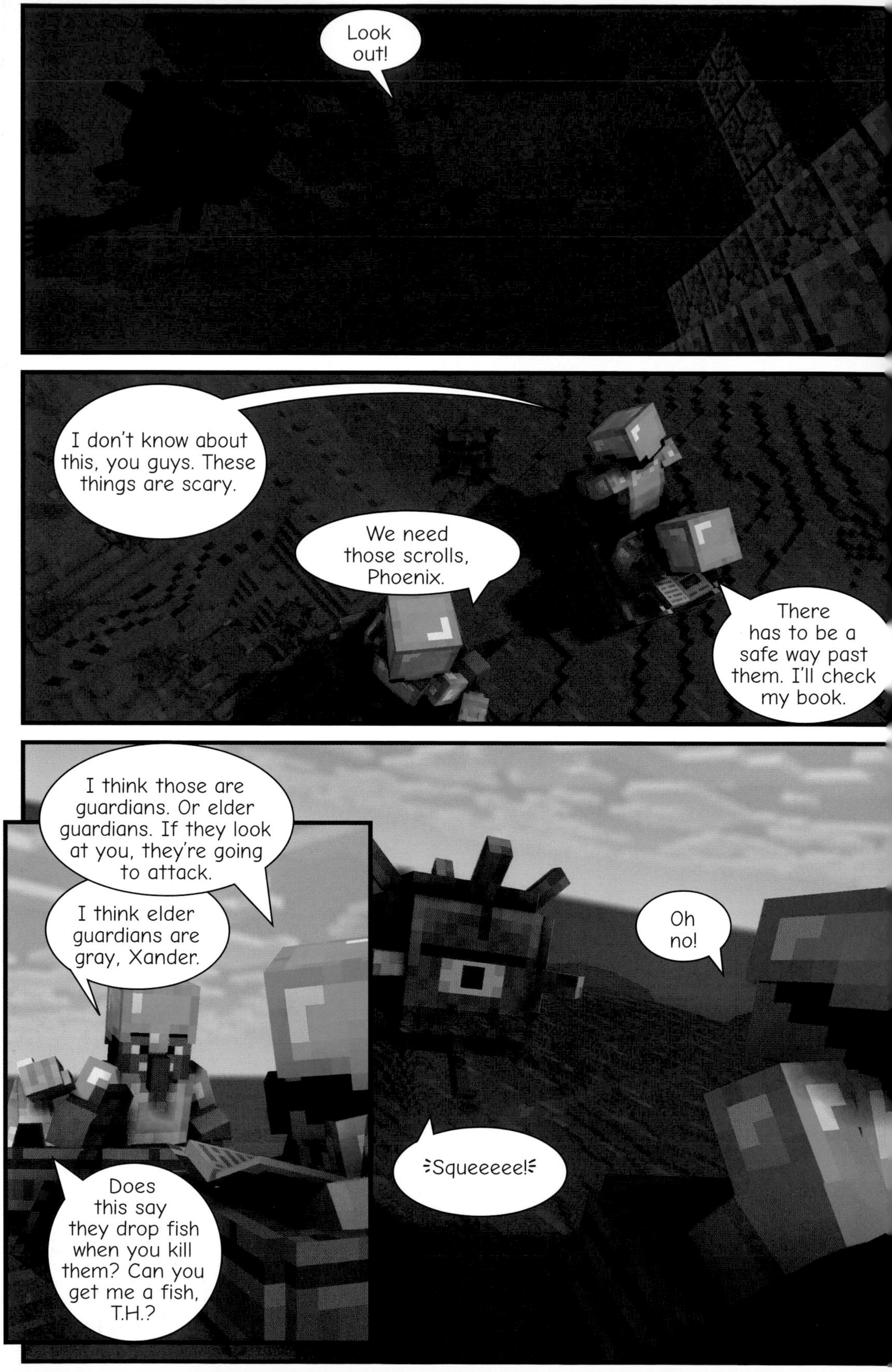
Look out!
I don't know about this, you guys. These things are scary.
We need those scrolls, Phoenix.
There has to be a safe way past them. I'll check my book.
I think those are guardians. Or elder guardians. If they look at you, they're going to attack.
I think elder guardians are gray, Xander.
Does this say they drop fish when you kill them? Can you get me a fish, T.H.?
Squeeeee!
Oh no!

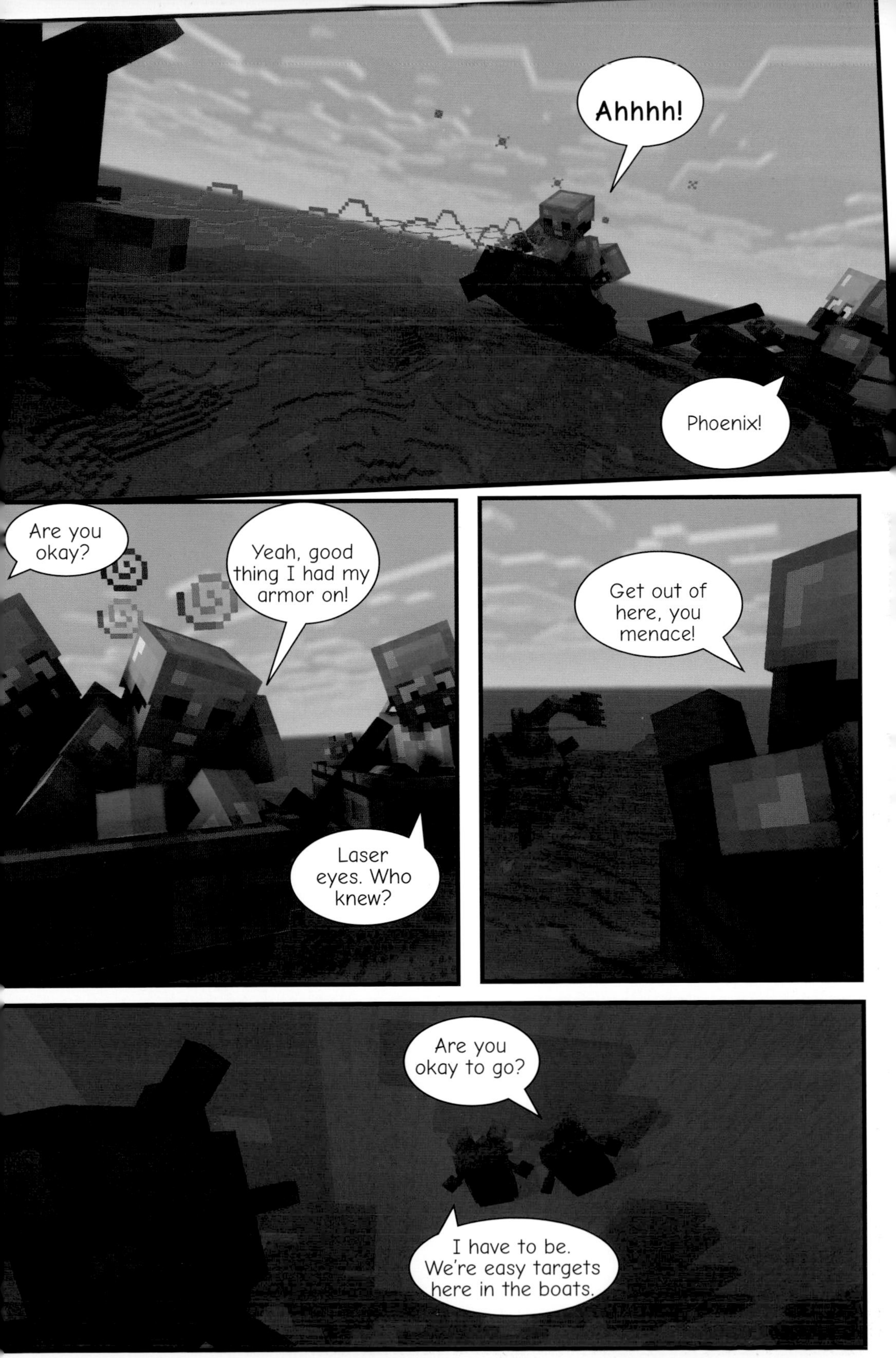
Ahhhh!
Phoenix!
Are you okay?
Yeah, good thing I had my armor on!
Laser eyes. Who knew?
Get out of here, you menace!
Are you okay to go?
I have to be. We're easy targets here in the boats.

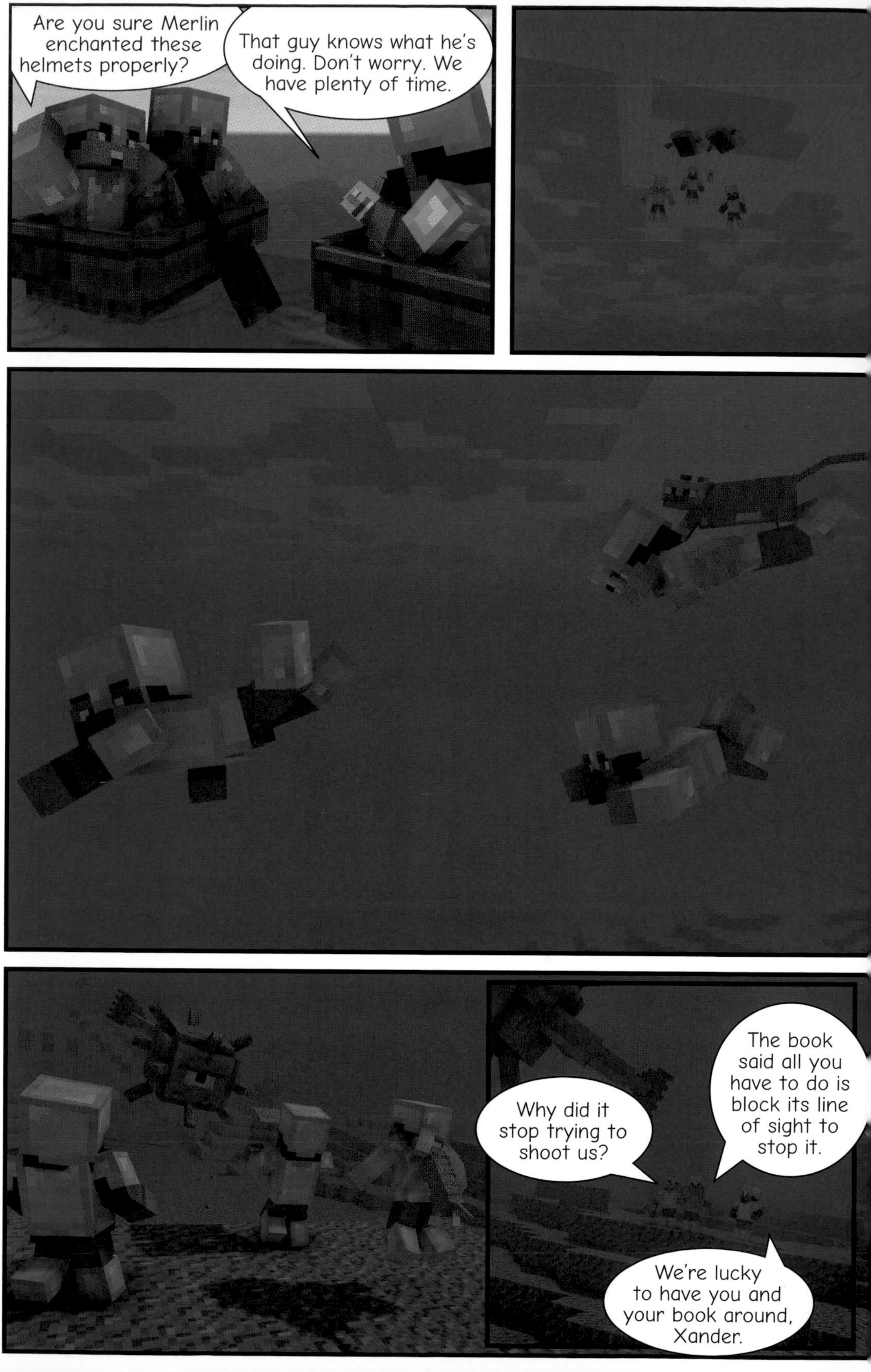
Are you sure Merlin enchanted these helmets properly?
That guy knows what he's doing. Don't worry. We have plenty of time.
Why did it stop trying to shoot us?
The book said all you have to do is block its line of sight to stop it.
We're lucky to have you and your book around, Xander.

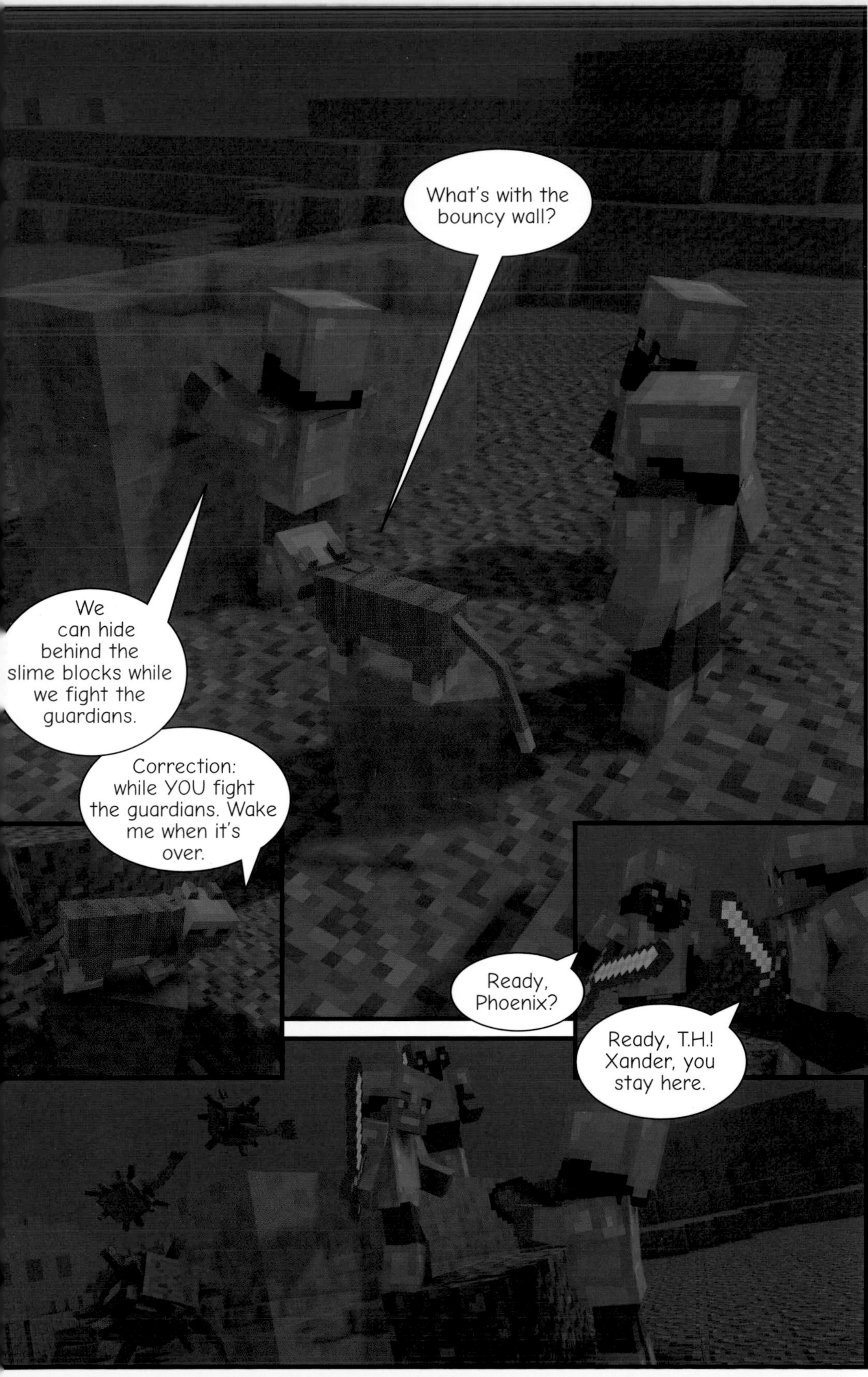
What's with the bouncy wall?
We can hide behind the slime blocks while we fight the guardians.
Correction: while YOU fight the guardians. Wake me when it's over.
Ready, Phoenix?
Ready, T.H.! Xander, you stay here.

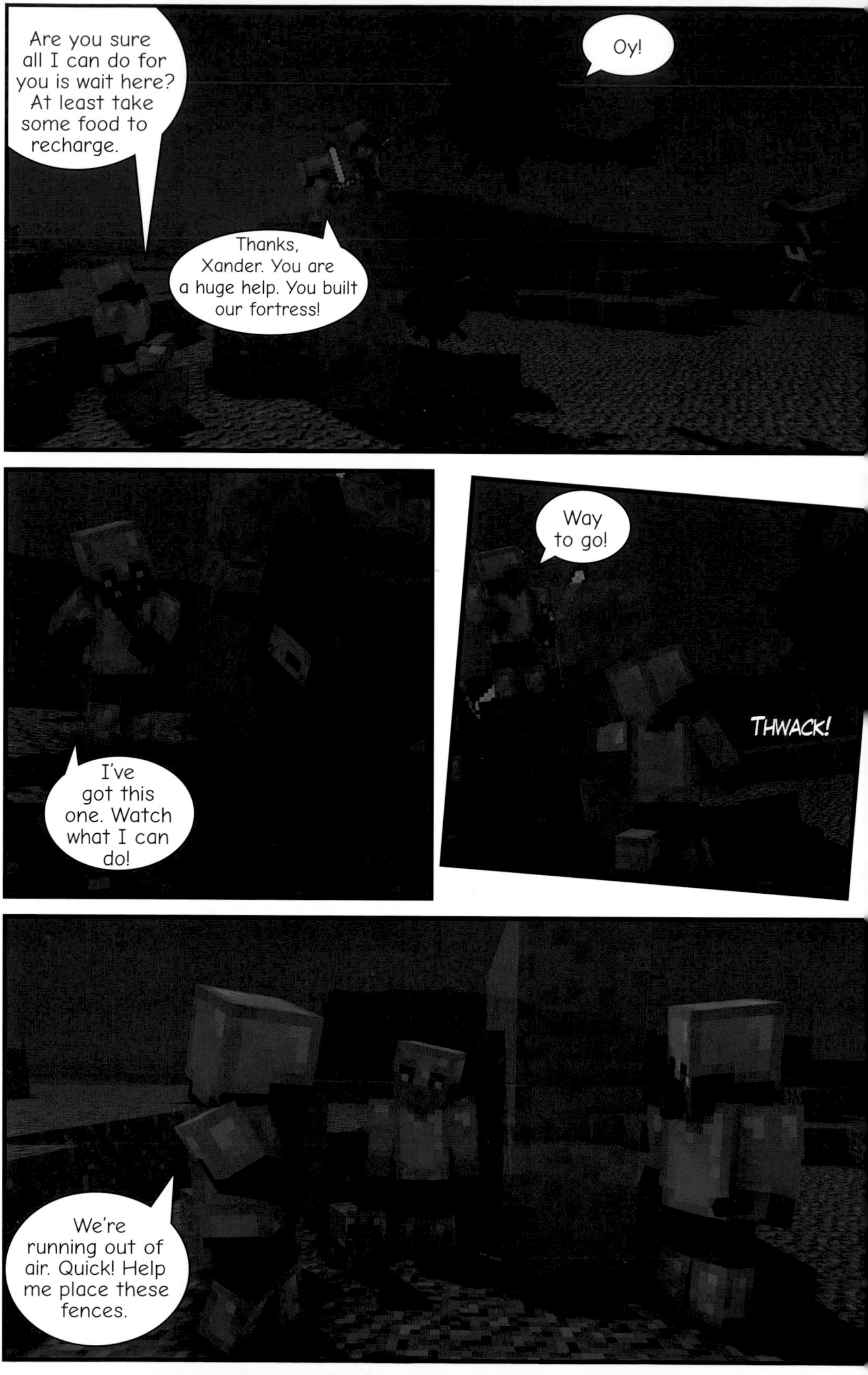
Are you sure all I can do for you is wait here? At least take some food to recharge.
Oy!
Thanks, Xander. You are a huge help. You built our fortress!
I've got this one. Watch what I can do!
Way to go!
THWACK!
We're running out of air. Quick! Help me place these fences.

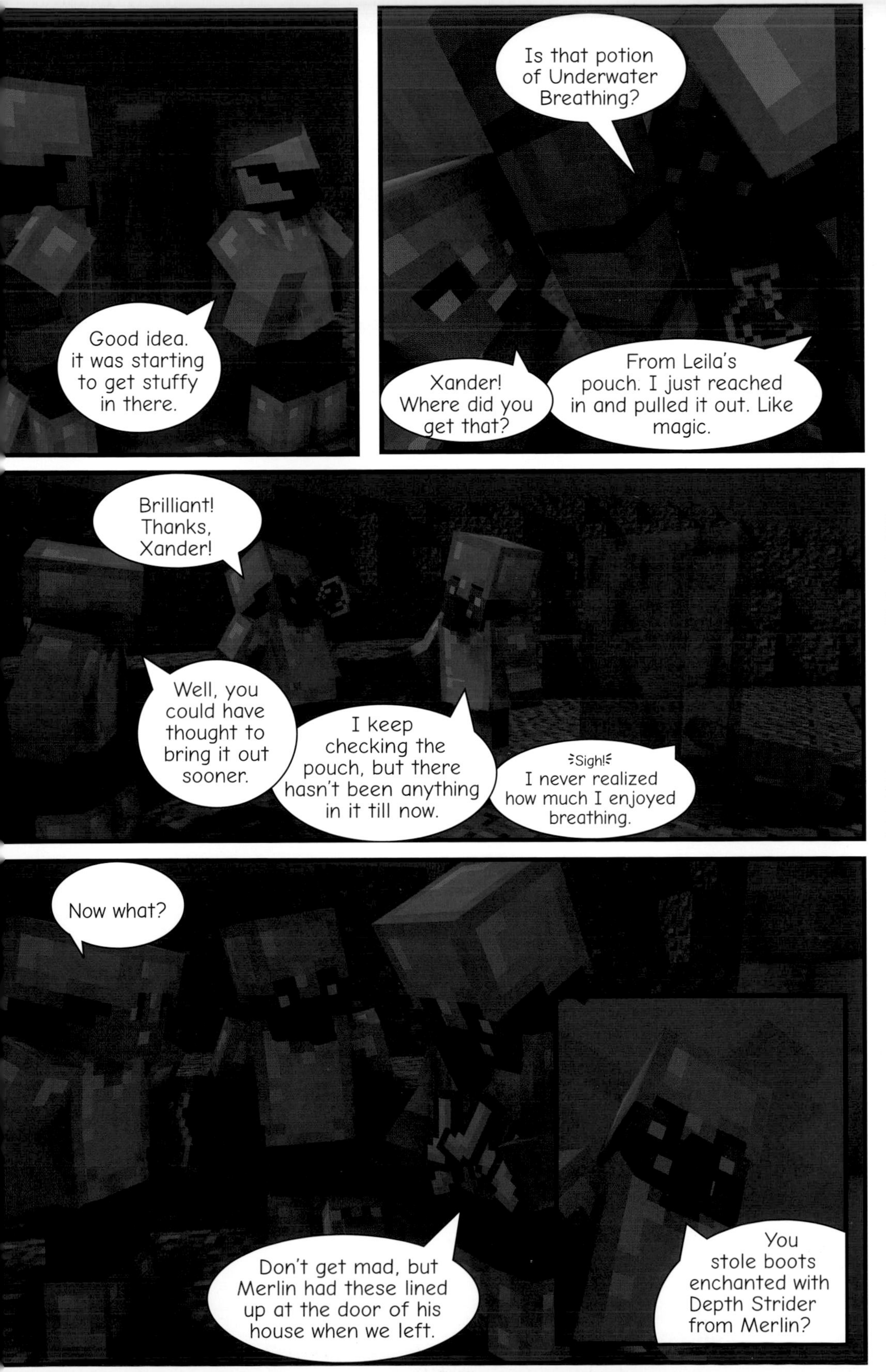
Good idea. it was starting to get stuffy in there.
Is that potion of Underwater Breathing?
Xander! Where did you get that?
From Leila's pouch. I just reached in and pulled it out. Like magic.
Brilliant! Thanks, Xander!
Well, you could have thought to bring it out sooner.
I keep checking the pouch, but there hasn't been anything in it till now.
Sigh!
I never realized how much I enjoyed breathing.
Now what?
Don't get mad, but Merlin had these lined up at the door of his house when we left.
You stole boots enchanted with Depth Strider from Merlin?

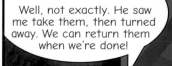

Well, not exactly. He saw me take them, then turned away. We can return them when we're done!

Fine. We'll wear them because they're here and we have a long way to go, but don't think I'm not going to tell Mom and Dad when we get home!

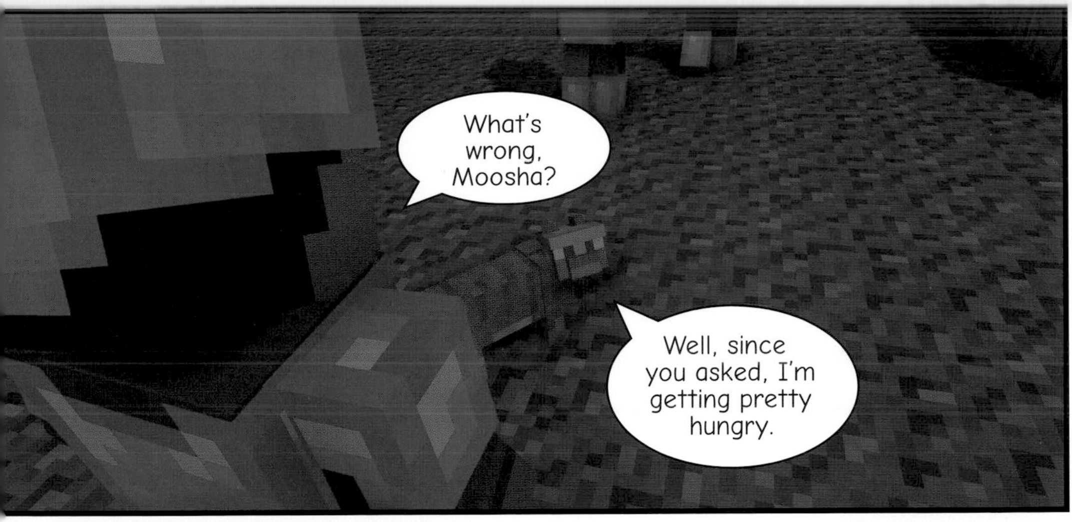
What's wrong, Moosha?
Well, since you asked, I'm getting pretty hungry.

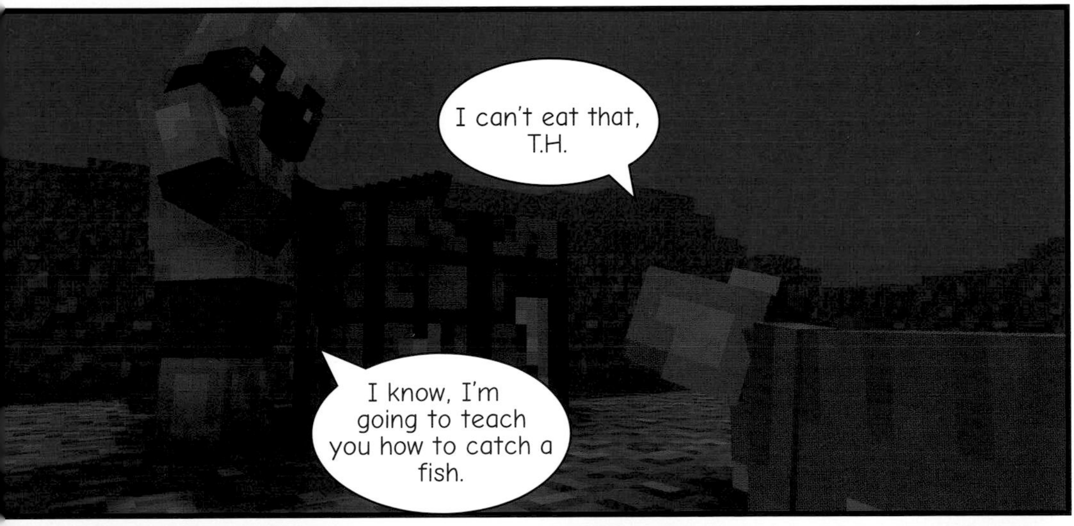
I can't eat that, T.H.
I know, I'm going to teach you how to catch a fish.

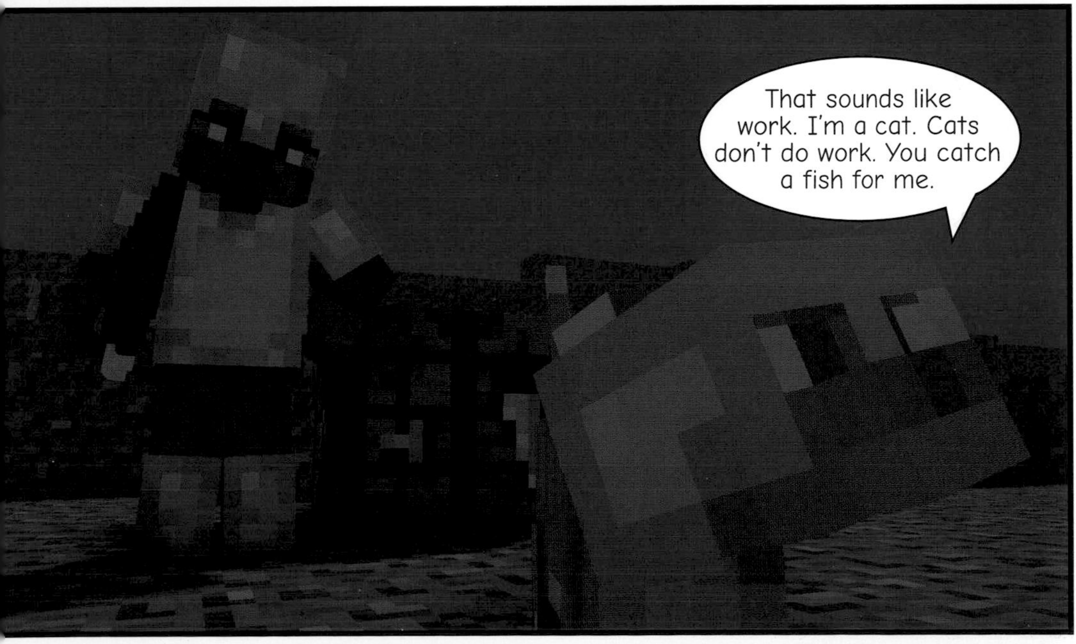
That sounds like work. I'm a cat. Cats don't do work. You catch a fish for me.

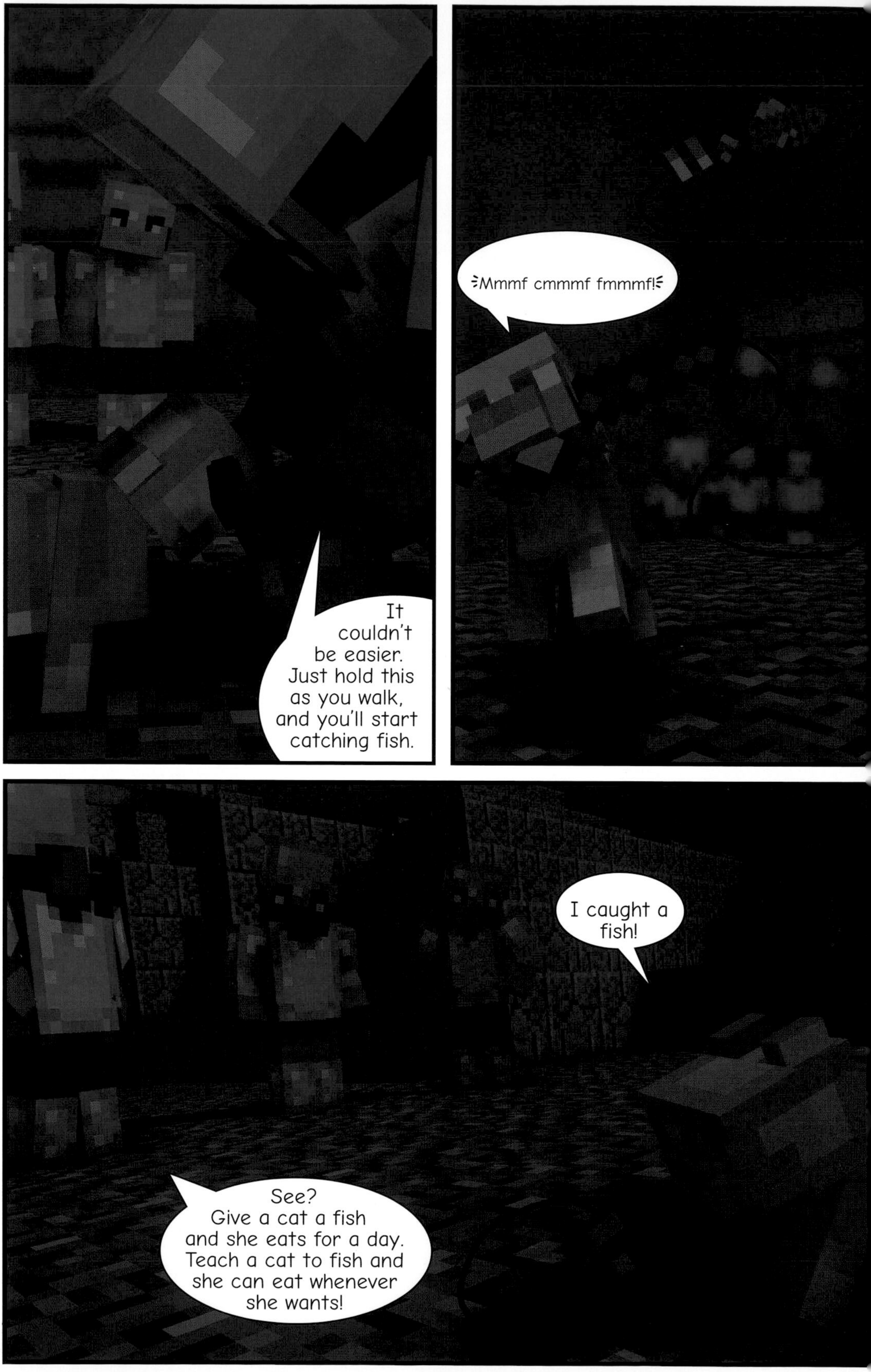
It couldn't be easier. Just hold this as you walk, and you'll start catching fish.
Mmmf cmmmf fmmmf!
I caught a fish!
See? Give a cat a fish and she eats for a day. Teach a cat to fish and she can eat whenever she wants!

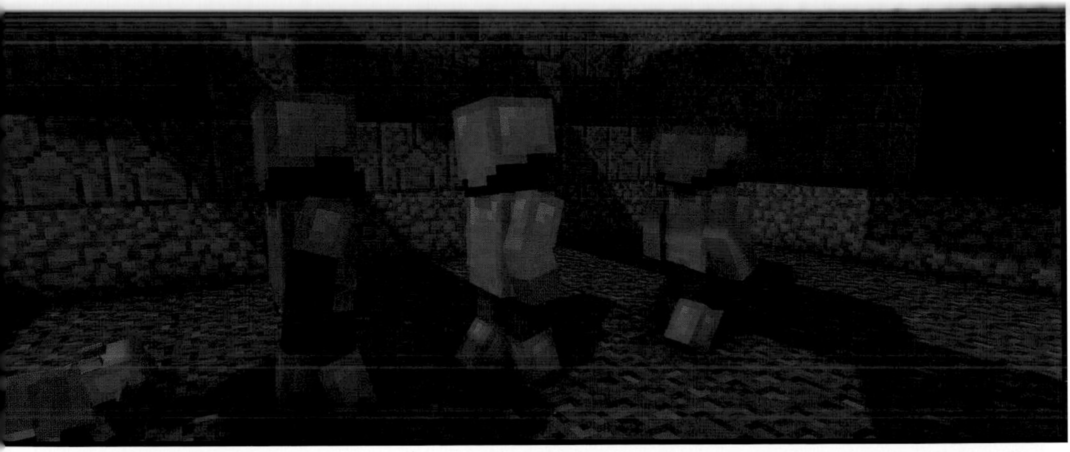

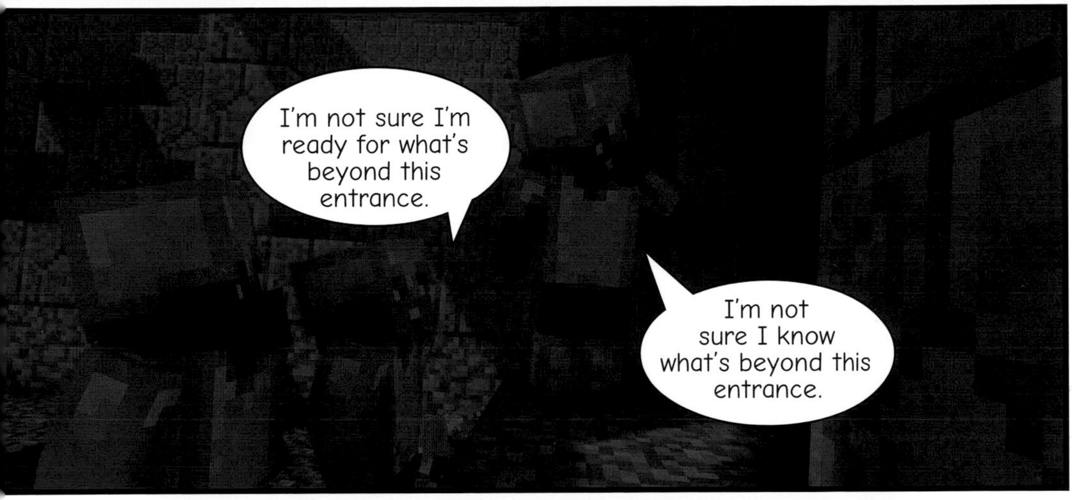
I'm not sure I'm ready for what's beyond this entrance.
I'm not sure I know what's beyond this entrance.

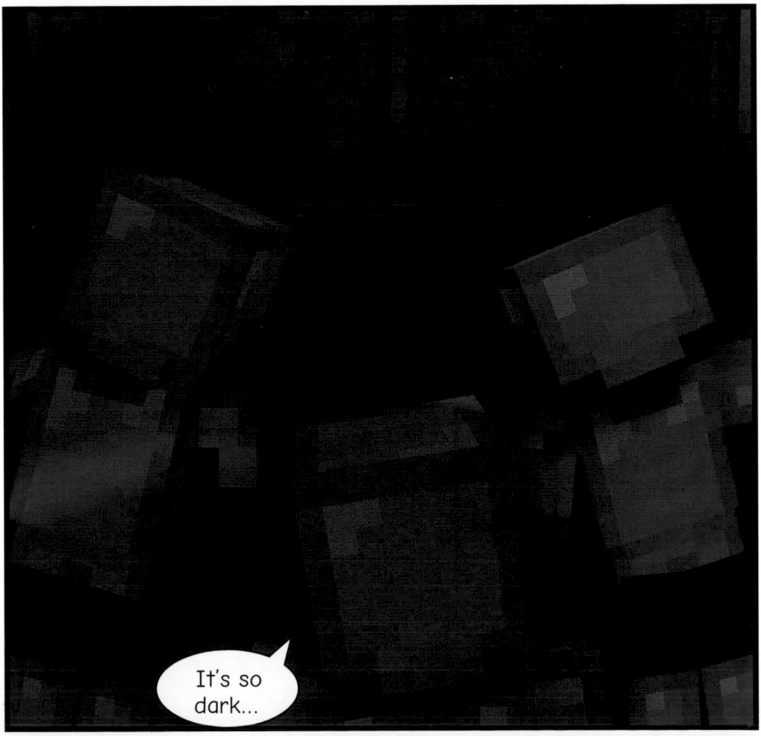
It's so dark...

CHAPTER 6

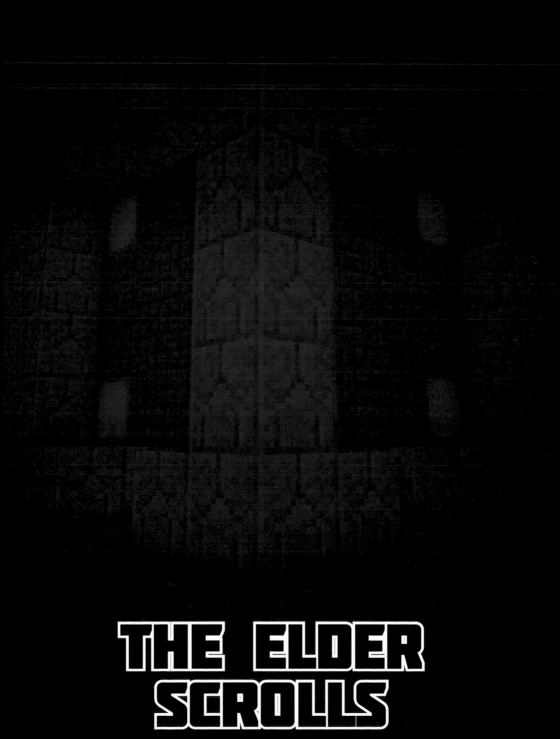

THE ELDER
SCROLLS

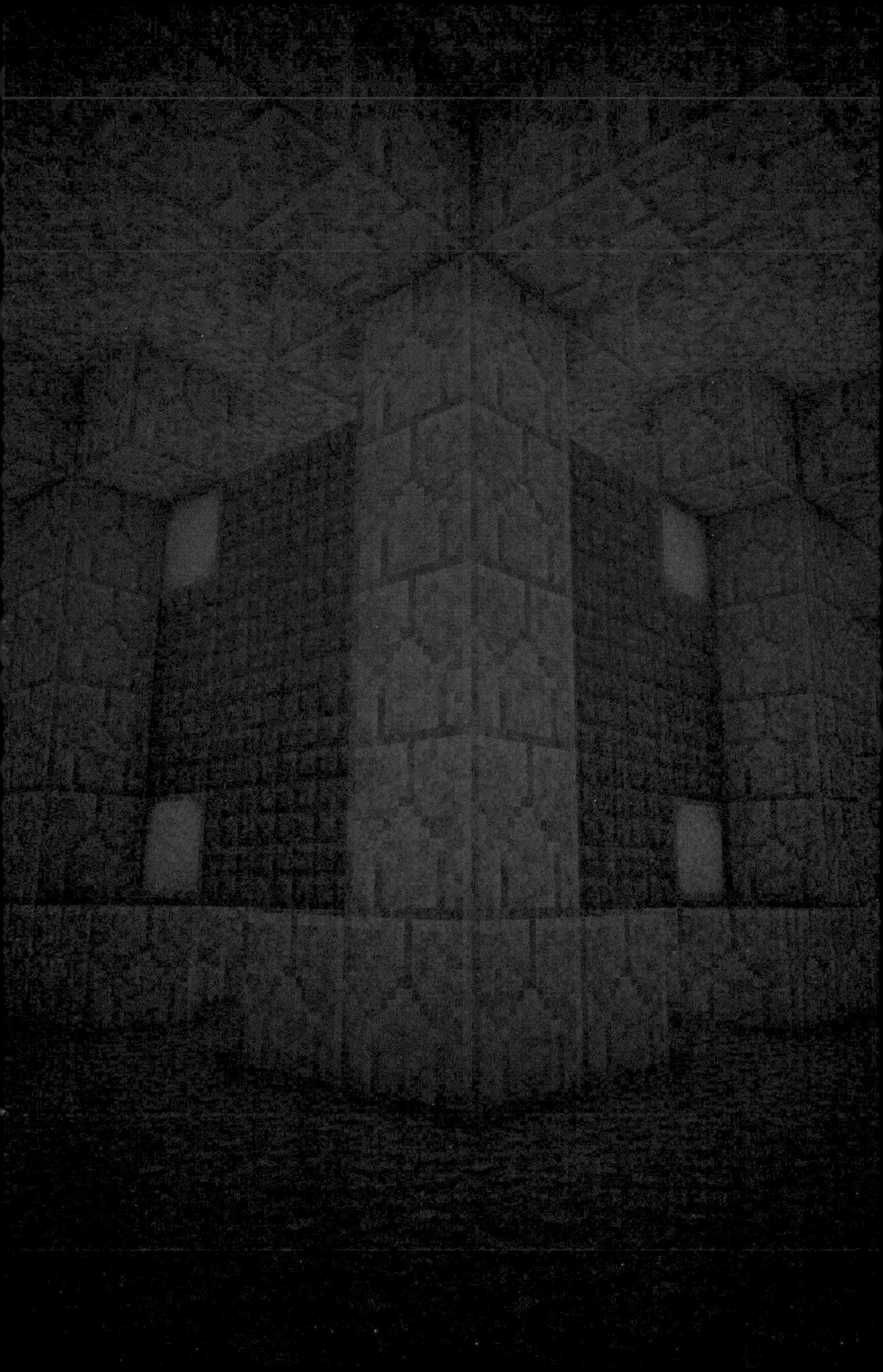

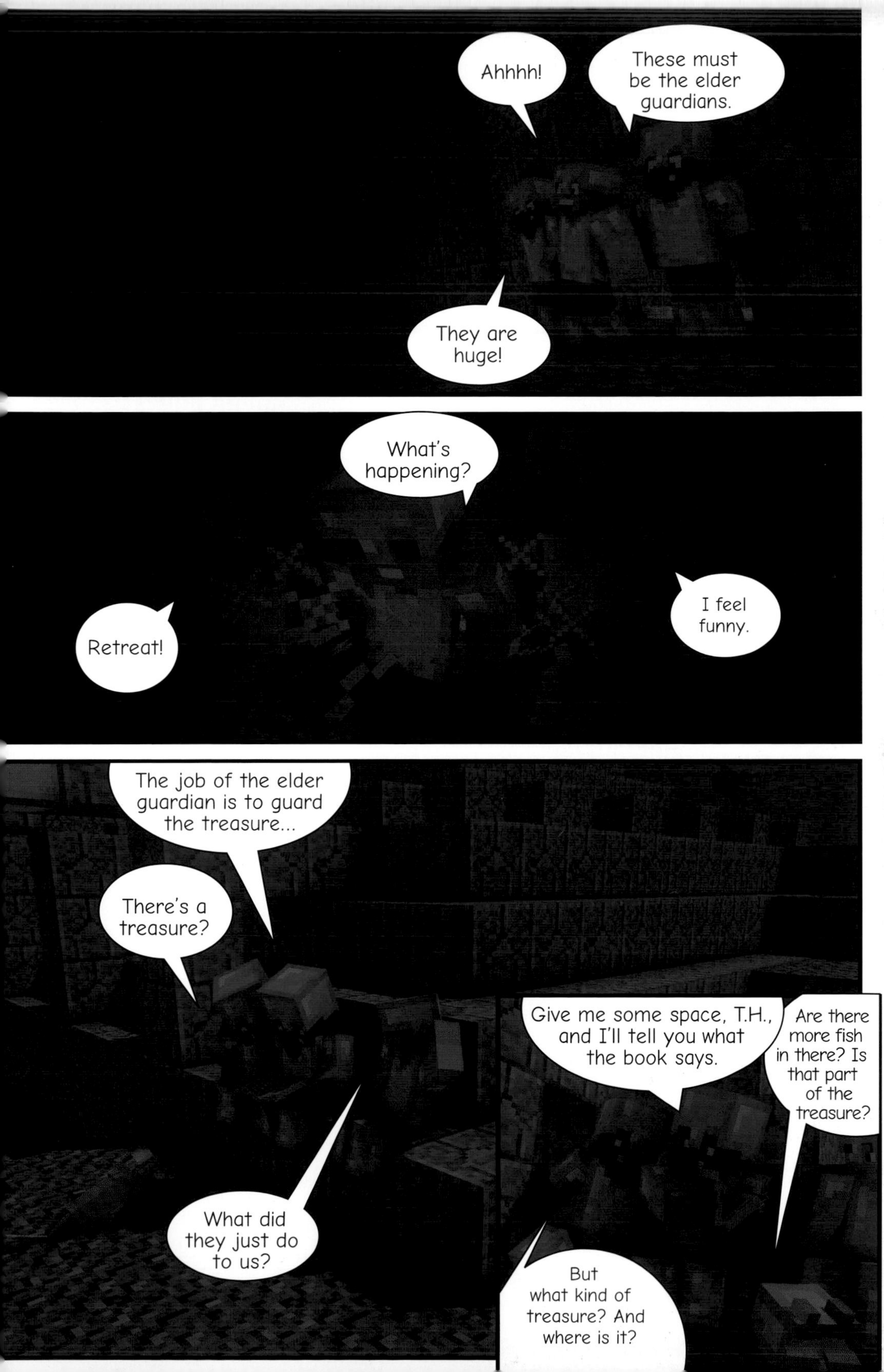

Ahhhh!
These must be the elder guardians.
They are huge!
What's happening?
Retreat!
I feel funny.
The job of the elder guardian is to guard the treasure...
There's a treasure?
What did they just do to us?
Give me some space, T.H., and I'll tell you what the book says.
Are there more fish in there? Is that part of the treasure?
But what kind of treasure? And where is it?

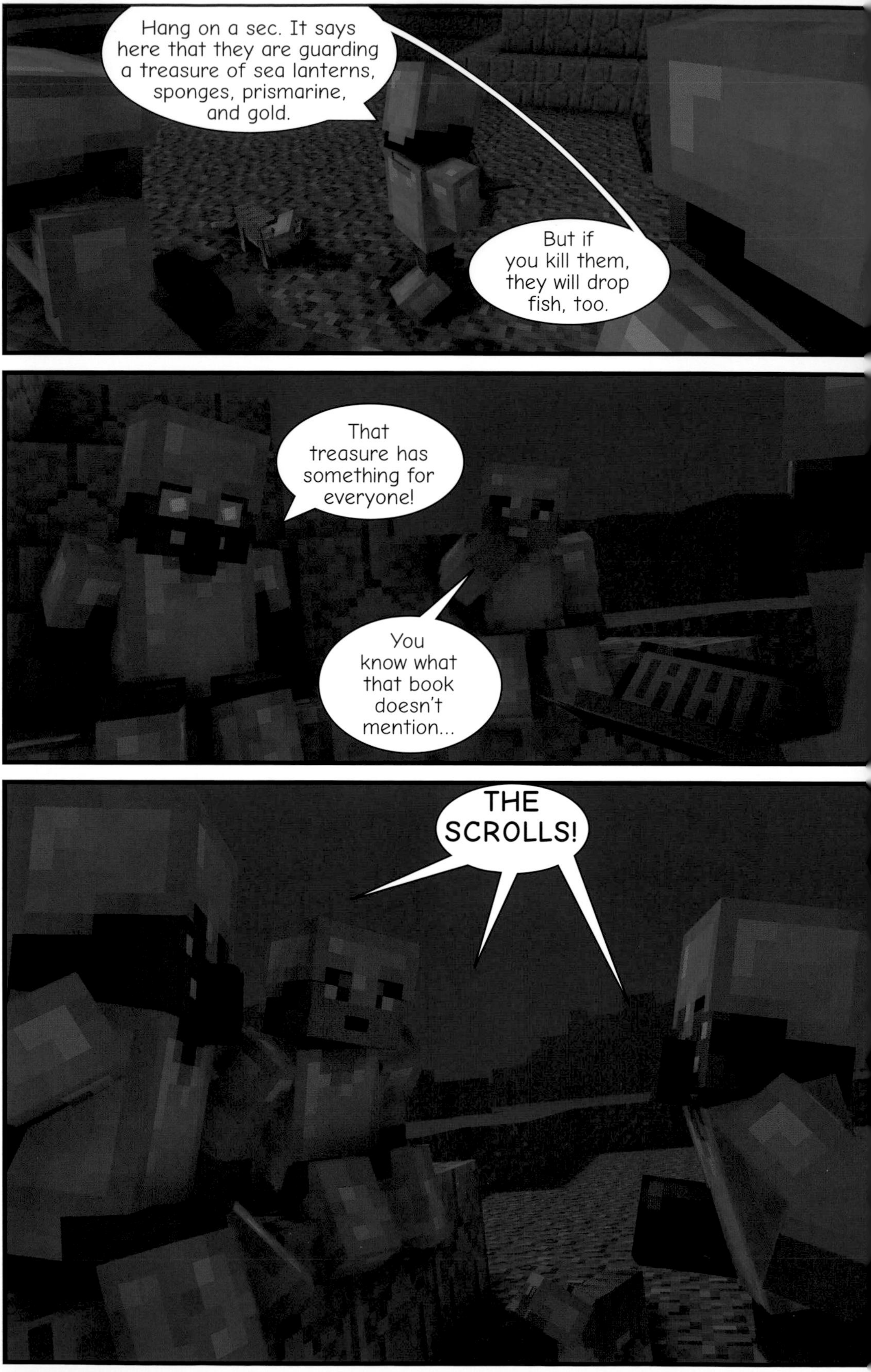
Hang on a sec. It says here that they are guarding a treasure of sea lanterns, sponges, prismarine, and gold.
But if you kill them, they will drop fish, too.
That treasure has something for everyone!
You know what that book doesn't mention...
THE SCROLLS!

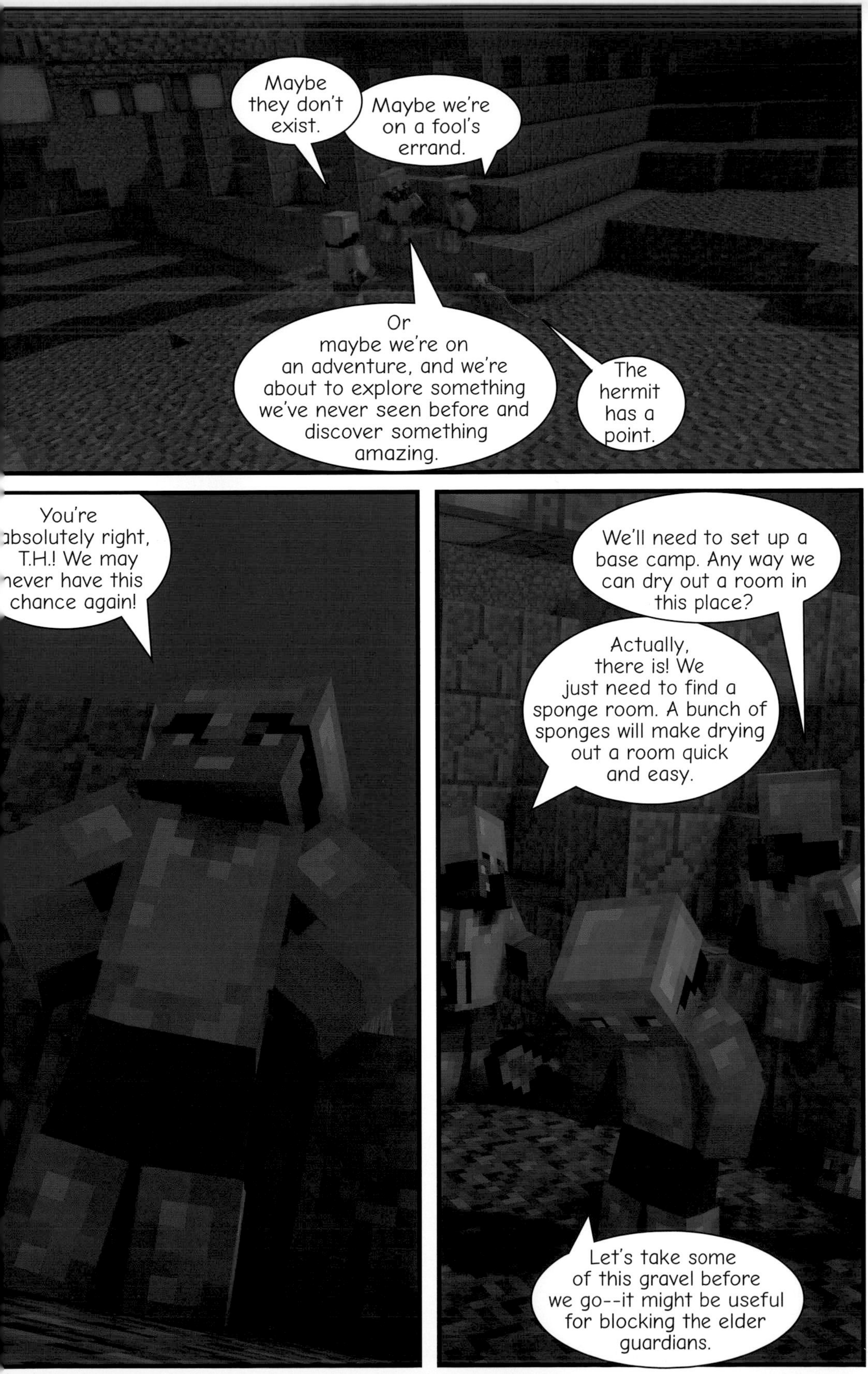
Maybe they don't exist.
Maybe we're on a fool's errand.
Or maybe we're on an adventure, and we're about to explore something we've never seen before and discover something amazing.
The hermit has a point.
You're absolutely right, T.H.! We may never have this chance again!
We'll need to set up a base camp. Any way we can dry out a room in this place?
Actually, there is! We just need to find a sponge room. A bunch of sponges will make drying out a room quick and easy.
Let's take some of this gravel before we go--it might be useful for blocking the elder guardians.

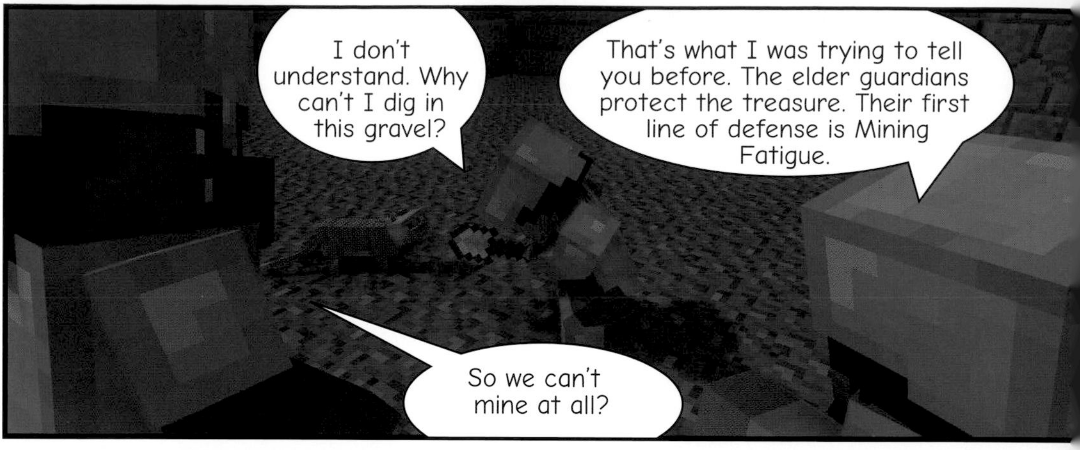

I don't understand. Why can't I dig in this gravel?
That's what I was trying to tell you before. The elder guardians protect the treasure. Their first line of defense is Mining Fatigue.
So we can't mine at all?

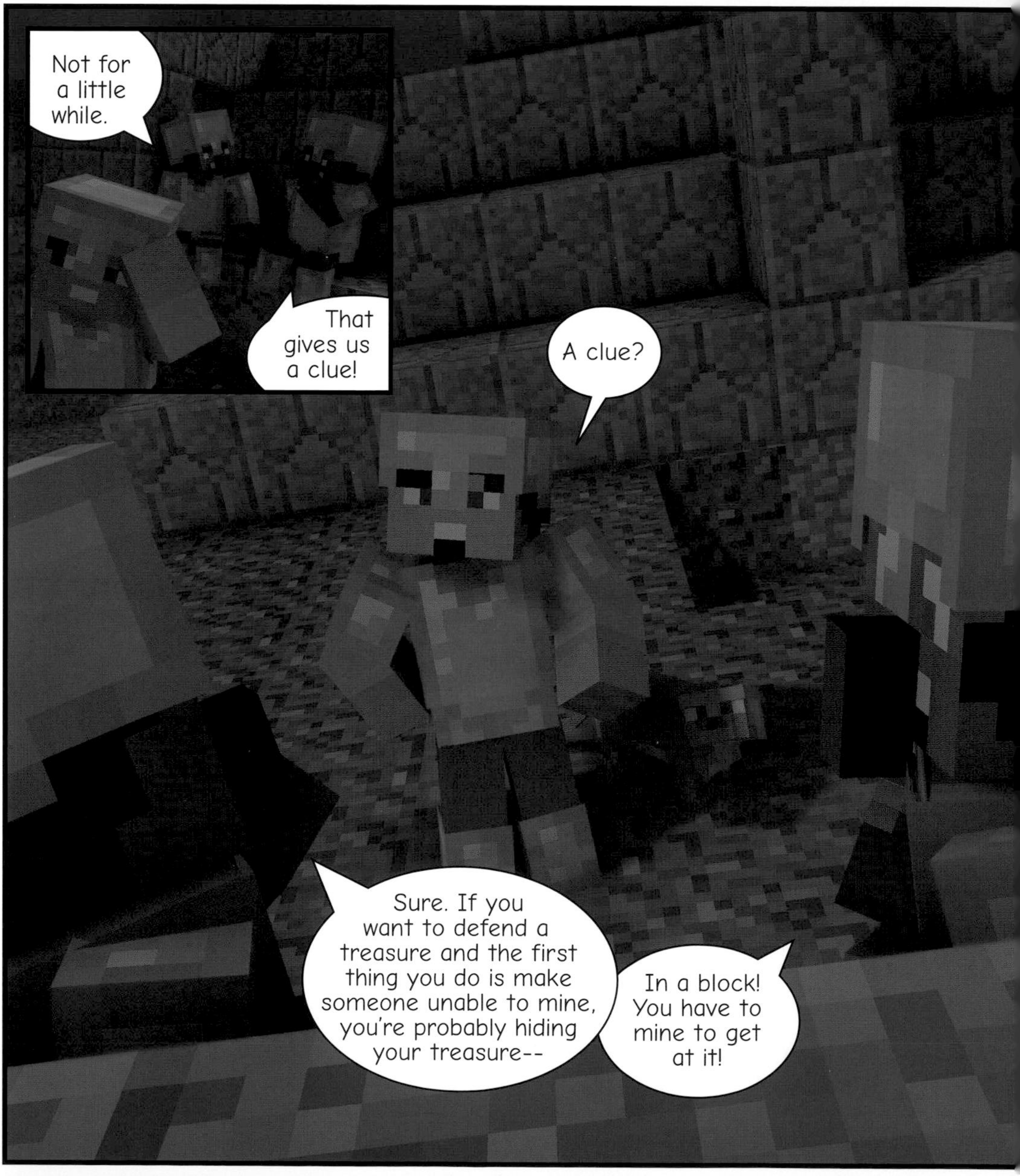

Not for a little while.
That gives us a clue!
A clue?
Sure. If you want to defend a treasure and the first thing you do is make someone unable to mine, you're probably hiding your treasure--
In a block! You have to mine to get at it!

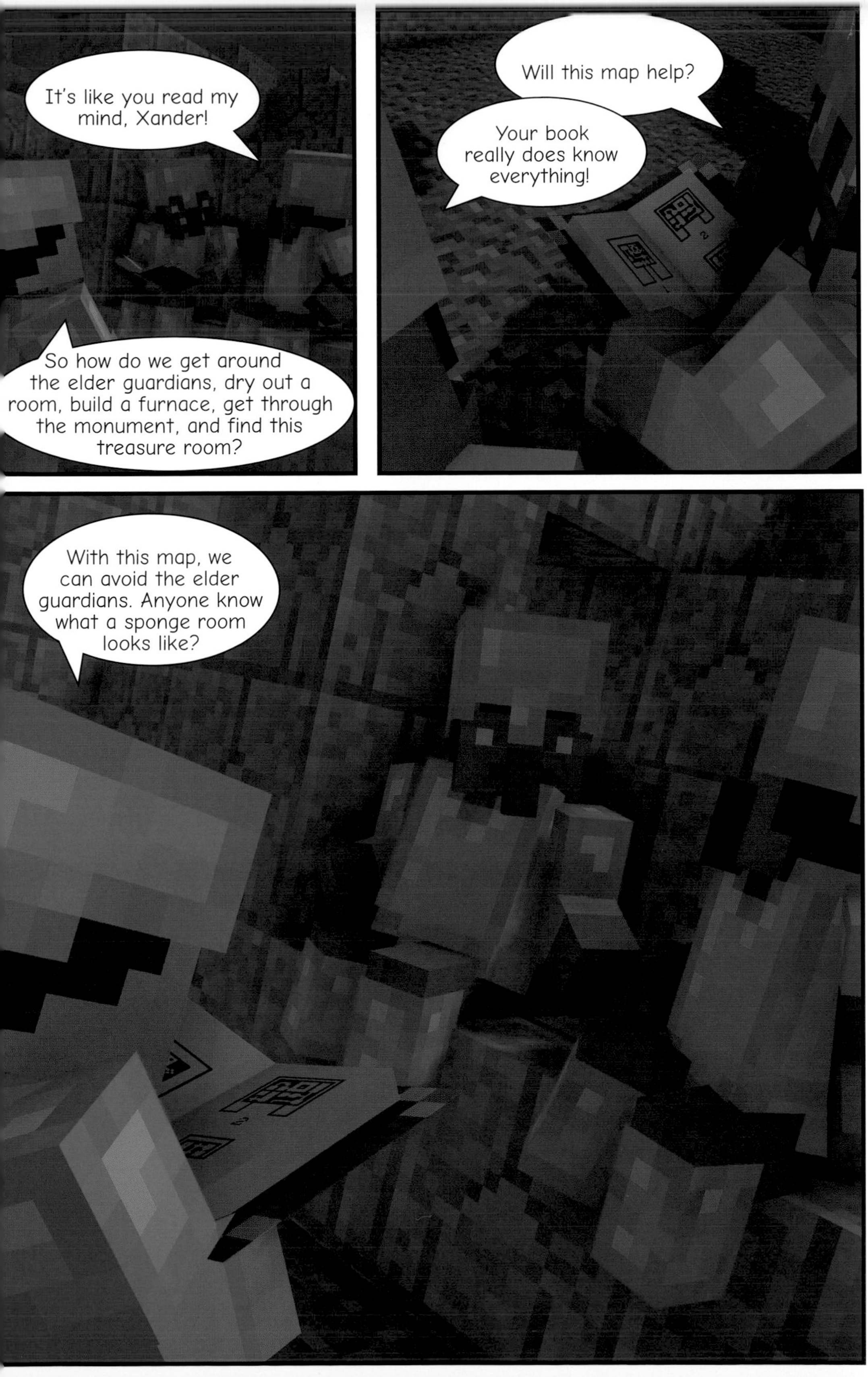
It's like you read my mind, Xander!
So how do we get around the elder guardians, dry out a room, build a furnace, get through the monument, and find this treasure room?
Will this map help?
Your book really does know everything!
With this map, we can avoid the elder guardians. Anyone know what a sponge room looks like?

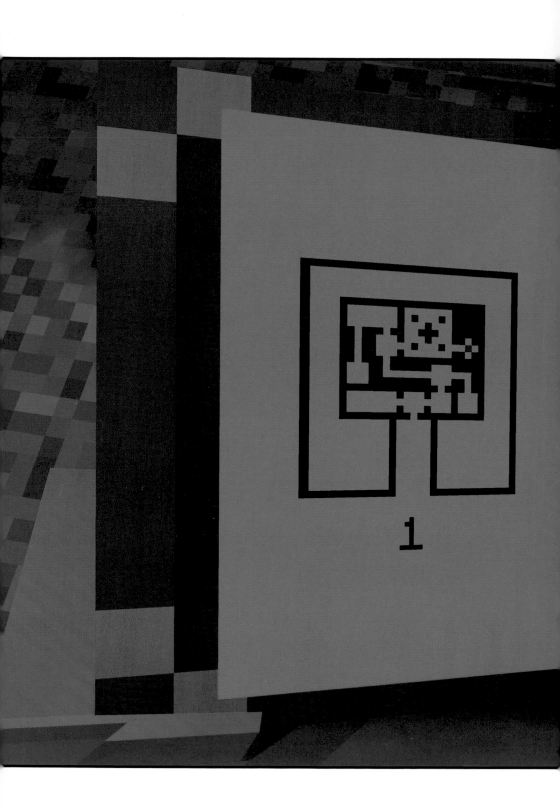

1

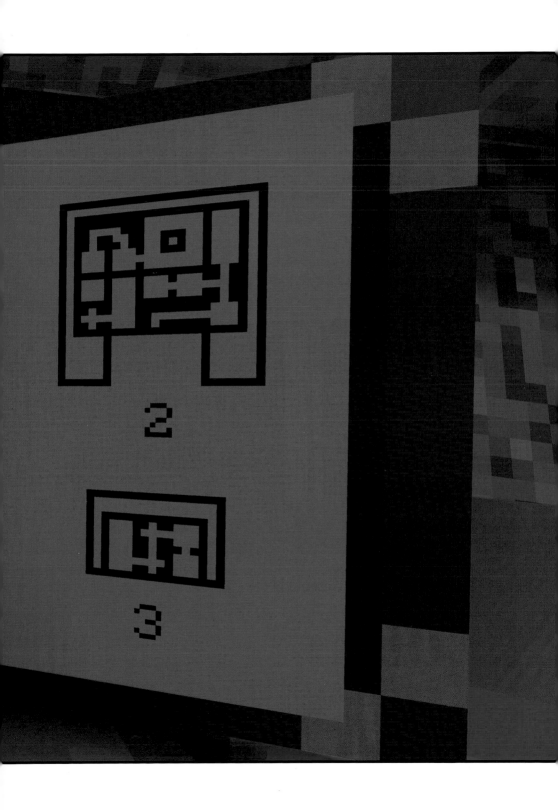

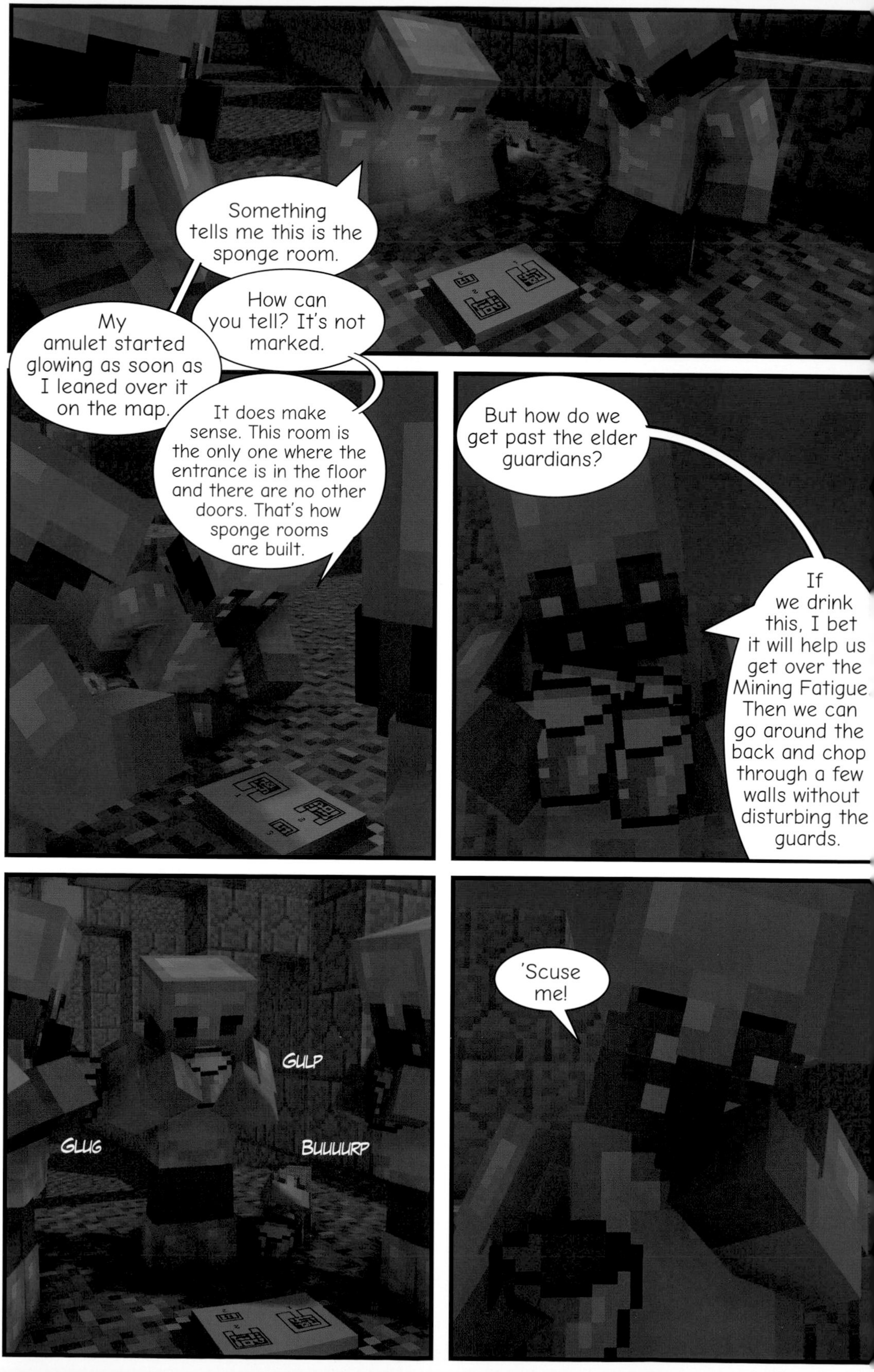
Something tells me this is the sponge room.
How can you tell? It's not marked.
My amulet started glowing as soon as I leaned over it on the map.
It does make sense. This room is the only one where the entrance is in the floor and there are no other doors. That's how sponge rooms are built.
But how do we get past the elder guardians?
If we drink this, I bet it will help us get over the Mining Fatigue. Then we can go around the back and chop through a few walls without disturbing the guards.
GULP
GLUG
BUUUURP
'Scuse me!

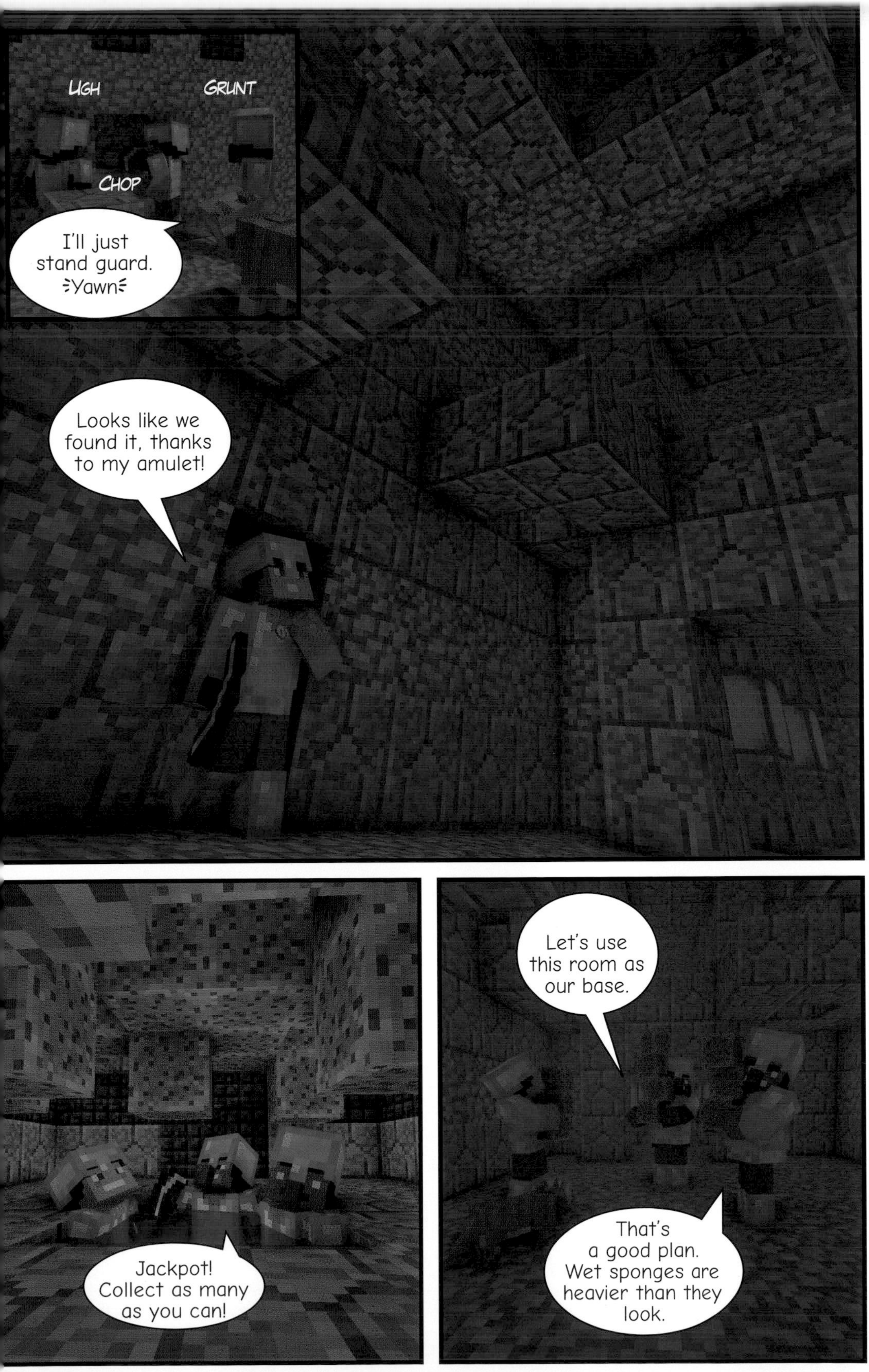
UGH
GRUNT
CHOP
I'll just stand guard. Yawn
Looks like we found it, thanks to my amulet!
Jackpot! Collect as many as you can!
Let's use this room as our base.
That's a good plan. Wet sponges are heavier than they look.

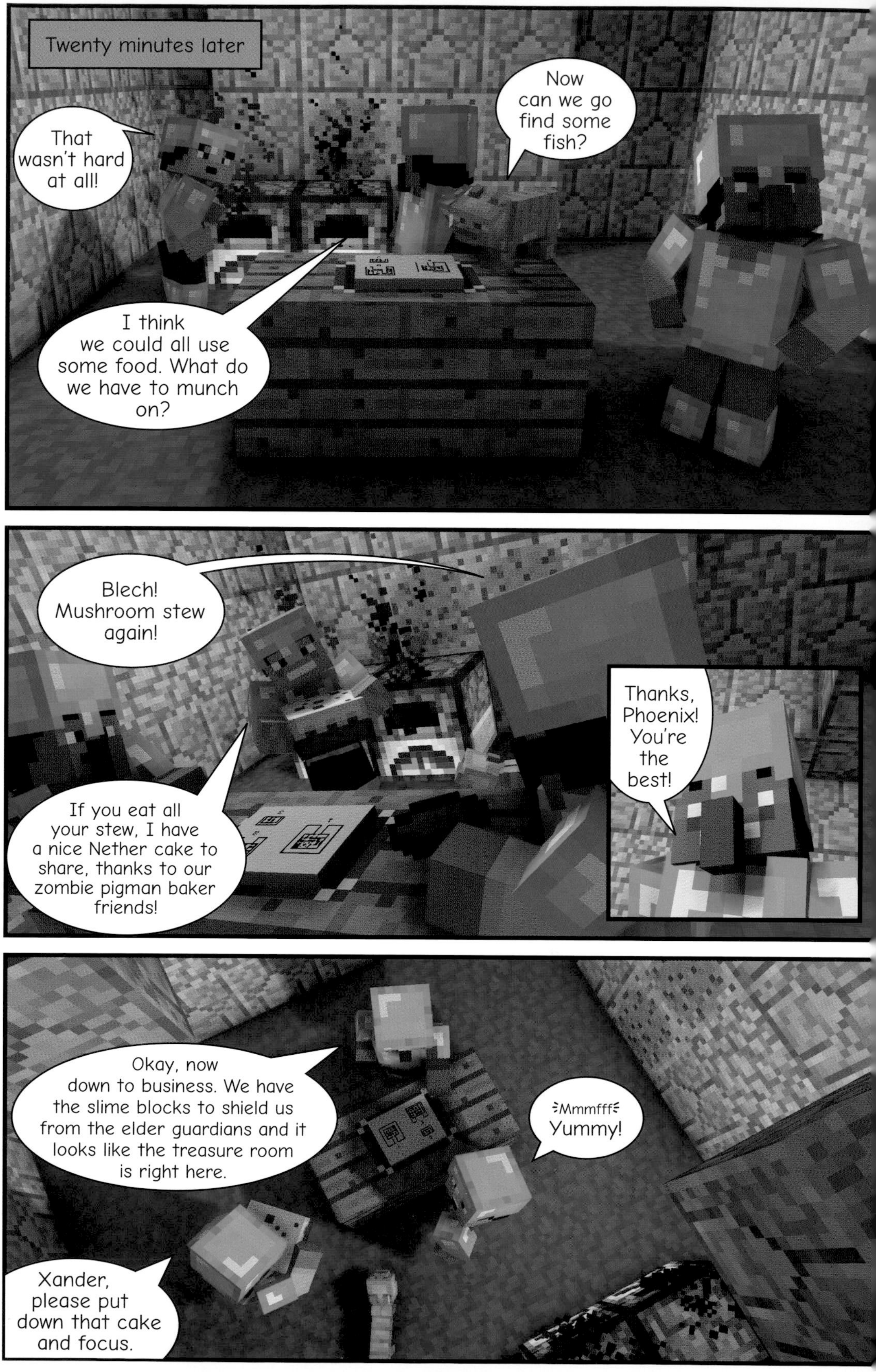
Twenty minutes later
That wasn't hard at all!
Now can we go find some fish?
I think we could all use some food. What do we have to munch on?
Blech! Mushroom stew again!
If you eat all your stew, I have a nice Nether cake to share, thanks to our zombie pigman baker friends!
Thanks, Phoenix! You're the best!
Okay, now down to business. We have the slime blocks to shield us from the elder guardians and it looks like the treasure room is right here.
Mmmfff Yummy!
Xander, please put down that cake and focus.

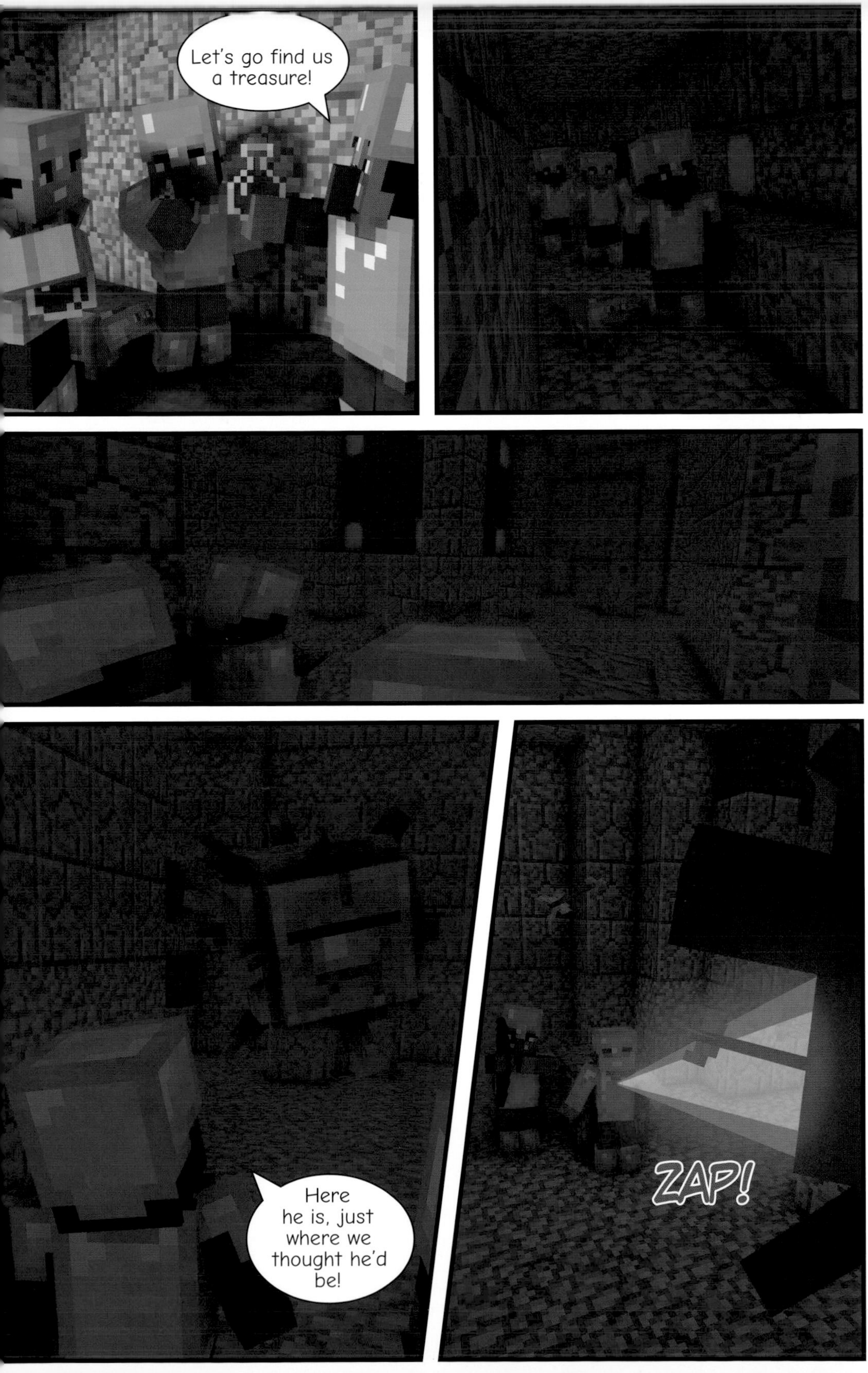
Let's go find us a treasure!
Here he is, just where we thought he'd be!
ZAP!

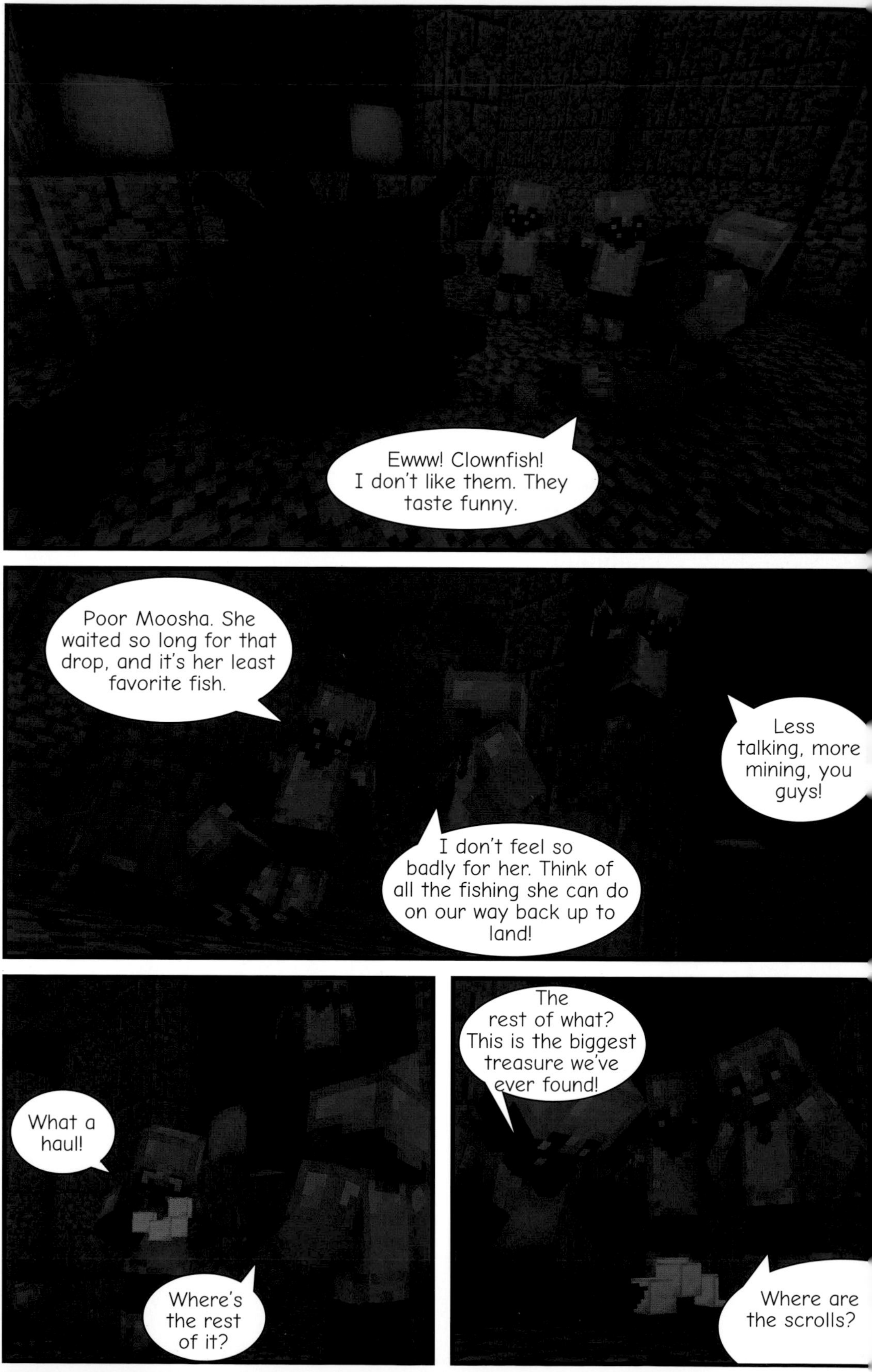
Ewww! Clownfish! I don't like them. They taste funny.
Poor Moosha. She waited so long for that drop, and it's her least favorite fish.
Less talking, more mining, you guys!
I don't feel so badly for her. Think of all the fishing she can do on our way back up to land!
What a haul!
Where's the rest of it?
The rest of what? This is the biggest treasure we've ever found!
Where are the scrolls?

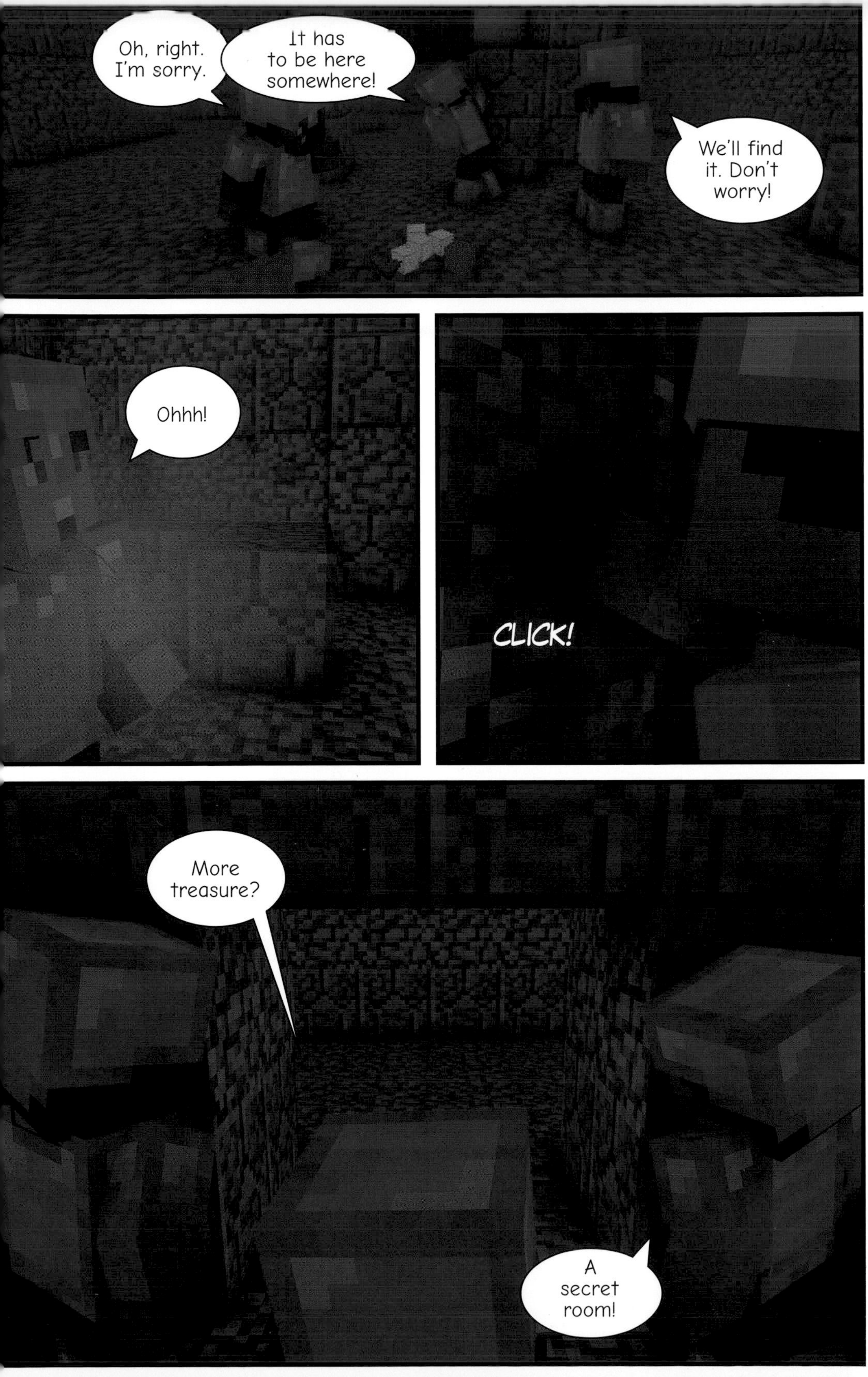
Oh, right. I'm sorry.
It has to be here somewhere!
We'll find it. Don't worry!
Ohhh!
CLICK!
More treasure?
A secret room!

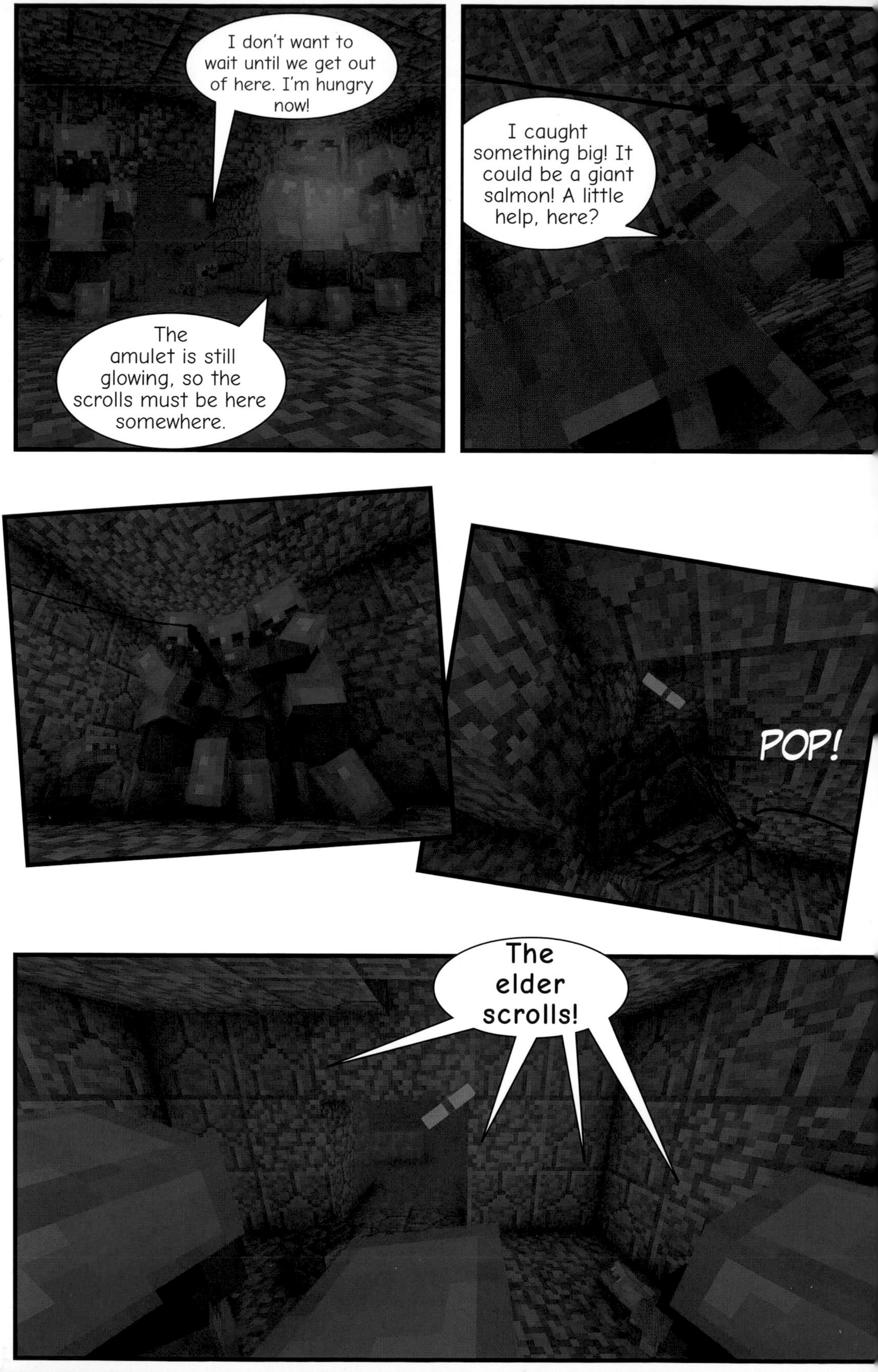
I don't want to wait until we get out of here. I'm hungry now!
The amulet is still glowing, so the scrolls must be here somewhere.
I caught something big! It could be a giant salmon! A little help, here?
POP!
The elder scrolls!

CHAPTER 7

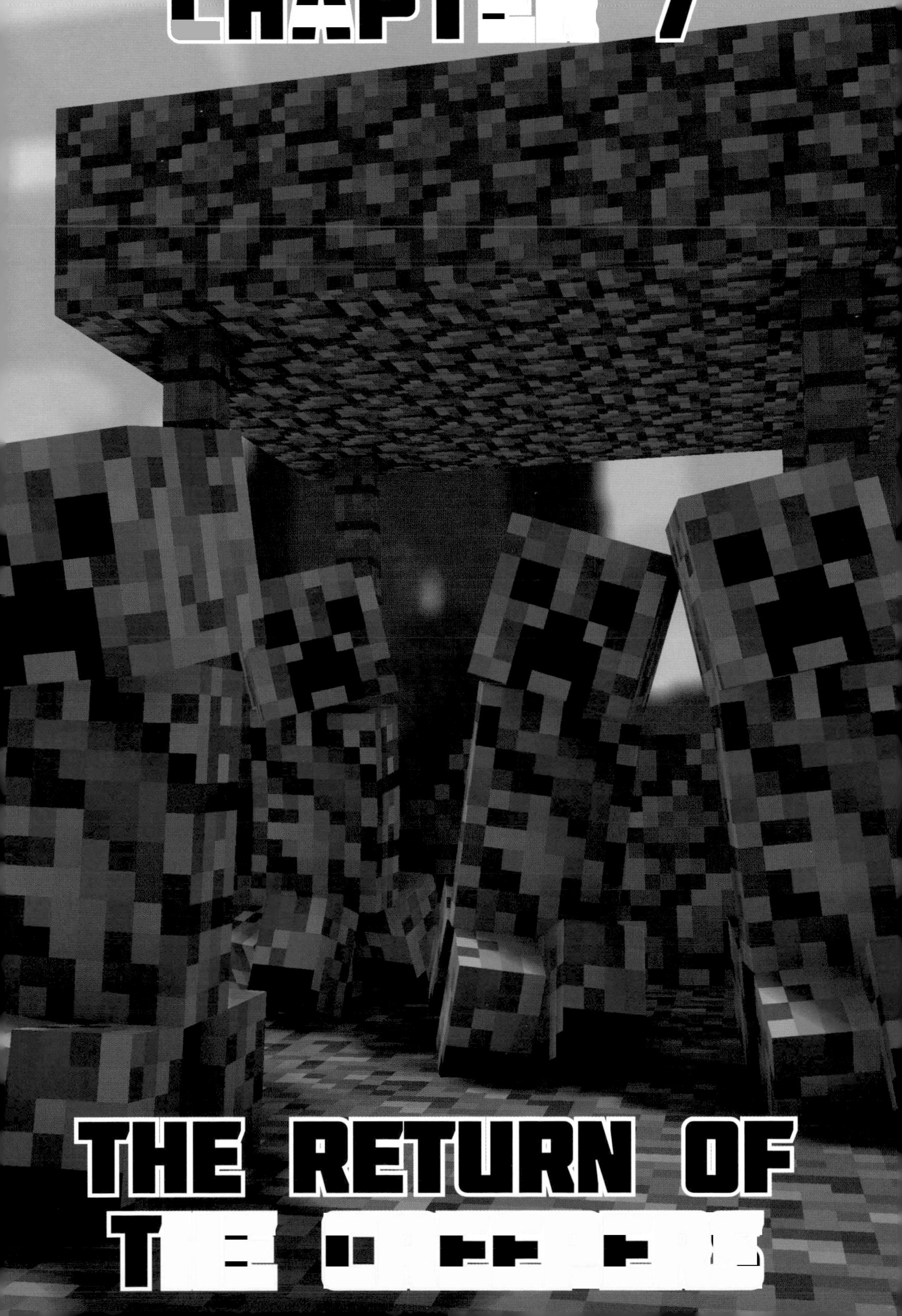

THE RETURN OF THE CREEPERS

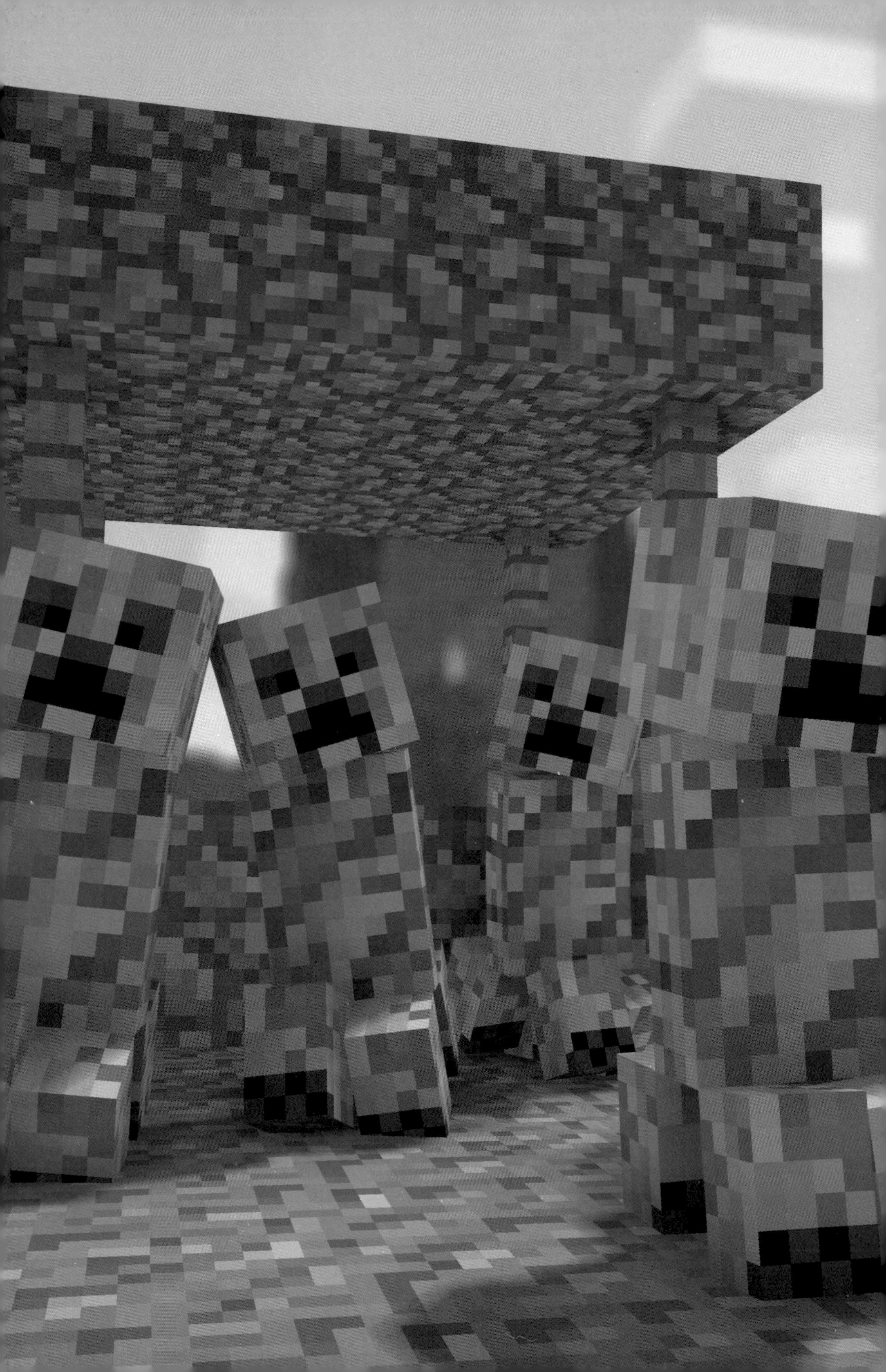

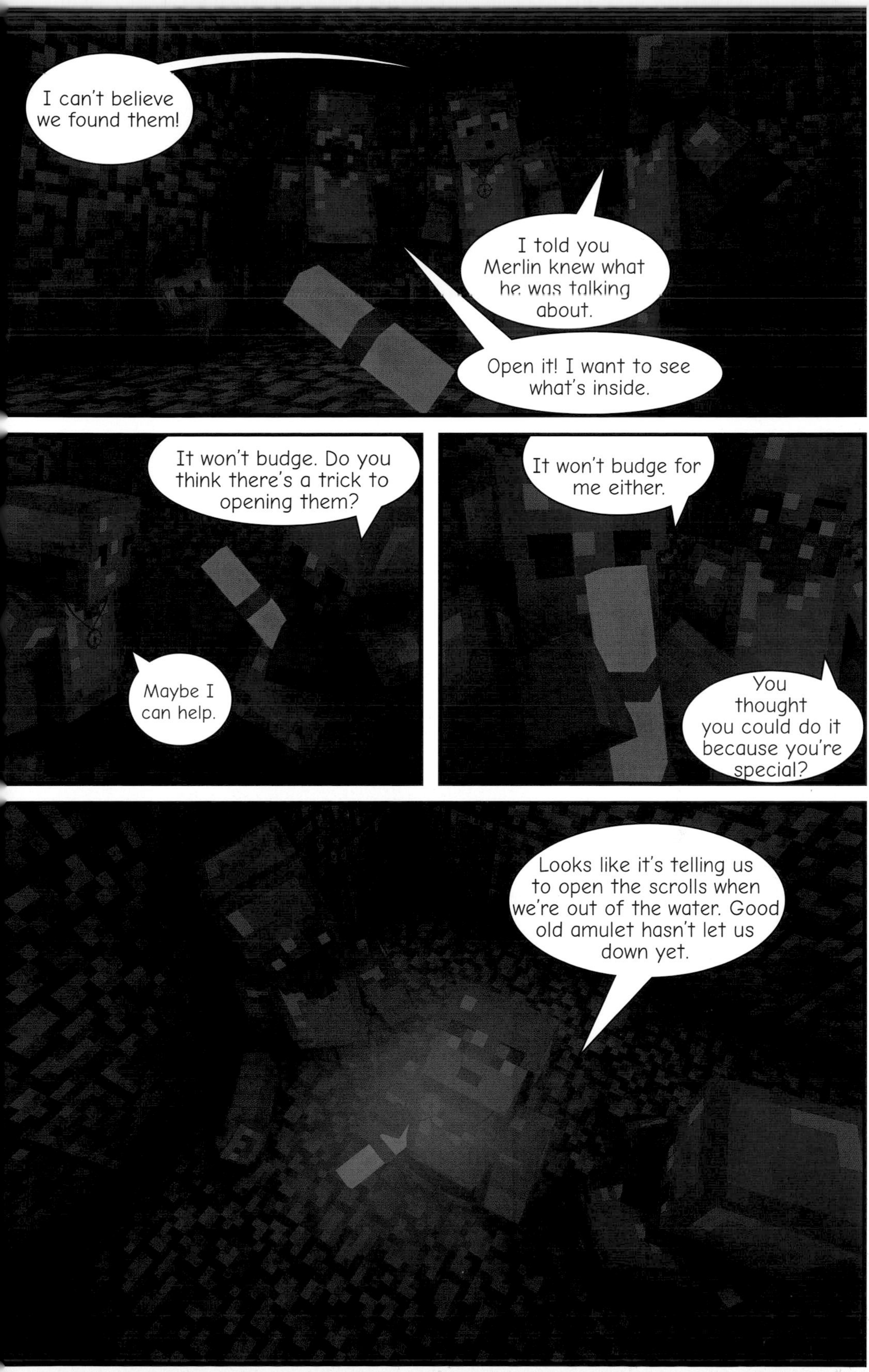
I can't believe we found them!
I told you Merlin knew what he was talking about.
Open it! I want to see what's inside.
It won't budge. Do you think there's a trick to opening them?
Maybe I can help.
It won't budge for me either.
You thought you could do it because you're special?
Looks like it's telling us to open the scrolls when we're out of the water. Good old amulet hasn't let us down yet.

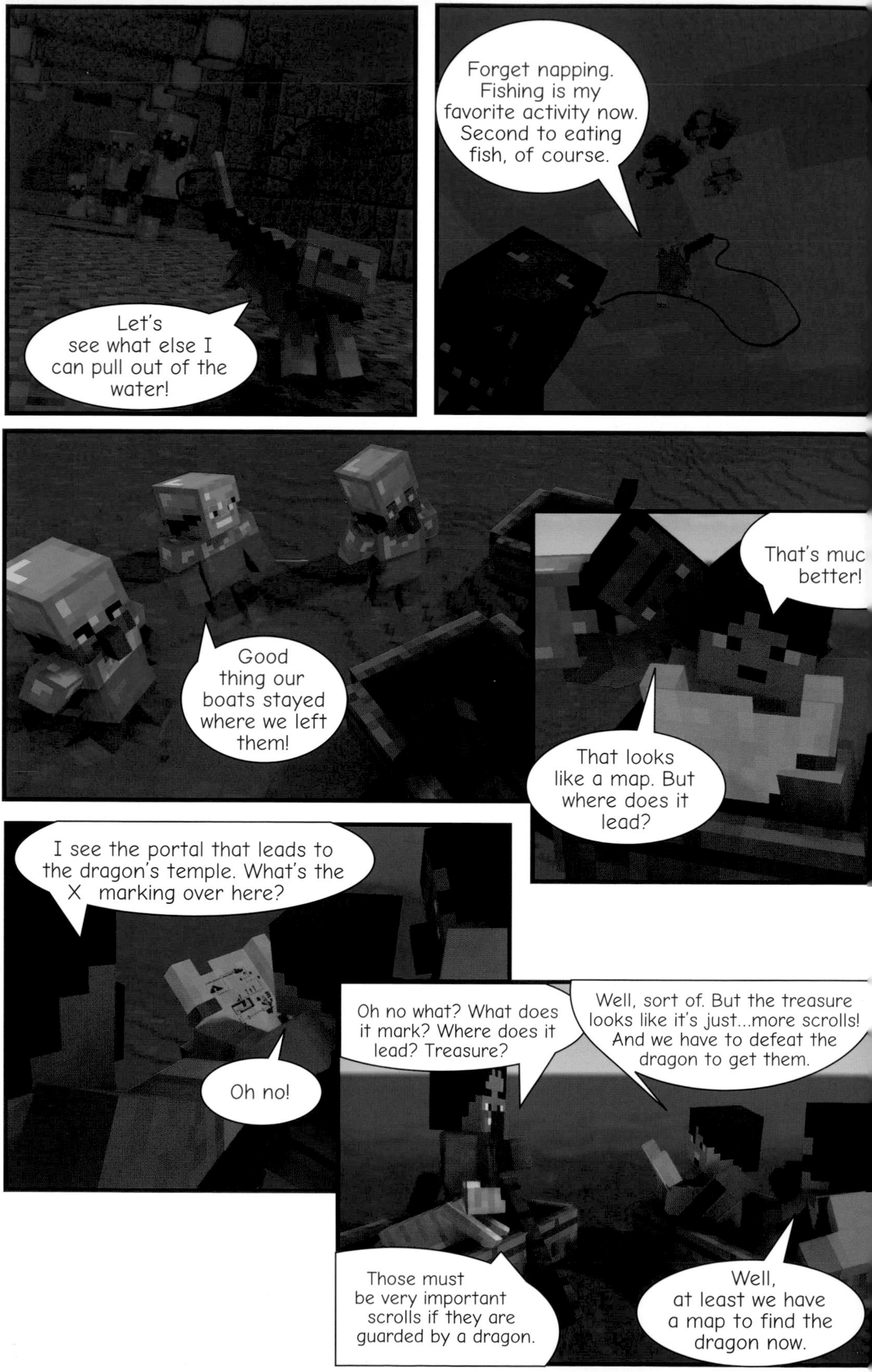
Let's see what else I can pull out of the water!
Forget napping. Fishing is my favorite activity now. Second to eating fish, of course.
Good thing our boats stayed where we left them!
That's muc better!
That looks like a map. But where does it lead?
I see the portal that leads to the dragon's temple. What's the X marking over here?
Oh no!
Oh no what? What does it mark? Where does it lead? Treasure?
Well, sort of. But the treasure looks like it's just...more scrolls! And we have to defeat the dragon to get them.
Those must be very important scrolls if they are guarded by a dragon.
Well, at least we have a map to find the dragon now.

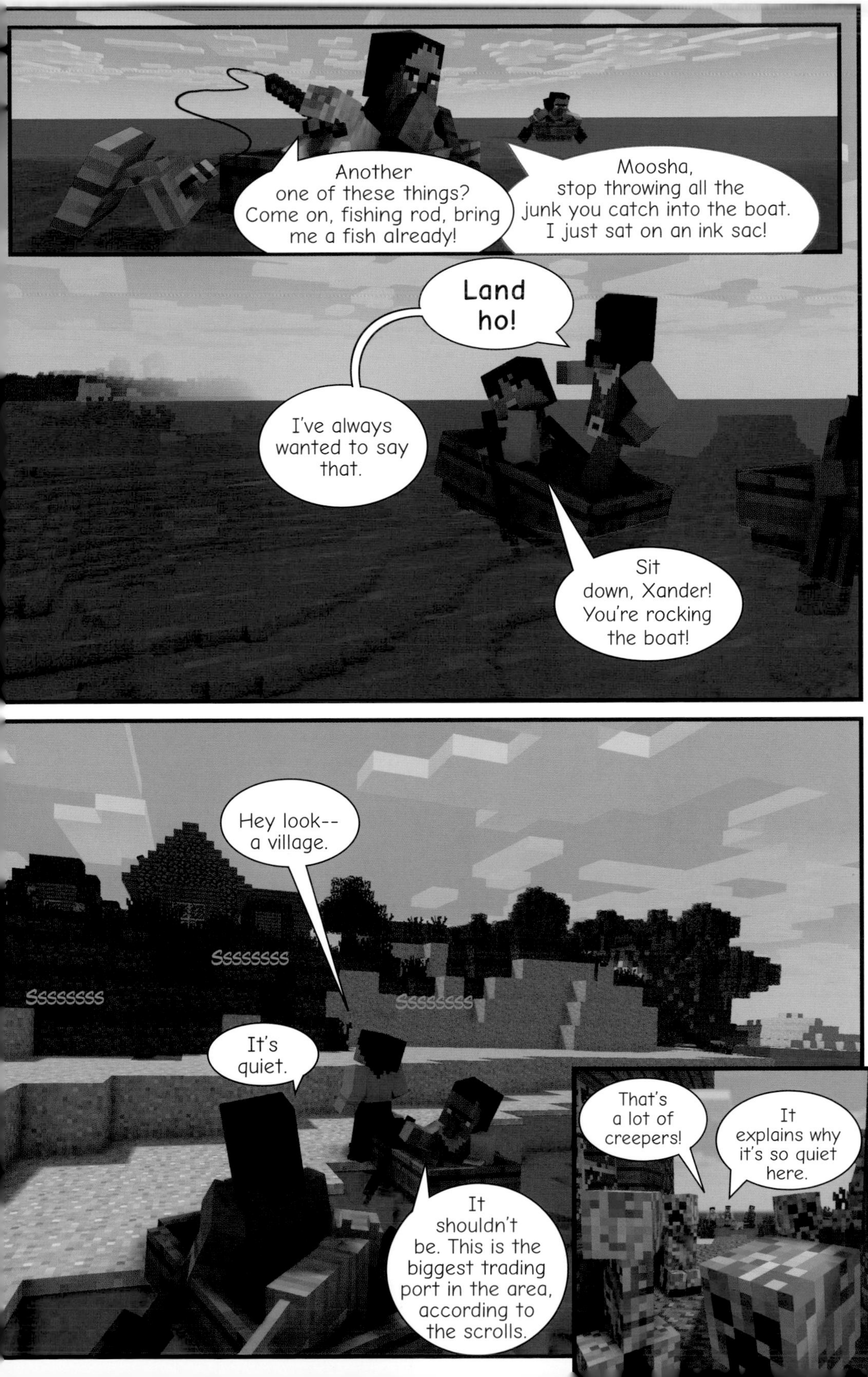
Another one of these things? Come on, fishing rod, bring me a fish already!
Moosha, stop throwing all the junk you catch into the boat. I just sat on an ink sac!
Land ho!
I've always wanted to say that.
Sit down, Xander! You're rocking the boat!
Hey look-- a village.
Ssssssss
Ssssssss
Ssssssss
It's quiet.
It shouldn't be. This is the biggest trading port in the area, according to the scrolls.
That's a lot of creepers!
It explains why it's so quiet here.

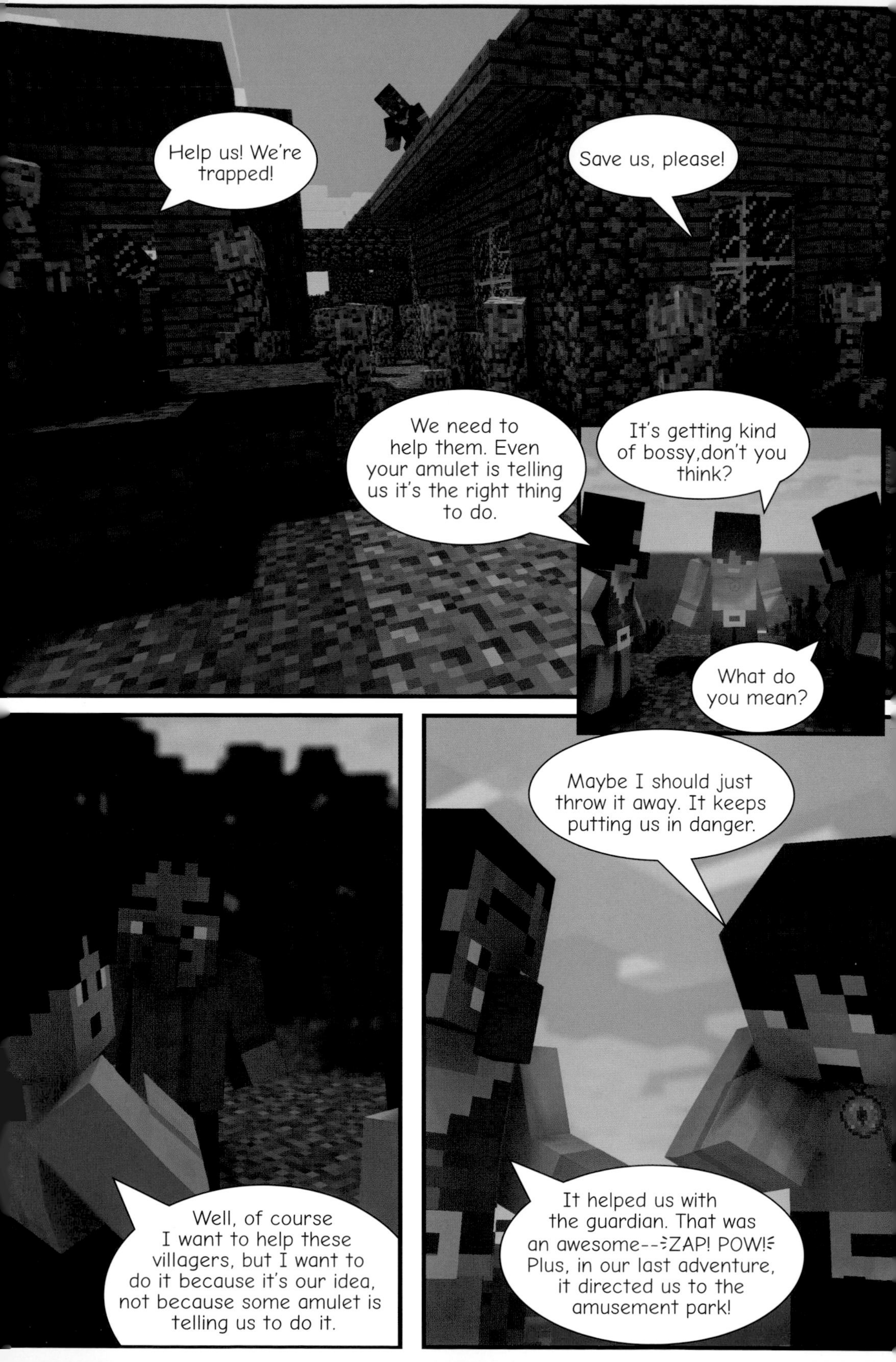
Help us! We're trapped!
Save us, please!
We need to help them. Even your amulet is telling us it's the right thing to do.
It's getting kind of bossy,don't you think?
What do you mean?
Well, of course I want to help these villagers, but I want to do it because it's our idea, not because some amulet is telling us to do it.
Maybe I should just throw it away. It keeps putting us in danger.
It helped us with the guardian. That was an awesome--ZAP! POW! Plus, in our last adventure, it directed us to the amusement park!

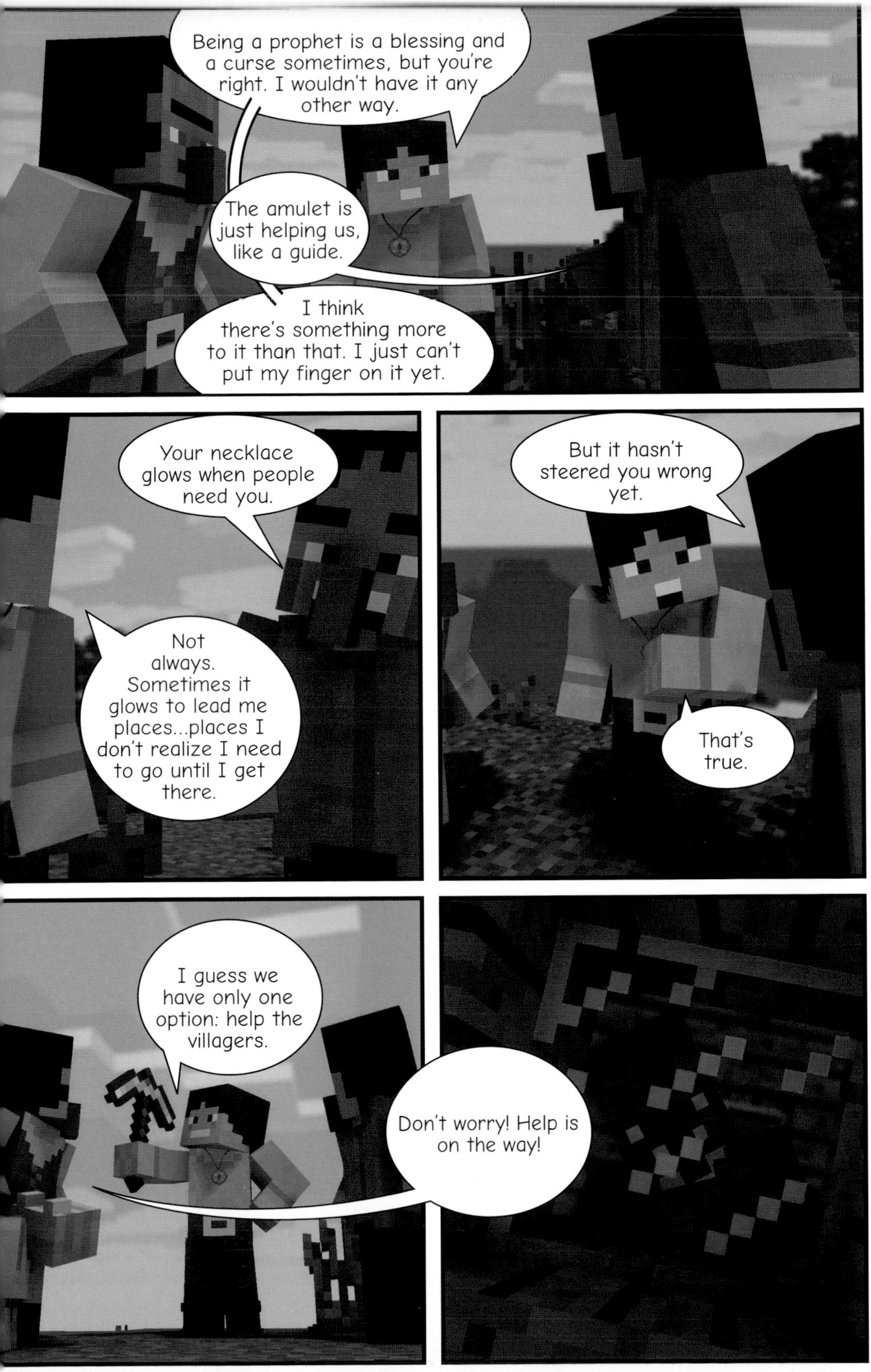
Being a prophet is a blessing and a curse sometimes, but you're right. I wouldn't have it any other way.
The amulet is just helping us, like a guide.
I think there's something more to it than that. I just can't put my finger on it yet.
Your necklace glows when people need you.
Not always. Sometimes it glows to lead me places...places I don't realize I need to go until I get there.
But it hasn't steered you wrong yet.
That's true.
I guess we have only one option: help the villagers.
Don't worry! Help is on the way!

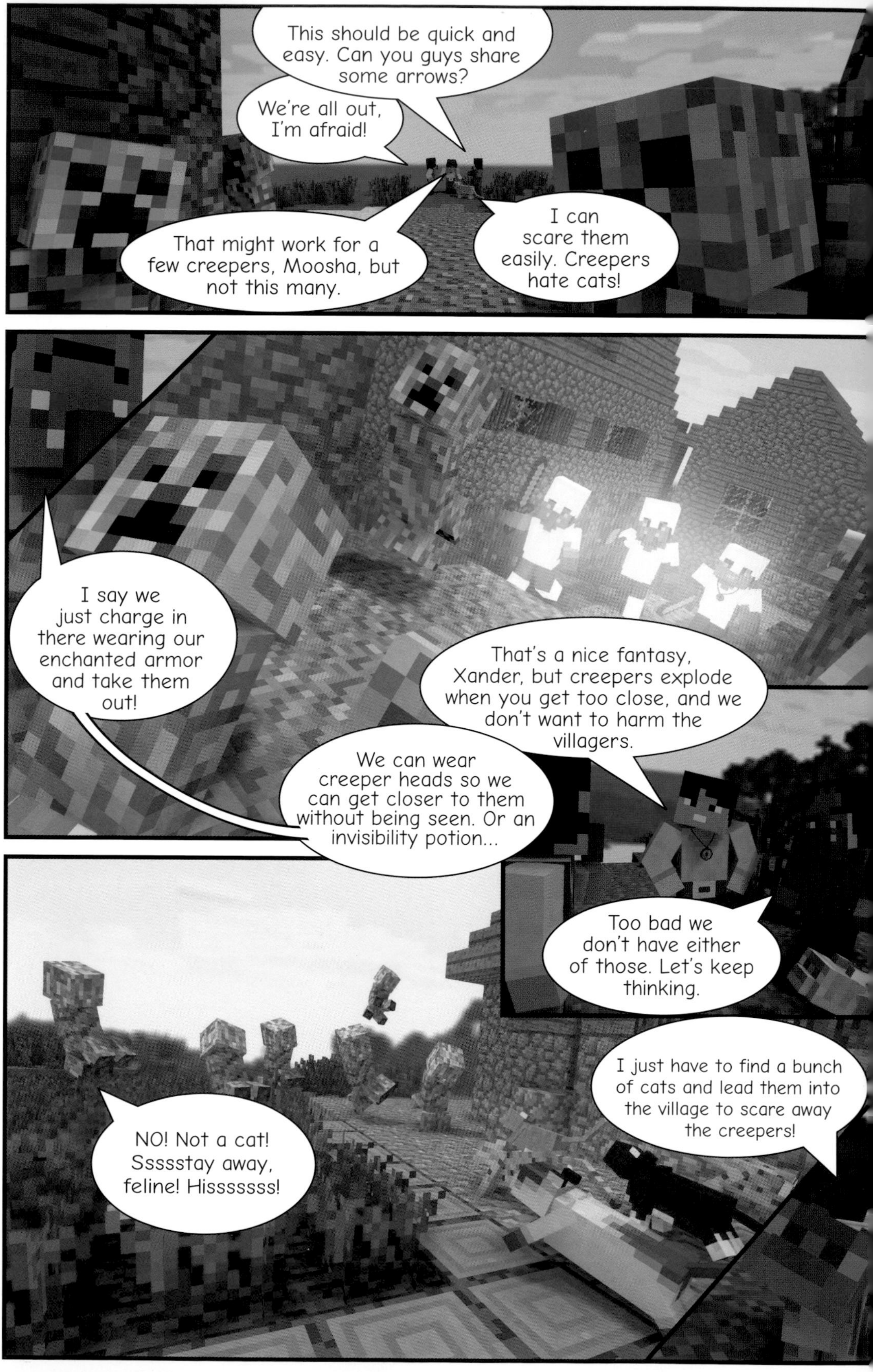
This should be quick and easy. Can you guys share some arrows?
We're all out, I'm afraid!
I can scare them easily. Creepers hate cats!
That might work for a few creepers, Moosha, but not this many.
I say we just charge in there wearing our enchanted armor and take them out!
That's a nice fantasy, Xander, but creepers explode when you get too close, and we don't want to harm the villagers.
We can wear creeper heads so we can get closer to them without being seen. Or an invisibility potion...
Too bad we don't have either of those. Let's keep thinking.
I just have to find a bunch of cats and lead them into the village to scare away the creepers!
NO! Not a cat! Sssssstay away, feline! Hisssssss!

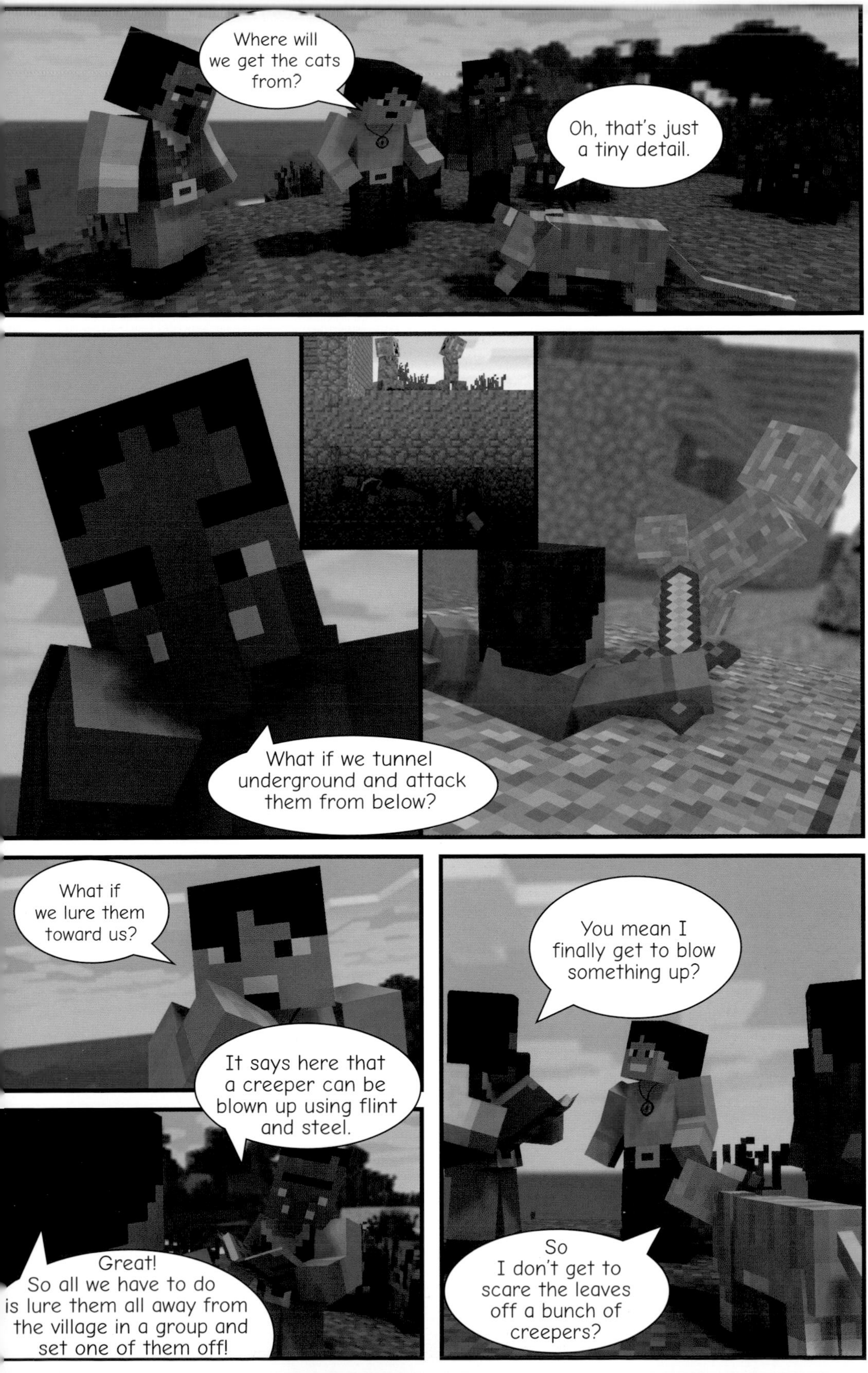

Where will we get the cats from?
Oh, that's just a tiny detail.
What if we tunnel underground and attack them from below?
What if we lure them toward us?
It says here that a creeper can be blown up using flint and steel.
Great! So all we have to do is lure them all away from the village in a group and set one of them off!
You mean I finally get to blow something up?
So I don't get to scare the leaves off a bunch of creepers?

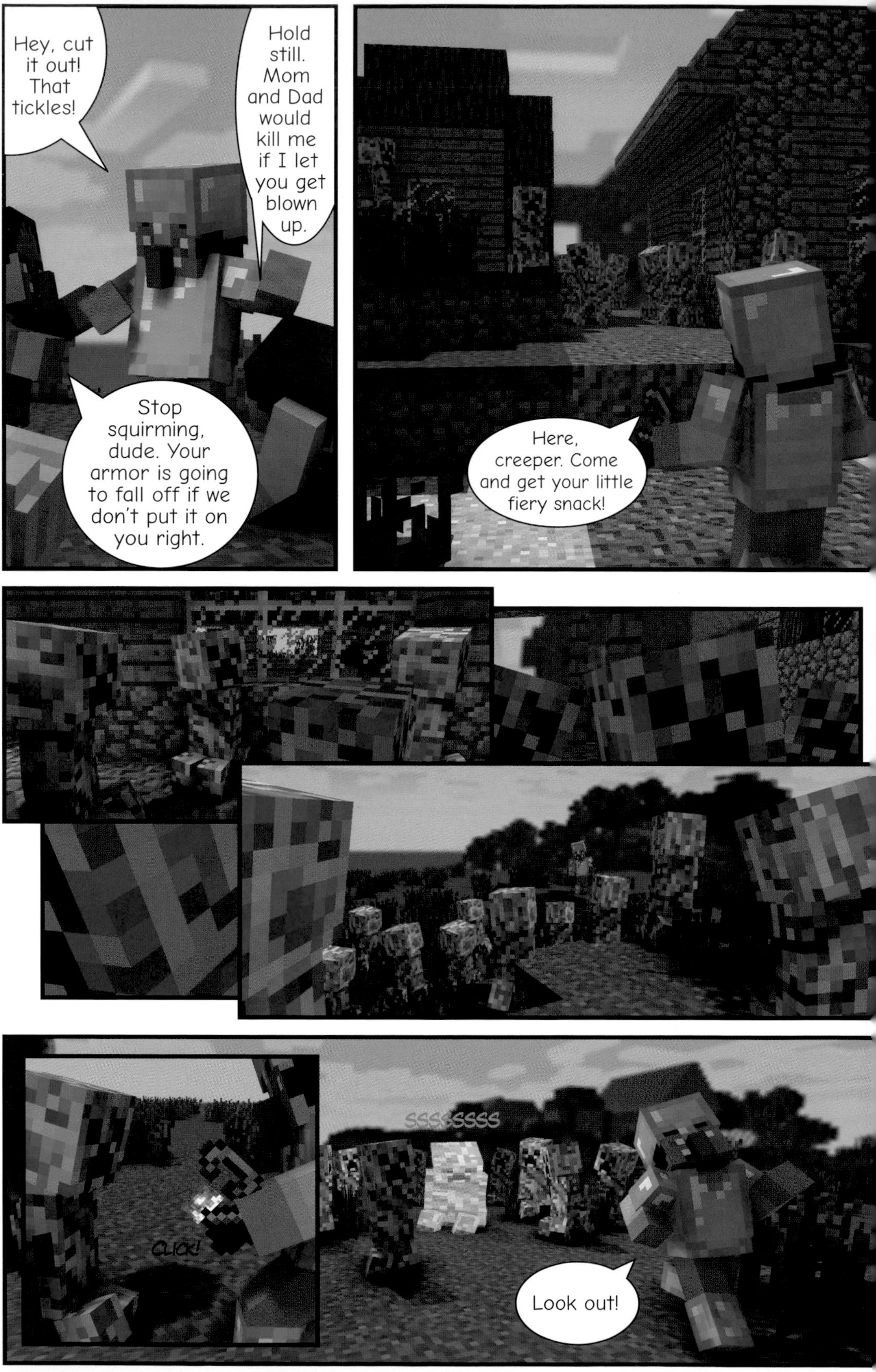
Hey, cut it out! That tickles!
Hold still. Mom and Dad would kill me if I let you get blown up.
Stop squirming, dude. Your armor is going to fall off if we don't put it on you right.
Here, creeper. Come and get your little fiery snack!
CLICK!
SSSSSSSS
Look out!

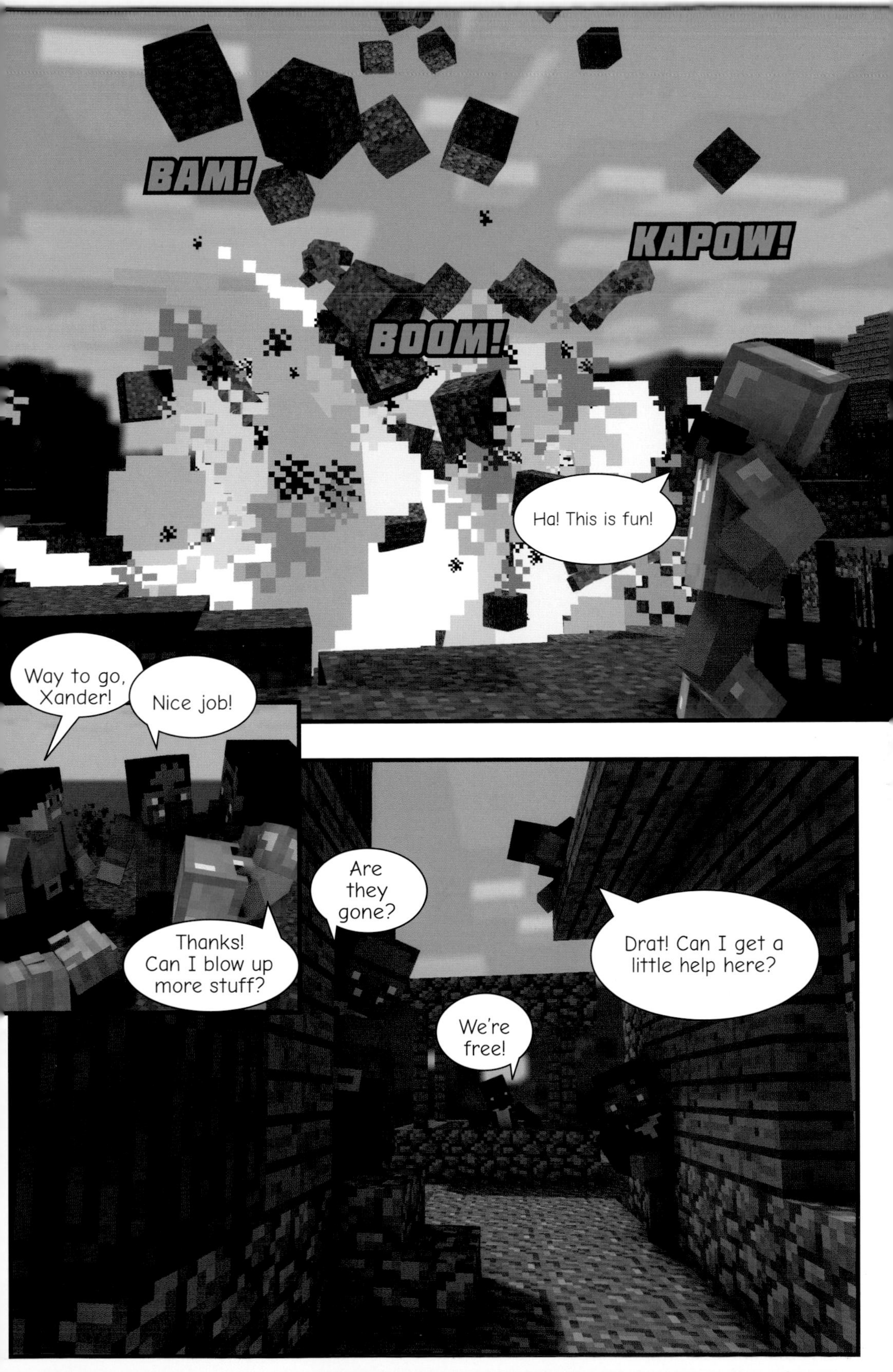
BAM!
KAPOW!
BOOM!
Ha! This is fun!
Way to go, Xander!
Nice job!
Thanks! Can I blow up more stuff?
Are they gone?
Drat! Can I get a little help here?
We're free!

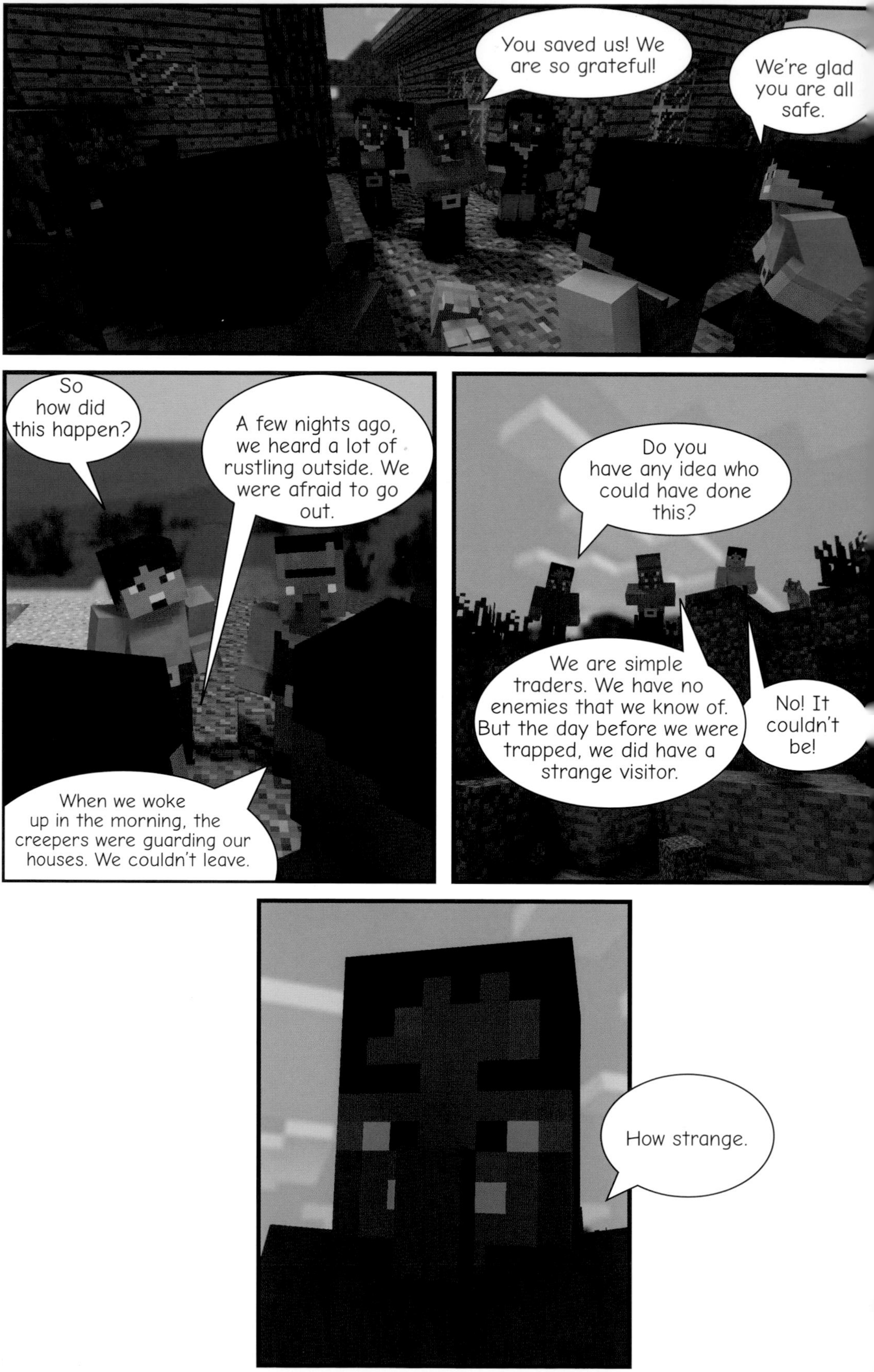
You saved us! We are so grateful!
We're glad you are all safe.
So how did this happen?
A few nights ago, we heard a lot of rustling outside. We were afraid to go out.
When we woke up in the morning, the creepers were guarding our houses. We couldn't leave.
Do you have any idea who could have done this?
We are simple traders. We have no enemies that we know of. But the day before we were trapped, we did have a strange visitor.
No! It couldn't be!
How strange.

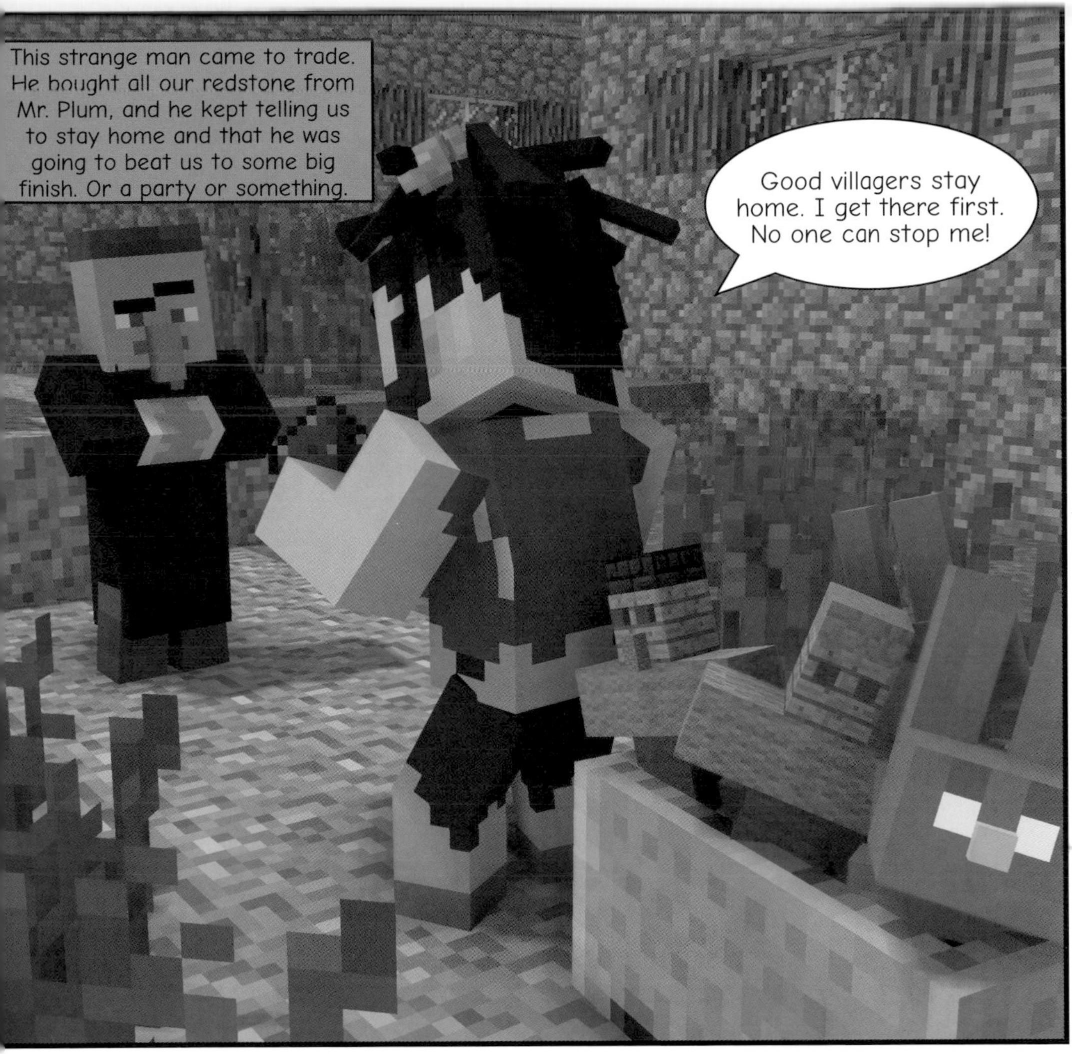
This strange man came to trade. He bought all our redstone from Mr. Plum, and he kept telling us to stay home and that he was going to beat us to some big finish. Or a party or something.
Good villagers stay home. I get there first. No one can stop me!

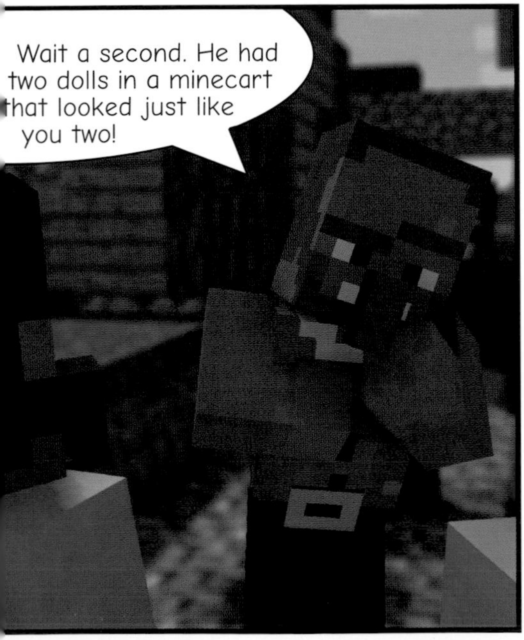
Wait a second. He had two dolls in a minecart that looked just like you two!

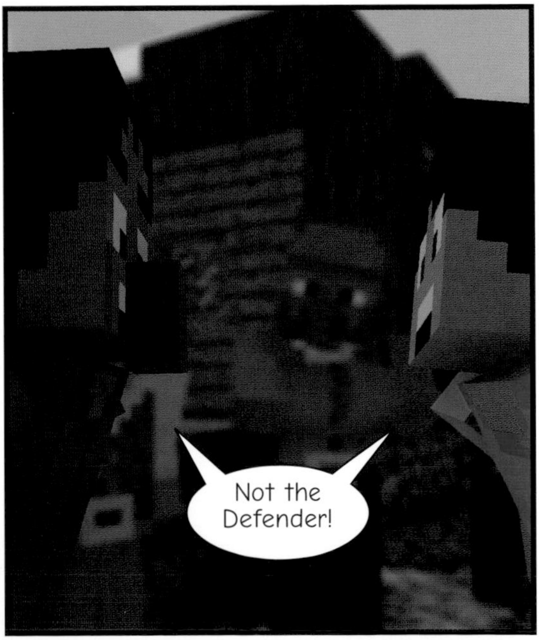
Not the Defender!

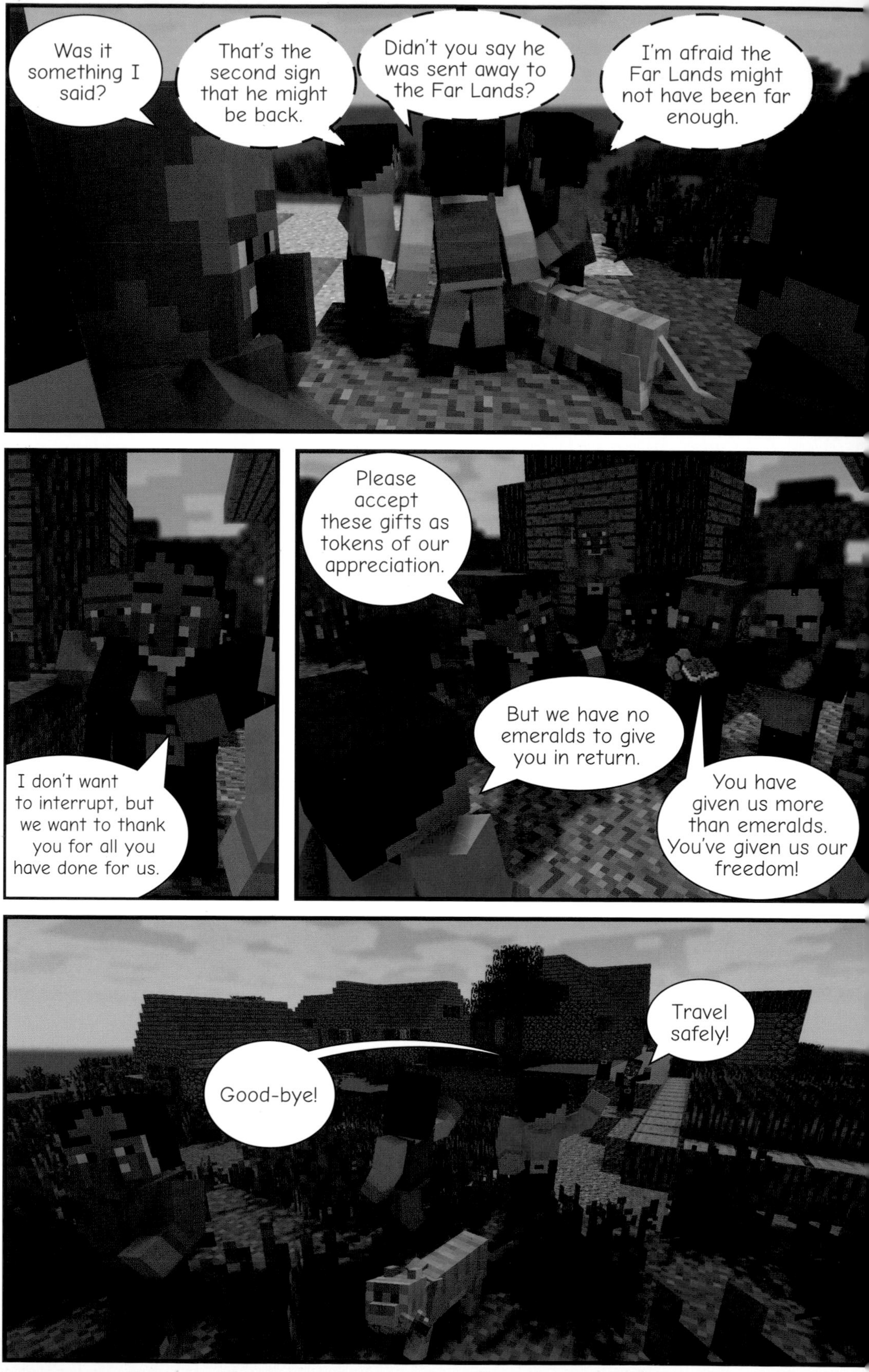
Was it something I said?
That's the second sign that he might be back.
Didn't you say he was sent away to the Far Lands?
I'm afraid the Far Lands might not have been far enough.
I don't want to interrupt, but we want to thank you for all you have done for us.
Please accept these gifts as tokens of our appreciation.
But we have no emeralds to give you in return.
You have given us more than emeralds. You've given us our freedom!
Good-bye!
Travel safely!

CHAPTER 8

ANGRY ZOMBIES

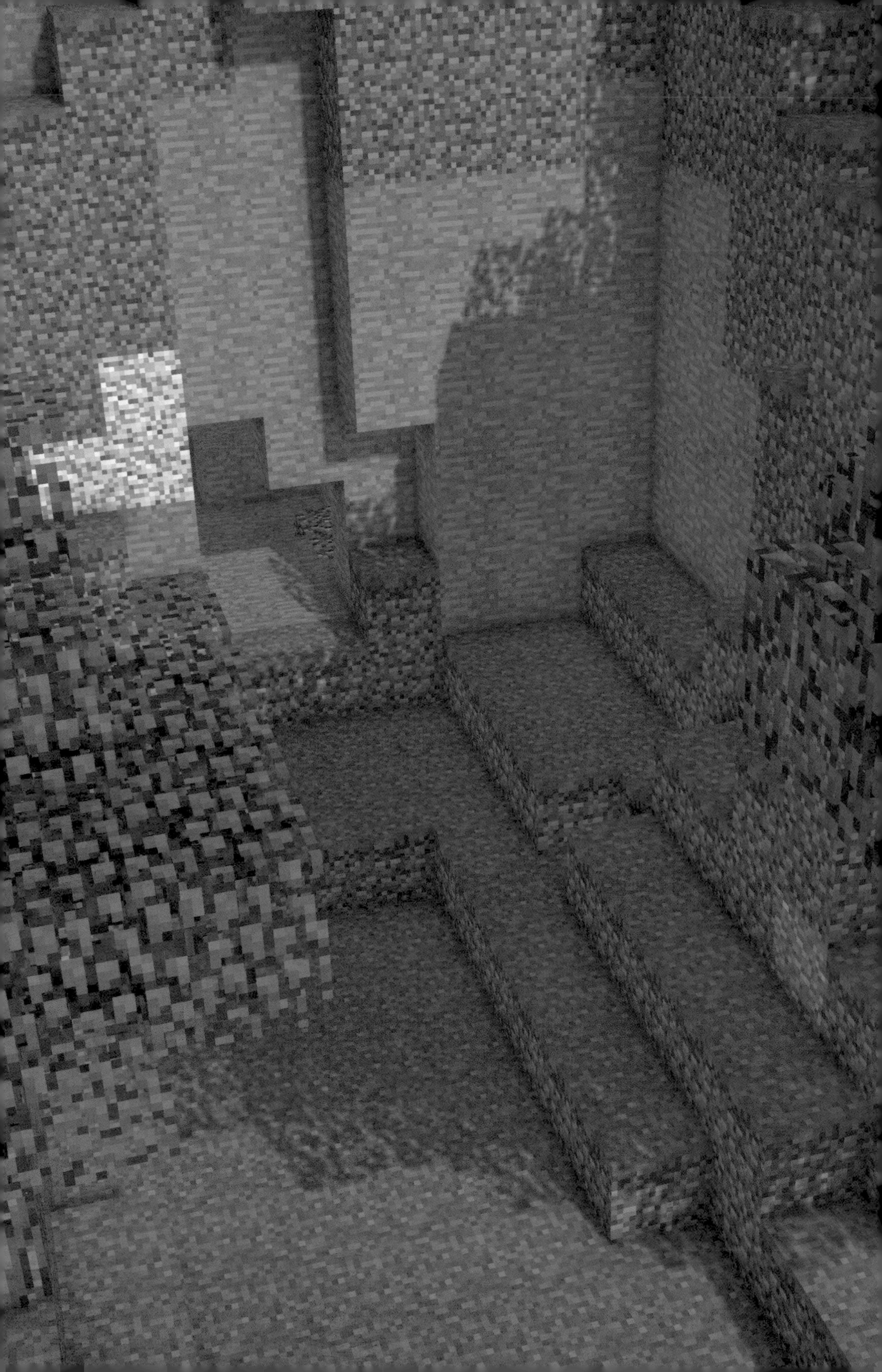

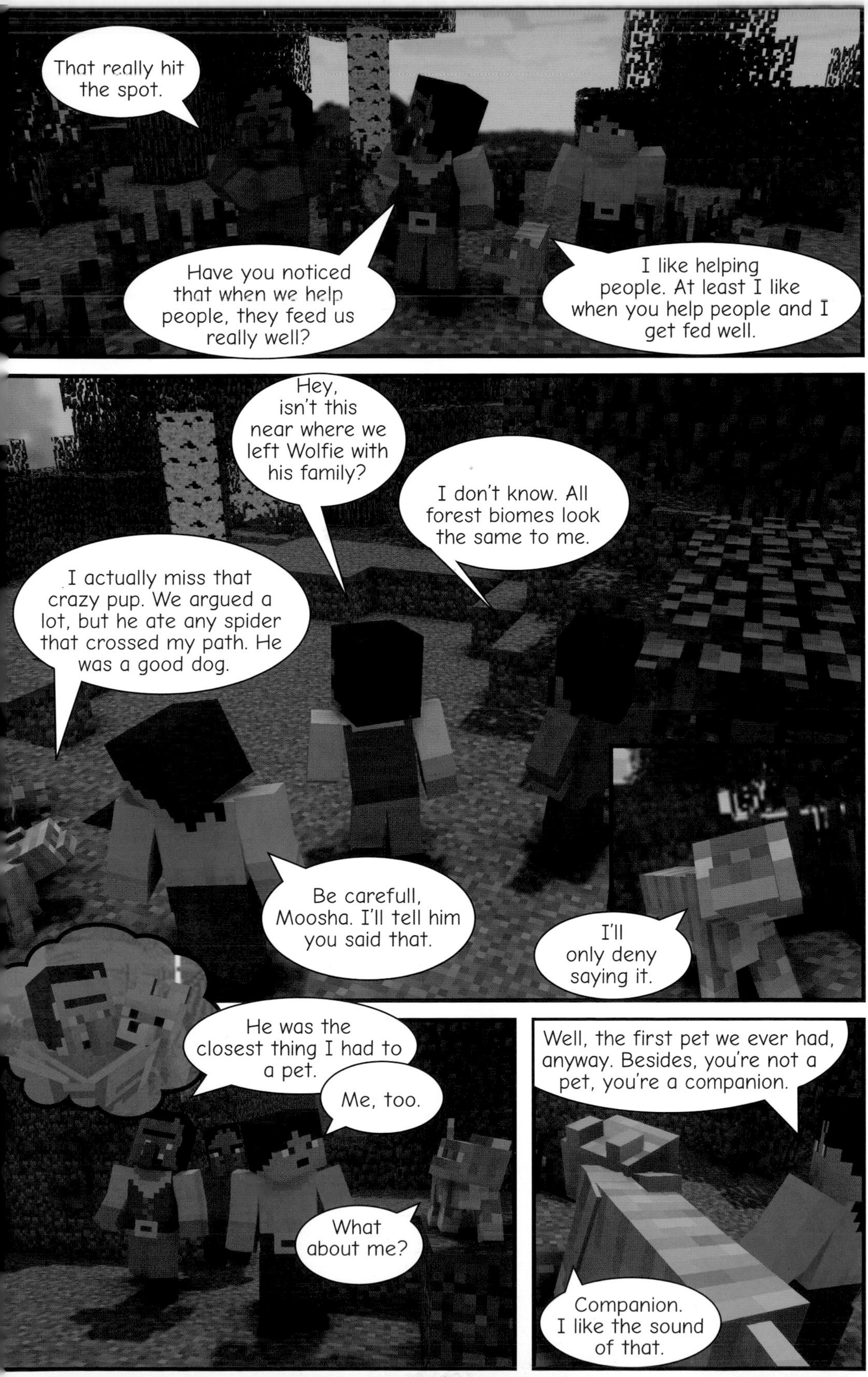
That really hit the spot.
Have you noticed that when we help people, they feed us really well?
I like helping people. At least I like when you help people and I get fed well.
Hey, isn't this near where we left Wolfie with his family?
I don't know. All forest biomes look the same to me.
I actually miss that crazy pup. We argued a lot, but he ate any spider that crossed my path. He was a good dog.
Be carefull, Moosha. I'll tell him you said that.
I'll only deny saying it.
He was the closest thing I had to a pet.
Me, too.
What about me?
Well, the first pet we ever had, anyway. Besides, you're not a pet, you're a companion.
Companion. I like the sound of that.

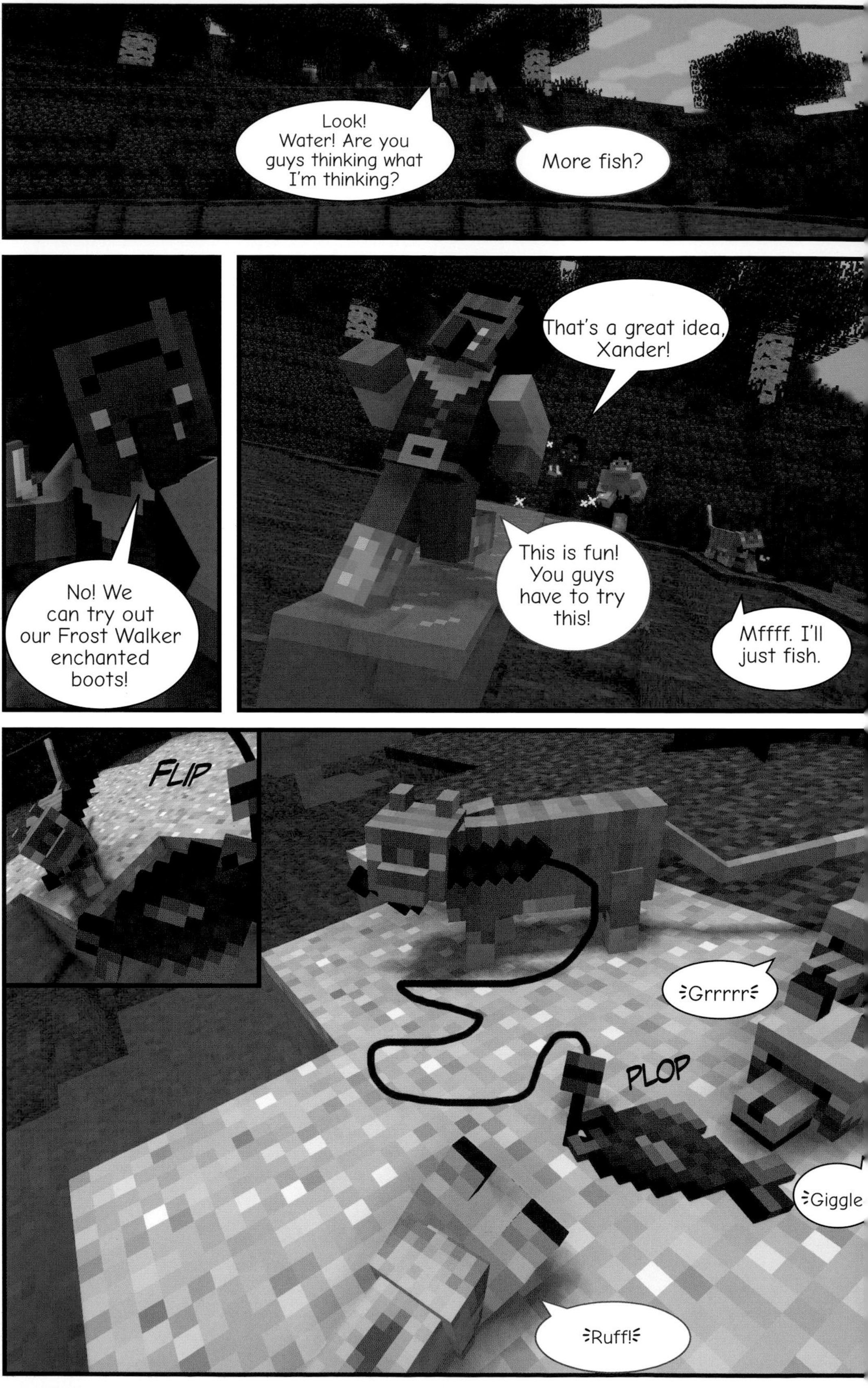
Look! Water! Are you guys thinking what I'm thinking?
More fish?
No! We can try out our Frost Walker enchanted boots!
That's a great idea, Xander!
This is fun! You guys have to try this!
Mffff. I'll just fish.
FLIP
Grrrrr
PLOP
Giggle
Ruff!

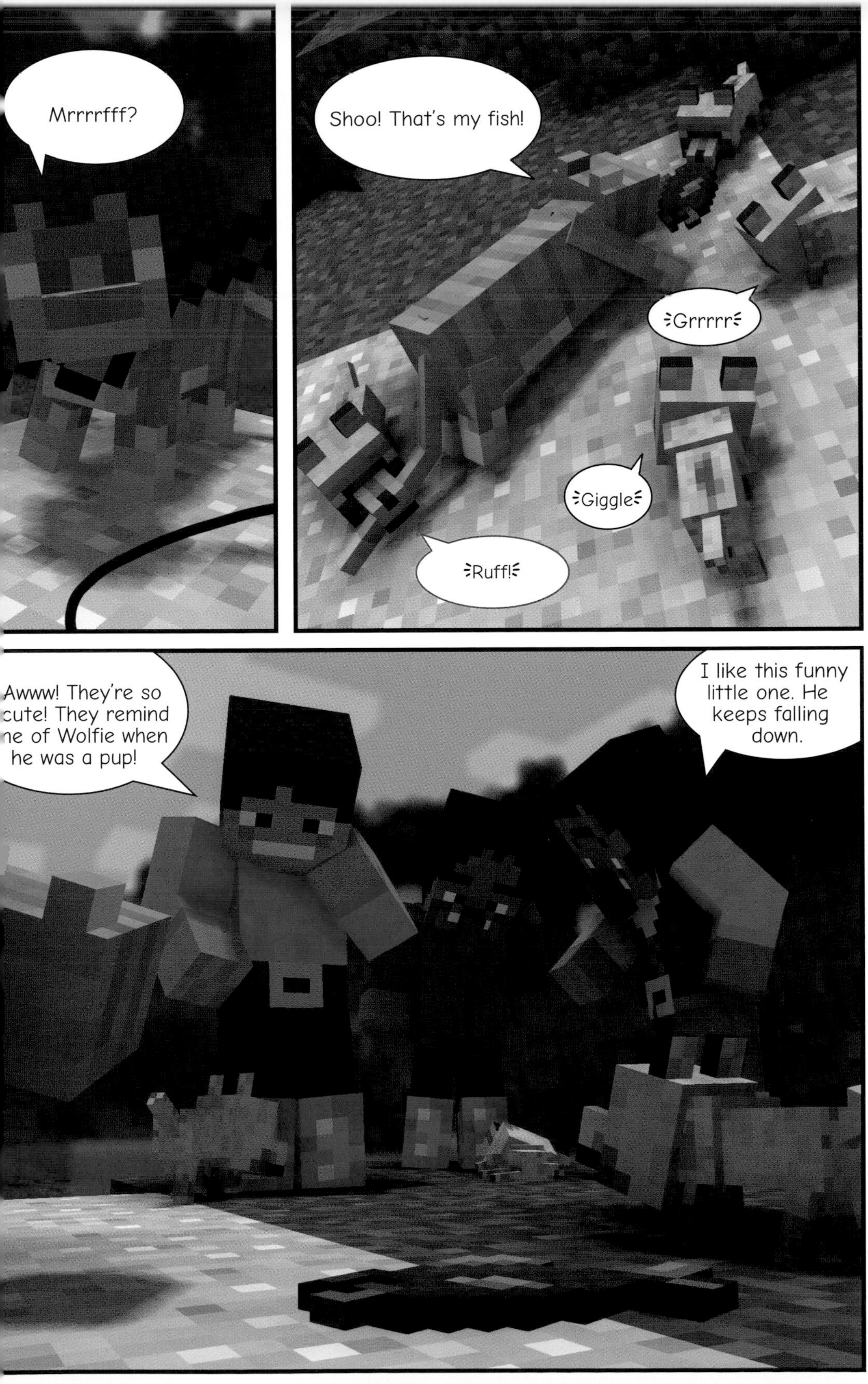

Mrrrrfff?
Shoo! That's my fish!
Grrrrr
Giggle
Ruff!
Awww! They're so cute! They remind ne of Wolfie when he was a pup!
I like this funny little one. He keeps falling down.

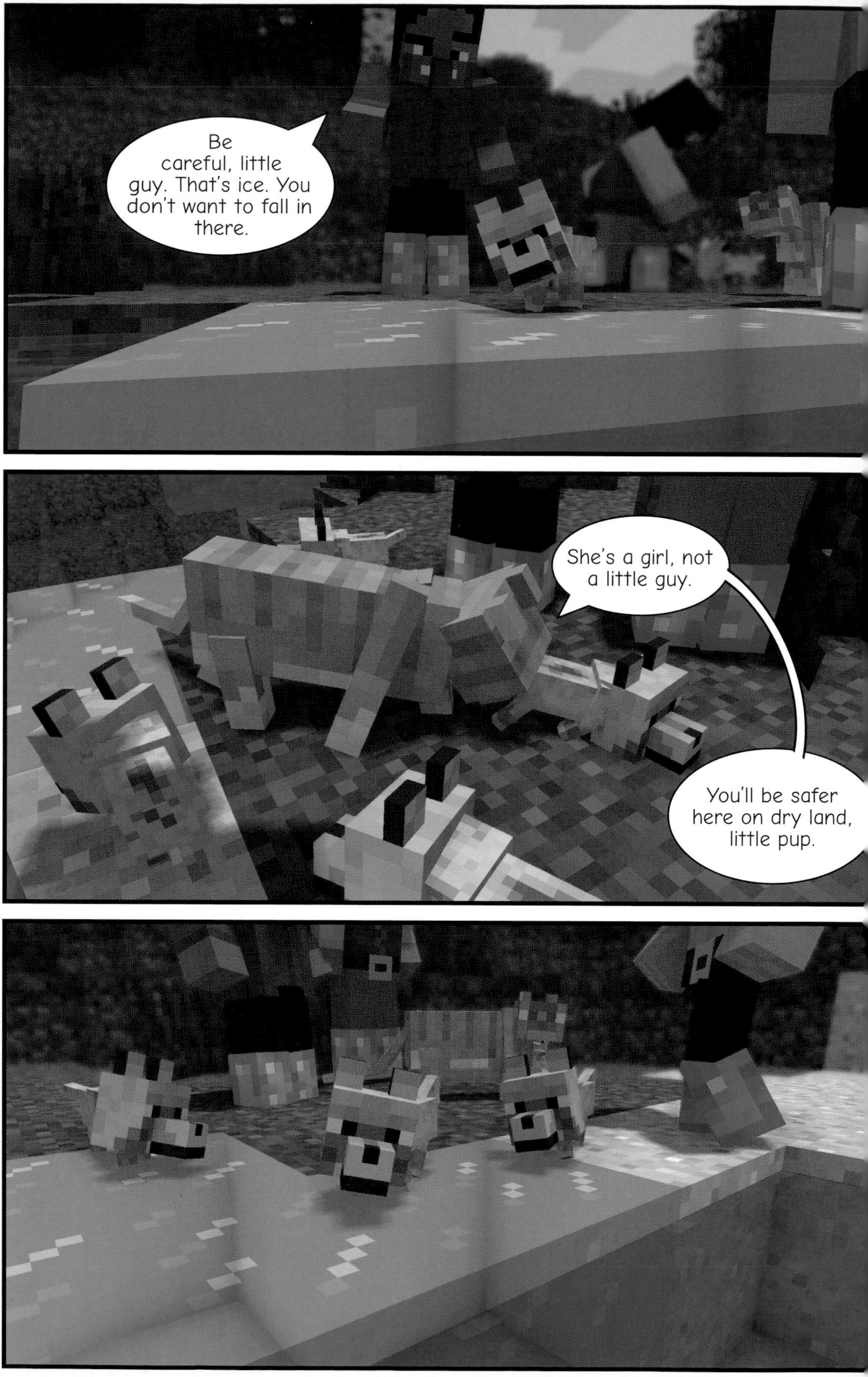
Be careful, little guy. That's ice. You don't want to fall in there.
She's a girl, not a little guy.
You'll be safer here on dry land, little pup.

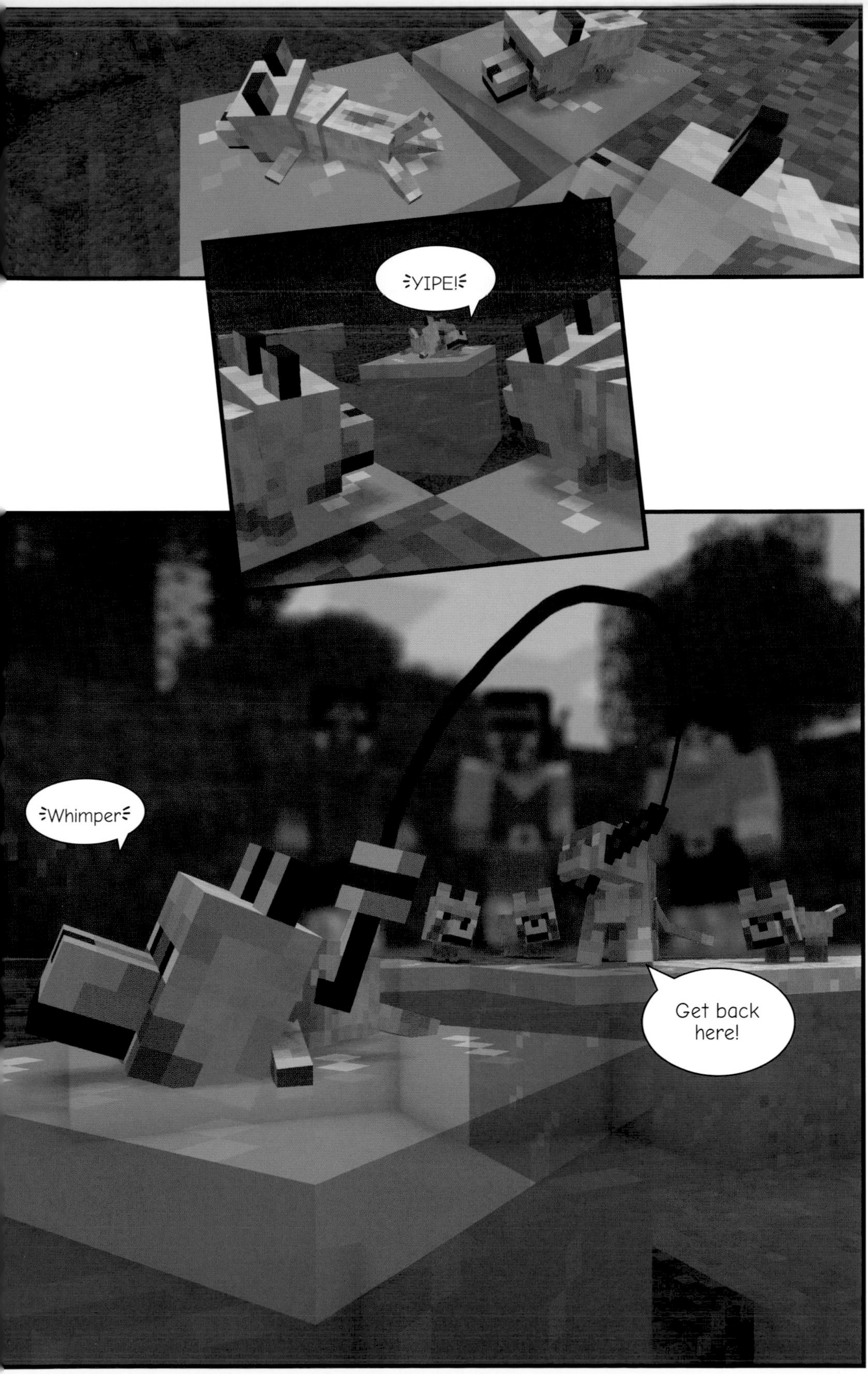
YIPE!
Whimper
Get back here!

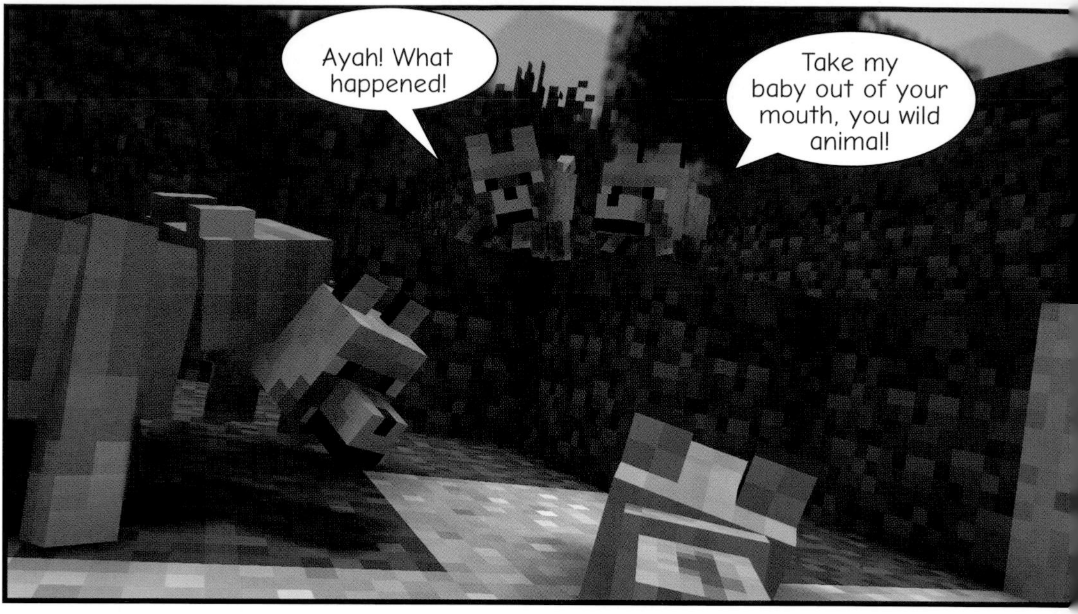
Ayah! What happened!
Take my baby out of your mouth, you wild animal!

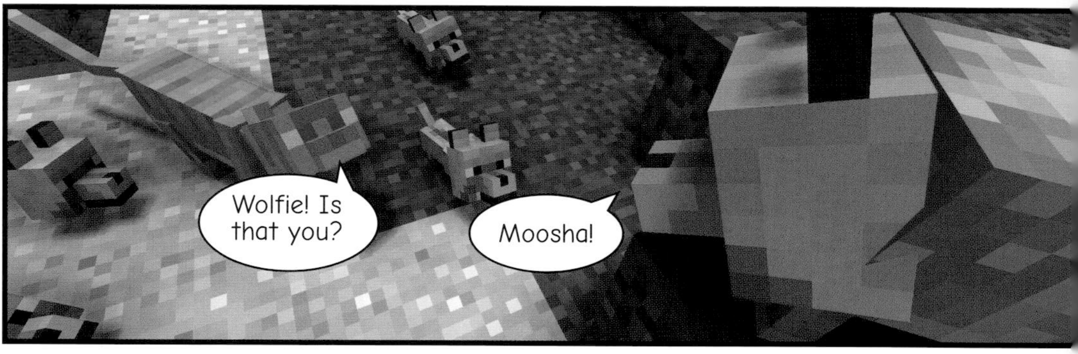
Wolfie! Is that you?
Moosha!

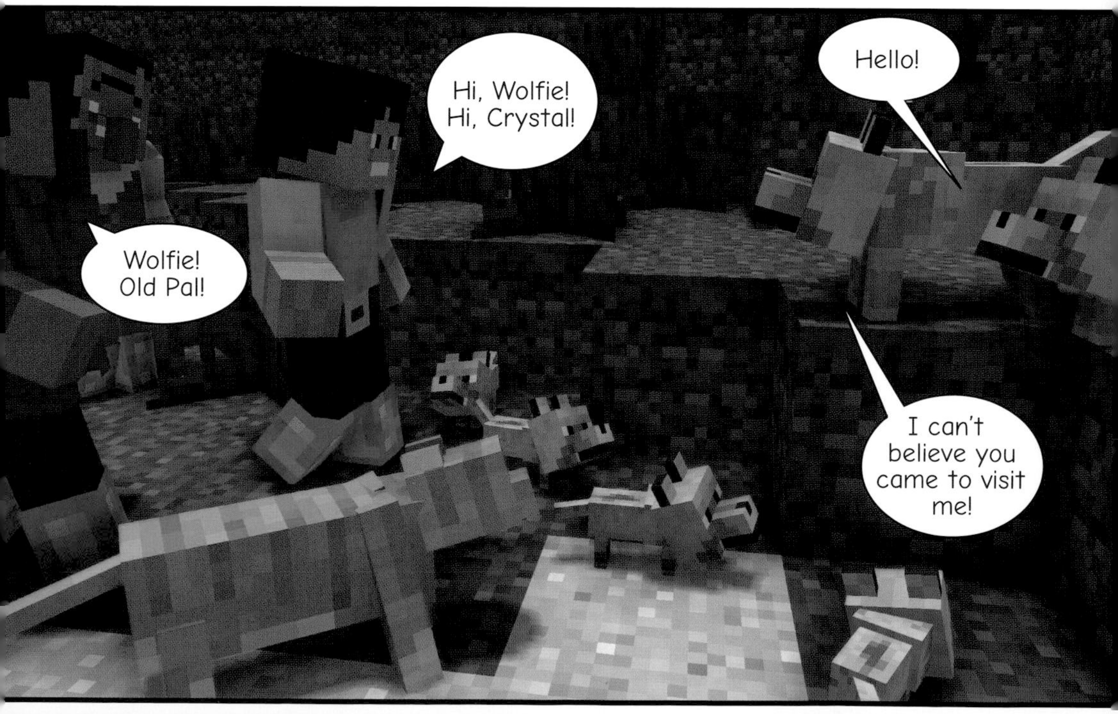
Wolfie! Old Pal!
Hi, Wolfie! Hi, Crystal!
Hello!
I can't believe you came to visit me!

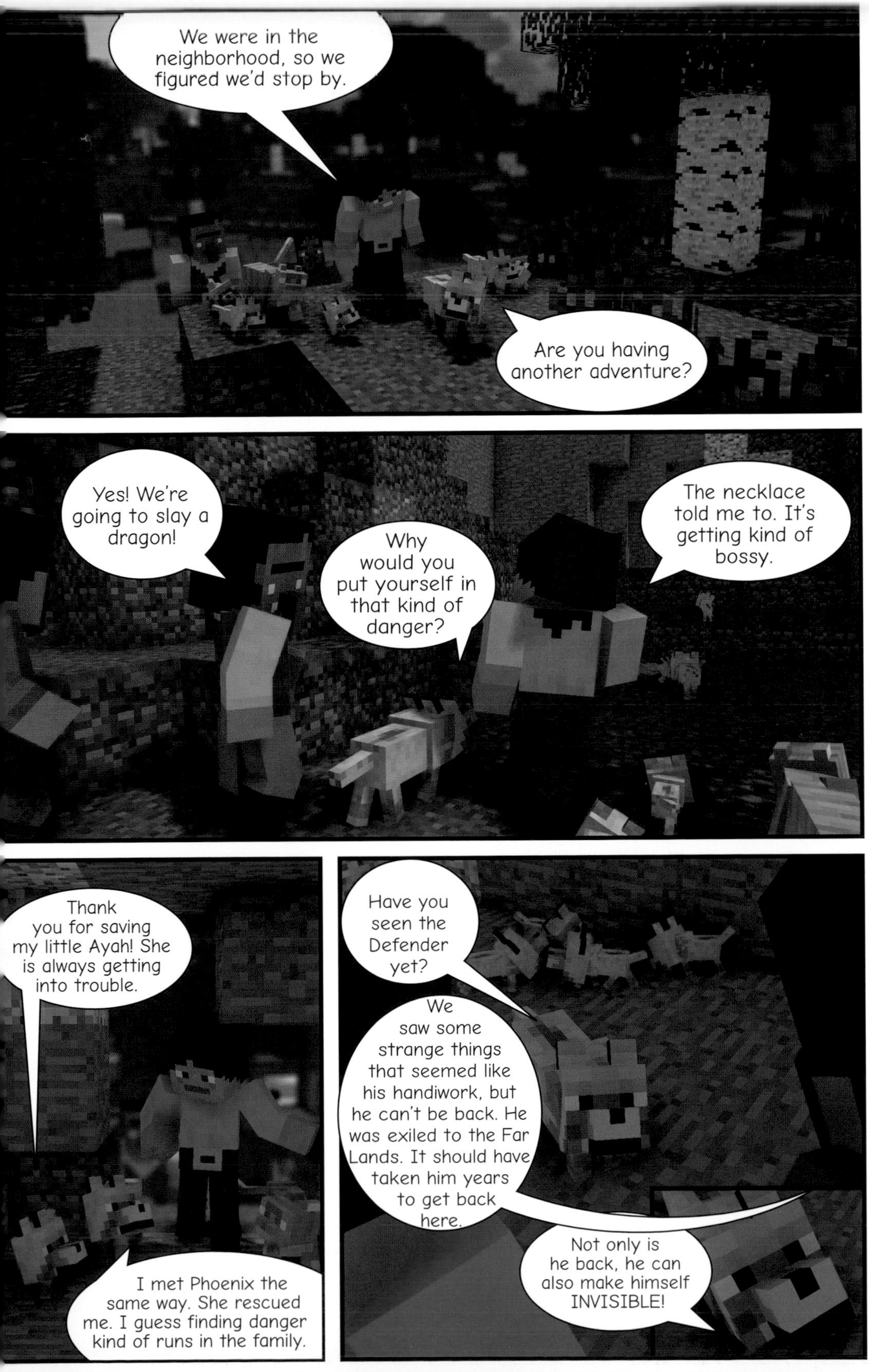
We were in the neighborhood, so we figured we'd stop by.
Are you having another adventure?
Yes! We're going to slay a dragon!
Why would you put yourself in that kind of danger?
The necklace told me to. It's getting kind of bossy.
Thank you for saving my little Ayah! She is always getting into trouble.
I met Phoenix the same way. She rescued me. I guess finding danger kind of runs in the family.
Have you seen the Defender yet?
We saw some strange things that seemed like his handiwork, but he can't be back. He was exiled to the Far Lands. It should have taken him years to get back here.
Not only is he back, he can also make himself INVISIBLE!

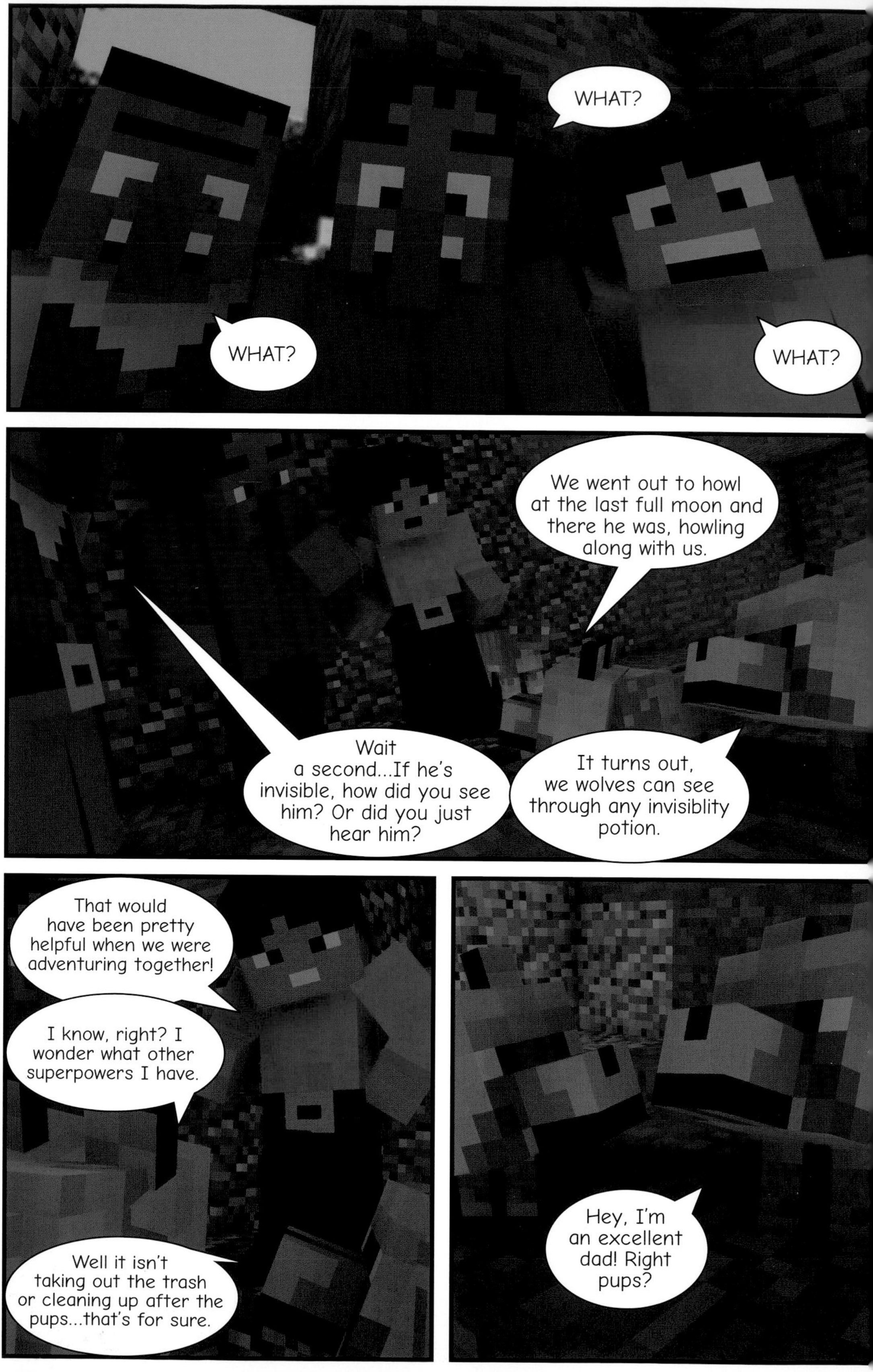
WHAT?
WHAT?
WHAT?
We went out to howl at the last full moon and there he was, howling along with us.
Wait a second...If he's invisible, how did you see him? Or did you just hear him?
It turns out, we wolves can see through any invisiblity potion.
That would have been pretty helpful when we were adventuring together!
I know, right? I wonder what other superpowers I have.
Well it isn't taking out the trash or cleaning up after the pups...that's for sure.
Hey, I'm an excellent dad! Right pups?

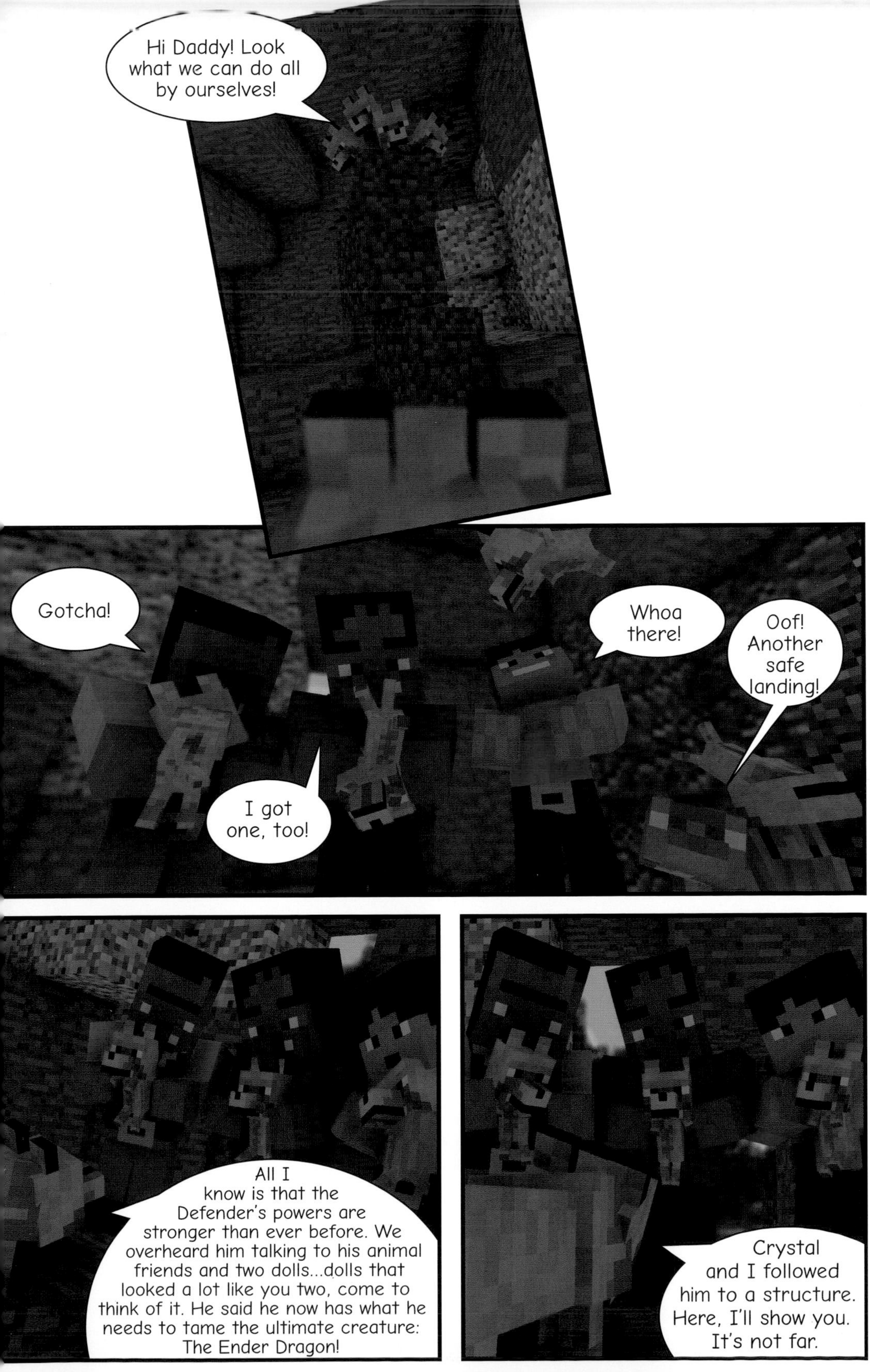

Hi Daddy! Look what we can do all by ourselves!
Gotcha!
I got one, too!
Whoa there!
Oof! Another safe landing!
All I know is that the Defender's powers are stronger than ever before. We overheard him talking to his animal friends and two dolls...dolls that looked a lot like you two, come to think of it. He said he now has what he needs to tame the ultimate creature: The Ender Dragon!
Crystal and I followed him to a structure. Here, I'll show you. It's not far.

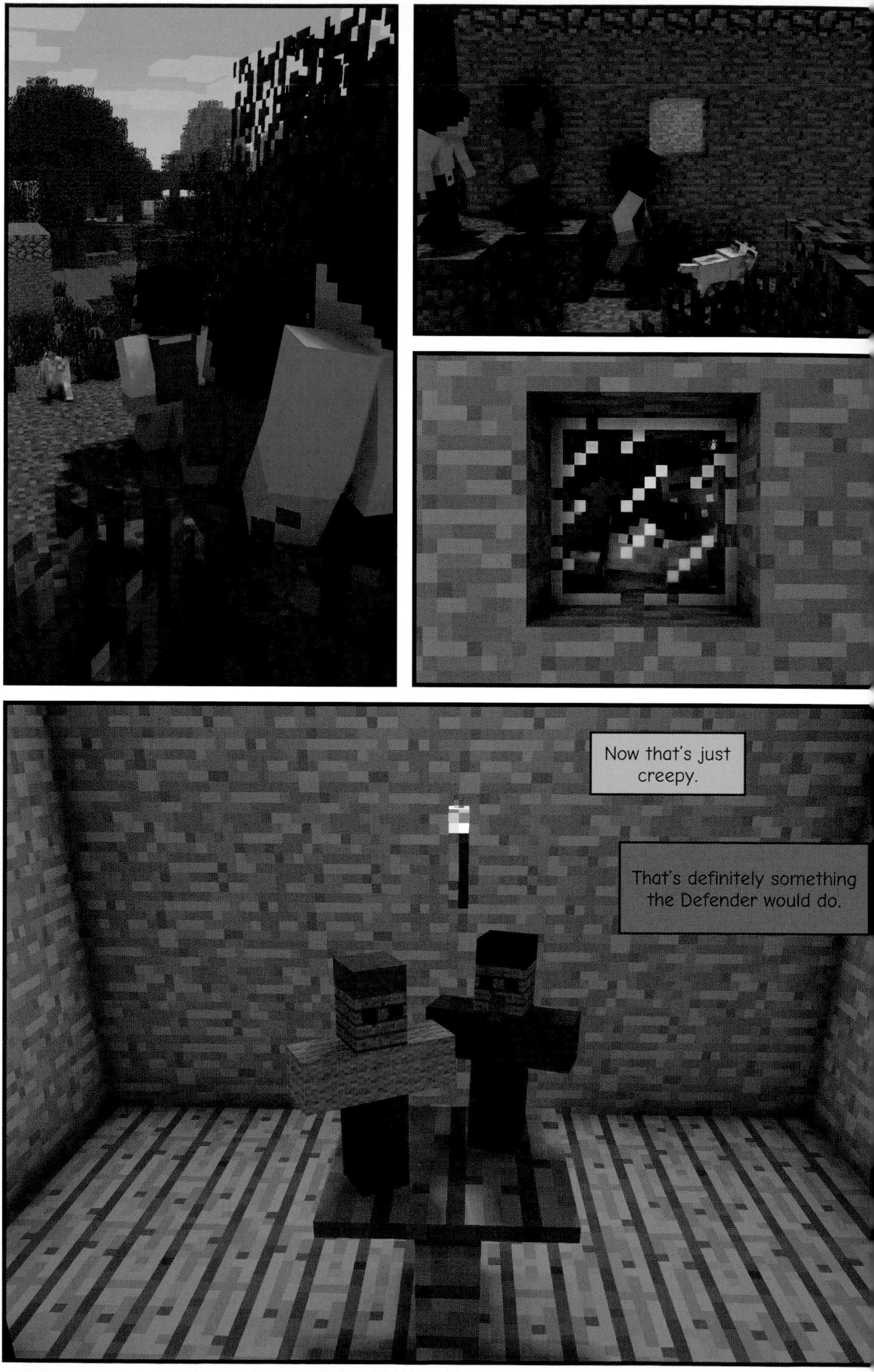
Now that's just creepy.
That's definitely something the Defender would do.

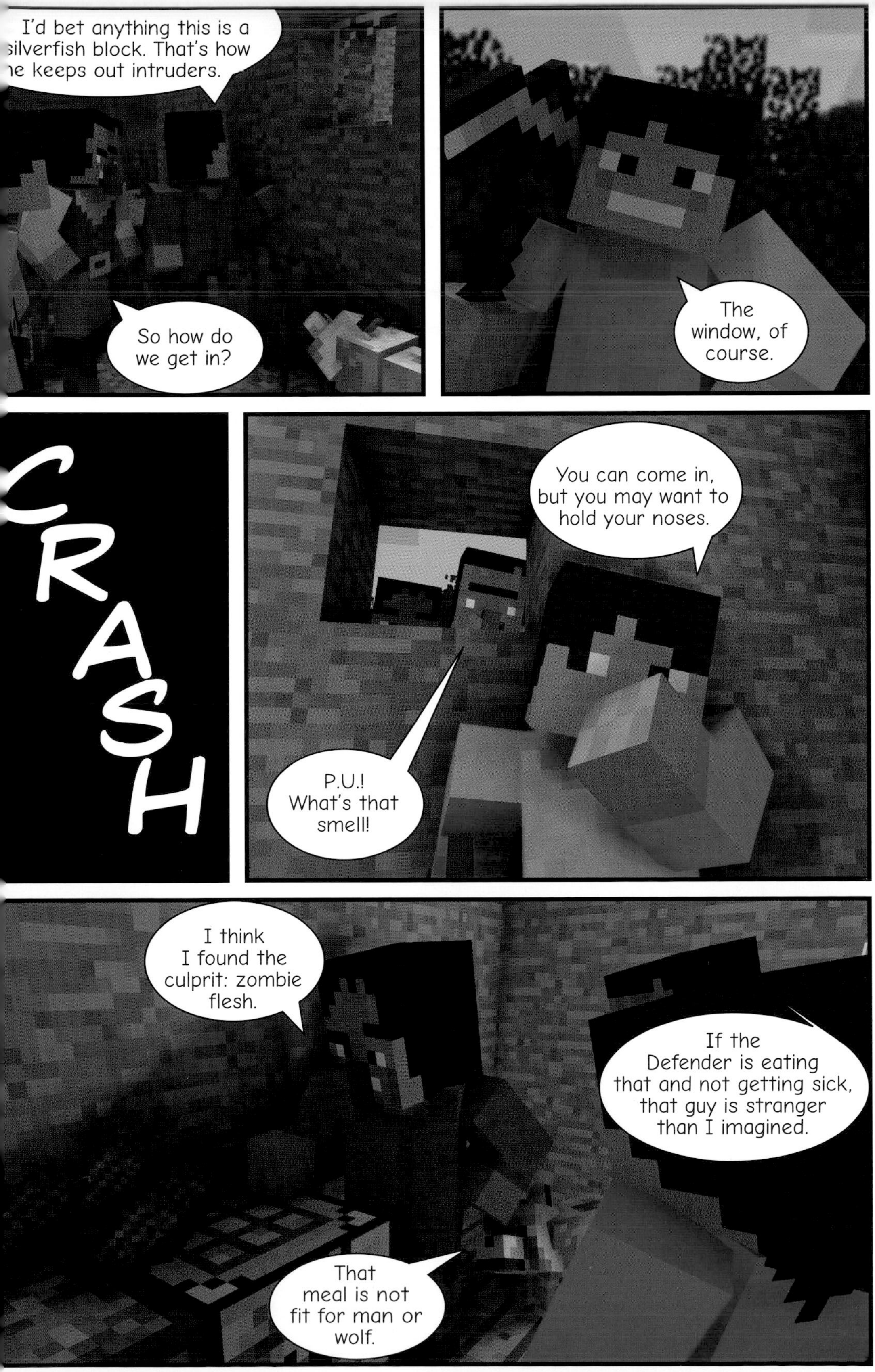
I'd bet anything this is a silverfish block. That's how he keeps out intruders.
So how do we get in?
The window, of course.
CRASH
You can come in, but you may want to hold your noses.
P.U.! What's that smell!
I think I found the culprit: zombie flesh.
If the Defender is eating that and not getting sick, that guy is stranger than I imagined.
That meal is not fit for man or wolf.

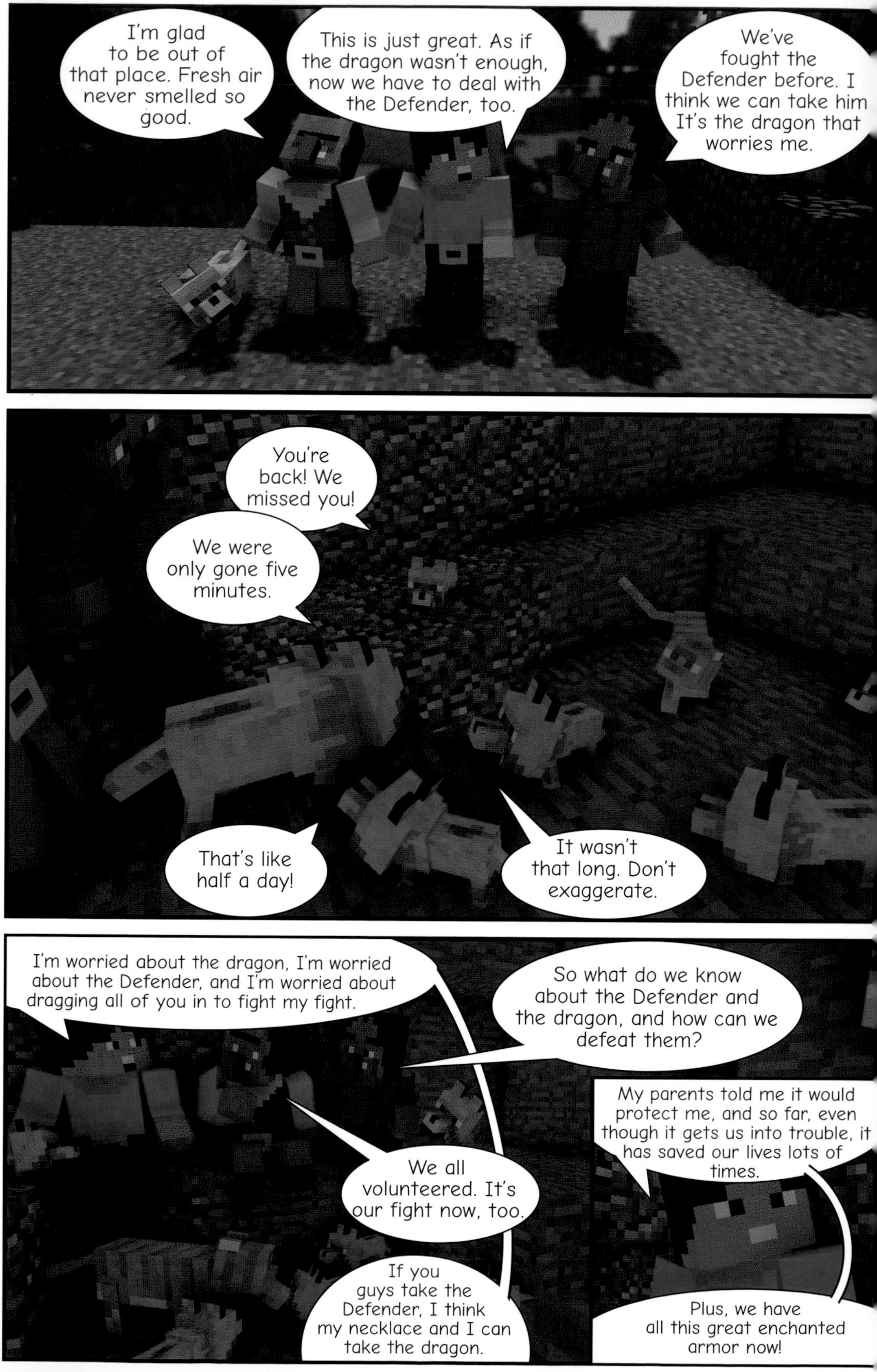
I'm glad to be out of that place. Fresh air never smelled so good.
This is just great. As if the dragon wasn't enough, now we have to deal with the Defender, too.
We've fought the Defender before. I think we can take him It's the dragon that worries me.
You're back! We missed you!
We were only gone five minutes.
That's like half a day!
It wasn't that long. Don't exaggerate.
I'm worried about the dragon, I'm worried about the Defender, and I'm worried about dragging all of you in to fight my fight.
So what do we know about the Defender and the dragon, and how can we defeat them?
We all volunteered. It's our fight now, too.
If you guys take the Defender, I think my necklace and I can take the dragon.
My parents told me it would protect me, and so far, even though it gets us into trouble, it has saved our lives lots of times.
Plus, we have all this great enchanted armor now!

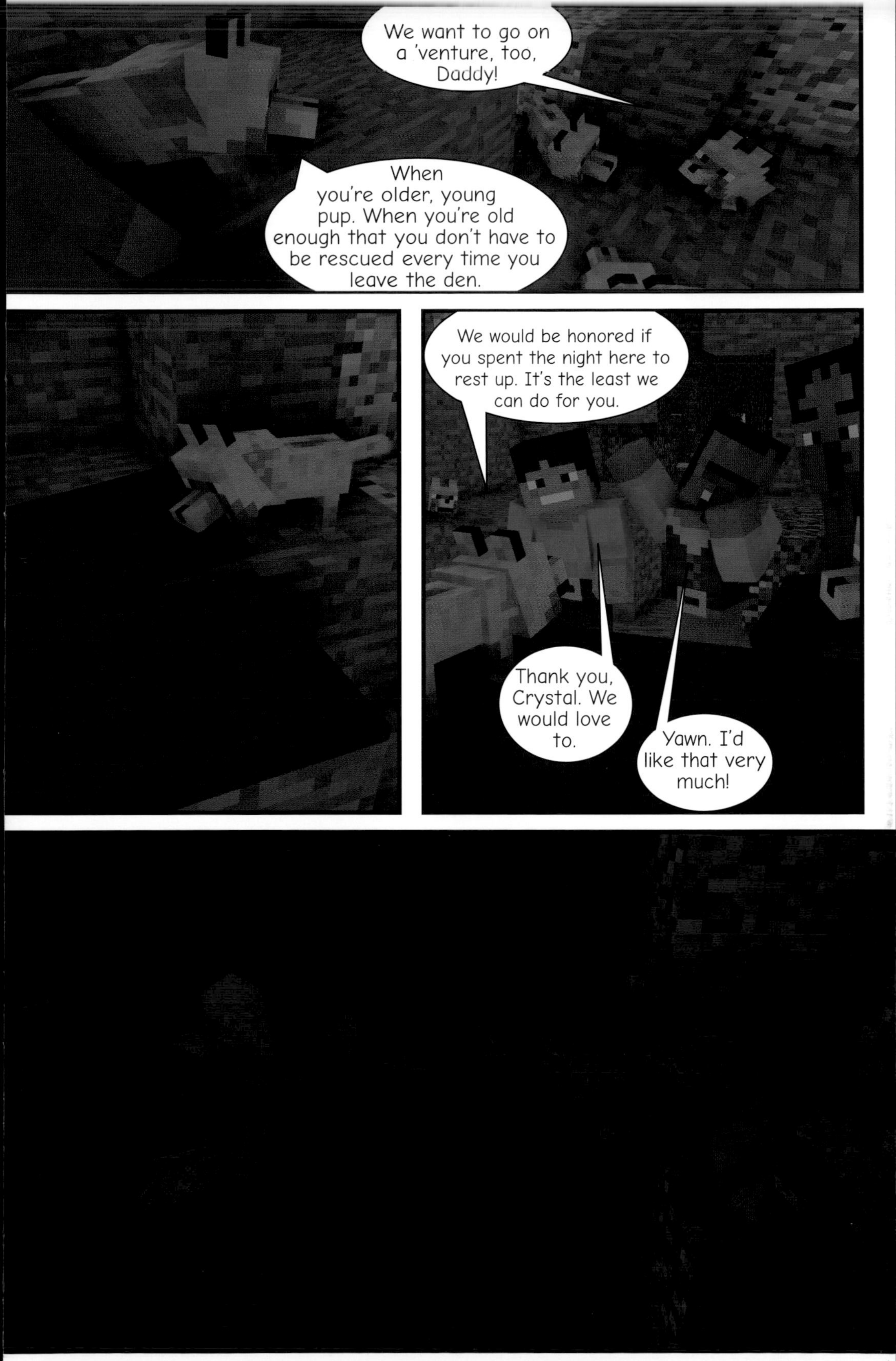
We want to go on a 'venture, too, Daddy!
When you're older, young pup. When you're old enough that you don't have to be rescued every time you leave the den.
We would be honored if you spent the night here to rest up. It's the least we can do for you.
Thank you, Crystal. We would love to.
Yawn. I'd like that very much!

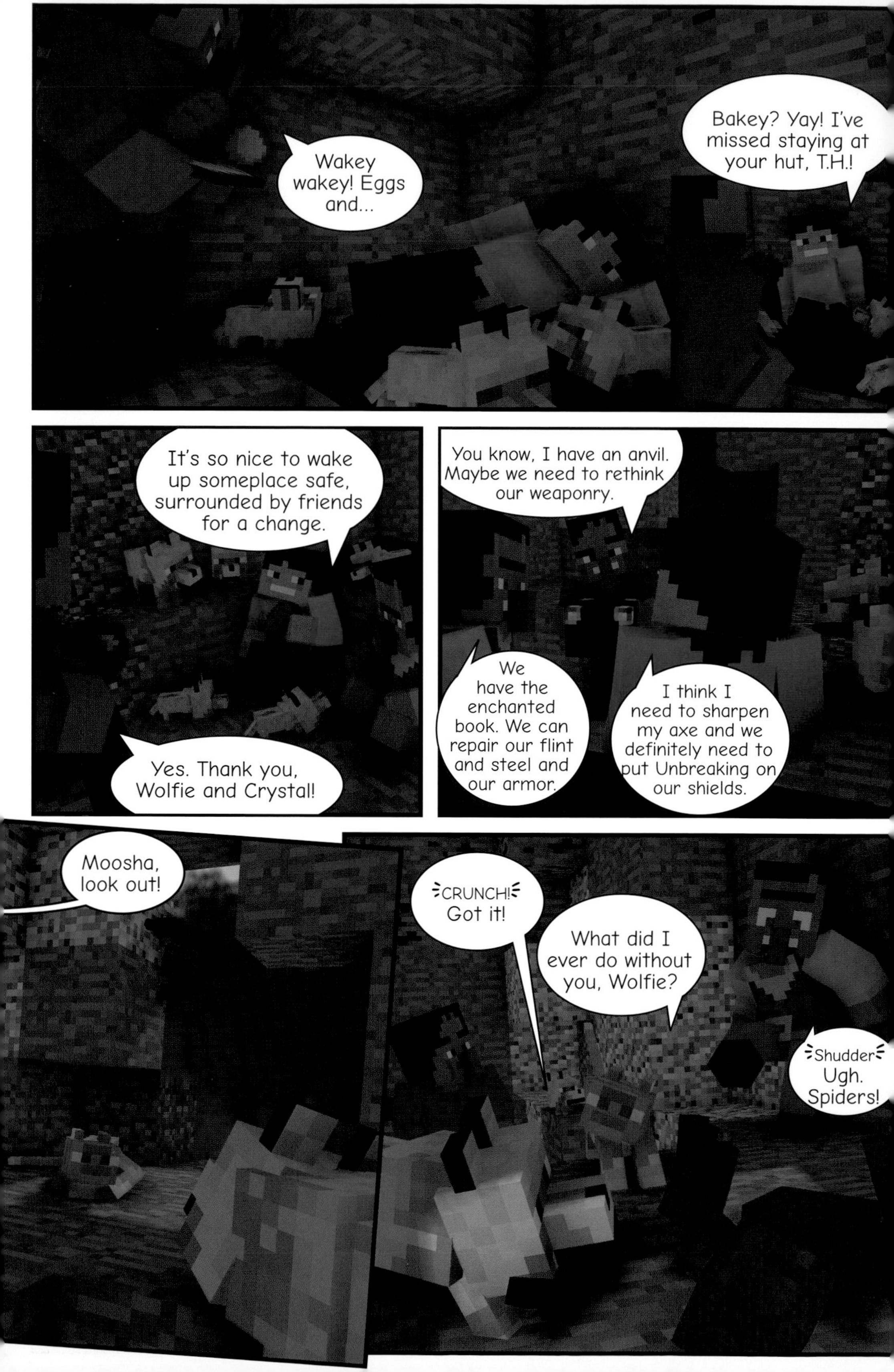

Wakey wakey! Eggs and...
Bakey? Yay! I've missed staying at your hut, T.H.!
It's so nice to wake up someplace safe, surrounded by friends for a change.
Yes. Thank you, Wolfie and Crystal!
You know, I have an anvil. Maybe we need to rethink our weaponry.
We have the enchanted book. We can repair our flint and steel and our armor.
I think I need to sharpen my axe and we definitely need to put Unbreaking on our shields.
Moosha, look out!
CRUNCH! Got it!
What did I ever do without you, Wolfie?
Shudder Ugh. Spiders!

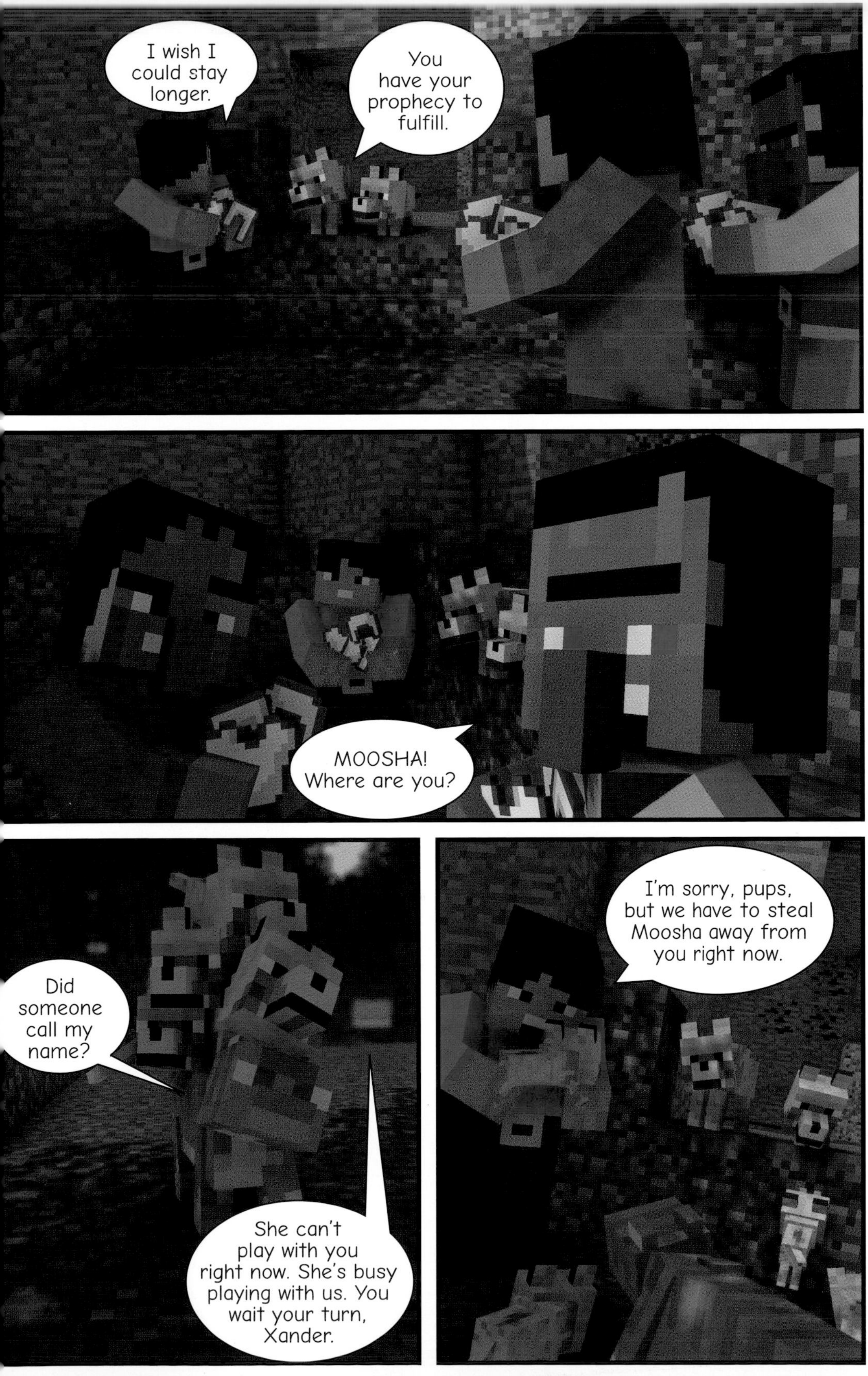
I wish I could stay longer.
You have your prophecy to fulfill.
MOOSHA! Where are you?
Did someone call my name?
She can't play with you right now. She's busy playing with us. You wait your turn, Xander.
I'm sorry, pups, but we have to steal Moosha away from you right now.

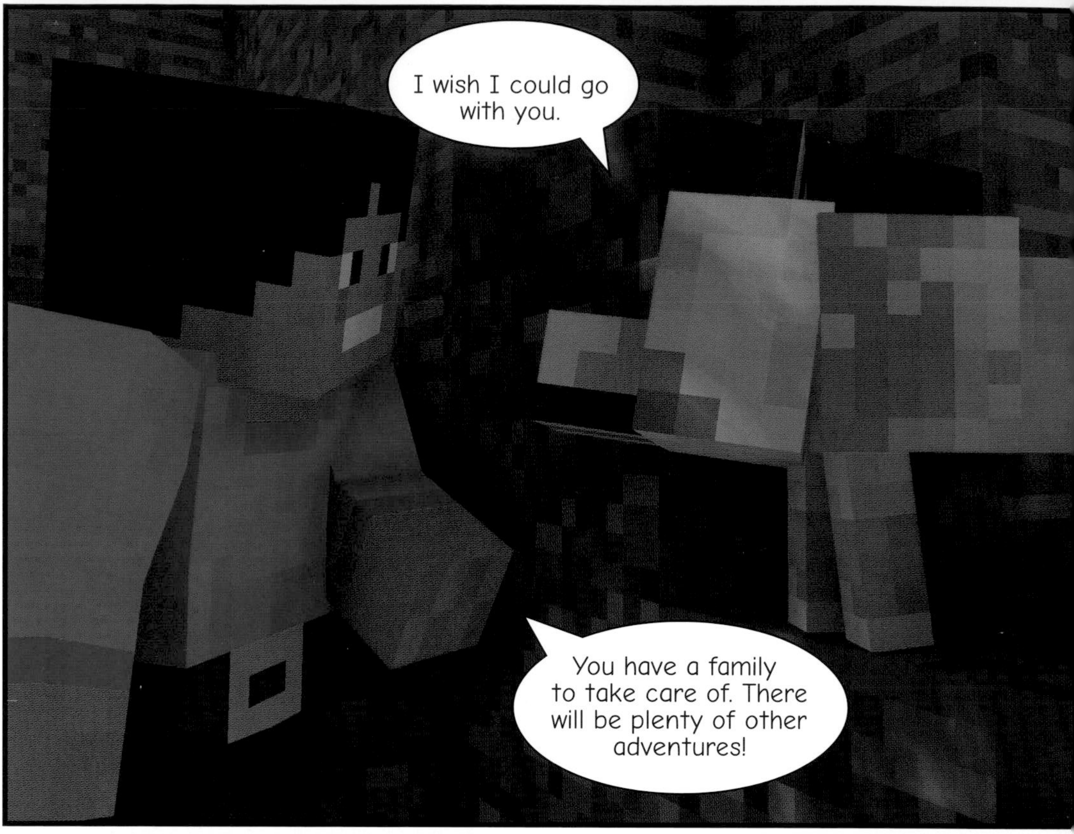
I wish I could go with you.
You have a family to take care of. There will be plenty of other adventures!

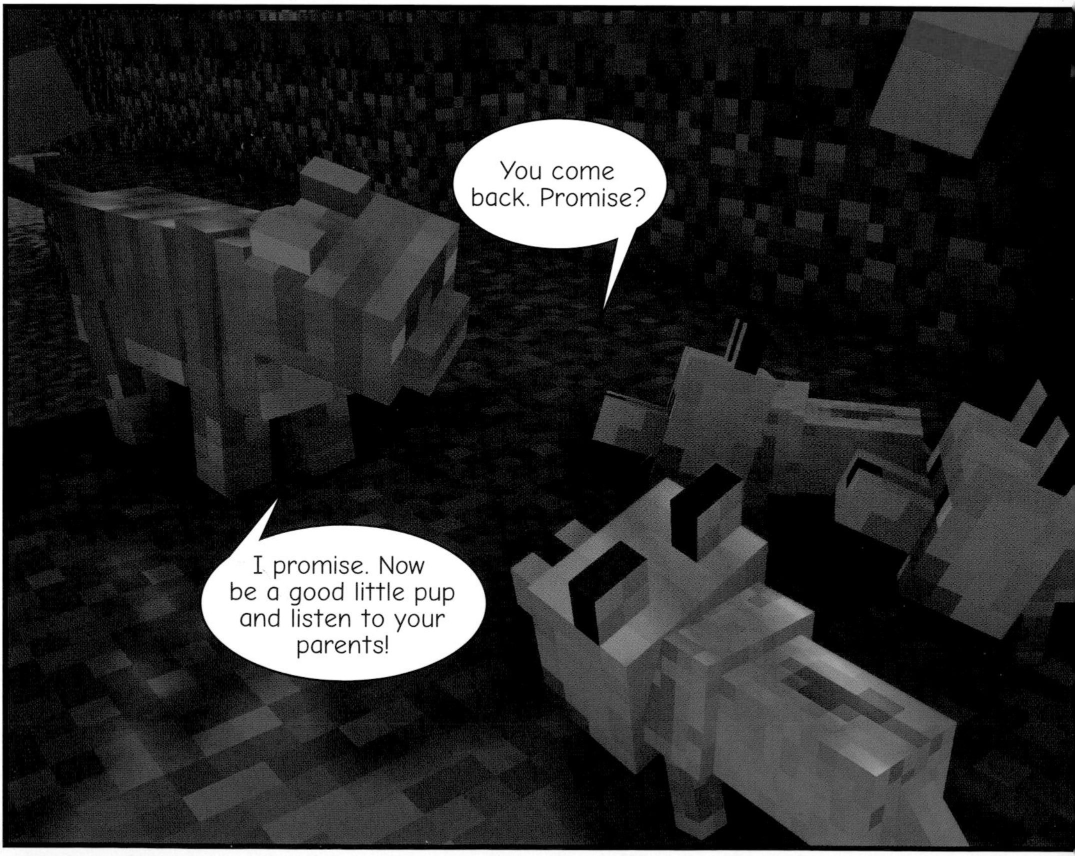
You come back. Promise?
I promise. Now be a good little pup and listen to your parents!

CHAPTER 9

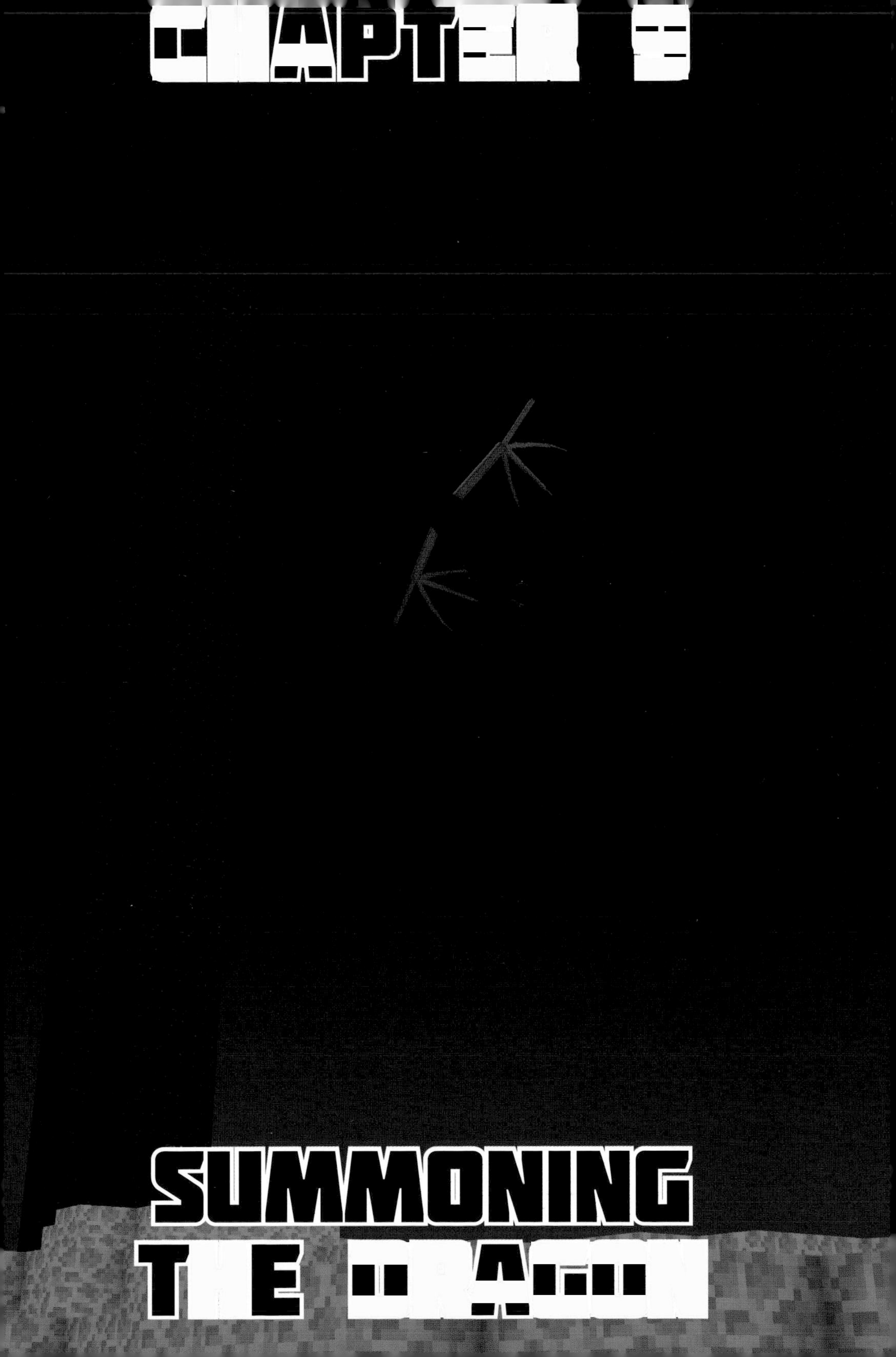

SUMMONING THE DRAGON

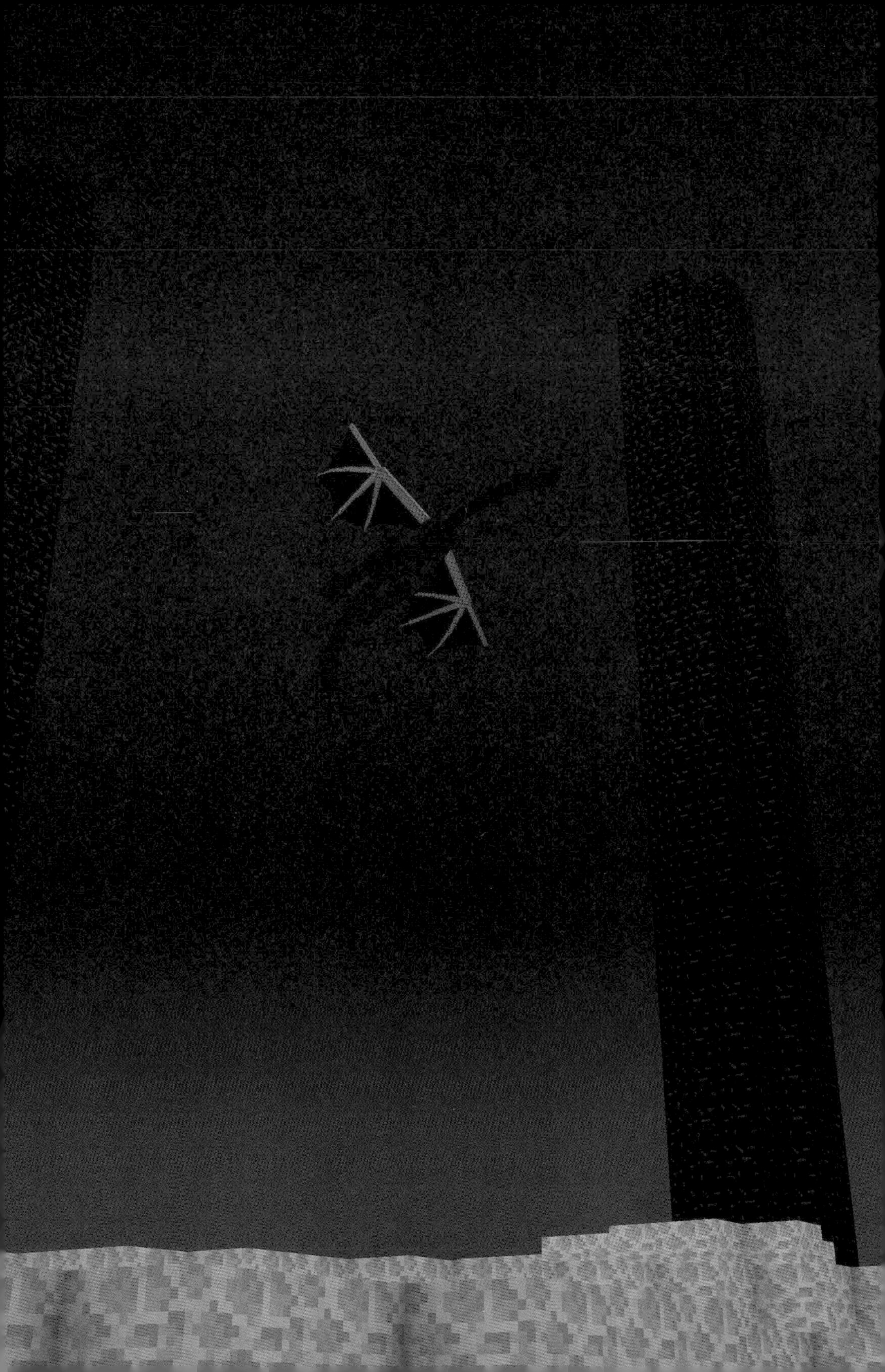

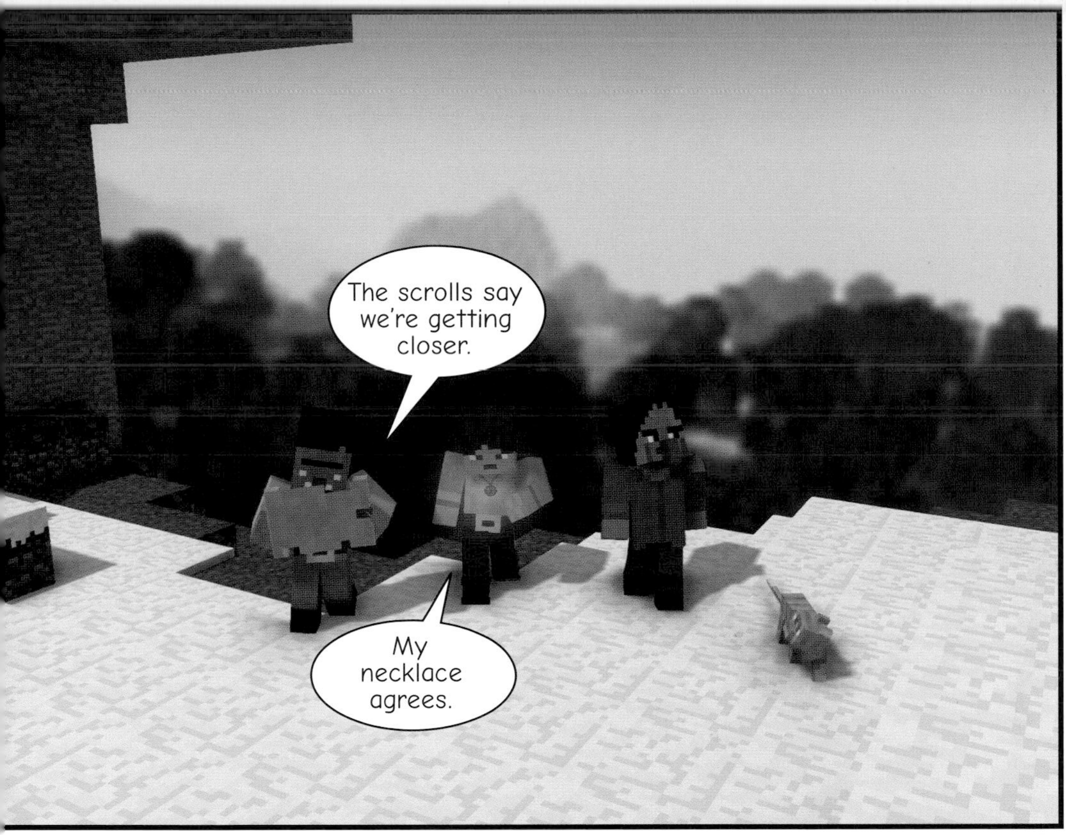
The scrolls say we're getting closer.
My necklace agrees.

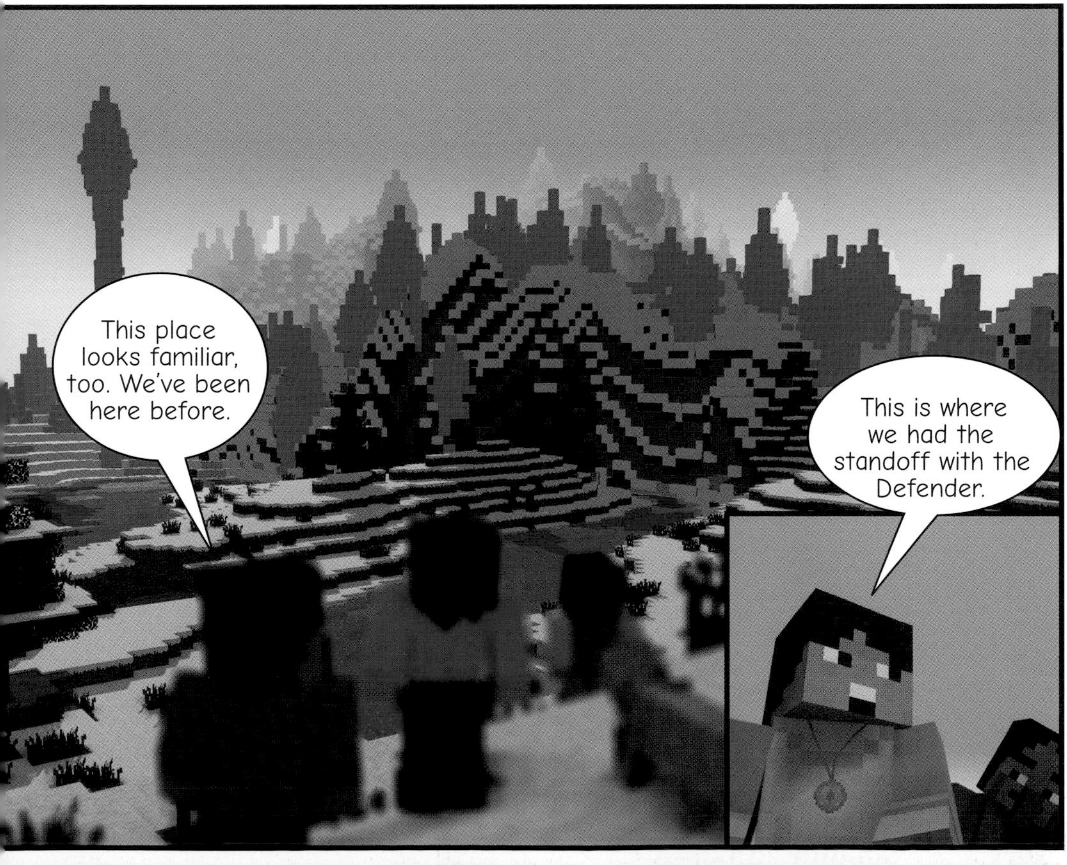
This place looks familiar, too. We've been here before.
This is where we had the standoff with the Defender.

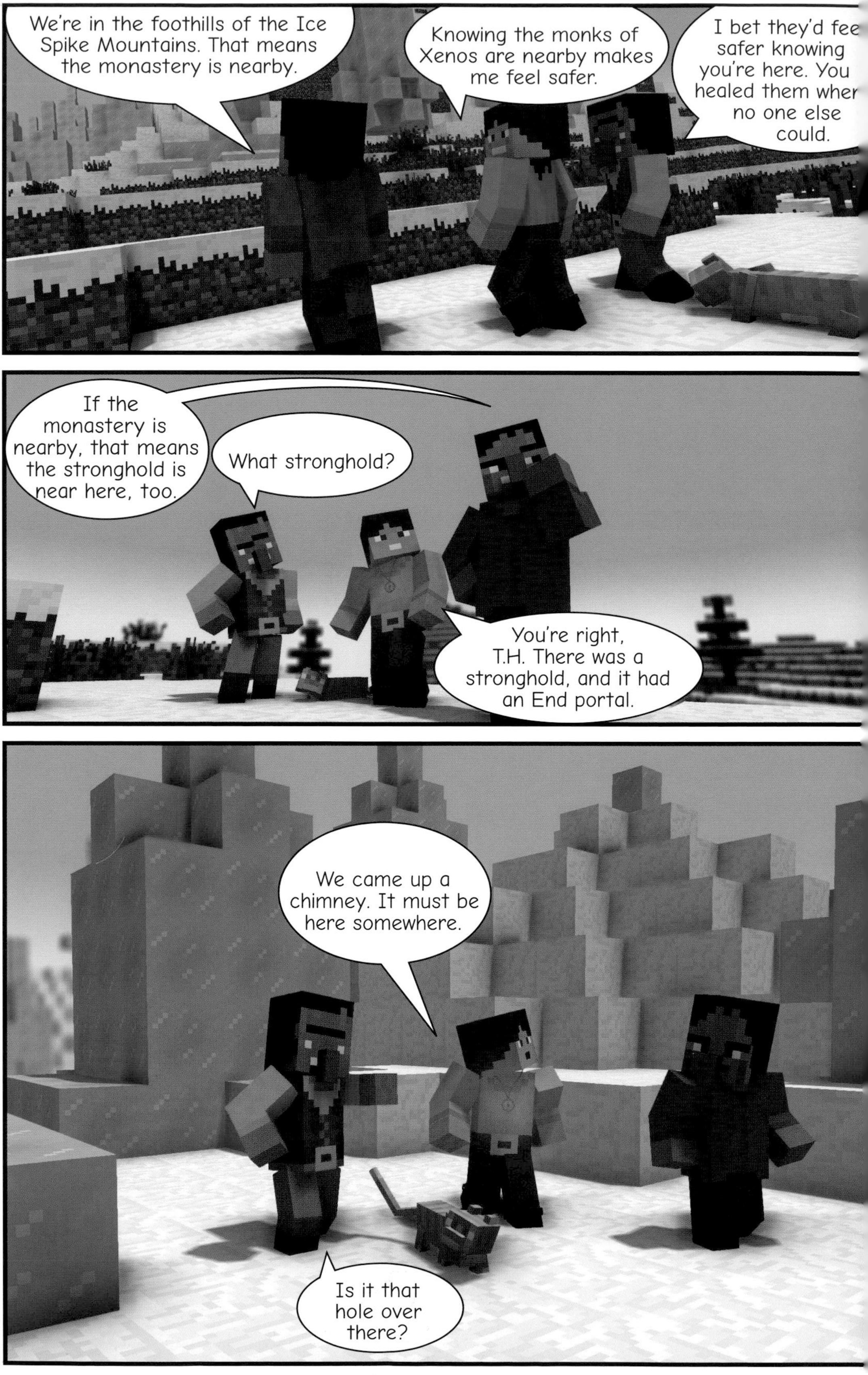

We're in the foothills of the Ice Spike Mountains. That means the monastery is nearby.
Knowing the monks of Xenos are nearby makes me feel safer.
I bet they'd fee safer knowing you're here. You healed them wher no one else could.
If the monastery is nearby, that means the stronghold is near here, too.
What stronghold?
You're right, T.H. There was a stronghold, and it had an End portal.
We came up a chimney. It must be here somewhere.
Is it that hole over there?

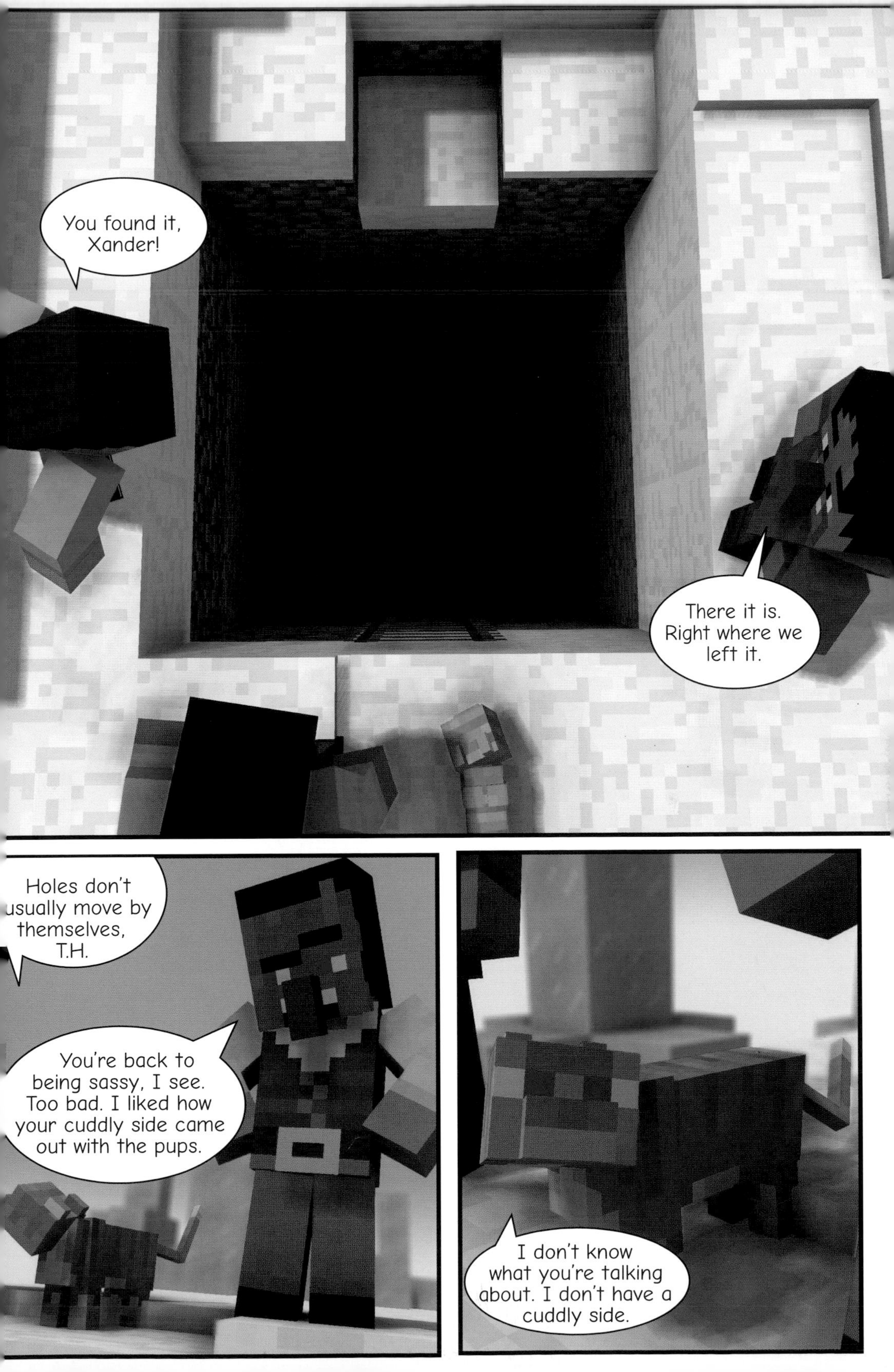
You found it, Xander!
There it is. Right where we left it.
Holes don't usually move by themselves, T.H.
You're back to being sassy, I see. Too bad. I liked how your cuddly side came out with the pups.
I don't know what you're talking about. I don't have a cuddly side.

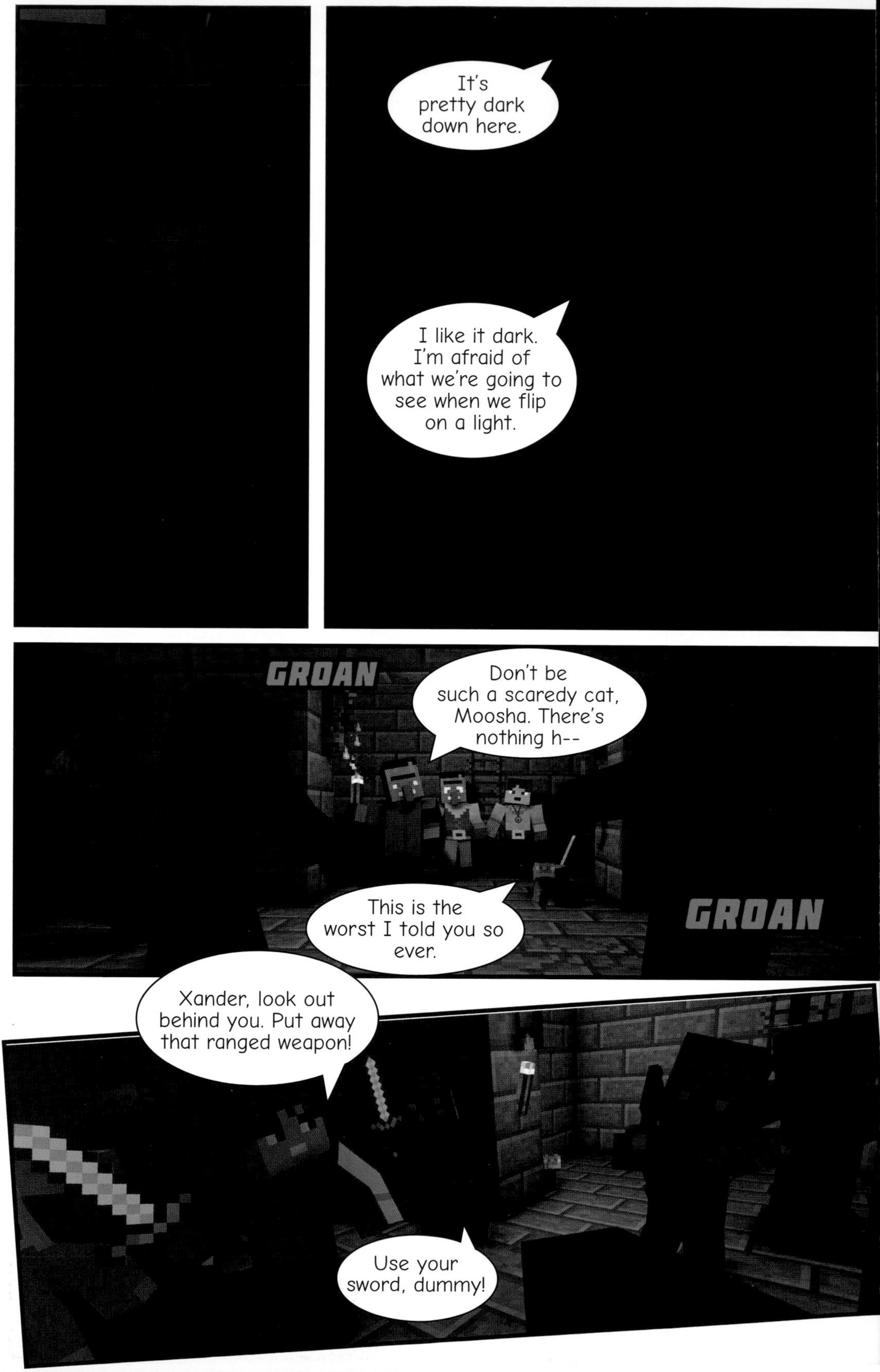
It's pretty dark down here.
I like it dark. I'm afraid of what we're going to see when we flip on a light.
GROAN
Don't be such a scaredy cat, Moosha. There's nothing h--
This is the worst I told you so ever.
GROAN
Xander, look out behind you. Put away that ranged weapon!
Use your sword, dummy!

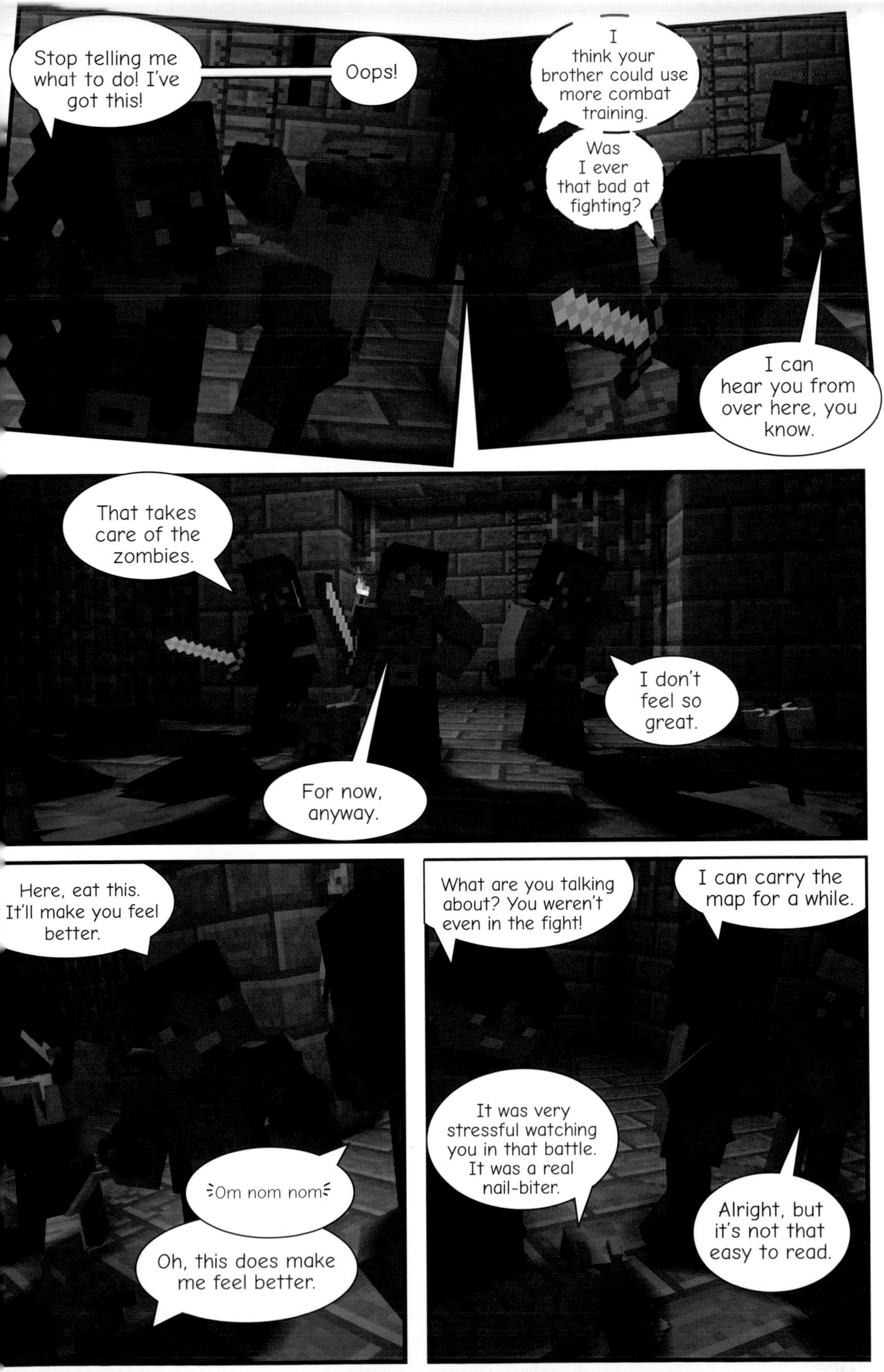
Stop telling me what to do! I've got this!
Oops!
I think your brother could use more combat training.
Was I ever that bad at fighting?
I can hear you from over here, you know.
That takes care of the zombies.
I don't feel so great.
For now, anyway.
Here, eat this. It'll make you feel better.
Om nom nom
Oh, this does make me feel better.
What are you talking about? You weren't even in the fight!
I can carry the map for a while.
It was very stressful watching you in that battle. It was a real nail-biter.
Alright, but it's not that easy to read.

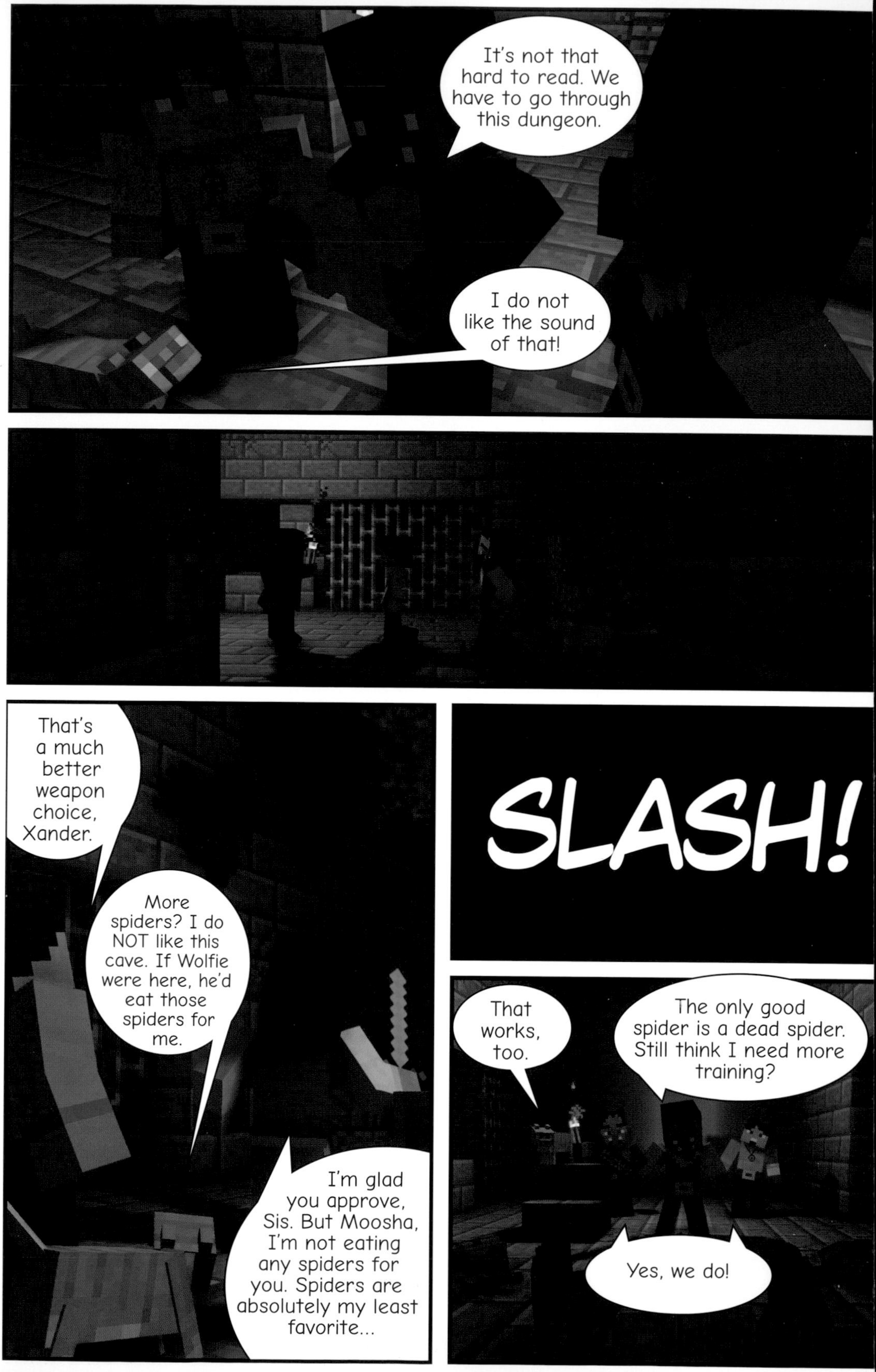
It's not that hard to read. We have to go through this dungeon.
I do not like the sound of that!
That's a much better weapon choice, Xander.
More spiders? I do NOT like this cave. If Wolfie were here, he'd eat those spiders for me.
I'm glad you approve, Sis. But Moosha, I'm not eating any spiders for you. Spiders are absolutely my least favorite...
SLASH!
That works, too.
The only good spider is a dead spider. Still think I need more training?
Yes, we do!

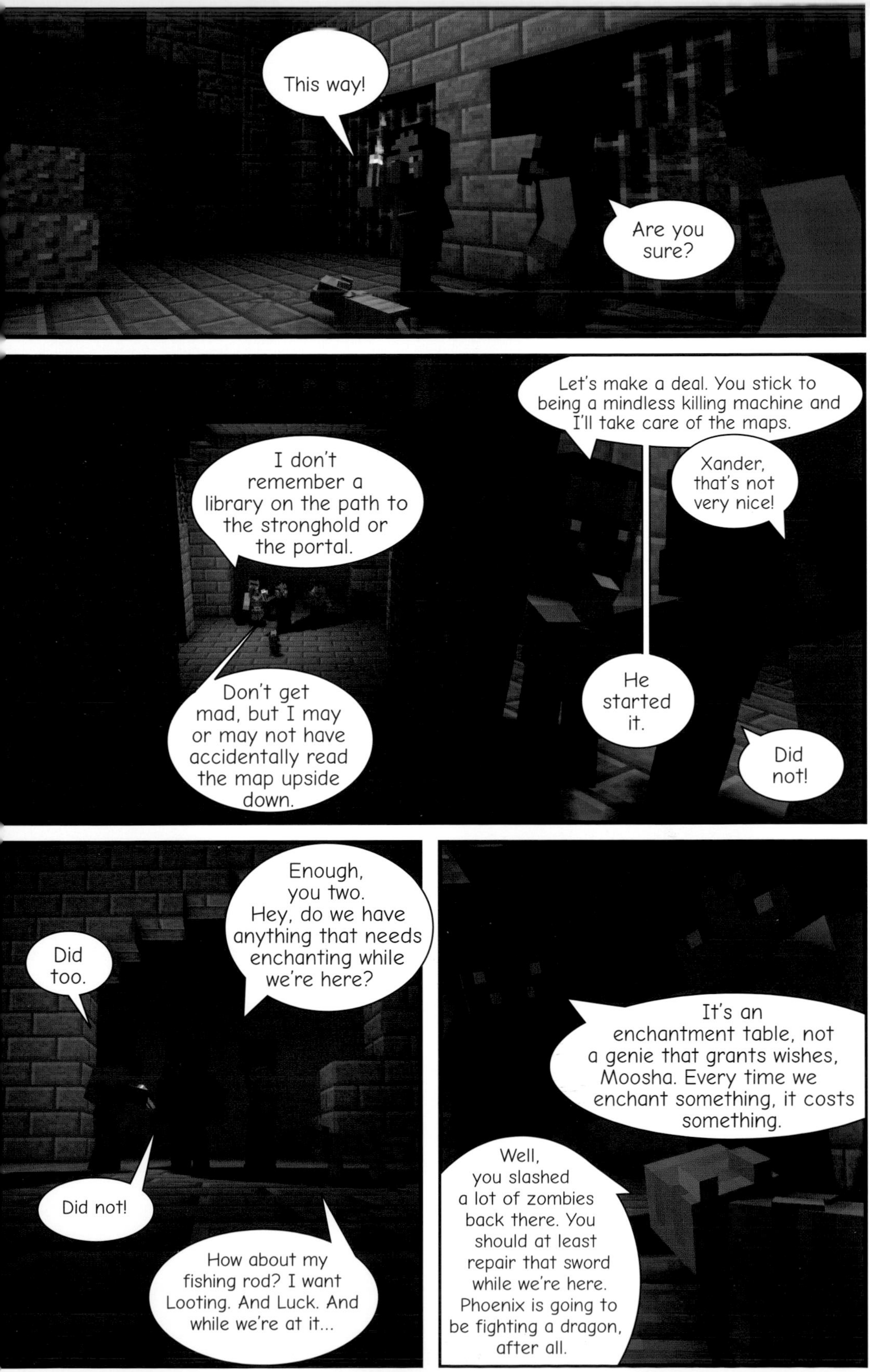
This way!
Are you sure?
Let's make a deal. You stick to being a mindless killing machine and I'll take care of the maps.
I don't remember a library on the path to the stronghold or the portal.
Xander, that's not very nice!
Don't get mad, but I may or may not have accidentally read the map upside down.
He started it.
Did not!
Did too.
Enough, you two. Hey, do we have anything that needs enchanting while we're here?
Did not!
How about my fishing rod? I want Looting. And Luck. And while we're at it...
It's an enchantment table, not a genie that grants wishes, Moosha. Every time we enchant something, it costs something.
Well, you slashed a lot of zombies back there. You should at least repair that sword while we're here. Phoenix is going to be fighting a dragon, after all.

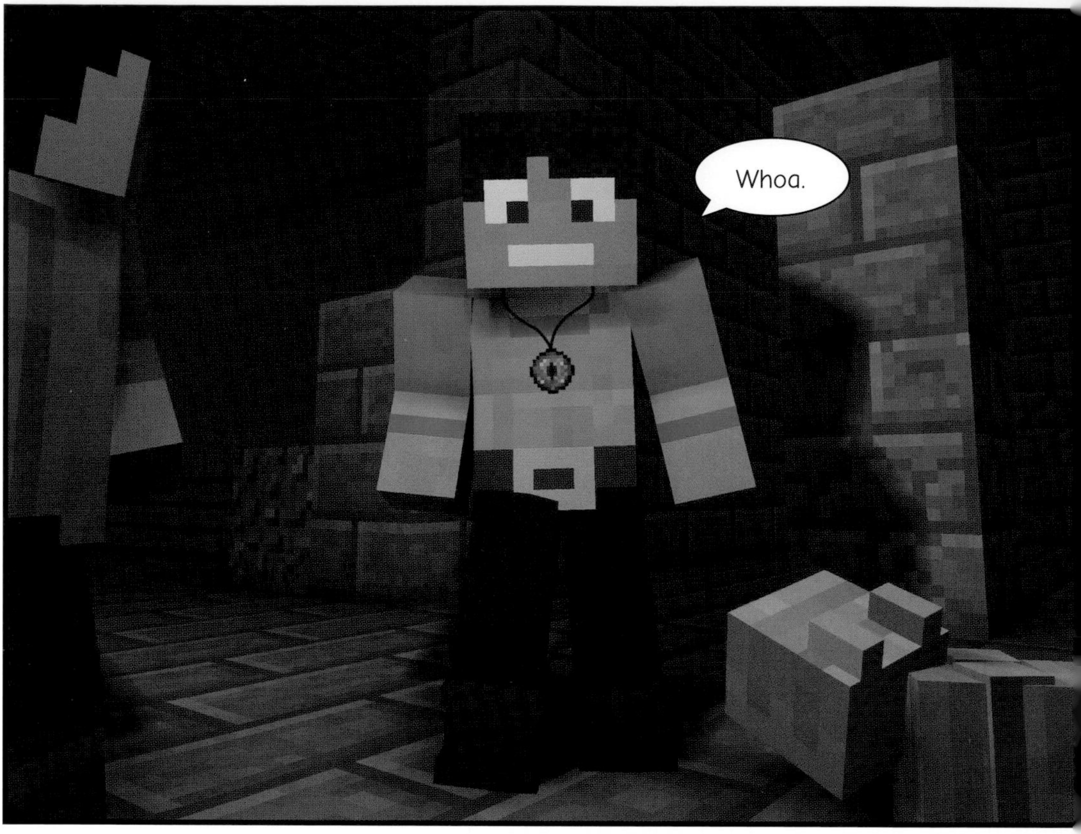
Whoa.

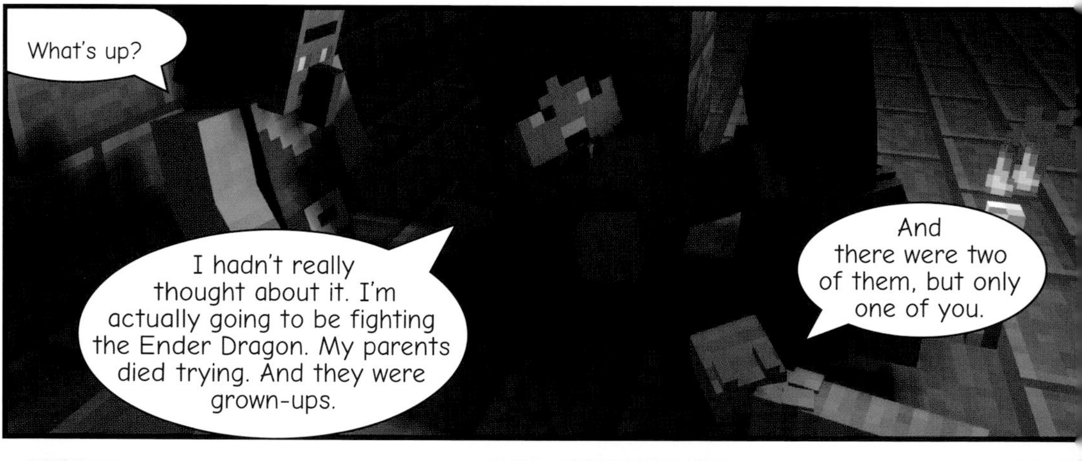
What's up?
I hadn't really thought about it. I'm actually going to be fighting the Ender Dragon. My parents died trying. And they were grown-ups.
And there were two of them, but only one of you.

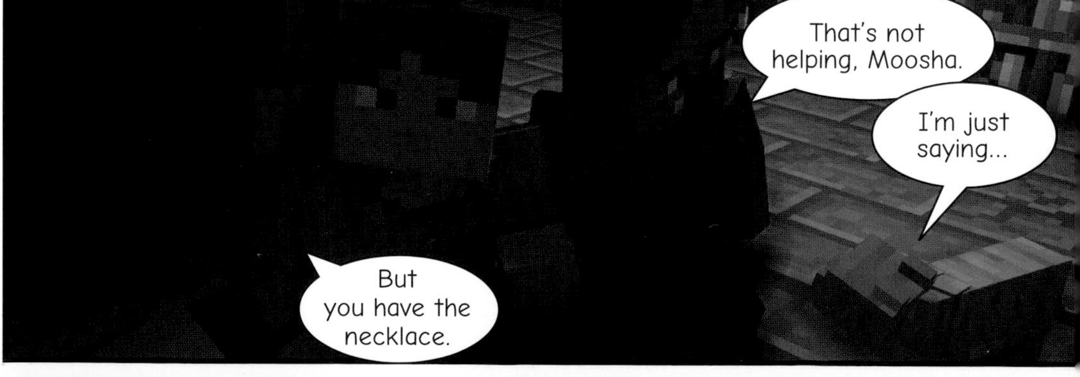
That's not helping, Moosha.
I'm just saying...
But you have the necklace.

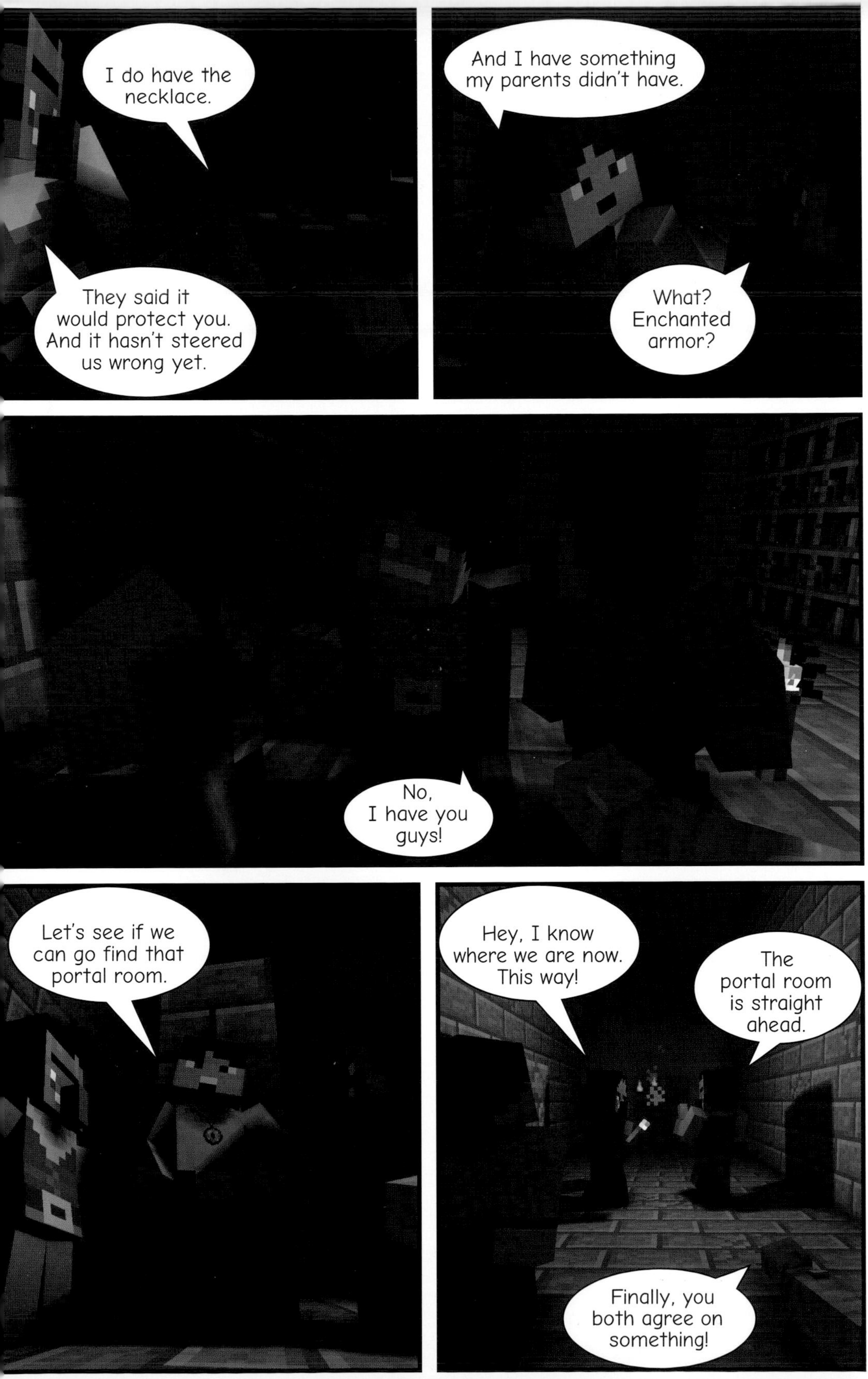
I do have the necklace.
They said it would protect you. And it hasn't steered us wrong yet.
And I have something my parents didn't have.
What? Enchanted armor?
No, I have you guys!
Let's see if we can go find that portal room.
Hey, I know where we are now. This way!
The portal room is straight ahead.
Finally, you both agree on something!

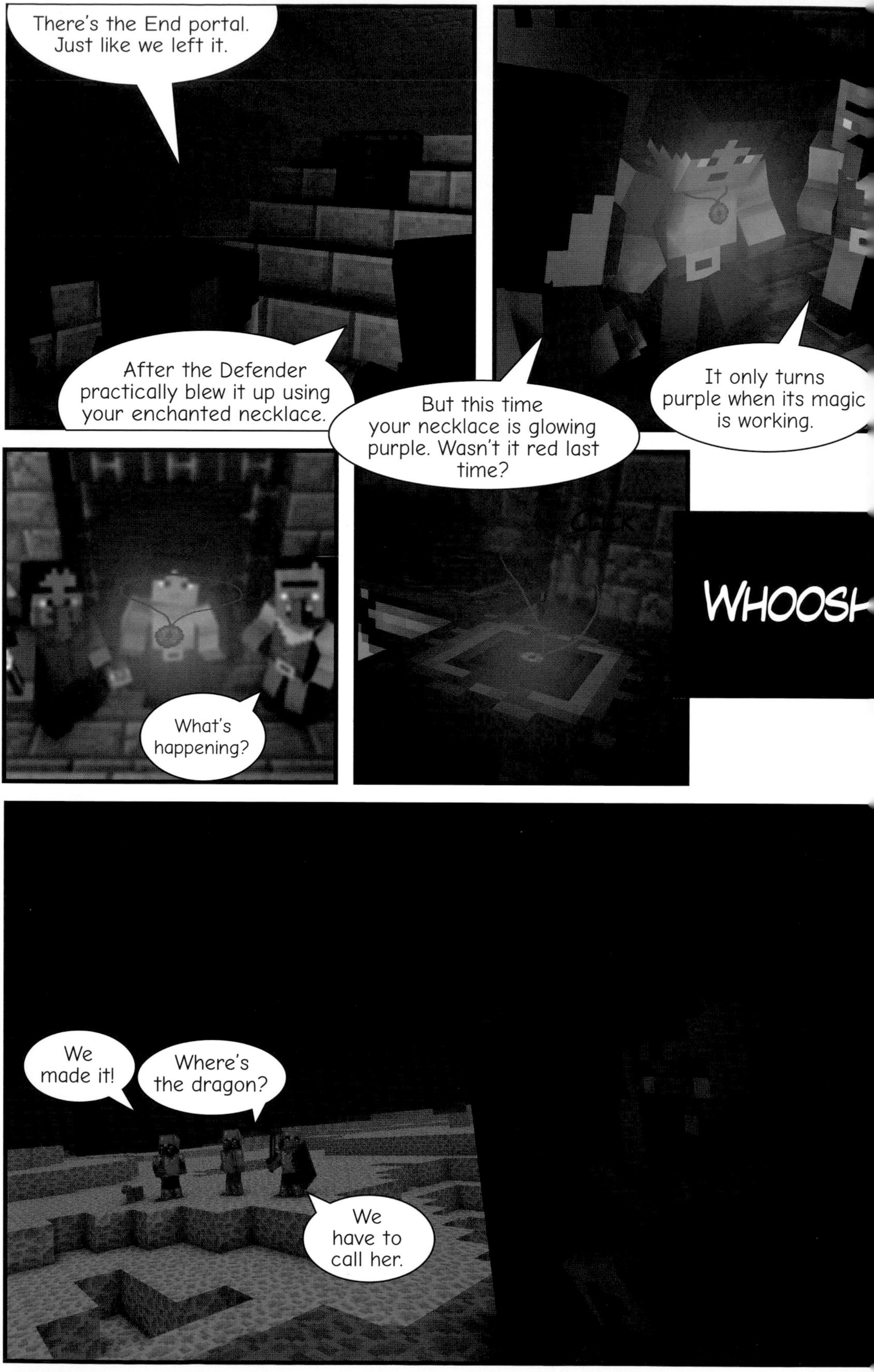
There's the End portal. Just like we left it.
After the Defender practically blew it up using your enchanted necklace.
But this time your necklace is glowing purple. Wasn't it red last time?
It only turns purple when its magic is working.
What's happening?
CLICK
WHOOSH
We made it!
Where's the dragon?
We have to call her.

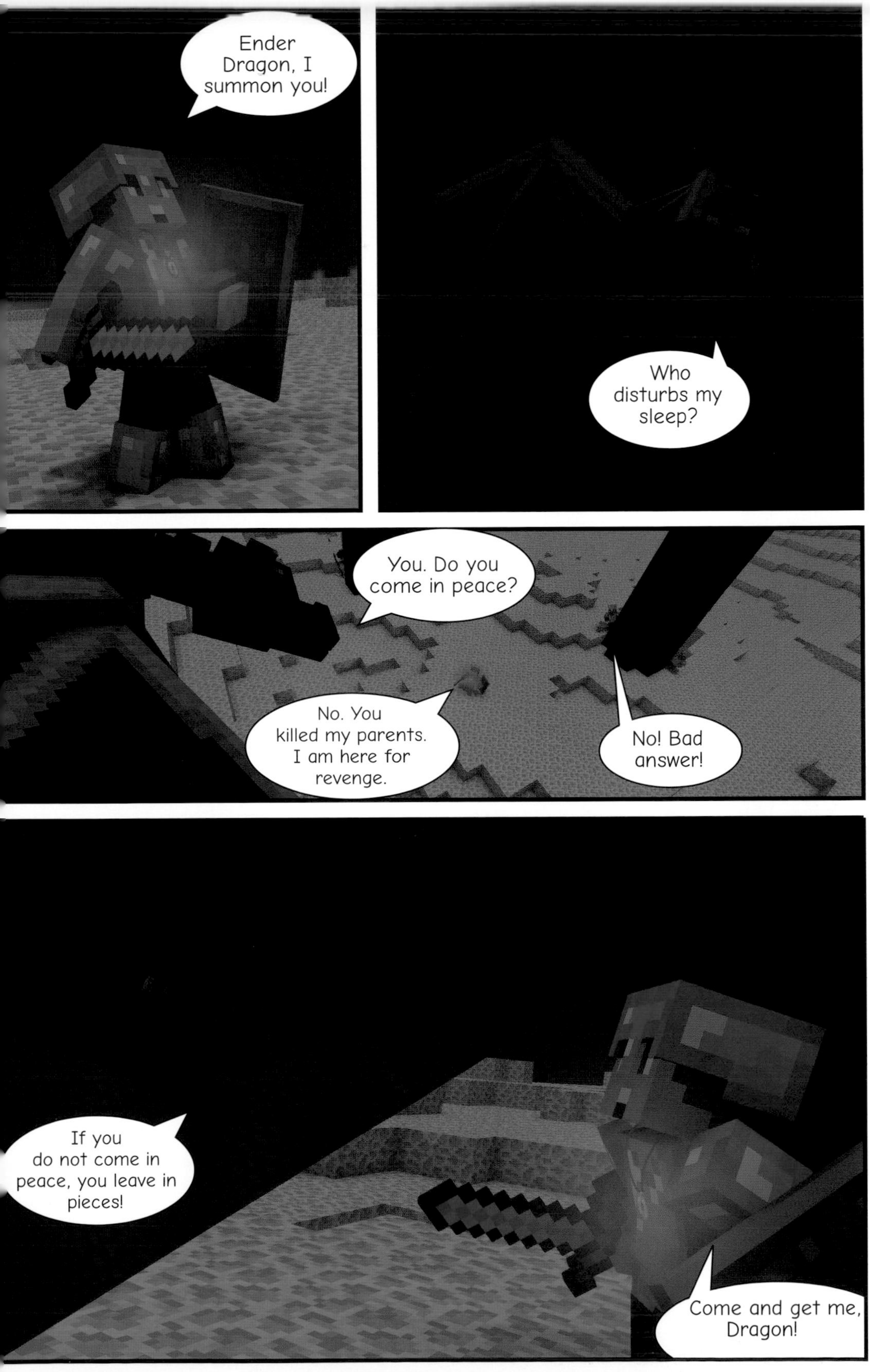
Ender Dragon, I summon you!
Who disturbs my sleep?
You. Do you come in peace?
No. You killed my parents. I am here for revenge.
No! Bad answer!
If you do not come in peace, you leave in pieces!
Come and get me, Dragon!

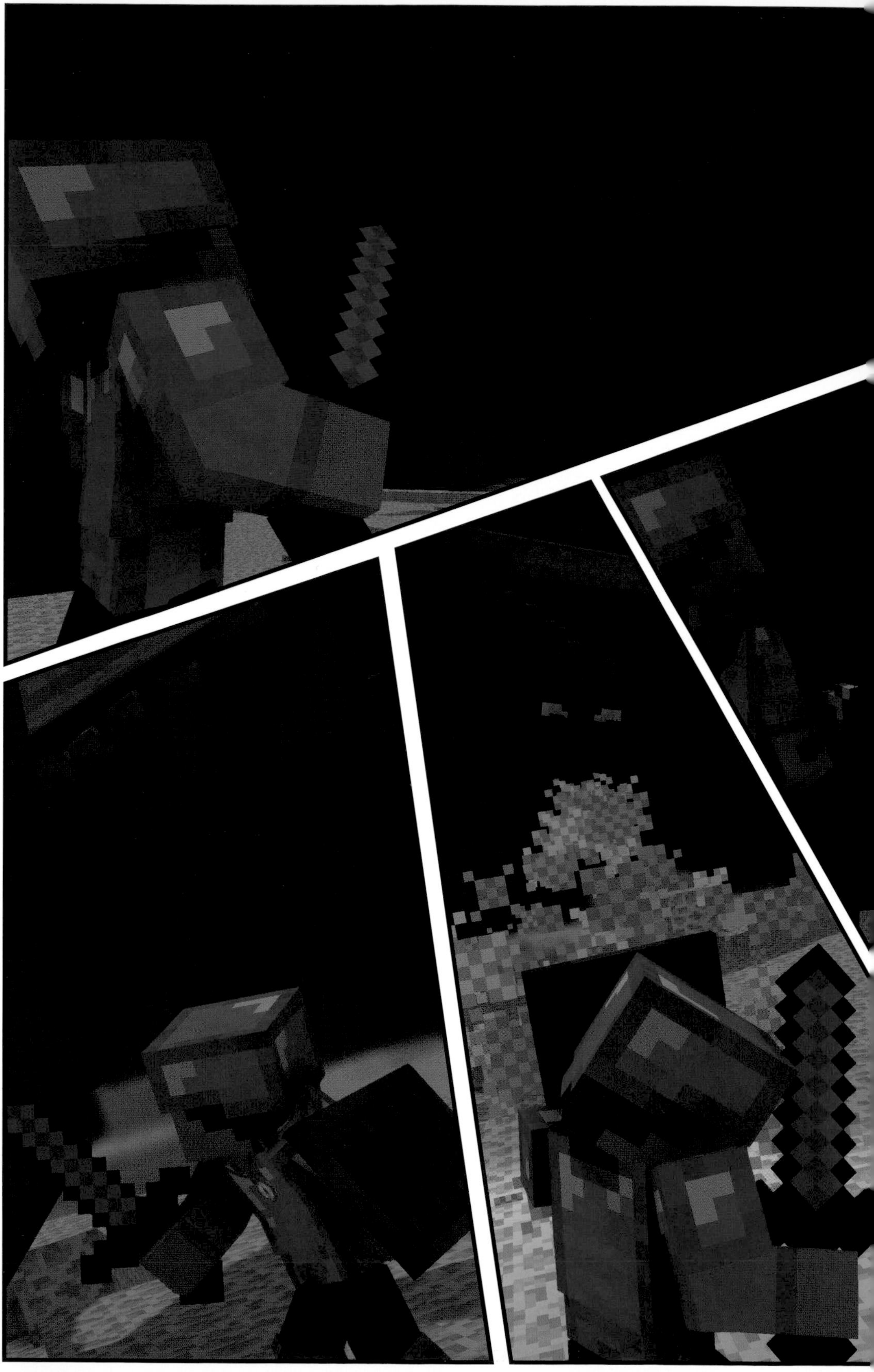

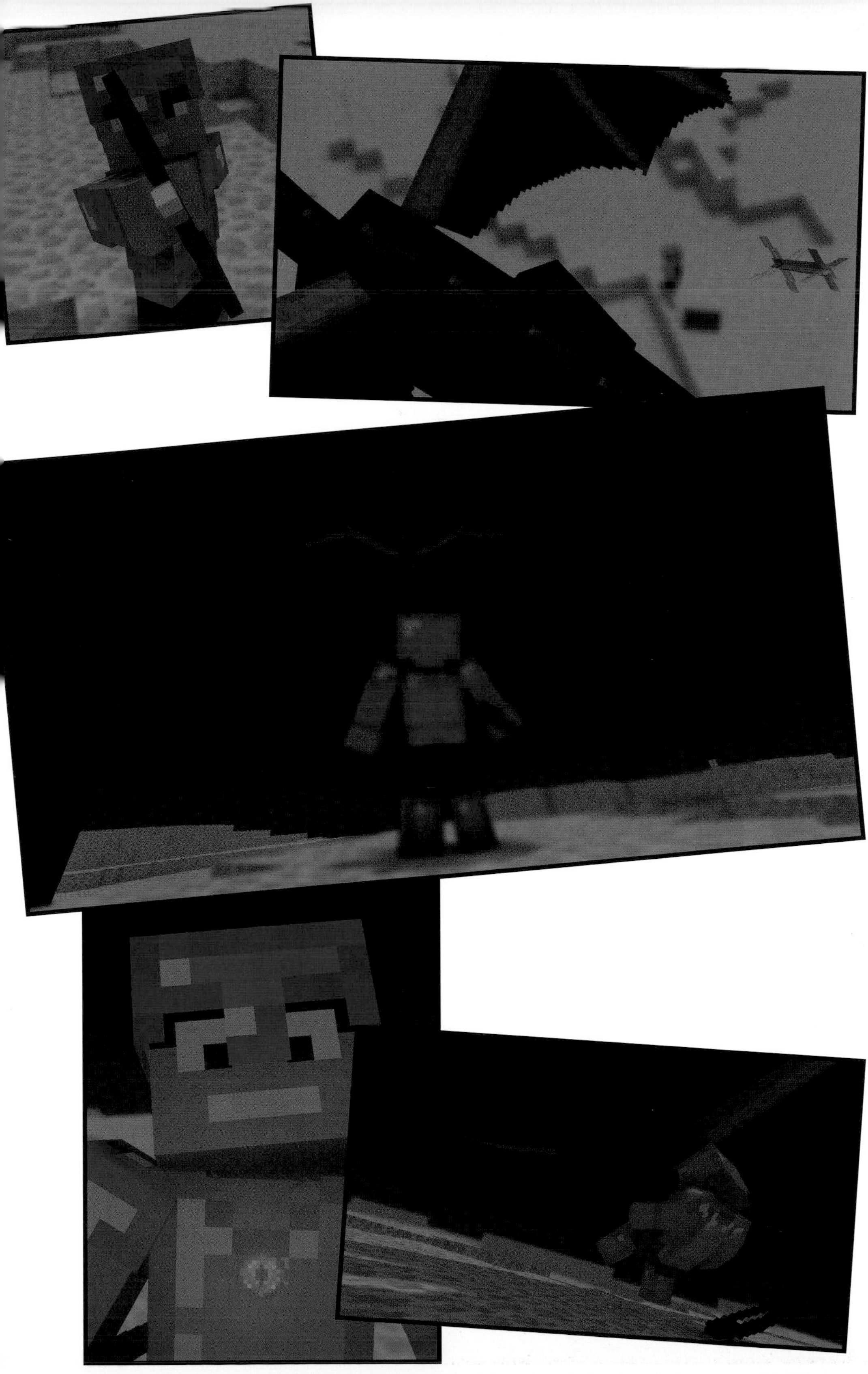

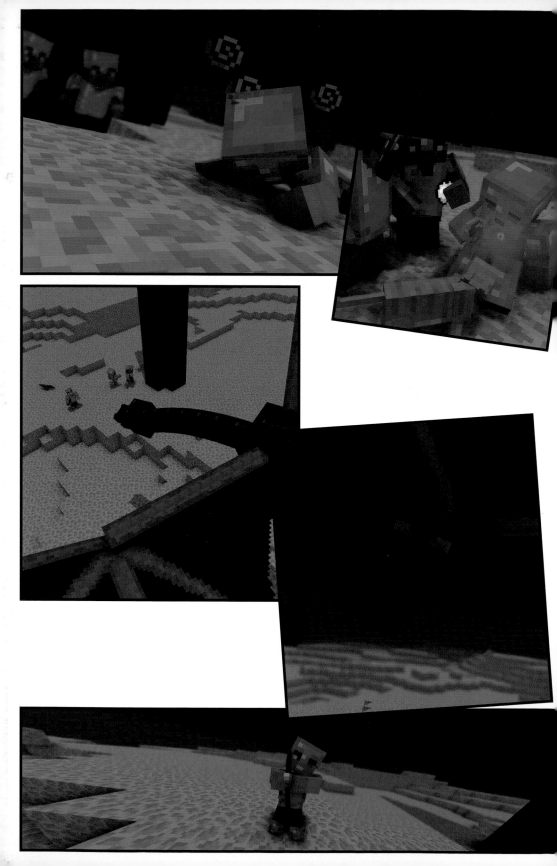

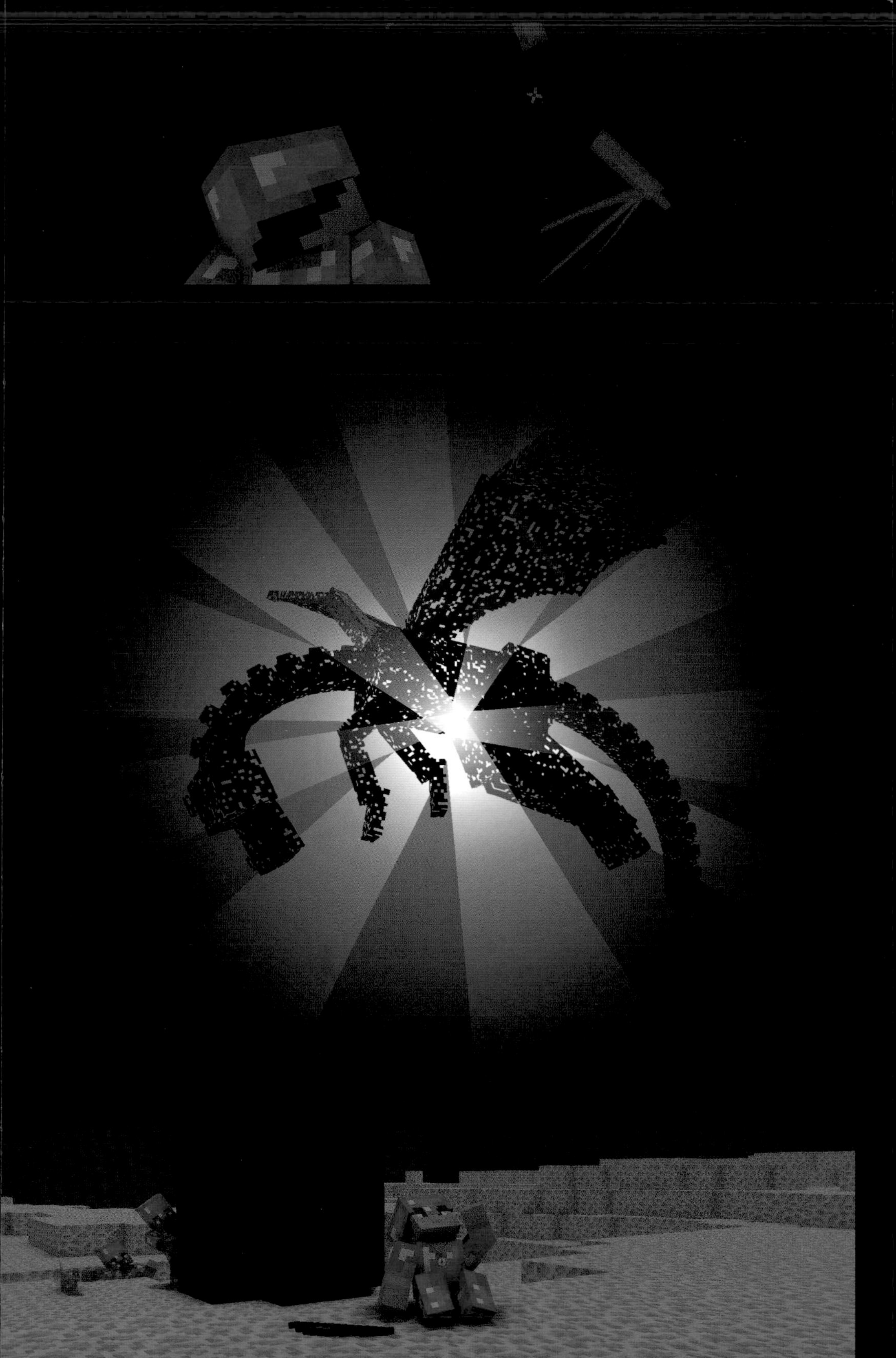

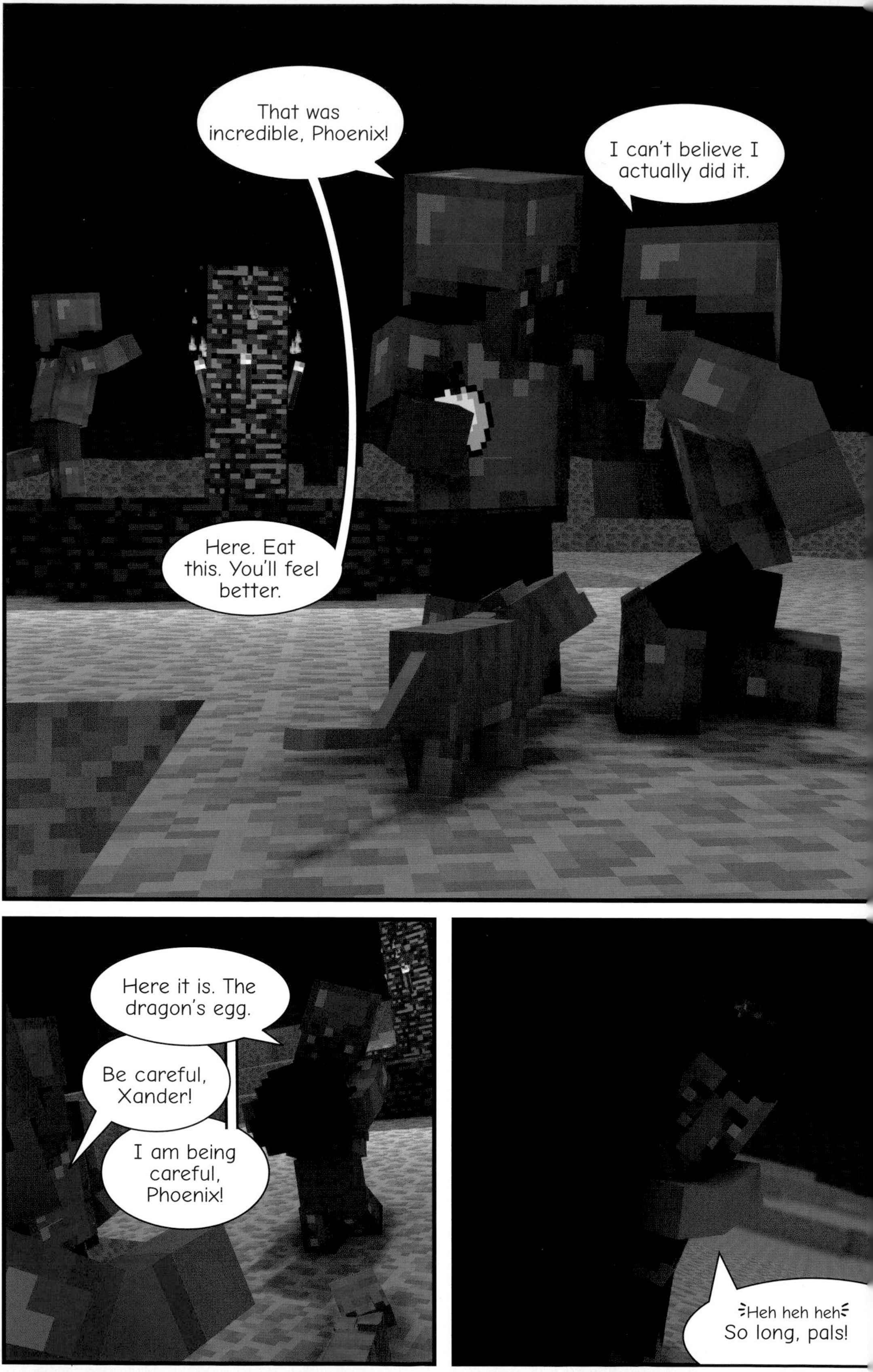
That was incredible, Phoenix!
I can't believe I actually did it.
Here. Eat this. You'll feel better.
Here it is. The dragon's egg.
Be careful, Xander!
I am being careful, Phoenix!
Heh heh heh
So long, pals!

CHAPTER 10

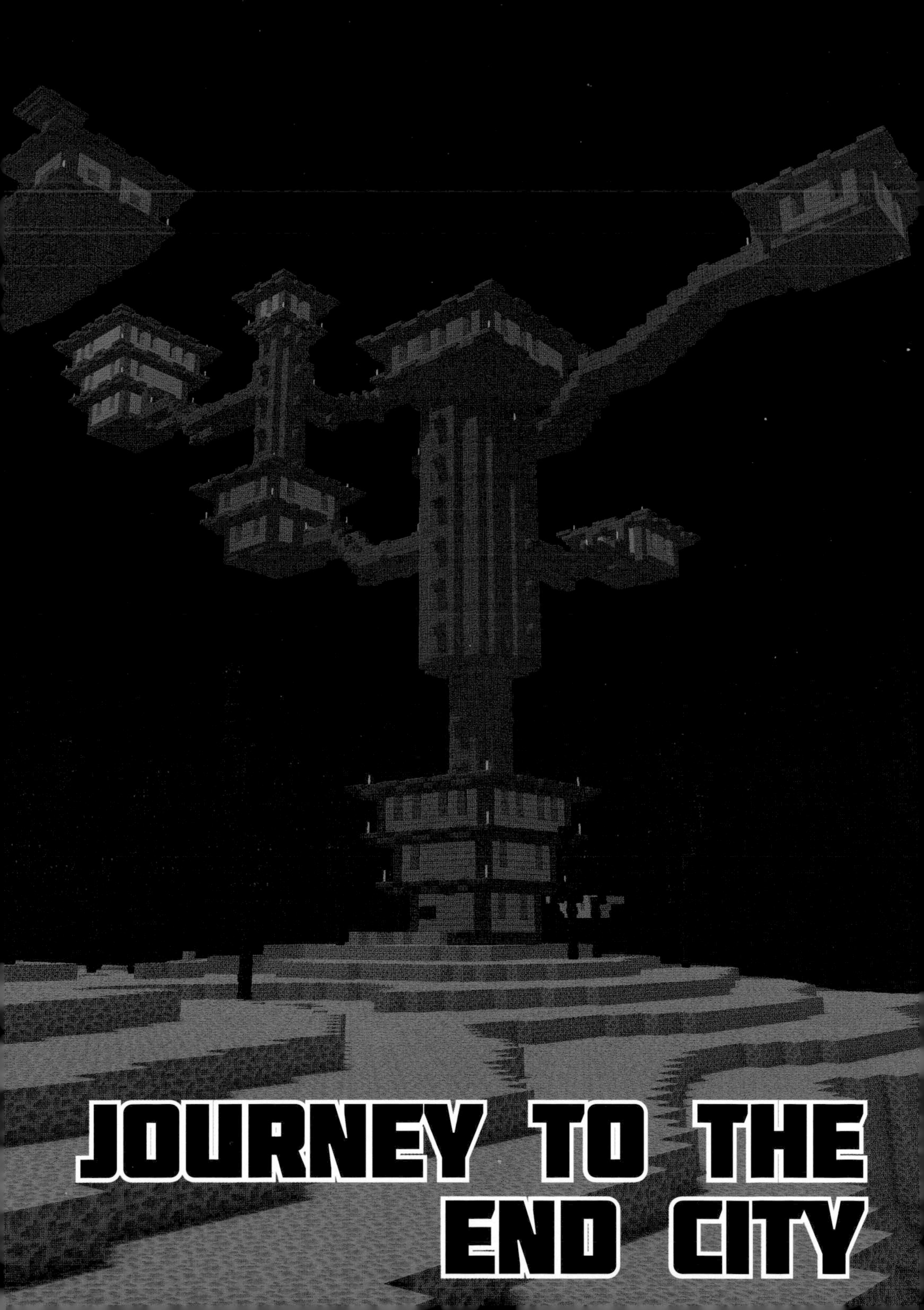

JOURNEY TO THE END CITY

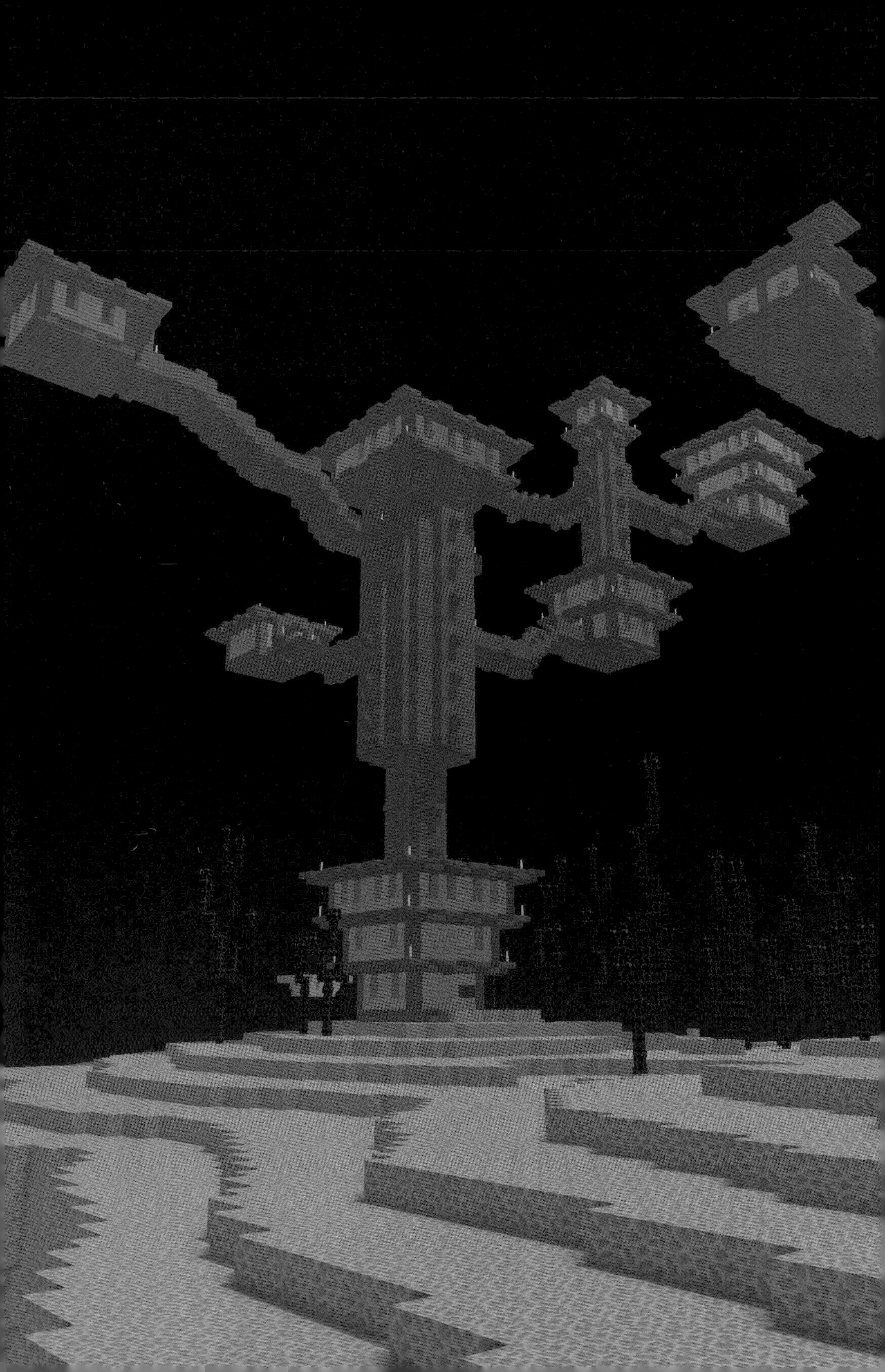

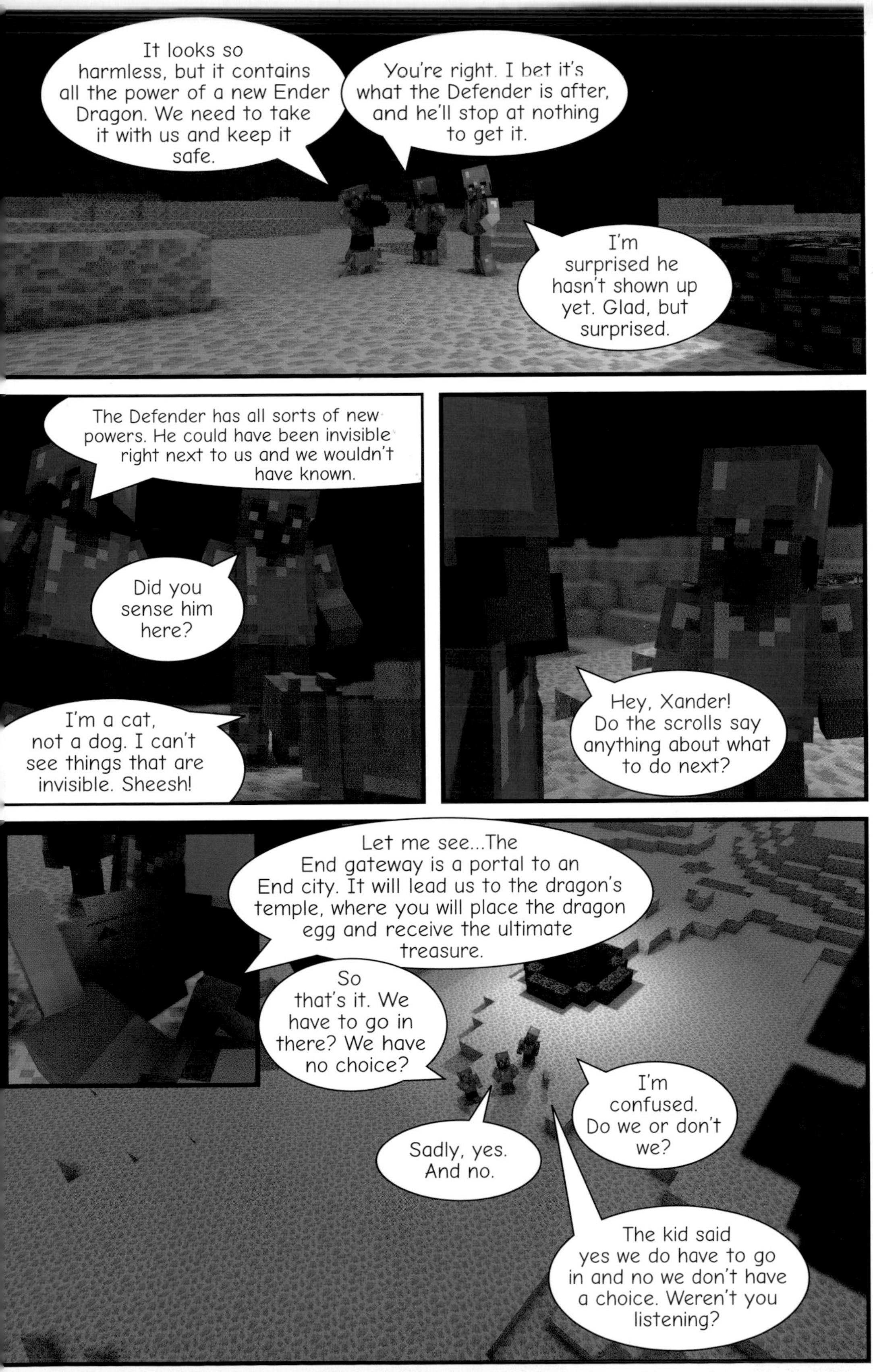
It looks so harmless, but it contains all the power of a new Ender Dragon. We need to take it with us and keep it safe.
You're right. I bet it's what the Defender is after, and he'll stop at nothing to get it.
I'm surprised he hasn't shown up yet. Glad, but surprised.
The Defender has all sorts of new powers. He could have been invisible right next to us and we wouldn't have known.
Did you sense him here?
I'm a cat, not a dog. I can't see things that are invisible. Sheesh!
Hey, Xander! Do the scrolls say anything about what to do next?
Let me see...The End gateway is a portal to an End city. It will lead us to the dragon's temple, where you will place the dragon egg and receive the ultimate treasure.
So that's it. We have to go in there? We have no choice?
Sadly, yes. And no.
I'm confused. Do we or don't we?
The kid said yes we do have to go in and no we don't have a choice. Weren't you listening?

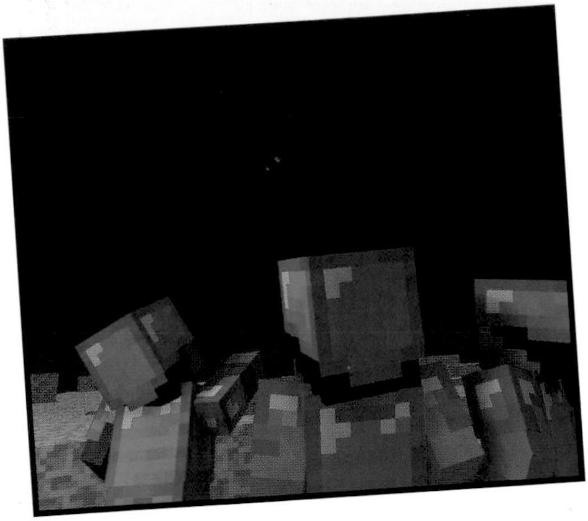

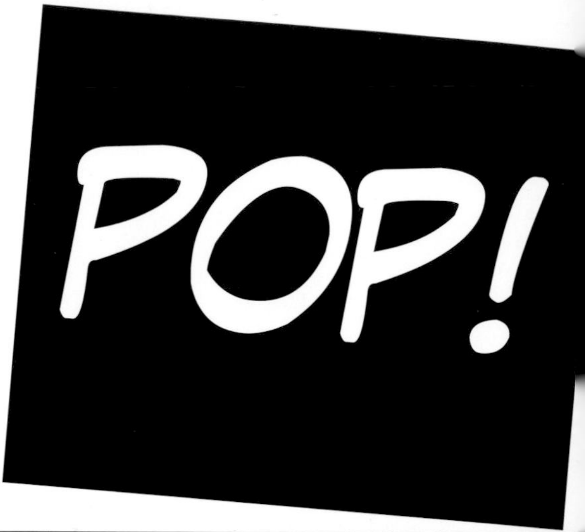
POP!

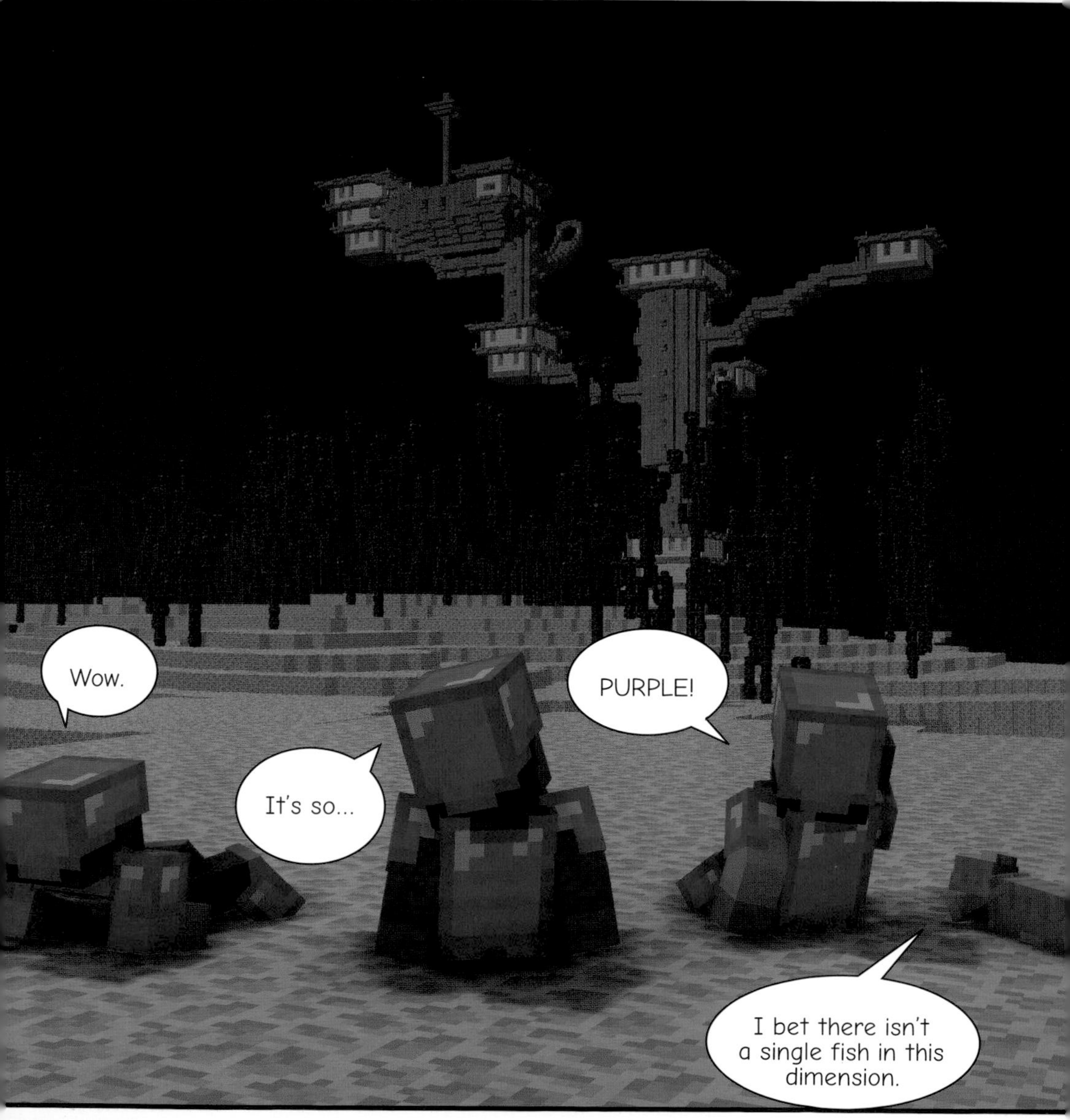
Wow.
It's so...
PURPLE!
I bet there isn't a single fish in this dimension.

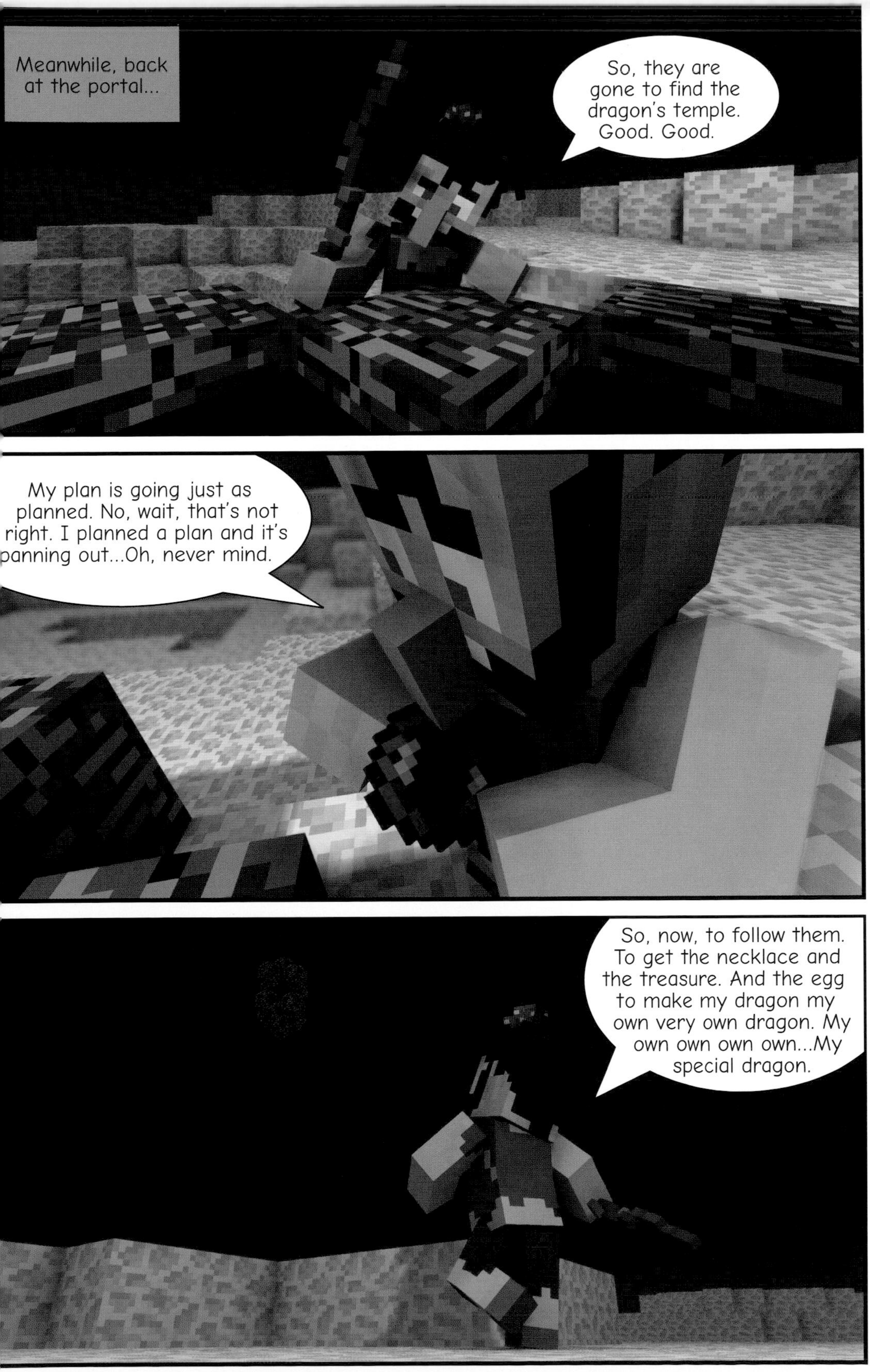

Meanwhile, back at the portal...
So, they are gone to find the dragon's temple. Good. Good.
My plan is going just as planned. No, wait, that's not right. I planned a plan and it's panning out...Oh, never mind.
So, now, to follow them. To get the necklace and the treasure. And the egg to make my dragon my own very own dragon. My own own own own...My special dragon.

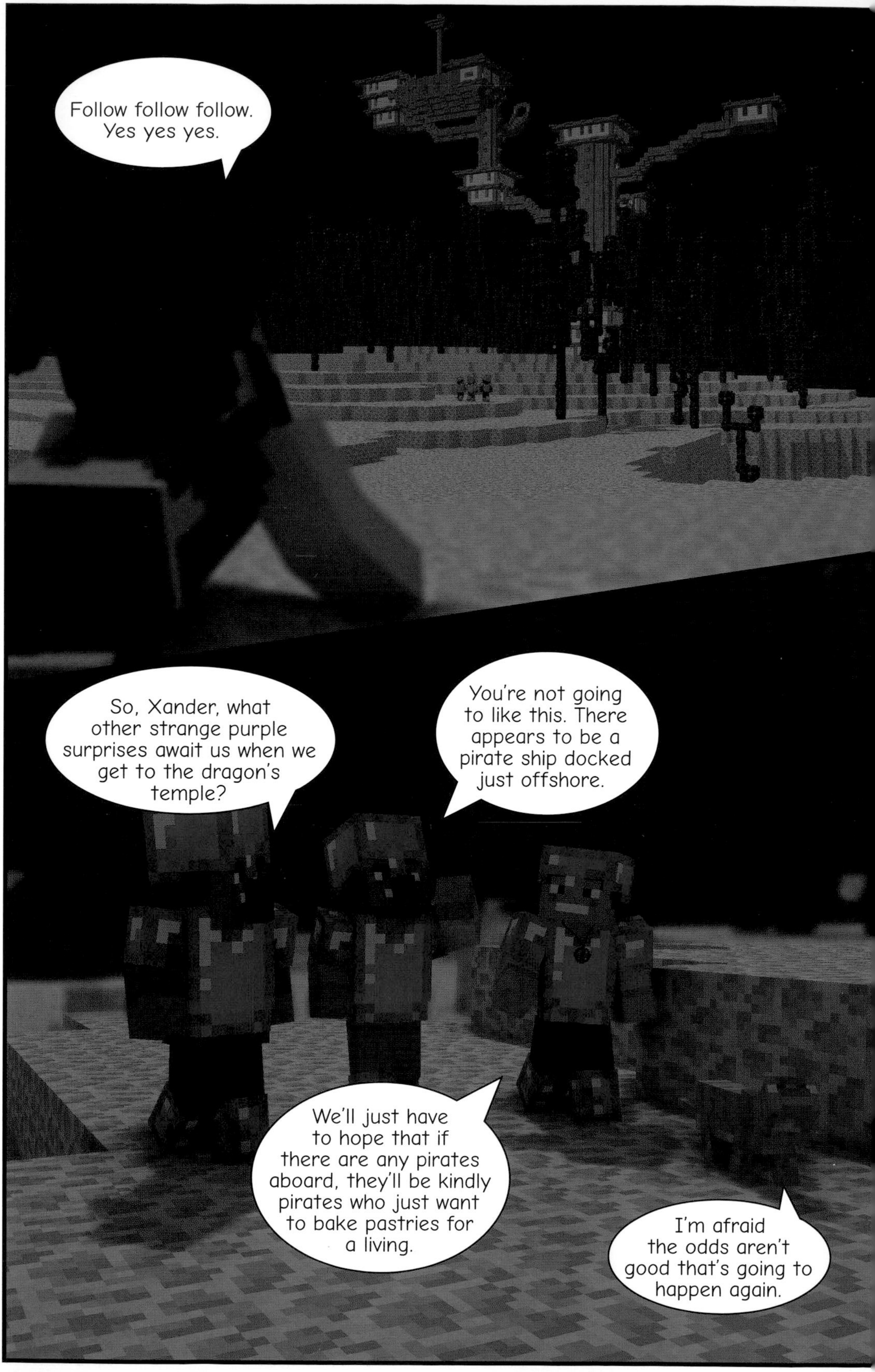
Follow follow follow. Yes yes yes.
So, Xander, what other strange purple surprises await us when we get to the dragon's temple?
You're not going to like this. There appears to be a pirate ship docked just offshore.
We'll just have to hope that if there are any pirates aboard, they'll be kindly pirates who just want to bake pastries for a living.
I'm afraid the odds aren't good that's going to happen again.

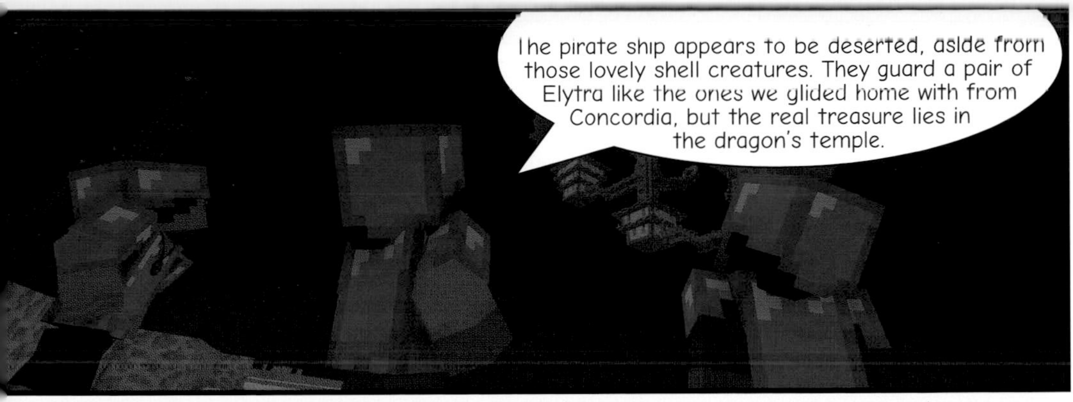
The pirate ship appears to be deserted, aside from those lovely shell creatures. They guard a pair of Elytra like the ones we glided home with from Concordia, but the real treasure lies in the dragon's temple.

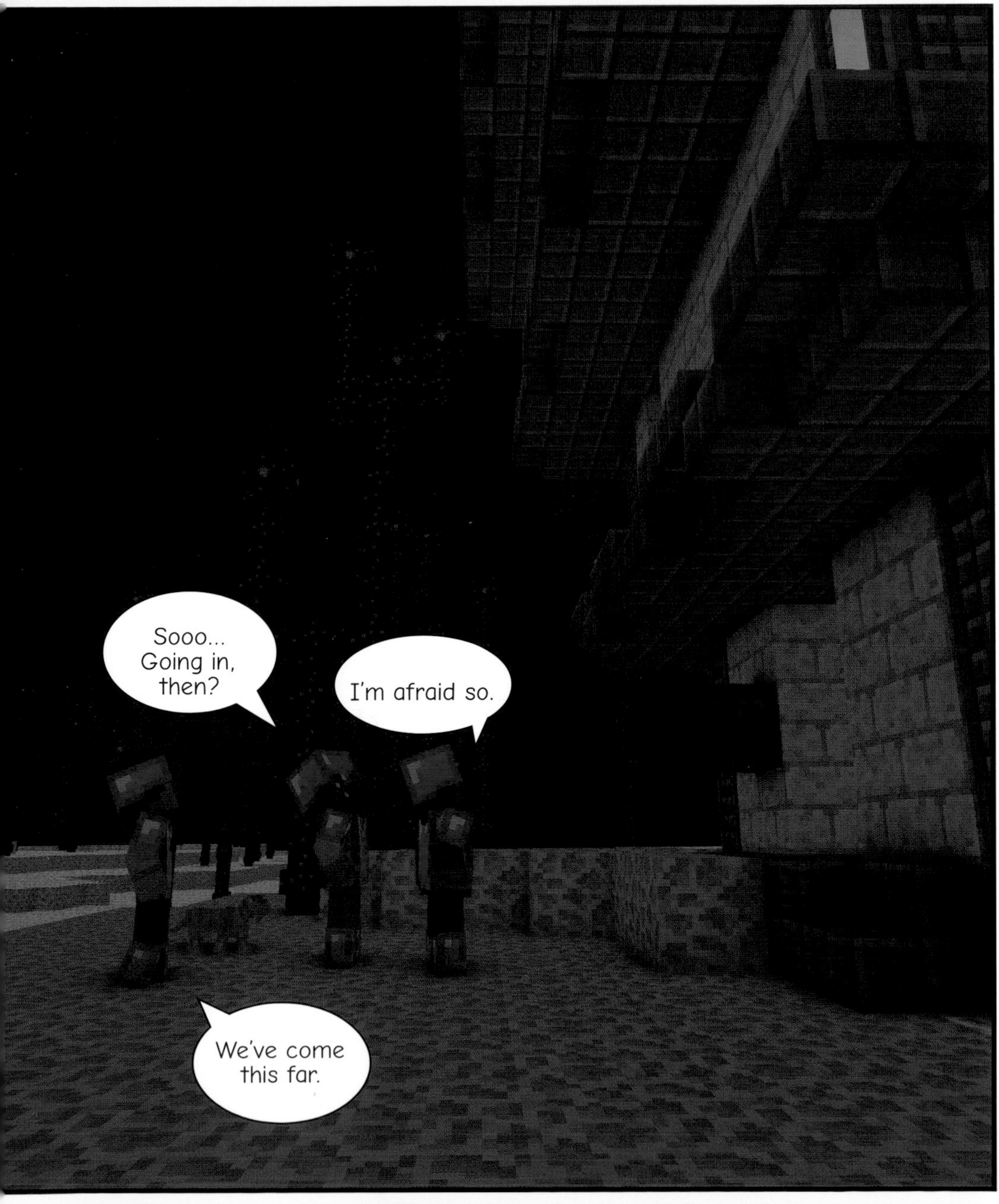
Sooo... Going in, then?
I'm afraid so.
We've come this far.

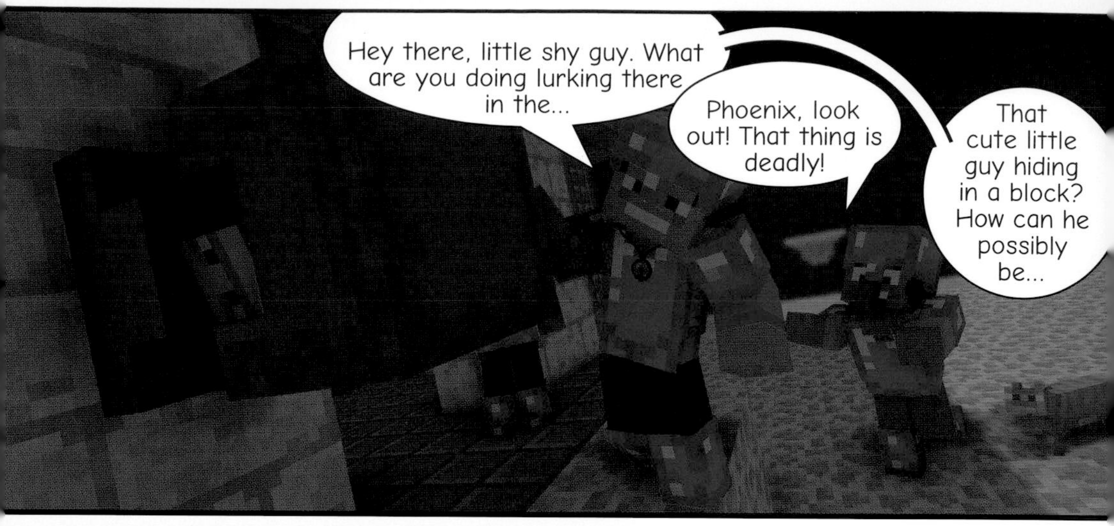
Hey there, little shy guy. What are you doing lurking there in the...
Phoenix, look out! That thing is deadly!
That cute little guy hiding in a block? How can he possibly be...

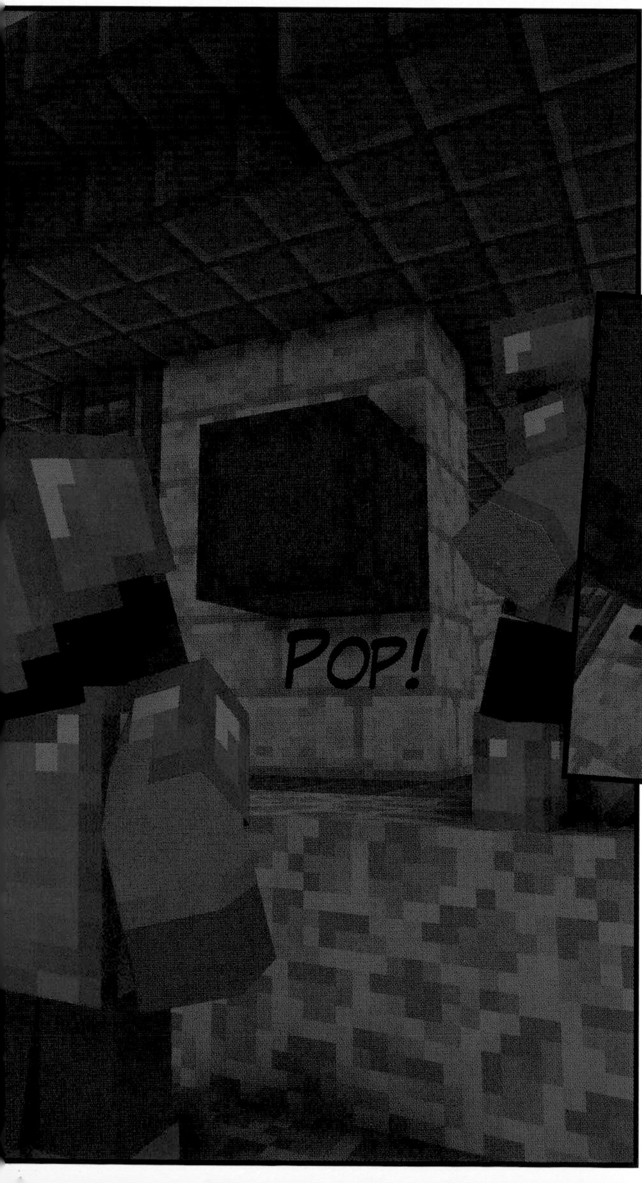
POP!

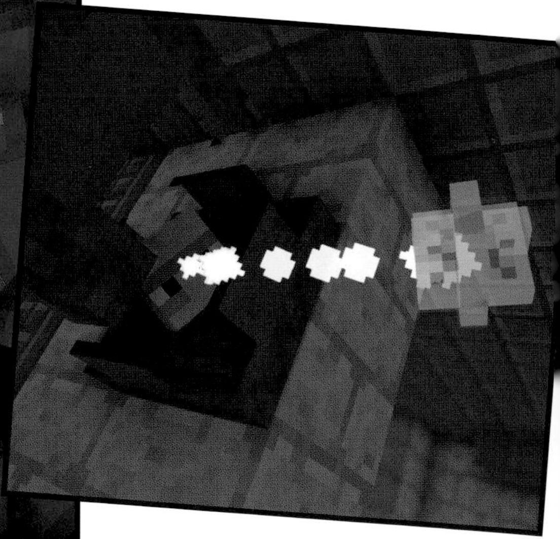

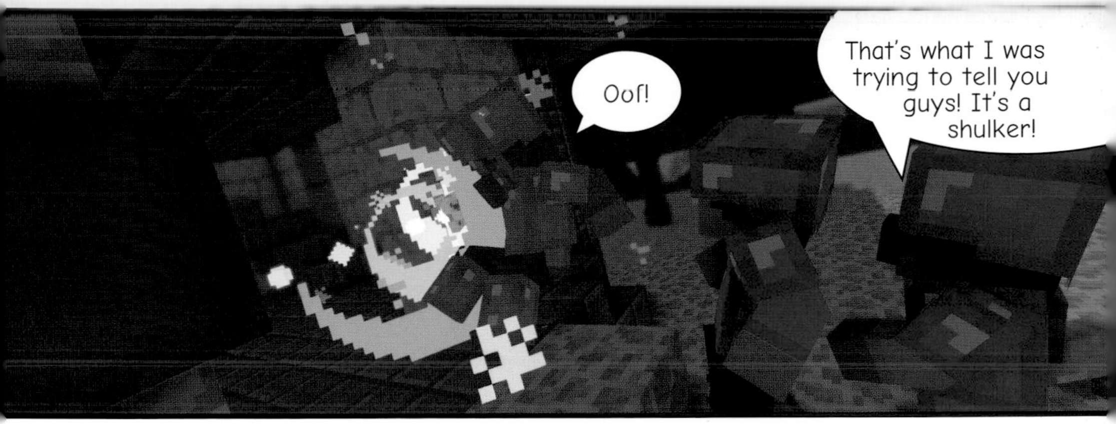
Oof!
That's what I was trying to tell you guys! It's a shulker!

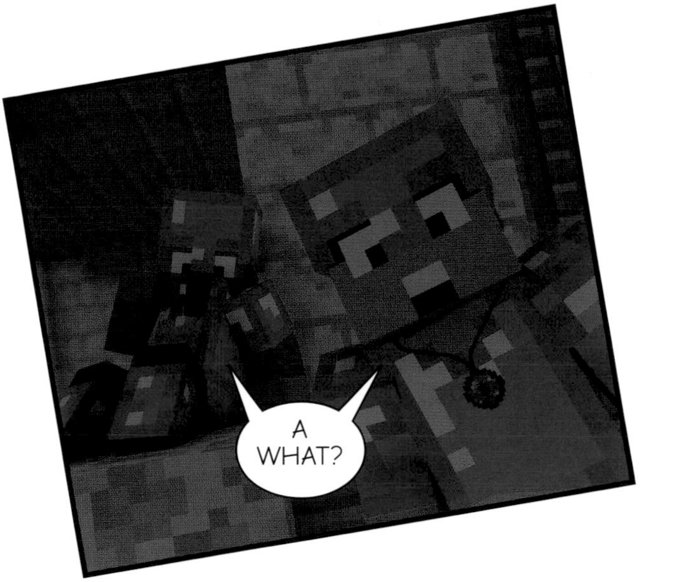
A WHAT?

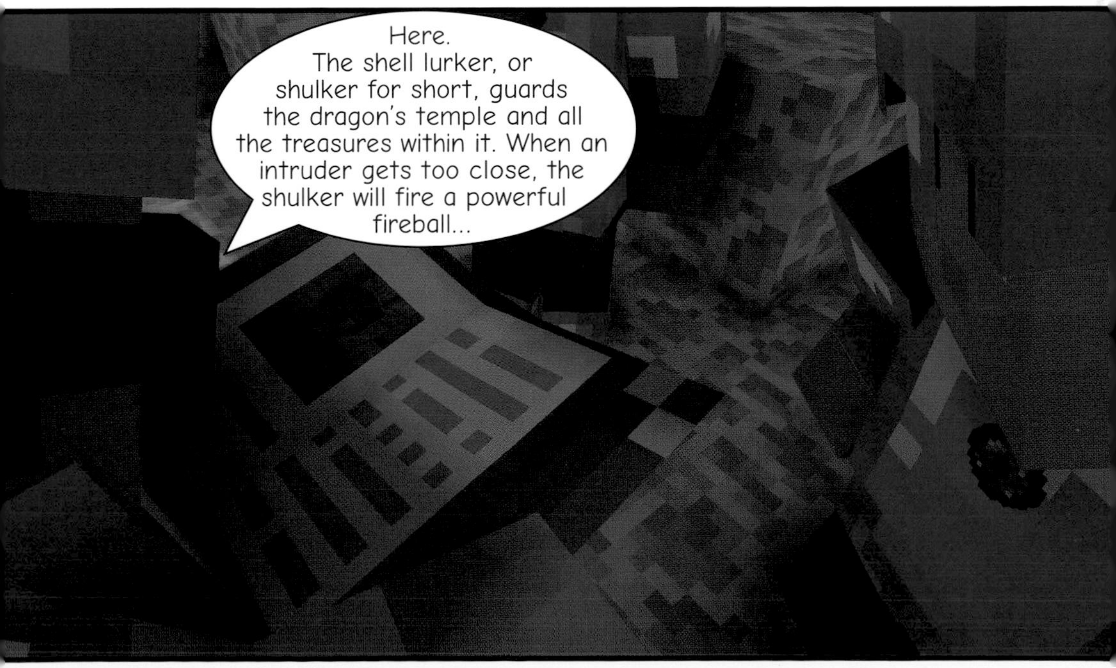
Here. The shell lurker, or shulker for short, guards the dragon's temple and all the treasures within it. When an intruder gets too close, the shulker will fire a powerful fireball...

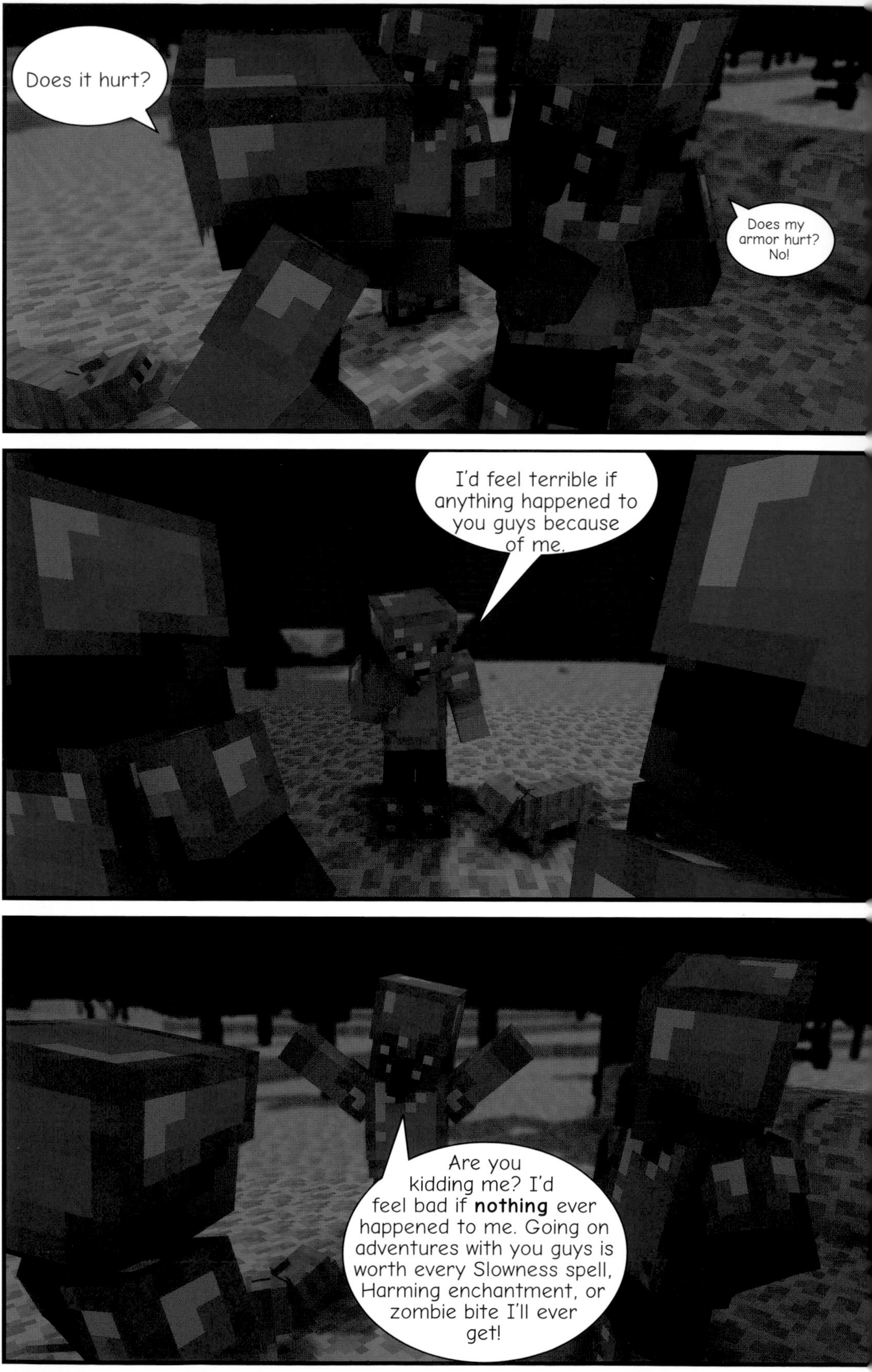

Does it hurt?
Does my armor hurt? No!
I'd feel terrible if anything happened to you guys because of me.
Are you kidding me? I'd feel bad if **nothing** ever happened to me. Going on adventures with you guys is worth every Slowness spell, Harming enchantment, or zombie bite I'll ever get!

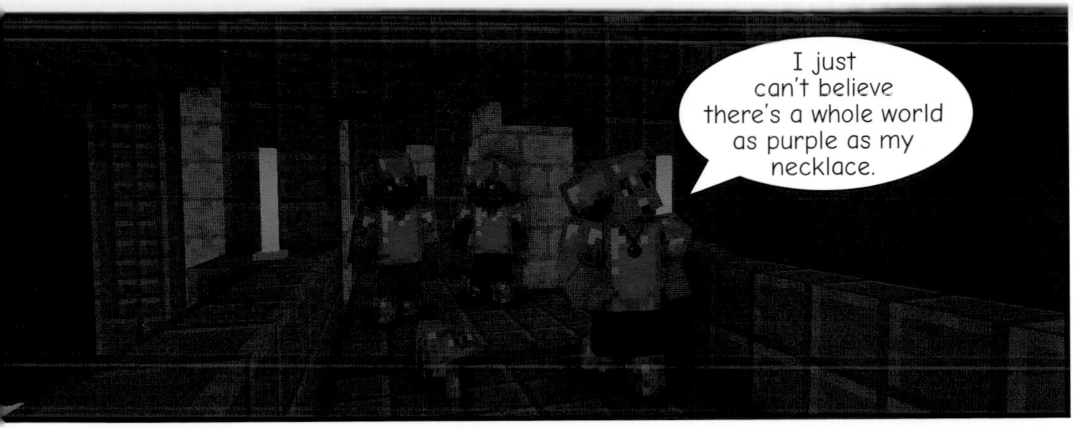
I just can't believe there's a whole world as purple as my necklace.

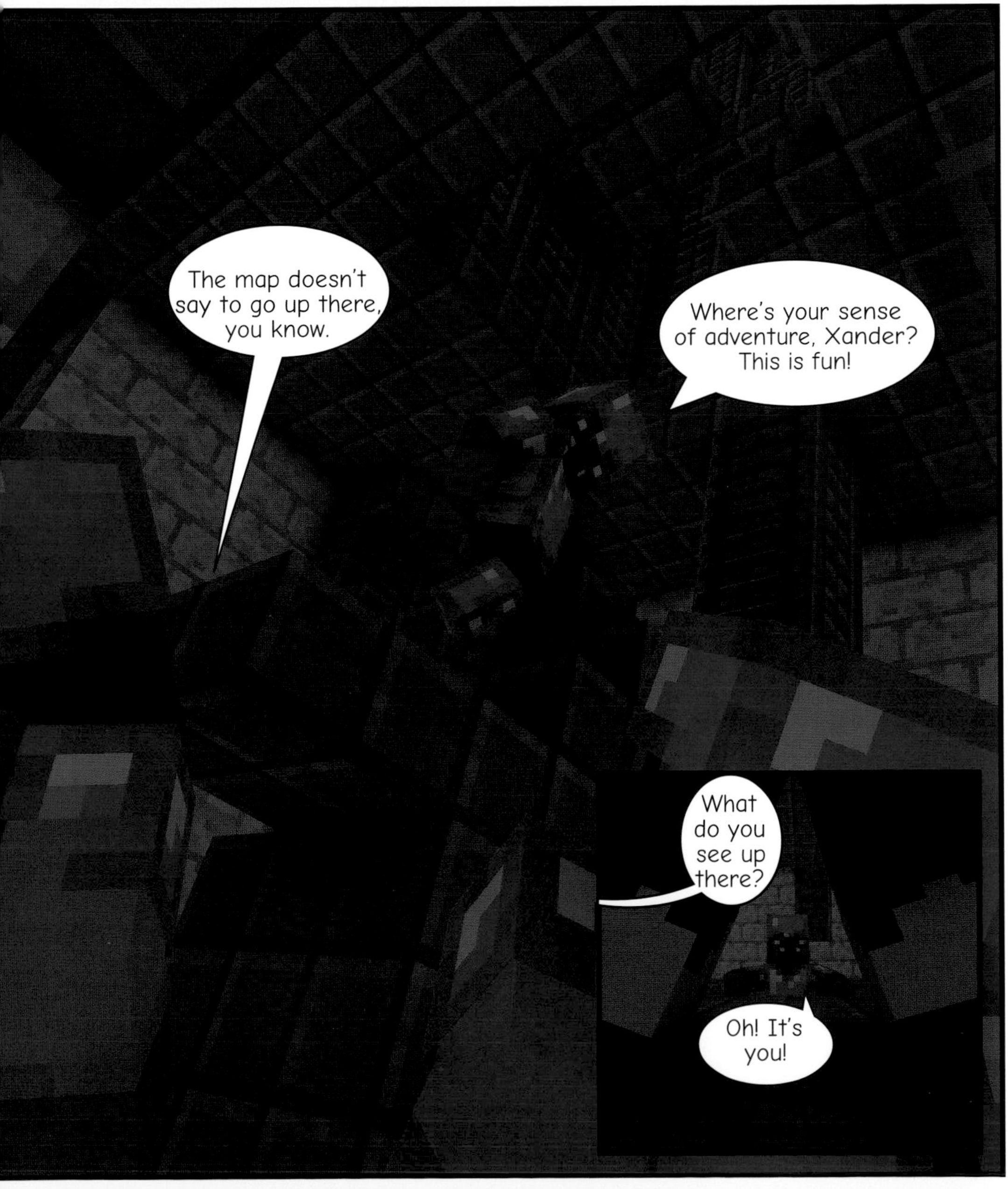
The map doesn't say to go up there, you know.
Where's your sense of adventure, Xander? This is fun!
What do you see up there?
Oh! It's you!

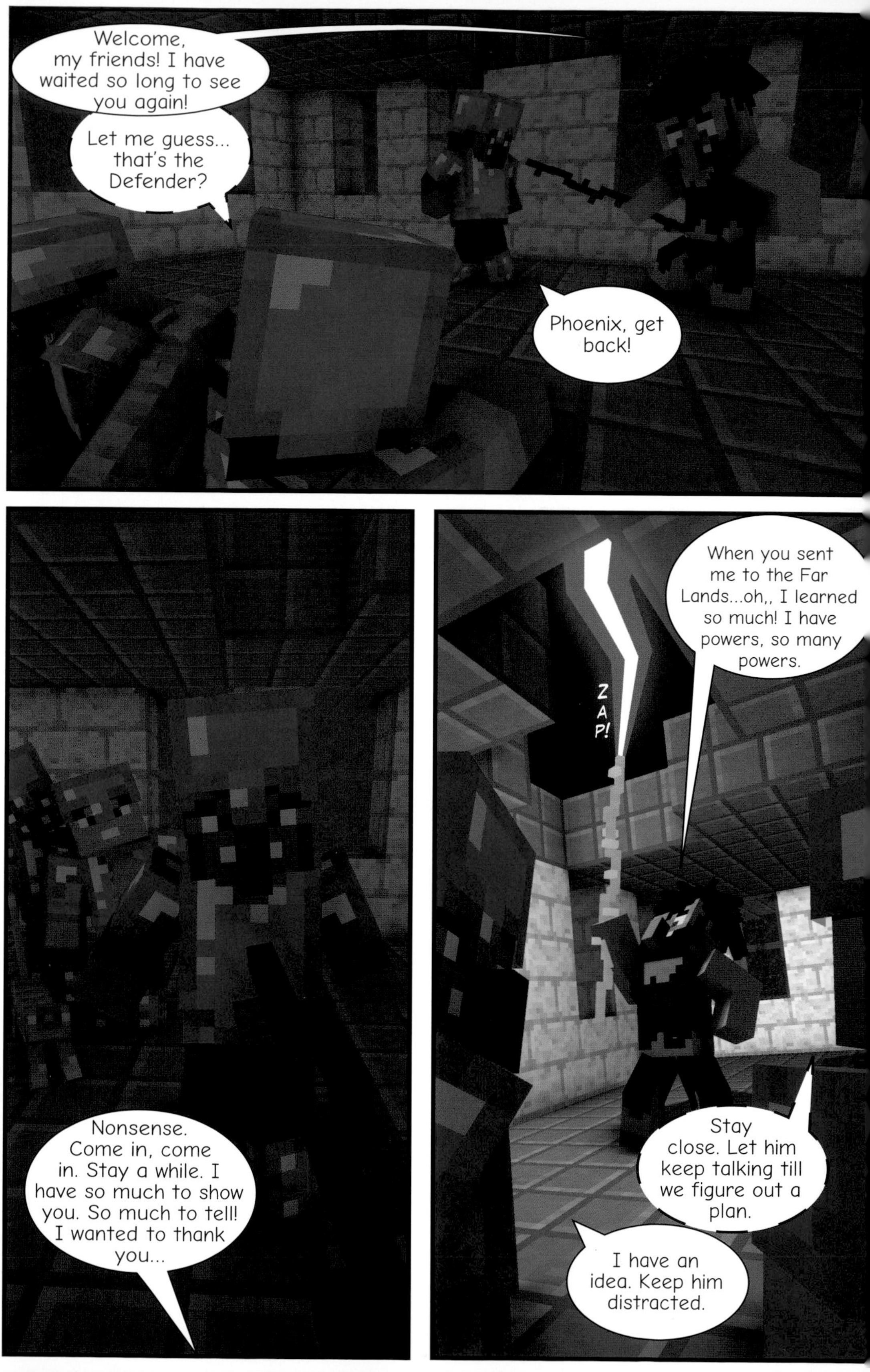
Welcome, my friends! I have waited so long to see you again!
Let me guess... that's the Defender?
Phoenix, get back!
Nonsense. Come in, come in. Stay a while. I have so much to show you. So much to tell! I wanted to thank you...
When you sent me to the Far Lands...oh,, I learned so much! I have powers, so many powers.
ZAP!
Stay close. Let him keep talking till we figure out a plan.
I have an idea. Keep him distracted.

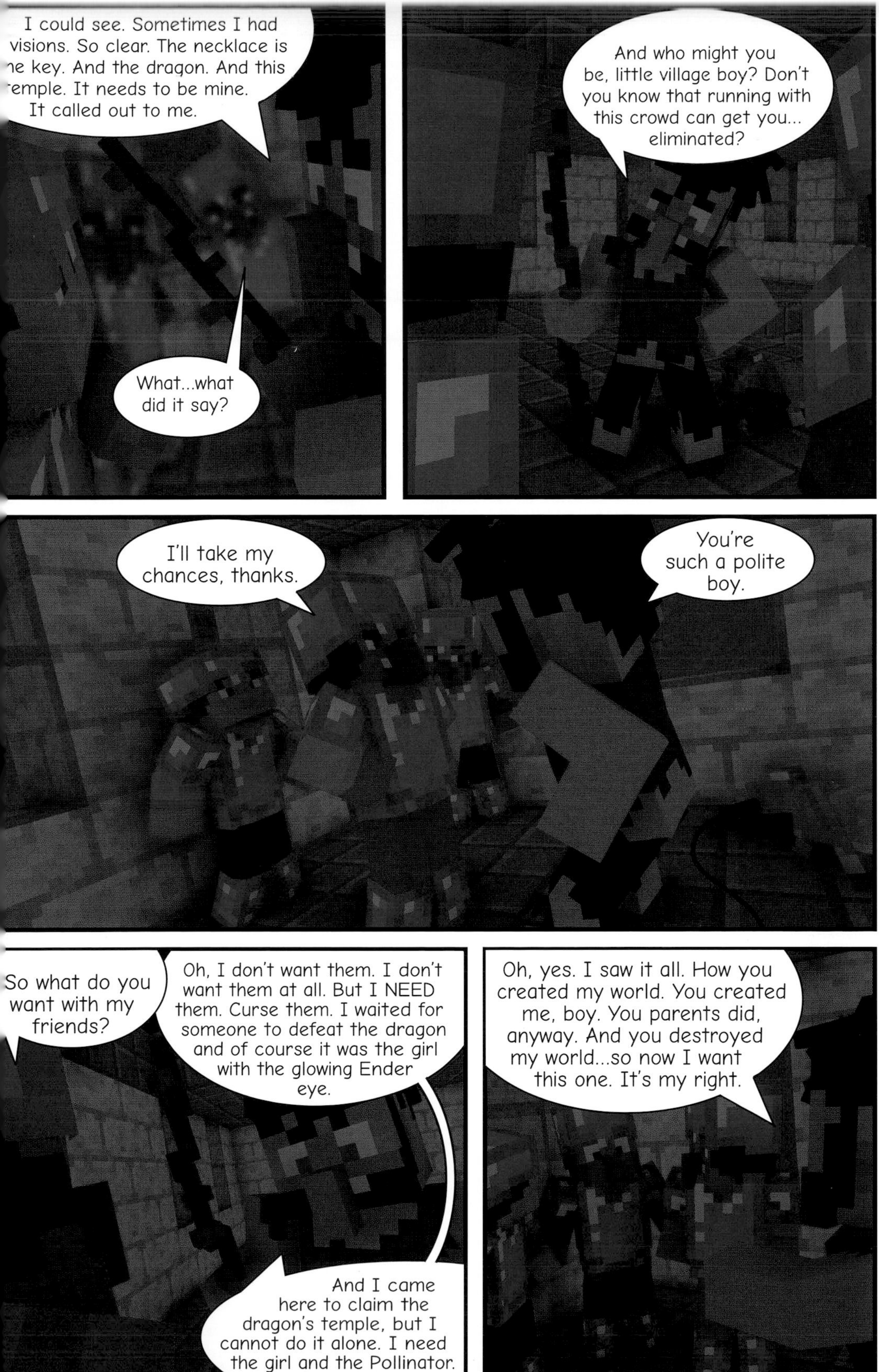
I could see. Sometimes I had visions. So clear. The necklace is he key. And the dragon. And this emple. It needs to be mine. It called out to me.
What...what did it say?
And who might you be, little village boy? Don't you know that running with this crowd can get you... eliminated?
I'll take my chances, thanks.
You're such a polite boy.
So what do you want with my friends?
Oh, I don't want them. I don't want them at all. But I NEED them. Curse them. I waited for someone to defeat the dragon and of course it was the girl with the glowing Ender eye.
And I came here to claim the dragon's temple, but I cannot do it alone. I need the girl and the Pollinator.
Oh, yes. I saw it all. How you created my world. You created me, boy. You parents did, anyway. And you destroyed my world...so now I want this one. It's my right.

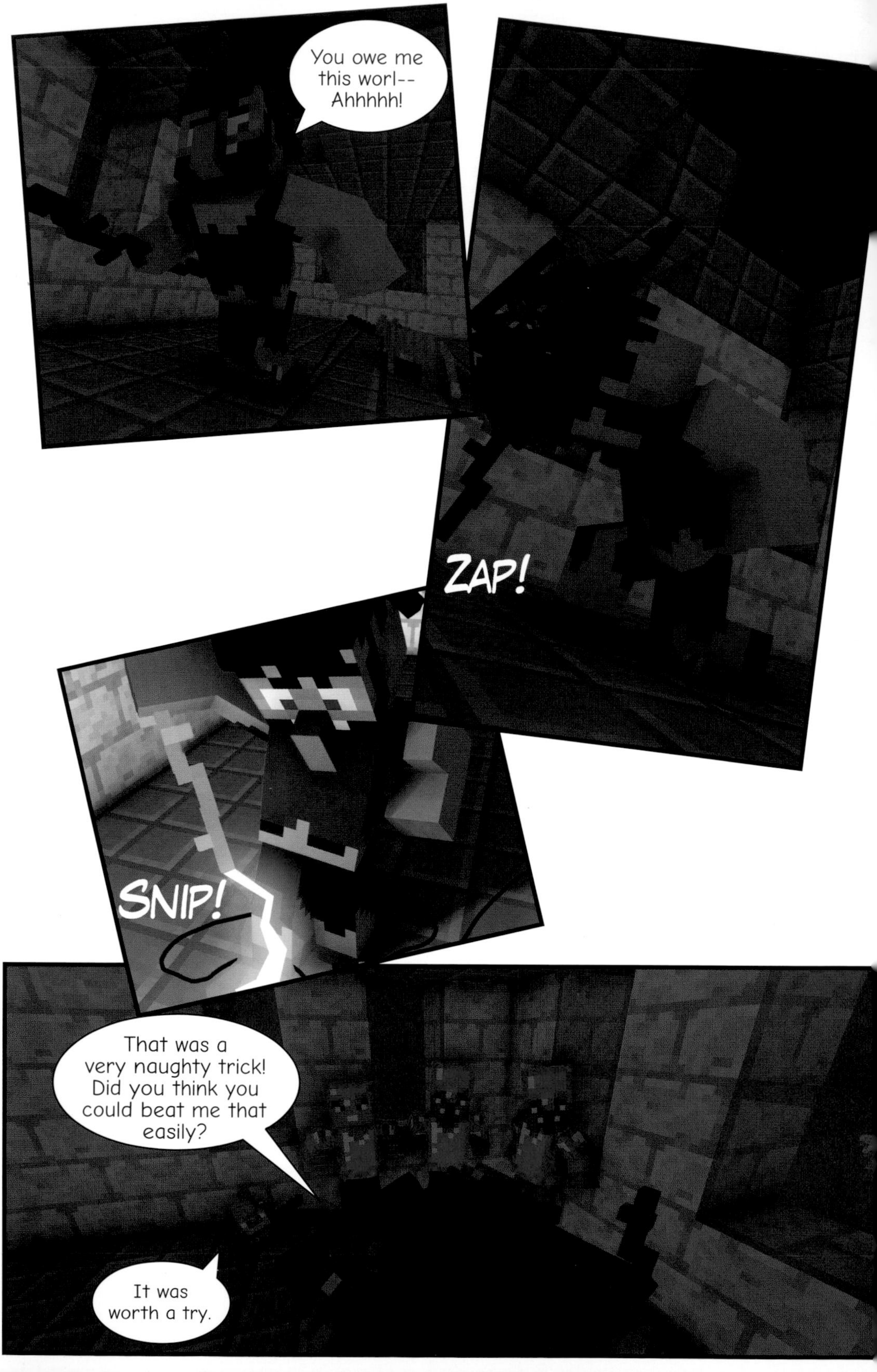
You owe me this worl-- Ahhhhh!
ZAP!
SNIP!
That was a very naughty trick! Did you think you could beat me that easily?
It was worth a try.

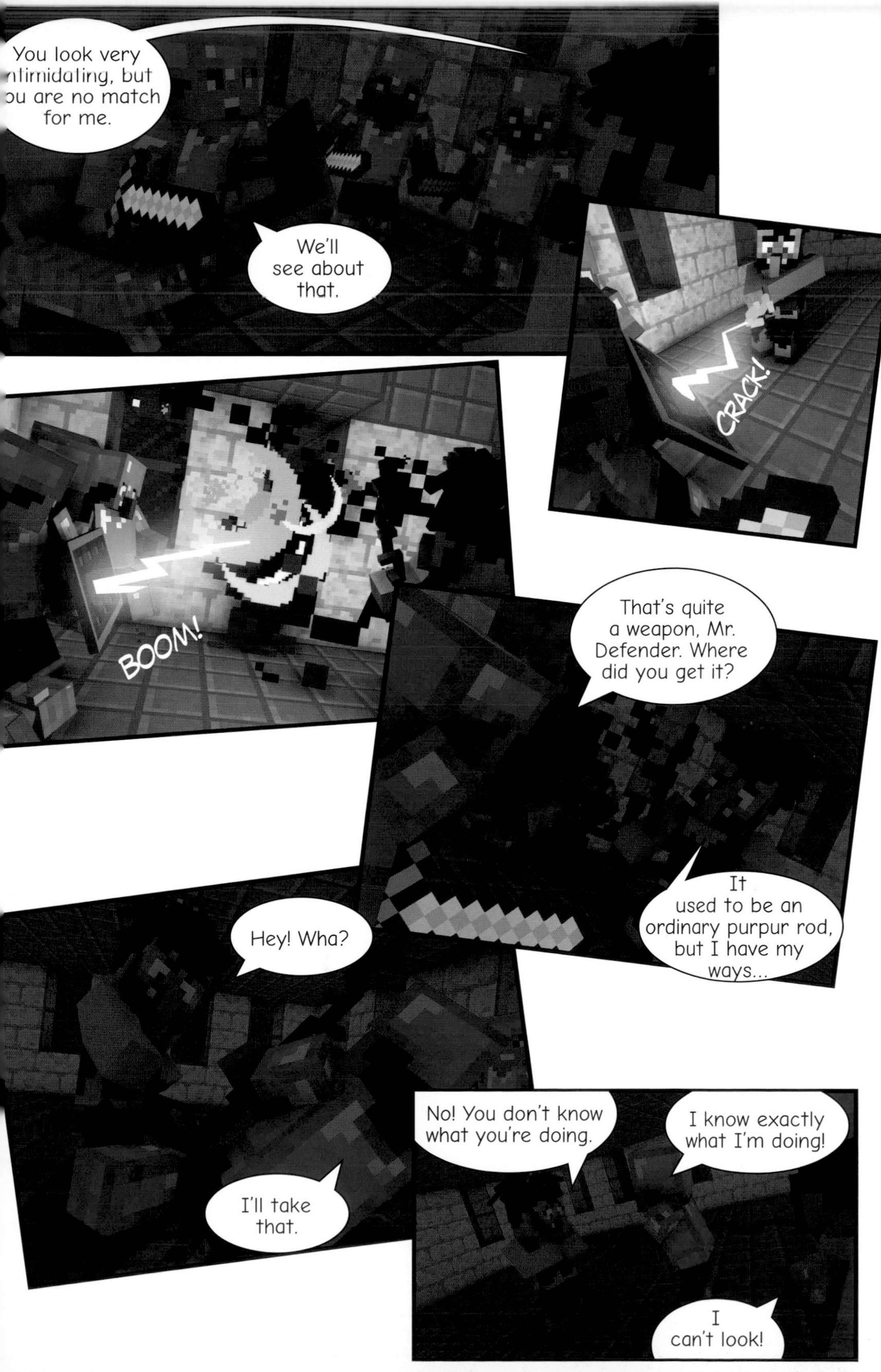
You look very ntimidating, but ou are no match for me.
We'll see about that.
CRACK!
BOOM!
That's quite a weapon, Mr. Defender. Where did you get it?
It used to be an ordinary purpur rod, but I have my ways...
Hey! Wha?
I'll take that.
No! You don't know what you're doing.
I know exactly what I'm doing!
I can't look!

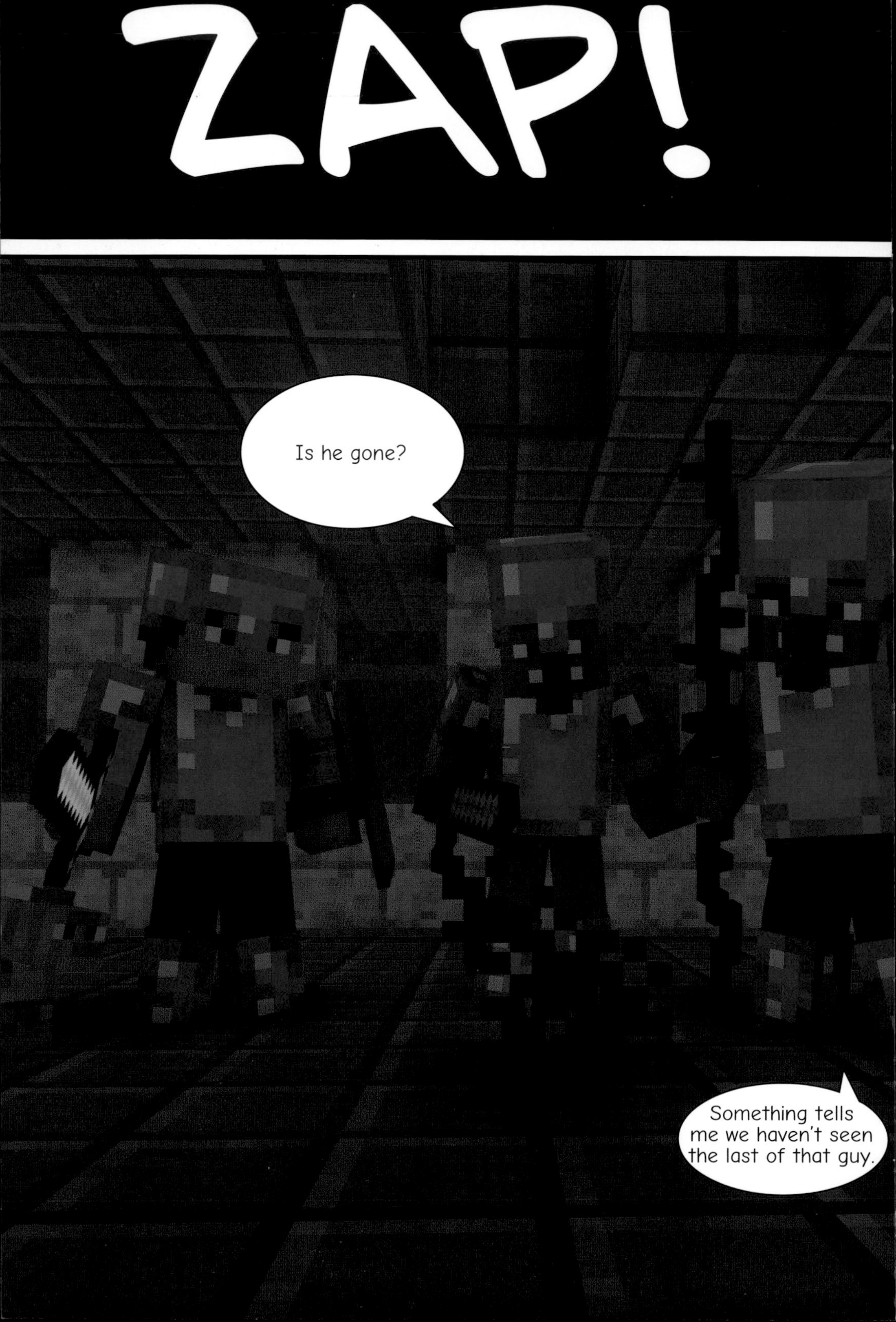
ZAP!
Is he gone?
Something tells me we haven't seen the last of that guy.

CHAPTER 11

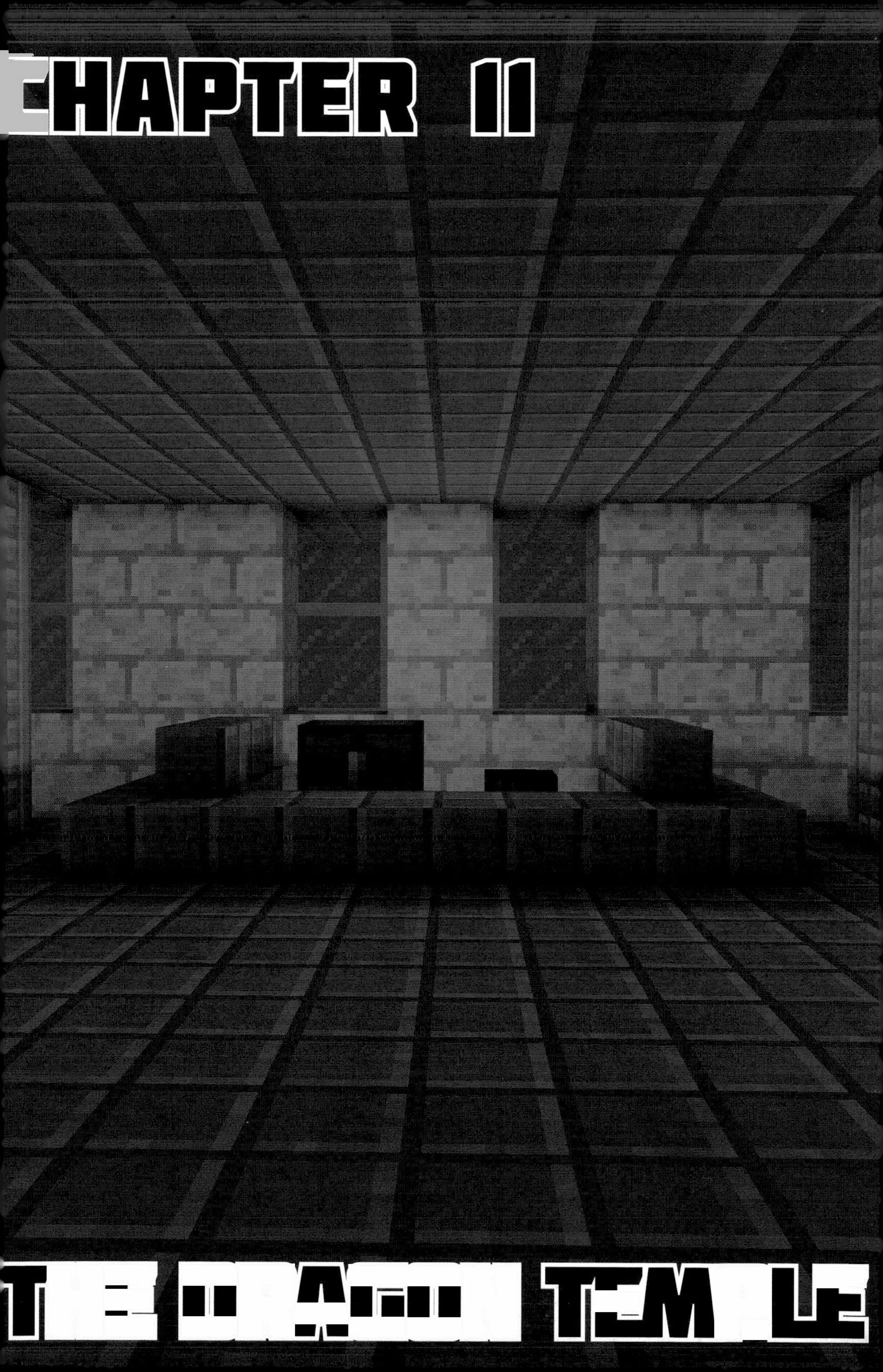

THE DRAGON TEMPLE

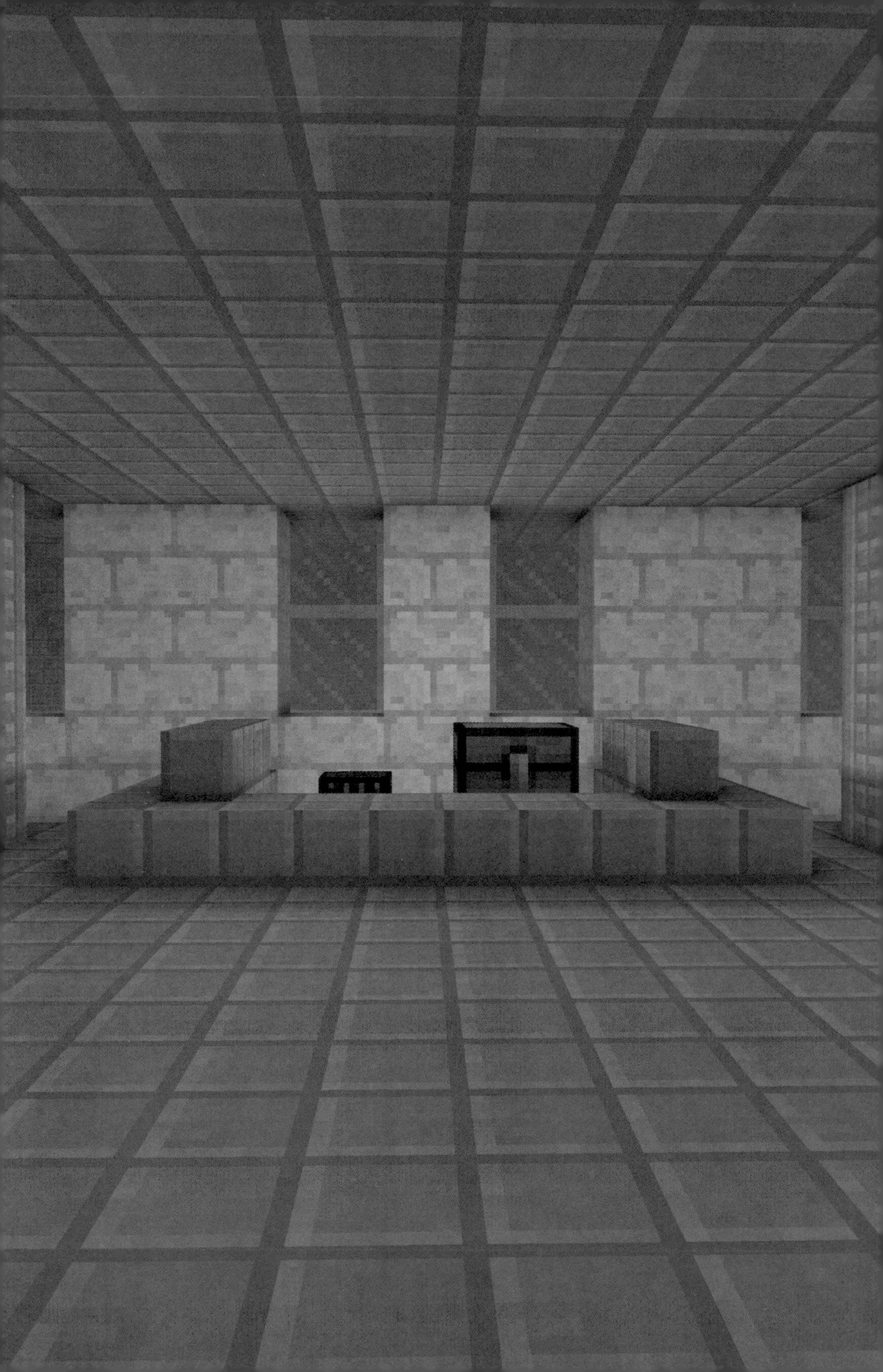

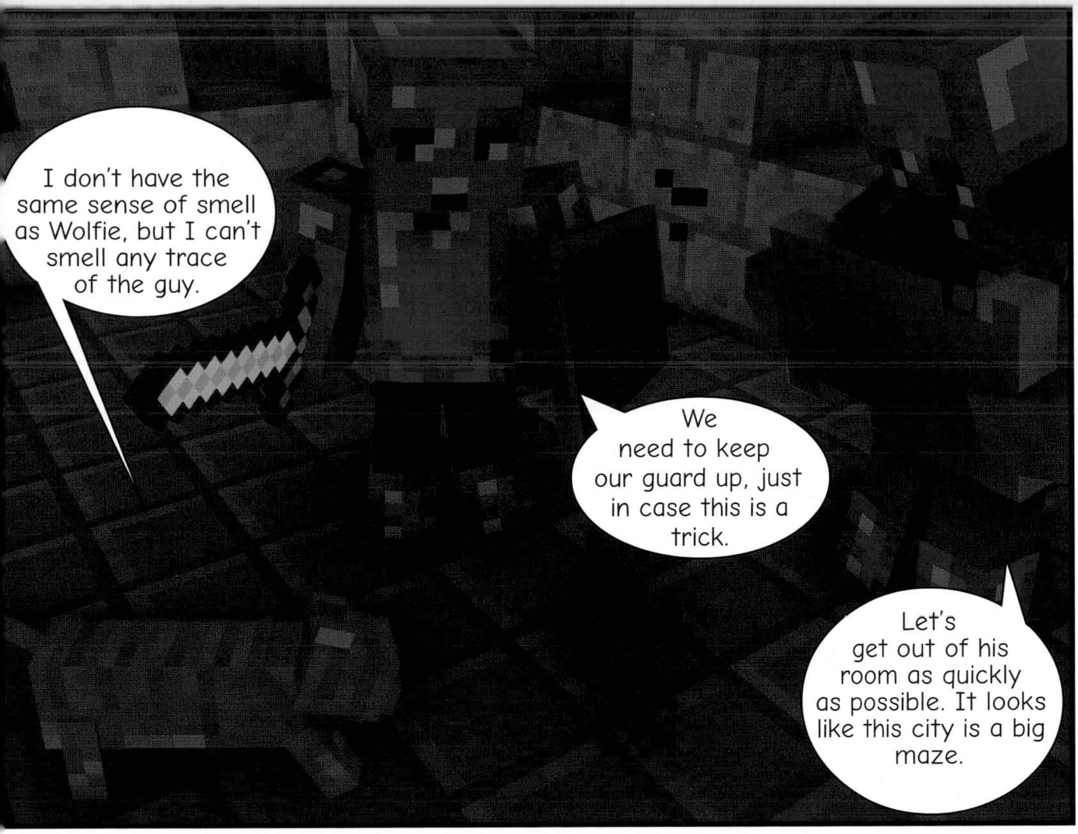
I don't have the same sense of smell as Wolfie, but I can't smell any trace of the guy.
We need to keep our guard up, just in case this is a trick.
Let's get out of his room as quickly as possible. It looks like this city is a big maze.

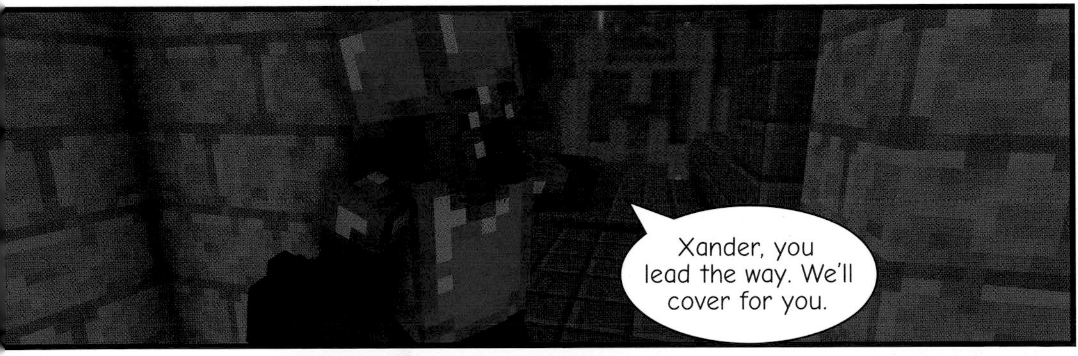
Xander, you lead the way. We'll cover for you.

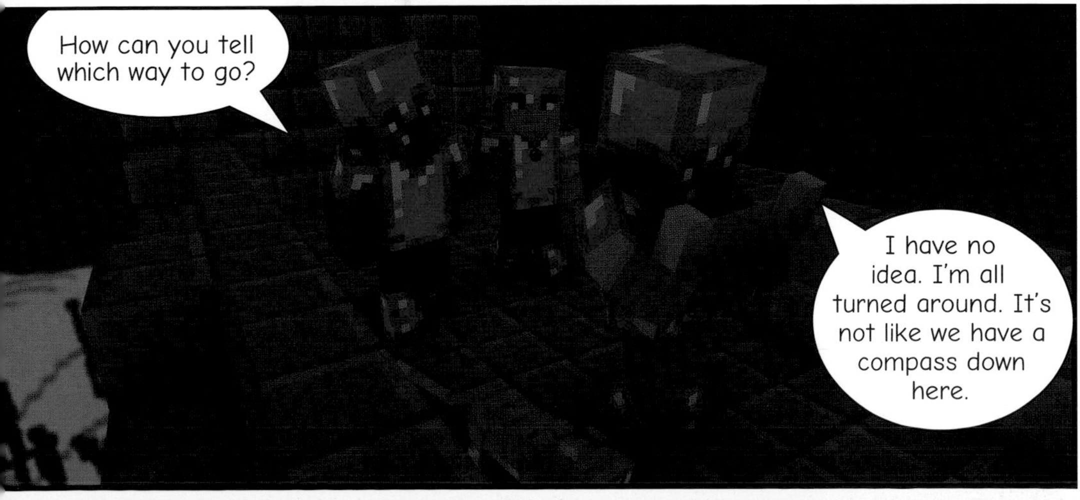
How can you tell which way to go?
I have no idea. I'm all turned around. It's not like we have a compass down here.

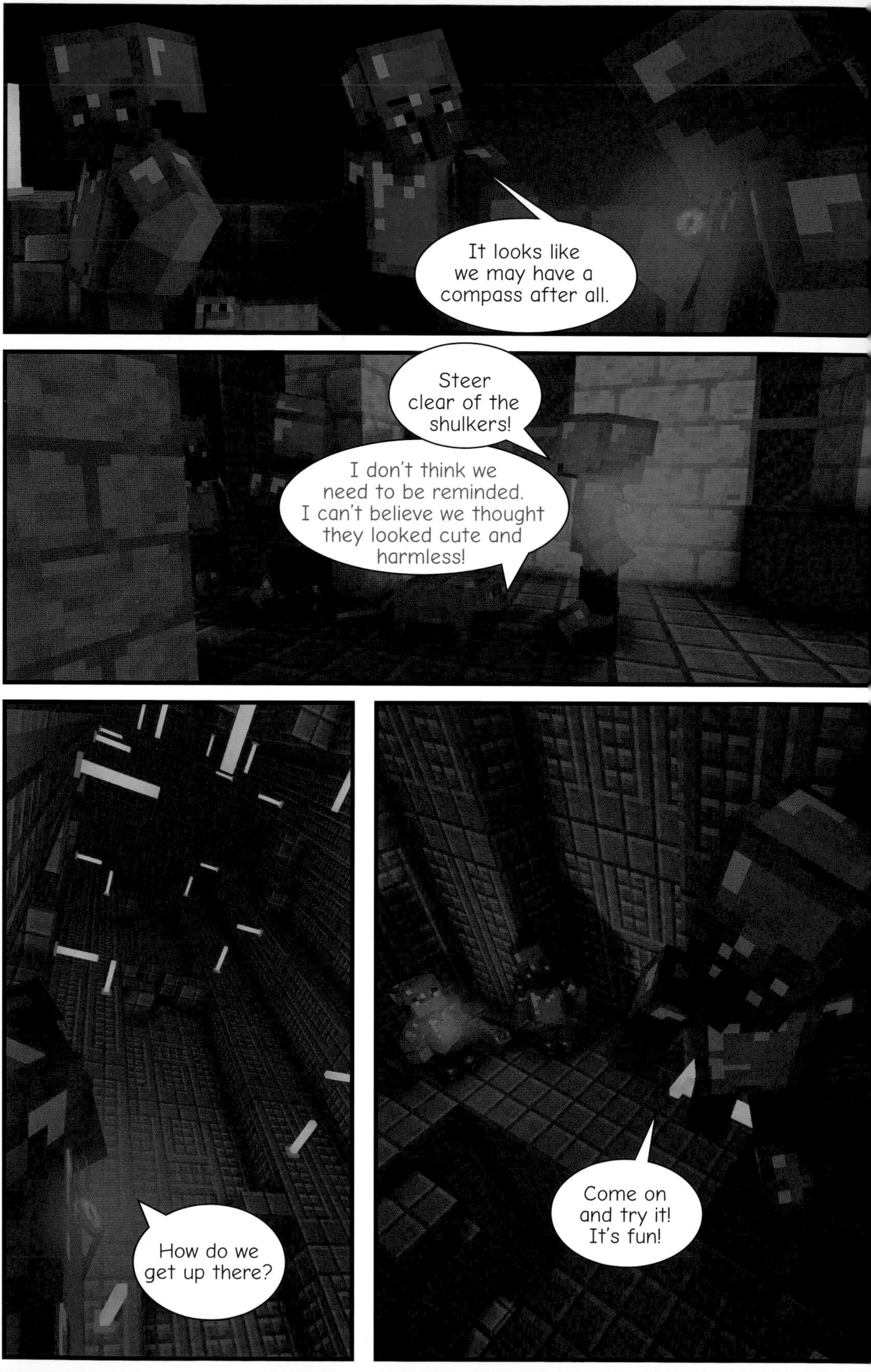
It looks like we may have a compass after all.
Steer clear of the shulkers!
I don't think we need to be reminded. I can't believe we thought they looked cute and harmless!
How do we get up there?
Come on and try it! It's fun!

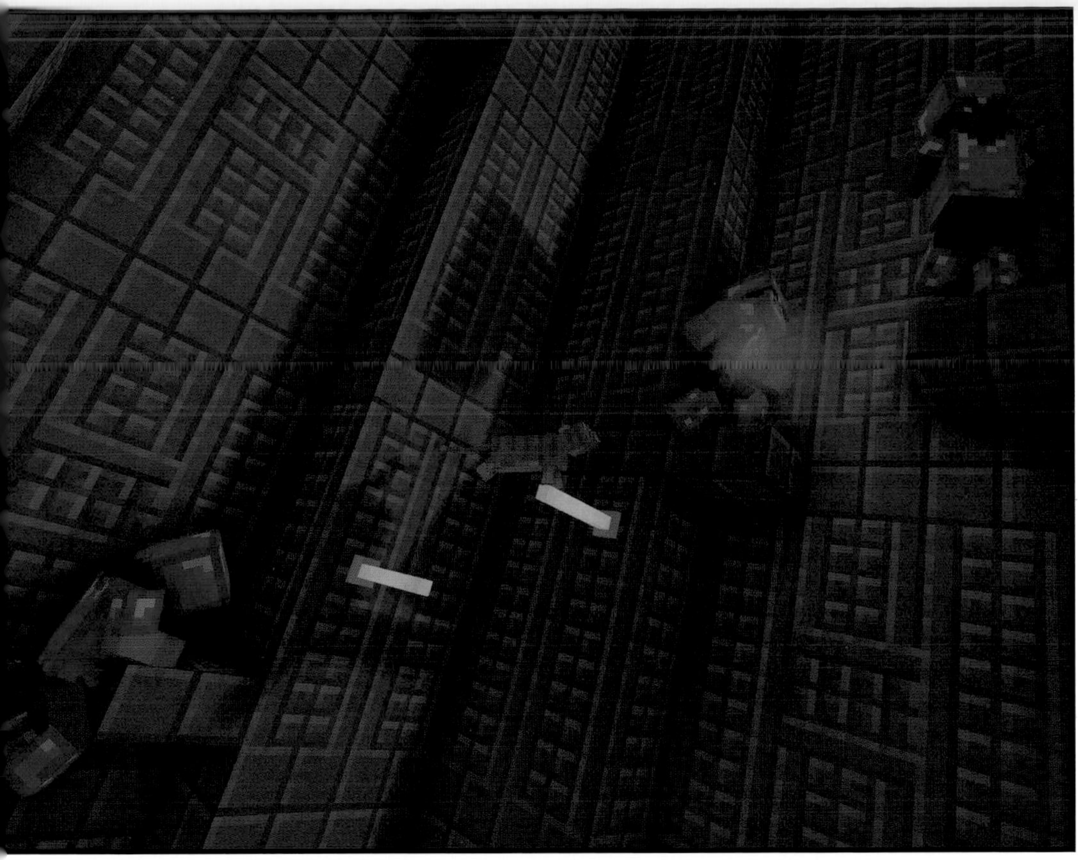

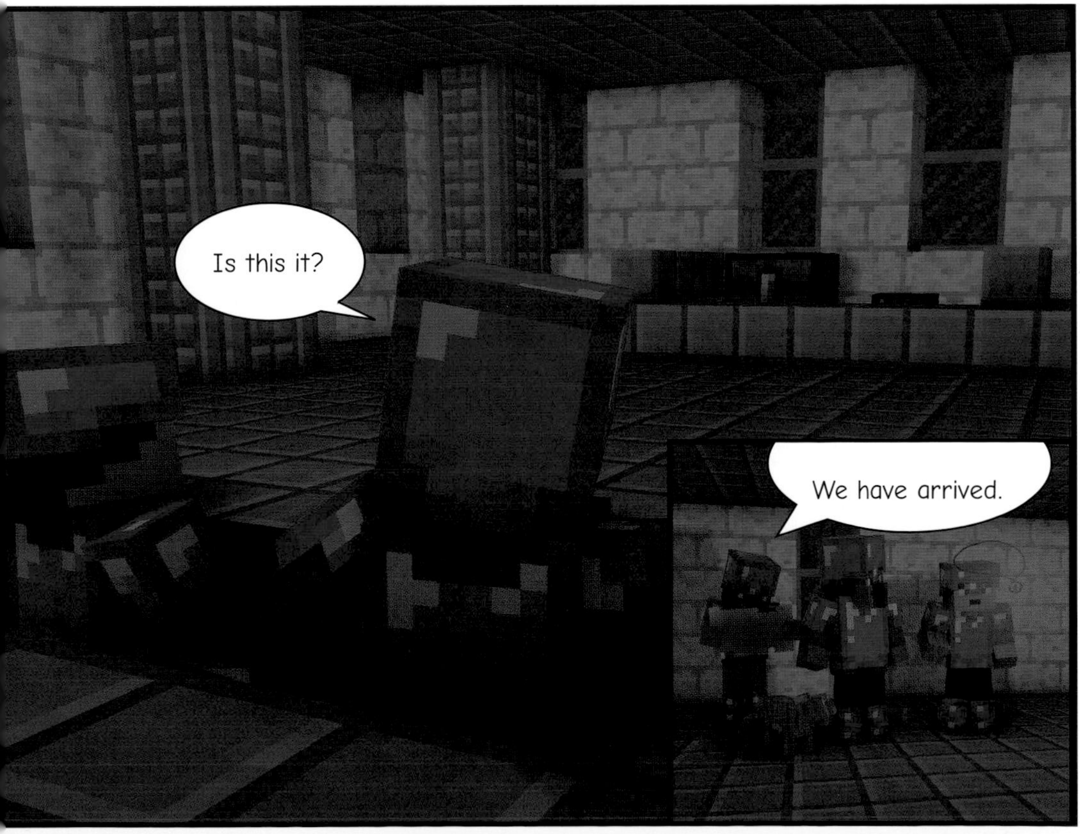
Is this it?
We have arrived.

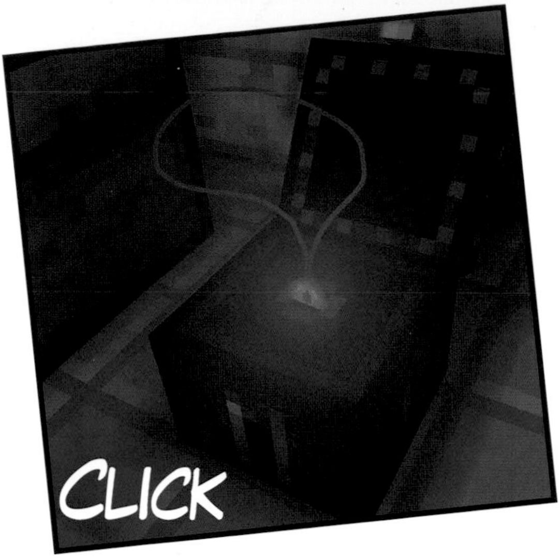
CLICK

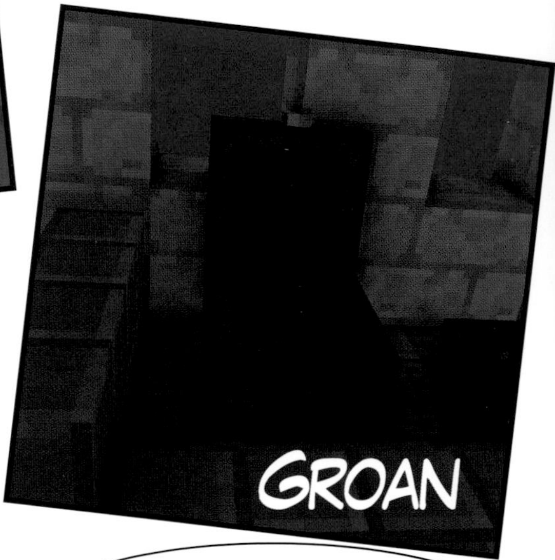
GROAN

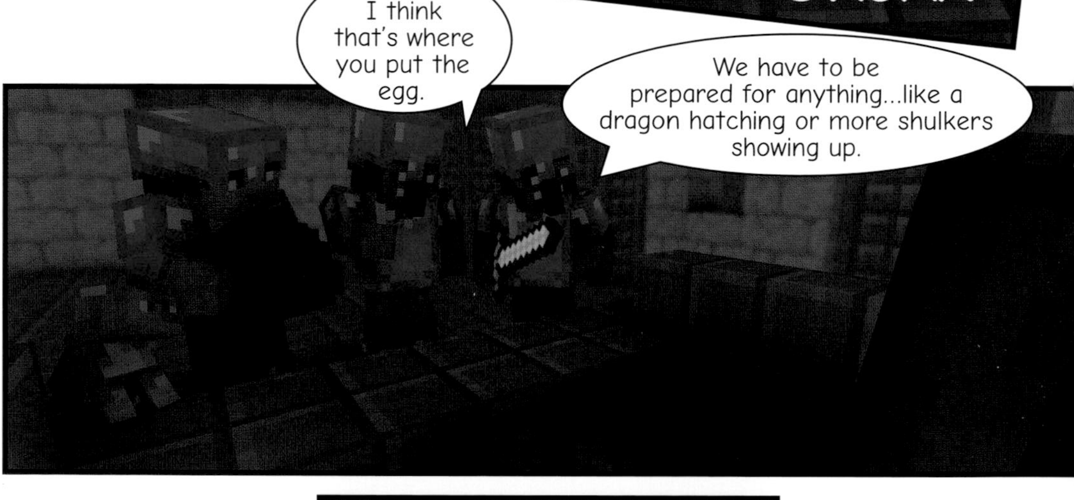
I think that's where you put the egg.
We have to be prepared for anything...like a dragon hatching or more shulkers showing up.

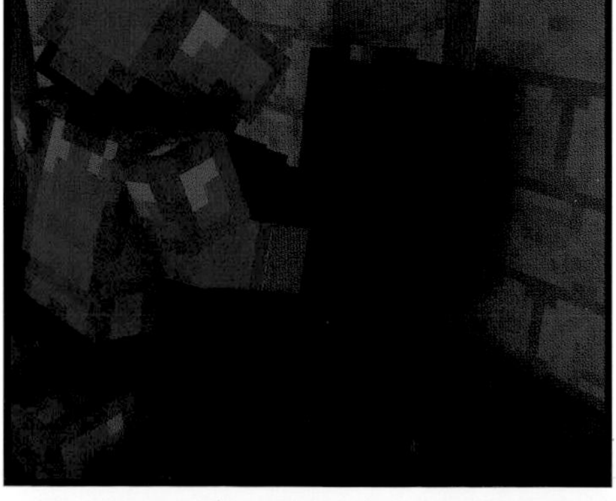

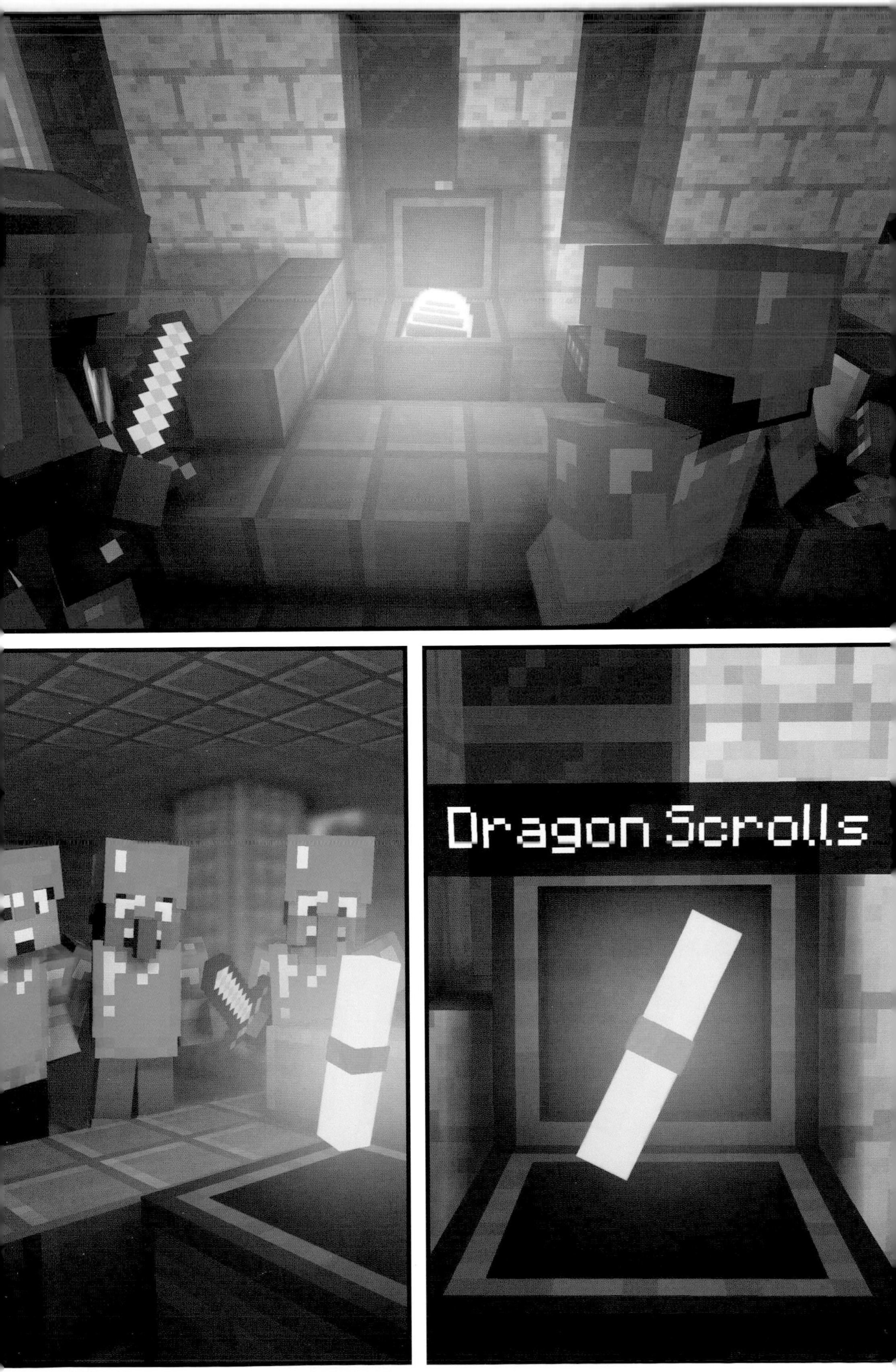
Dragon Scrolls

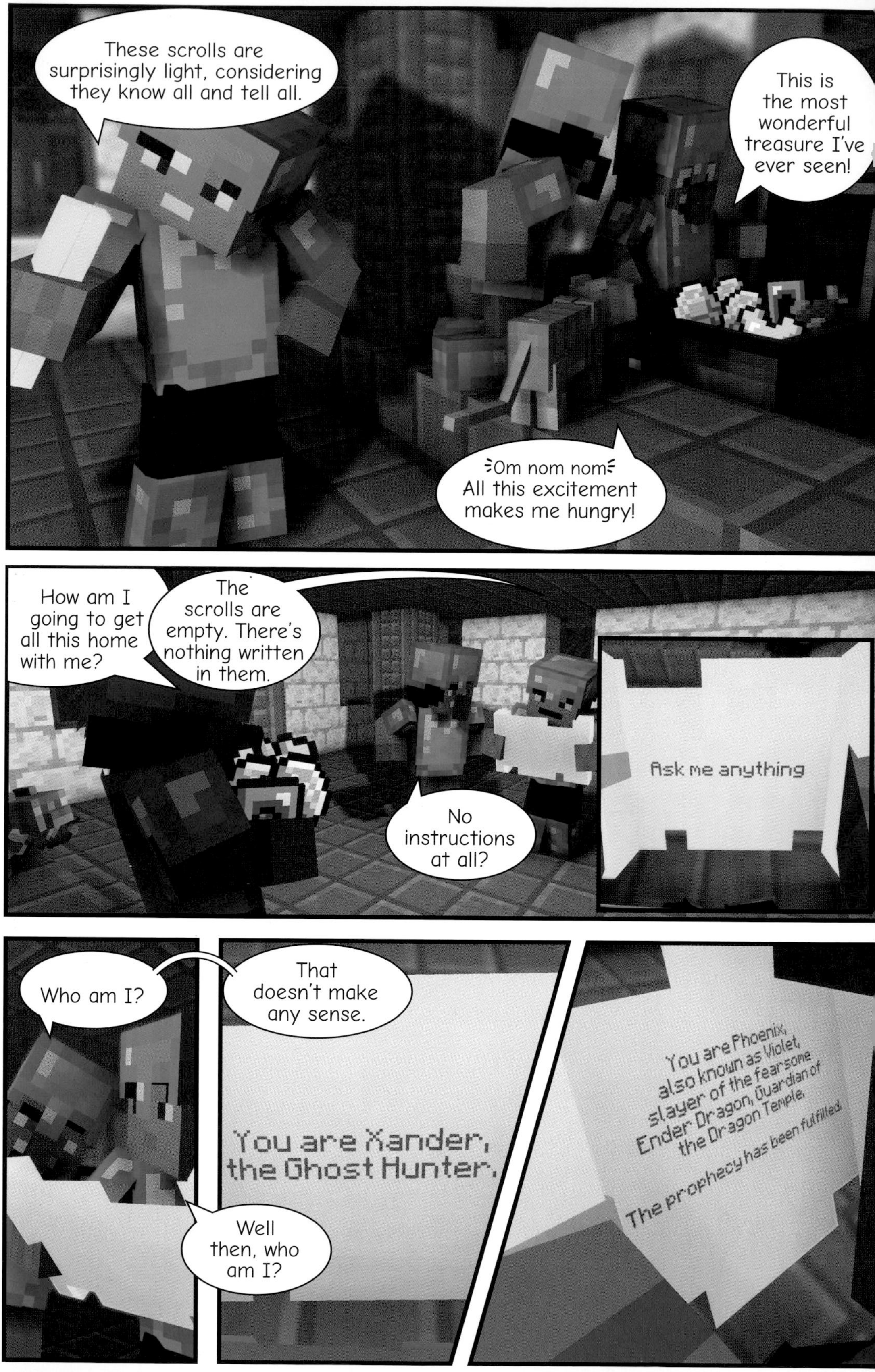

These scrolls are surprisingly light, considering they know all and tell all.
This is the most wonderful treasure I've ever seen!
Om nom nom
All this excitement makes me hungry!
How am I going to get all this home with me?
The scrolls are empty. There's nothing written in them.
No instructions at all?
Ask me anything
Who am I?
That doesn't make any sense.
You are Xander, the Ghost Hunter.
Well then, who am I?
You are Phoenix, also known as Violet, slayer of the fearsome Ender Dragon, Guardian of the Dragon Temple.
The prophecy has been fulfilled.

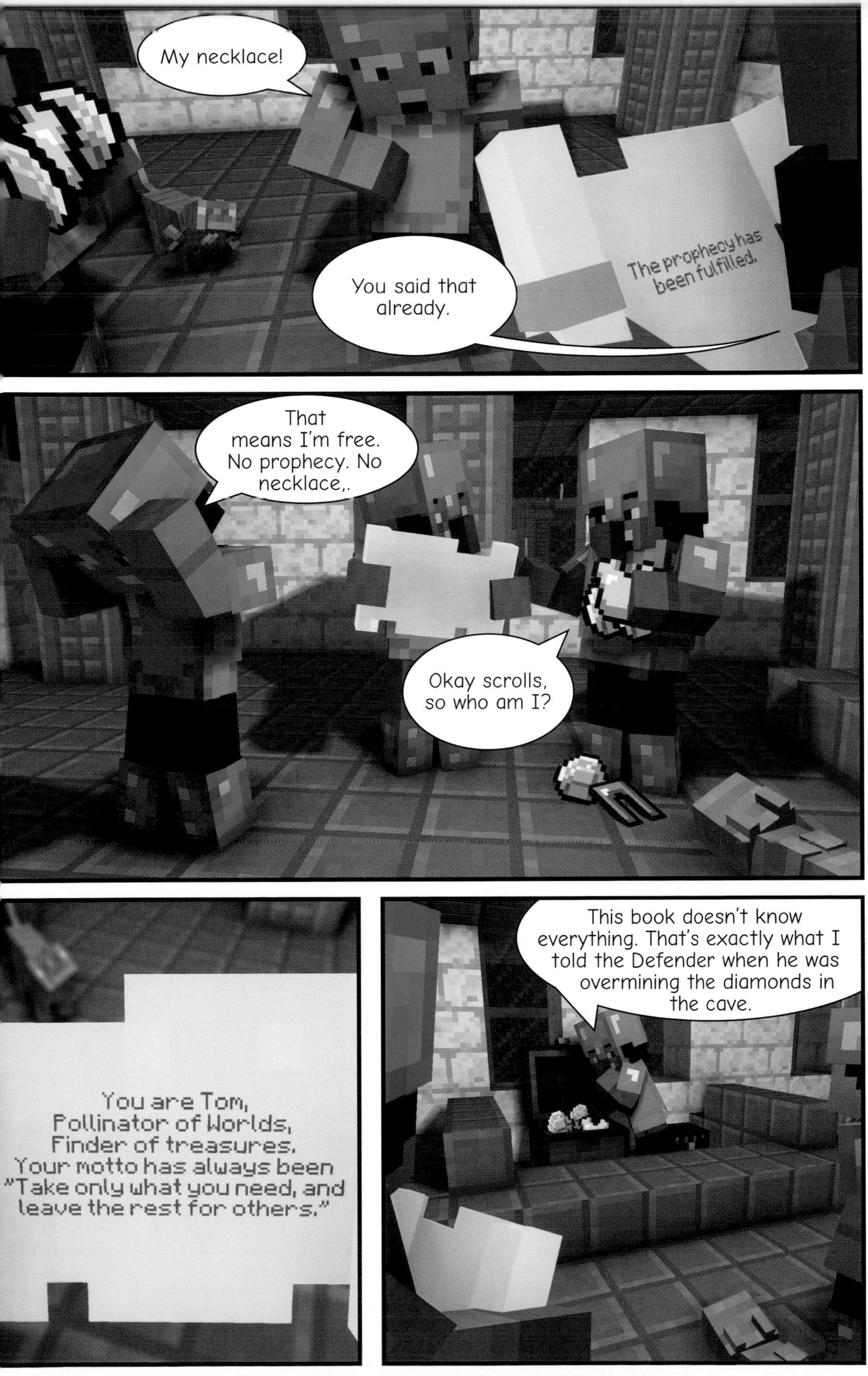
My necklace!
The prophecy has been fulfilled.
You said that already.
That means I'm free. No prophecy. No necklace,.
Okay scrolls, so who am I?
You are Tom, Pollinator of Worlds, Finder of treasures. Your motto has always been "Take only what you need, and leave the rest for others."
This book doesn't know everything. That's exactly what I told the Defender when he was overmining the diamonds in the cave.

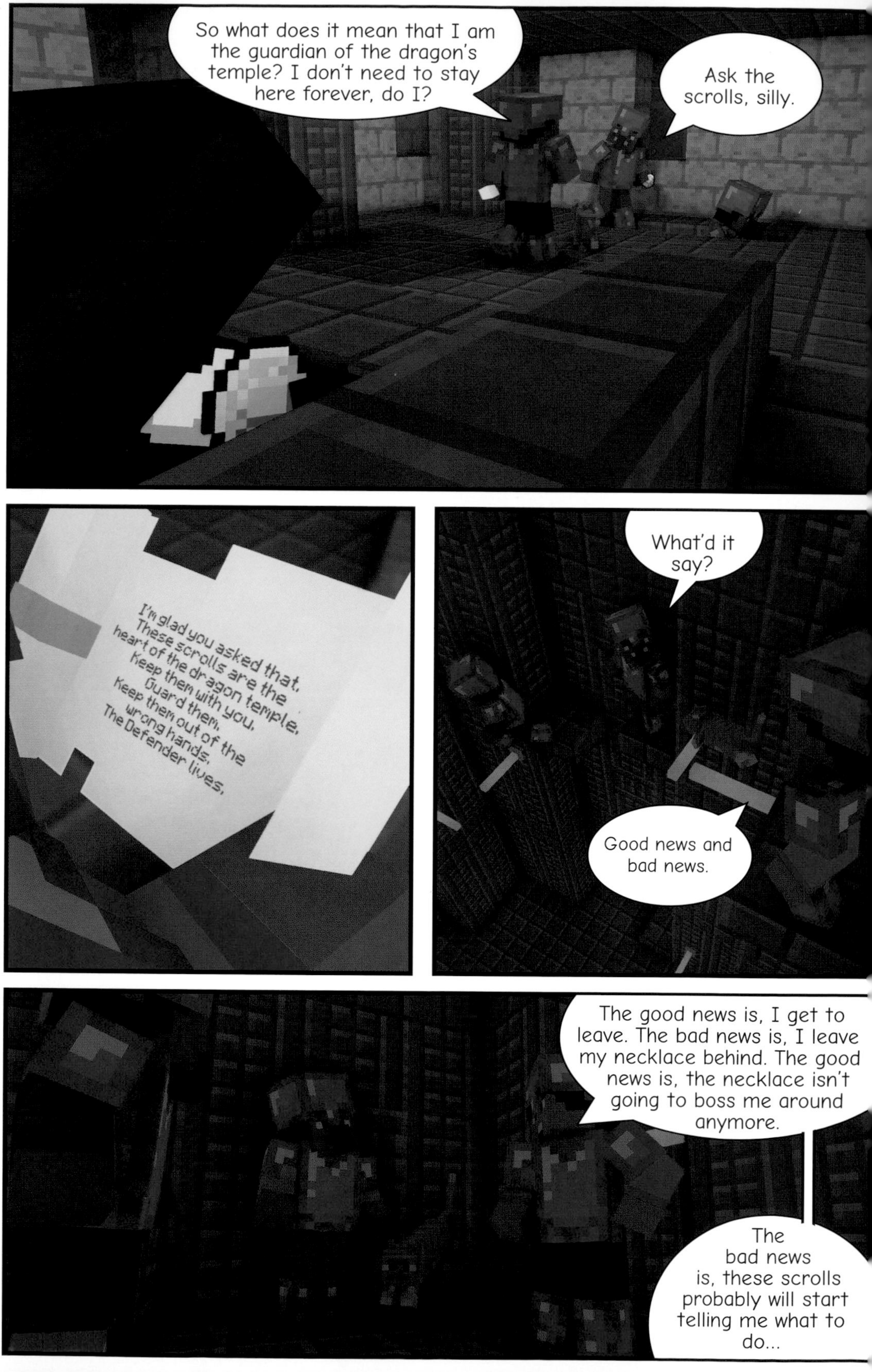
So what does it mean that I am the guardian of the dragon's temple? I don't need to stay here forever, do I?
Ask the scrolls, silly.
I'm glad you asked that. These scrolls are the heart of the dragon temple. Keep them with you. Guard them. Keep them out of the wrong hands. The Defender lives.
What'd it say?
Good news and bad news.
The good news is, I get to leave. The bad news is, I leave my necklace behind. The good news is, the necklace isn't going to boss me around anymore.
The bad news is, these scrolls probably will start telling me what to do...

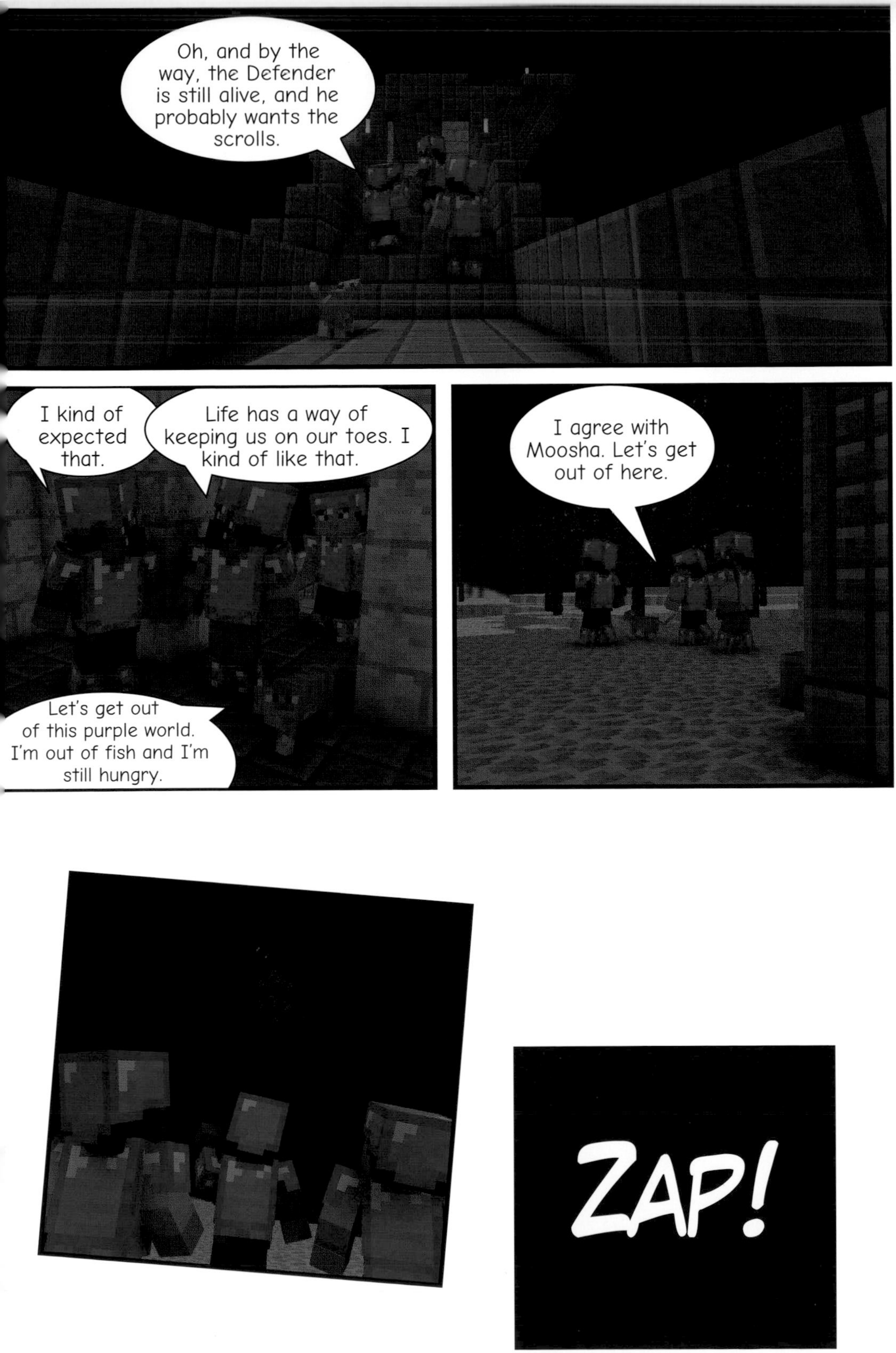
Oh, and by the way, the Defender is still alive, and he probably wants the scrolls.
I kind of expected that.
Life has a way of keeping us on our toes. I kind of like that.
Let's get out of this purple world. I'm out of fish and I'm still hungry.
I agree with Moosha. Let's get out of here.
ZAP!

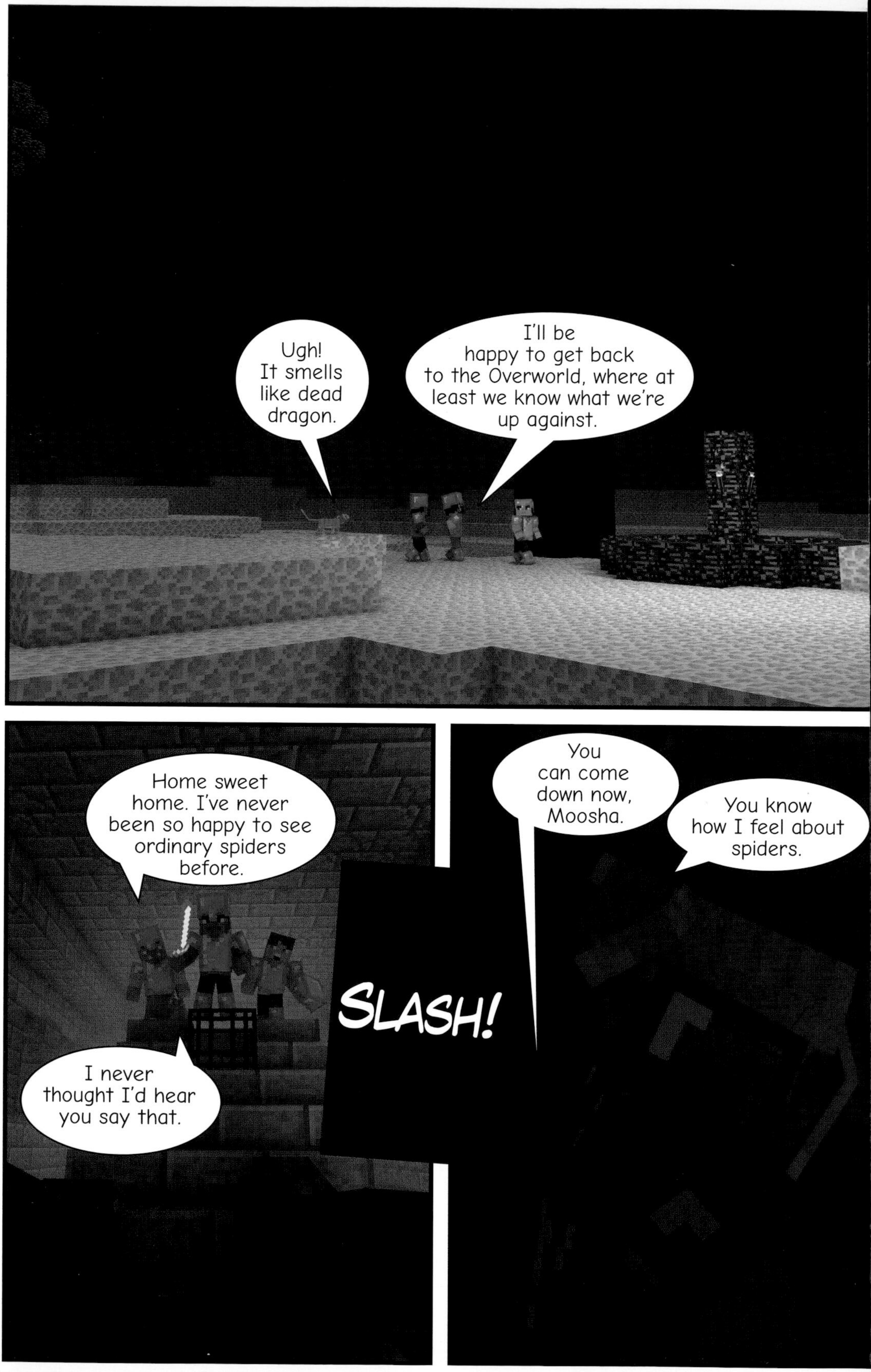

Ugh! It smells like dead dragon.
I'll be happy to get back to the Overworld, where at least we know what we're up against.
Home sweet home. I've never been so happy to see ordinary spiders before.
I never thought I'd hear you say that.
SLASH!
You can come down now, Moosha.
You know how I feel about spiders.

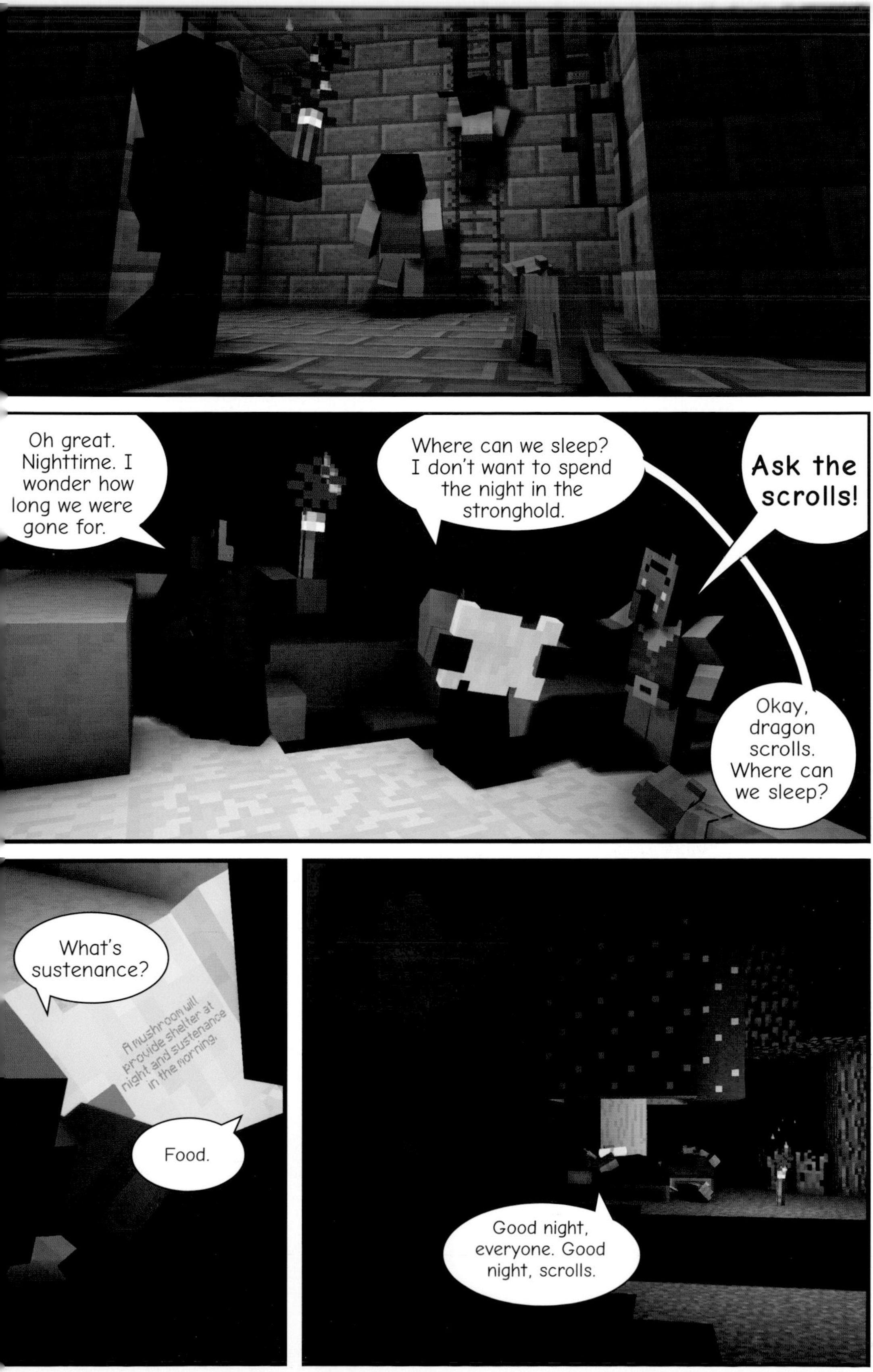
Oh great. Nighttime. I wonder how long we were gone for.
Where can we sleep? I don't want to spend the night in the stronghold.
Ask the scrolls!
Okay, dragon scrolls. Where can we sleep?
A mushroom will provide shelter at night and sustenance in the morning.
What's sustenance?
Food.
Good night, everyone. Good night, scrolls.

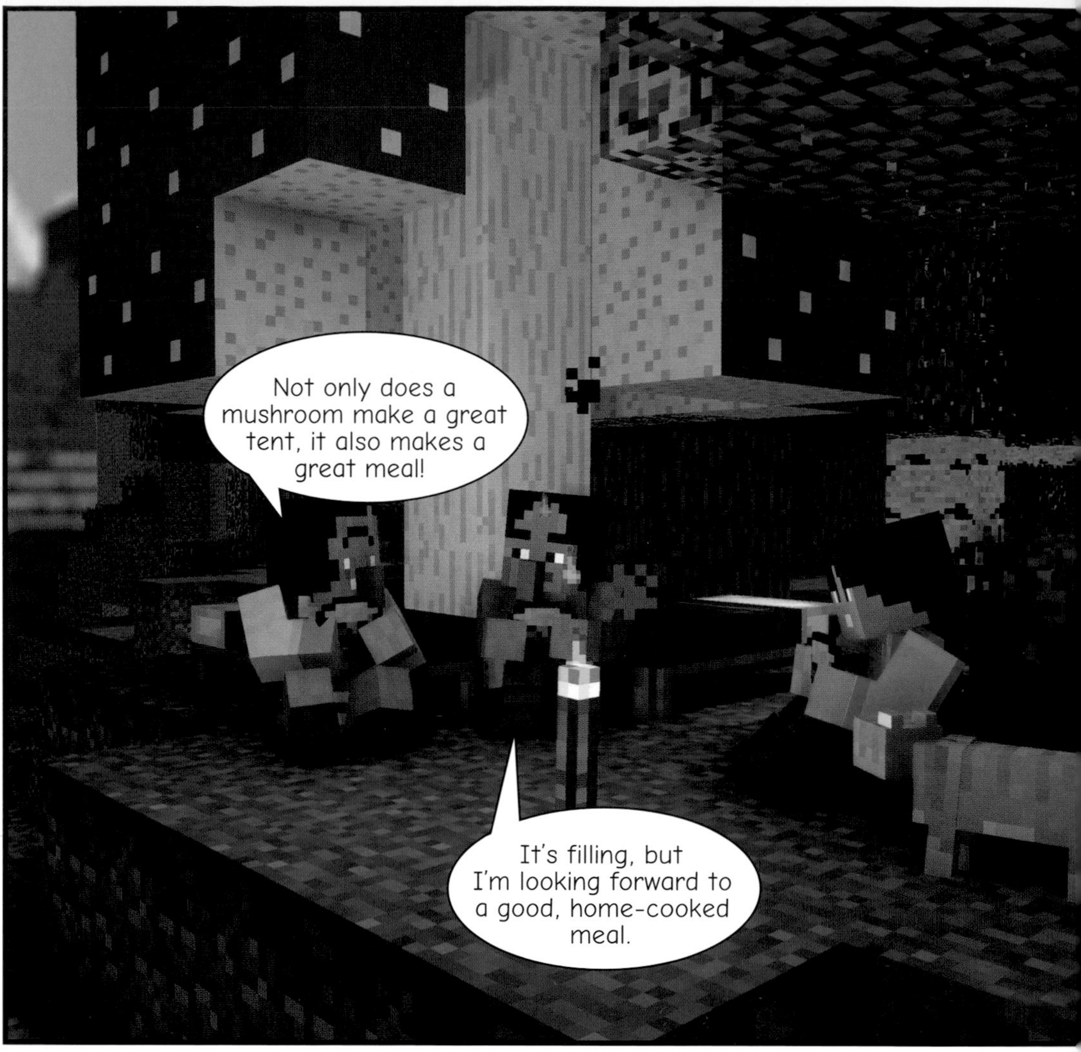
Not only does a mushroom make a great tent, it also makes a great meal!
It's filling, but I'm looking forward to a good, home-cooked meal.

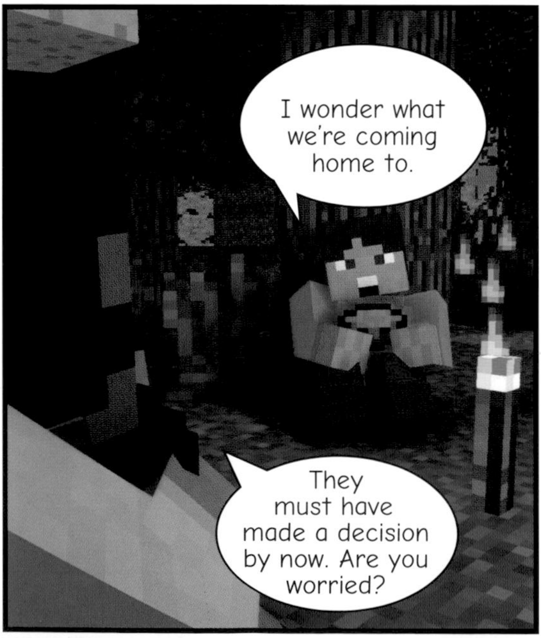
I wonder what we're coming home to.
They must have made a decision by now. Are you worried?

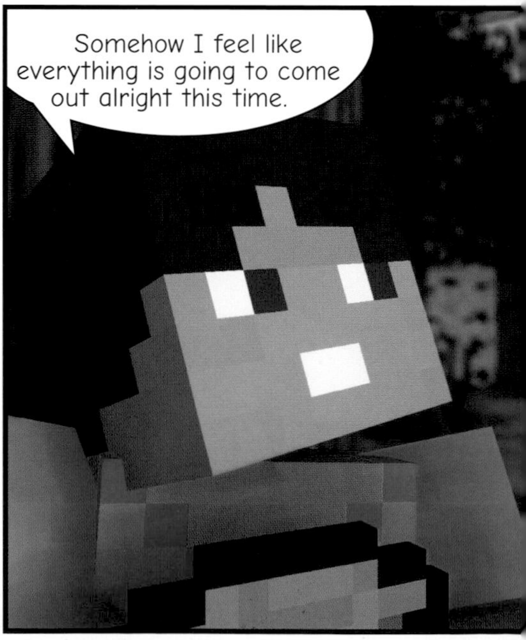
Somehow I feel like everything is going to come out alright this time.

CHAPTER 12

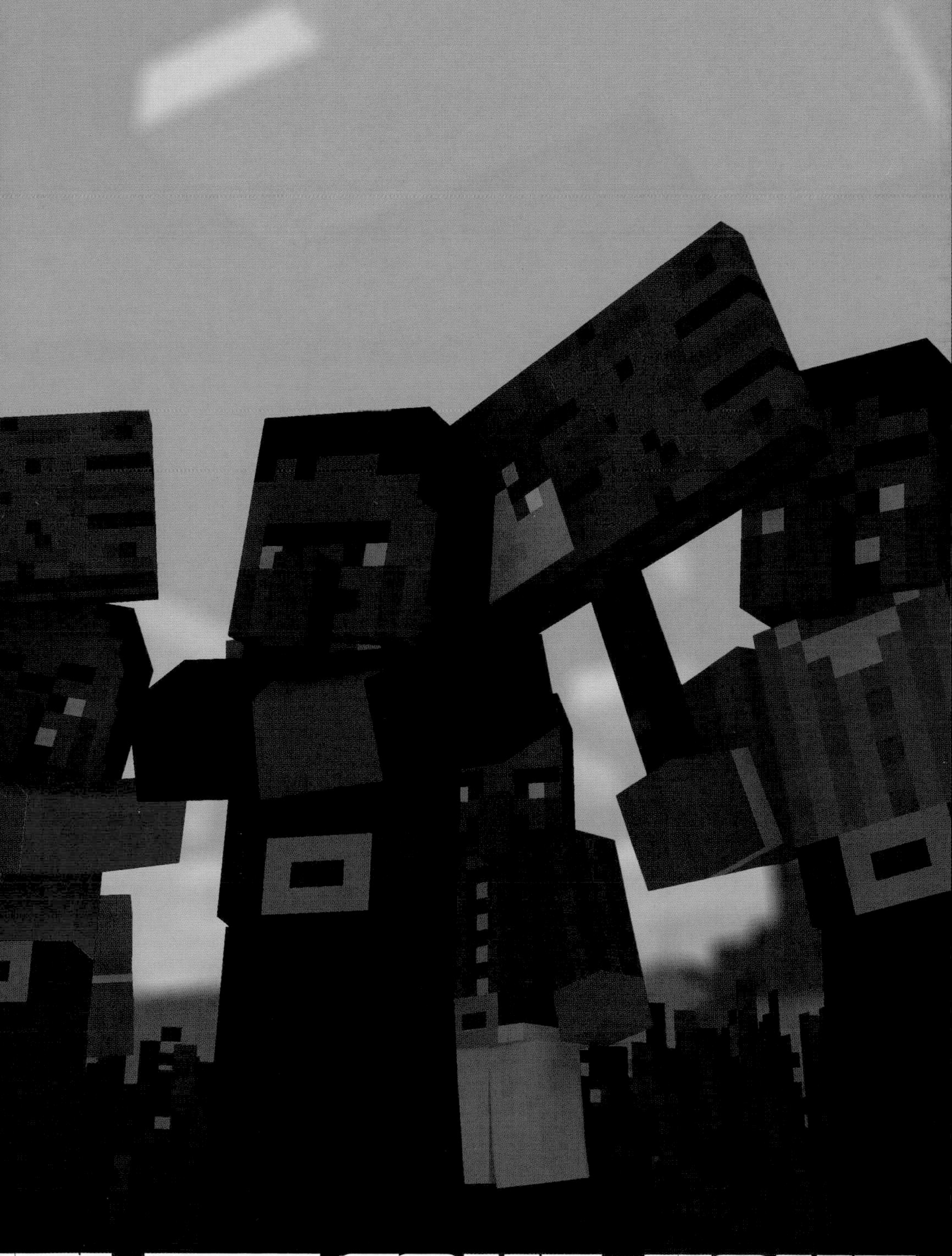

UN-WELCOME HOME

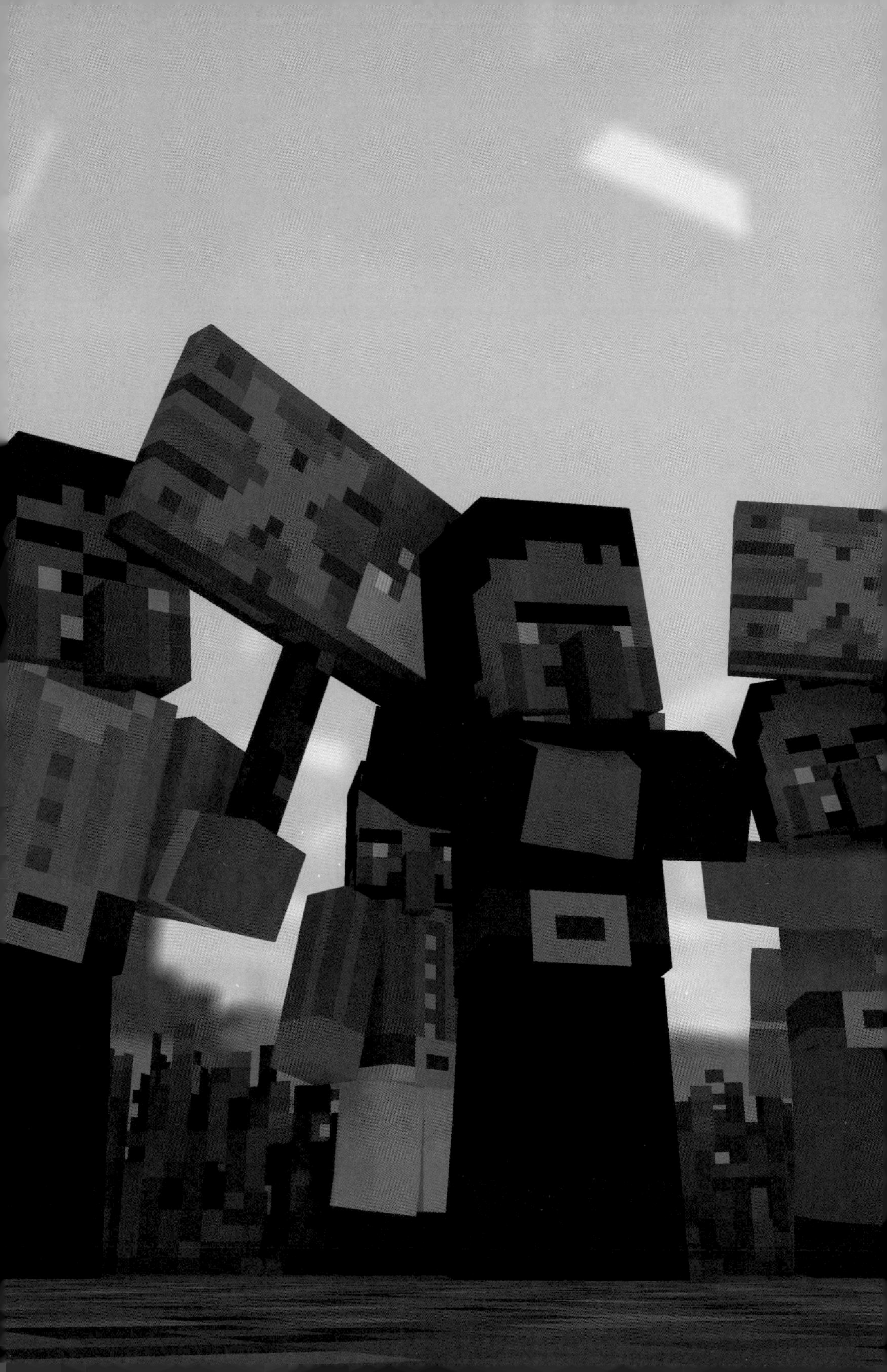

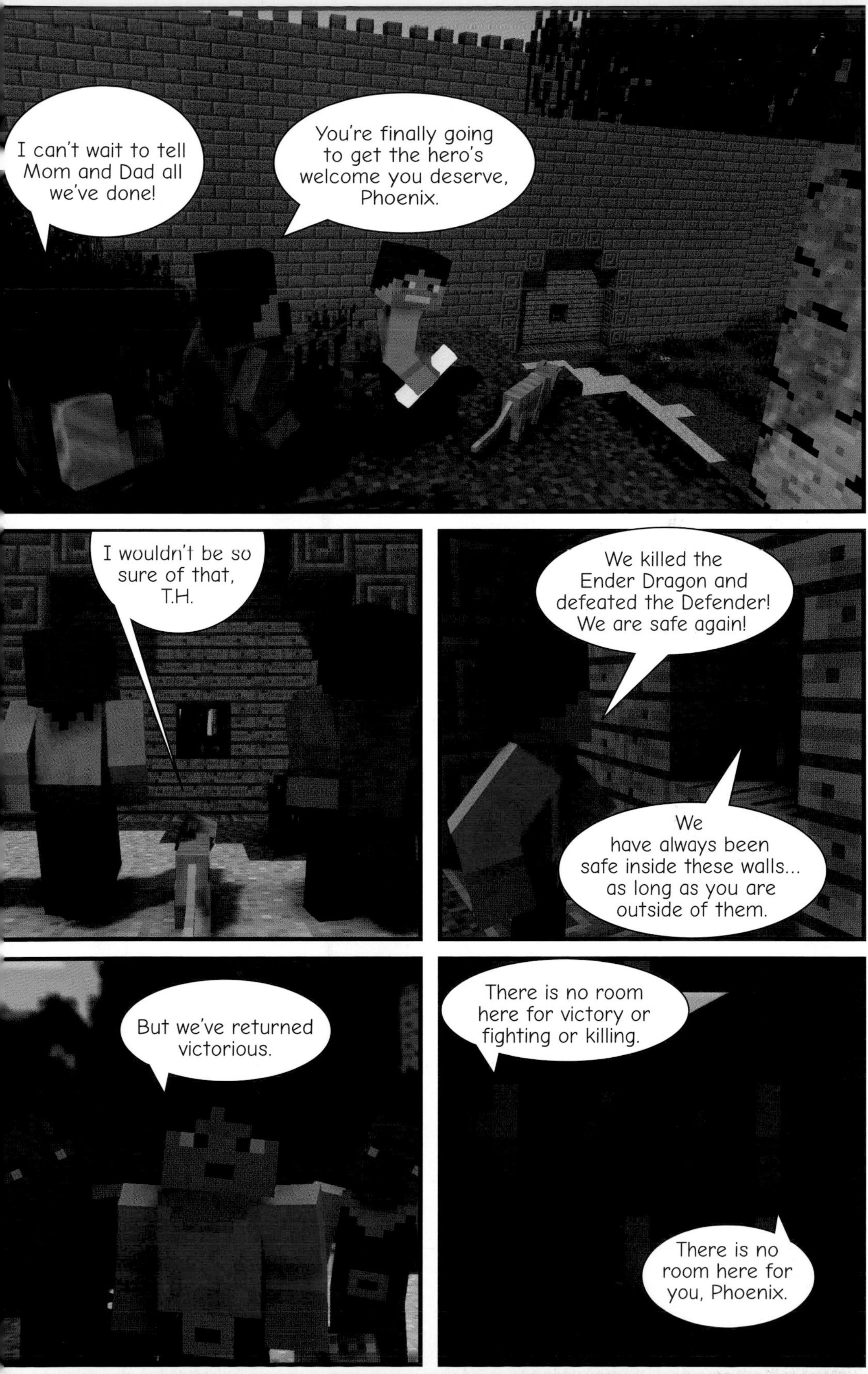
I can't wait to tell Mom and Dad all we've done!
You're finally going to get the hero's welcome you deserve, Phoenix.
I wouldn't be so sure of that, T.H.
We killed the Ender Dragon and defeated the Defender! We are safe again!
We have always been safe inside these walls... as long as you are outside of them.
But we've returned victorious.
There is no room here for victory or fighting or killing.
There is no room here for you, Phoenix.

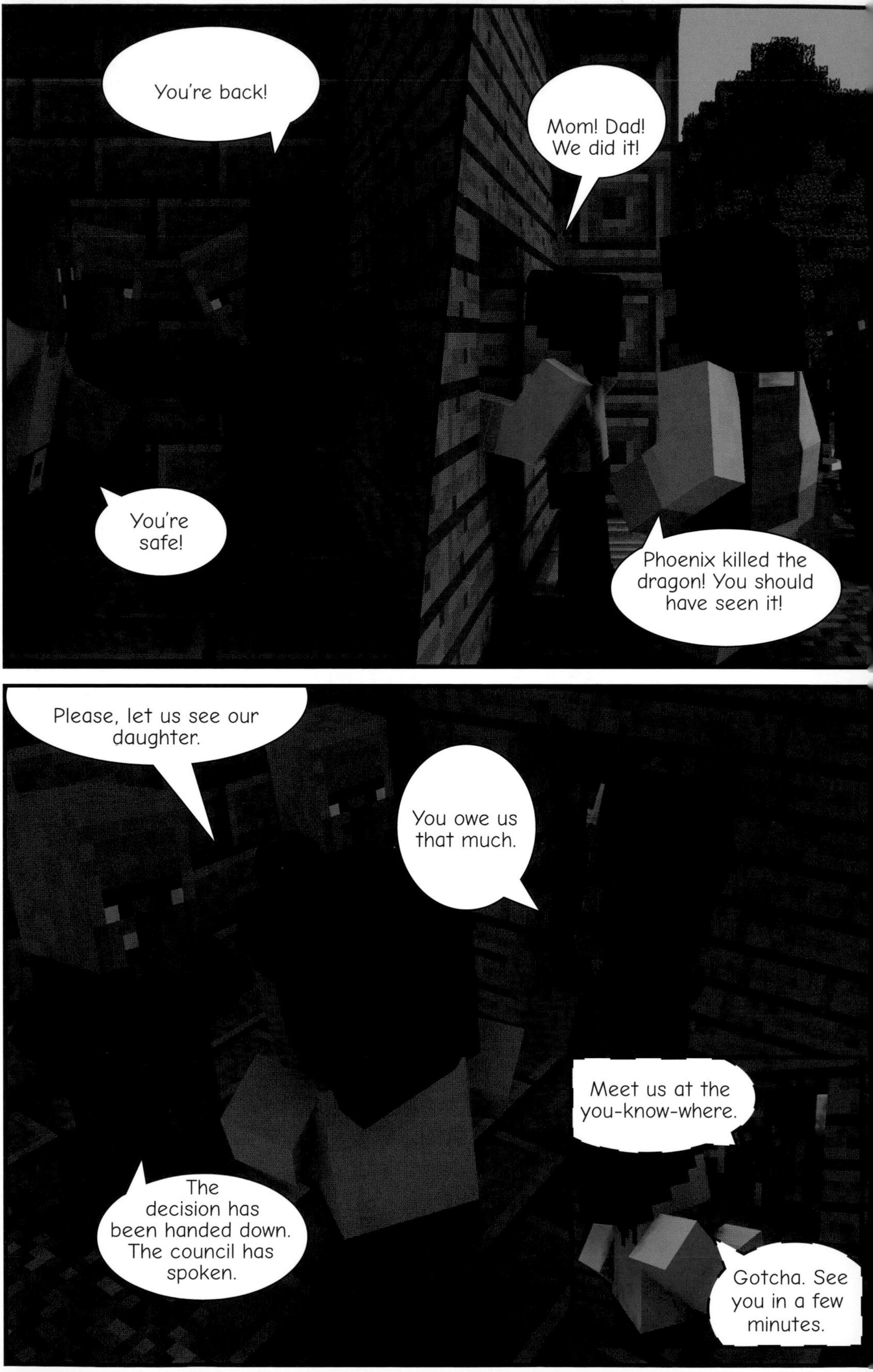
You're back!
Mom! Dad! We did it!
You're safe!
Phoenix killed the dragon! You should have seen it!
Please, let us see our daughter.
You owe us that much.
Meet us at the you-know-where.
The decision has been handed down. The council has spoken.
Gotcha. See you in a few minutes.

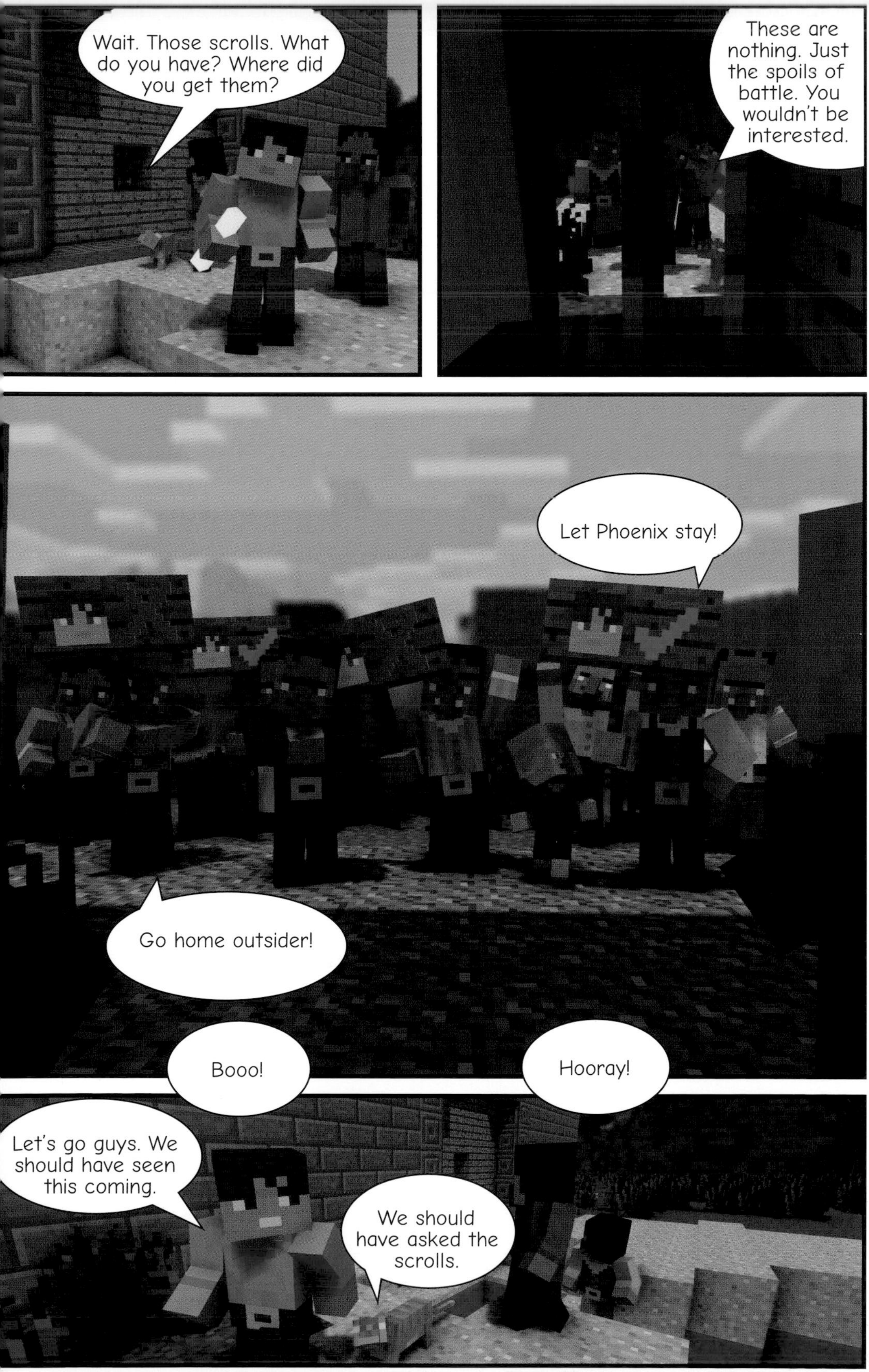
Wait. Those scrolls. What do you have? Where did you get them?
These are nothing. Just the spoils of battle. You wouldn't be interested.
Let Phoenix stay!
Go home outsider!
Booo!
Hooray!
Let's go guys. We should have seen this coming.
We should have asked the scrolls.

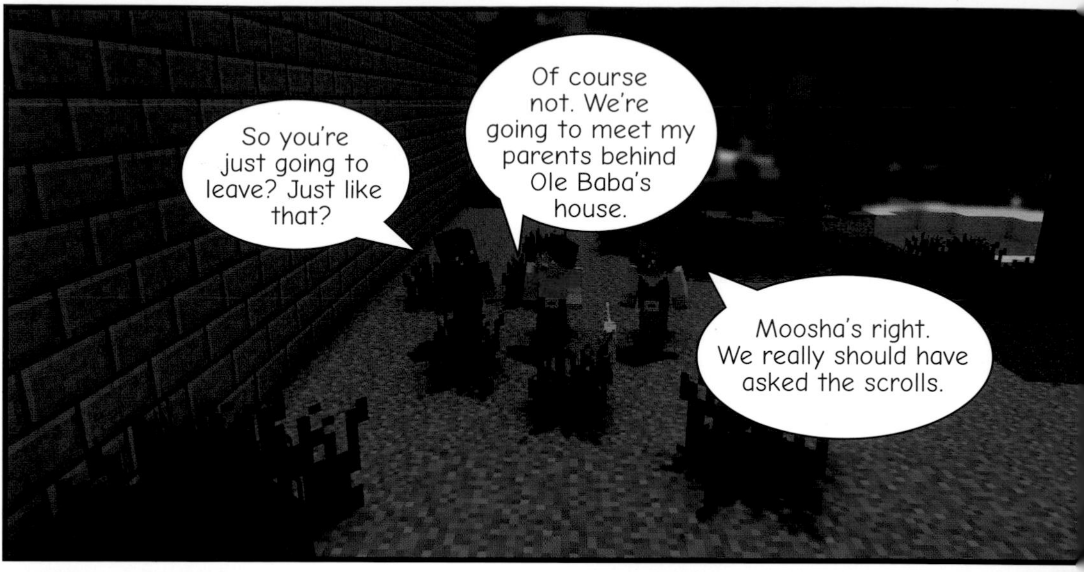
So you're just going to leave? Just like that?
Of course not. We're going to meet my parents behind Ole Baba's house.
Moosha's right. We really should have asked the scrolls.

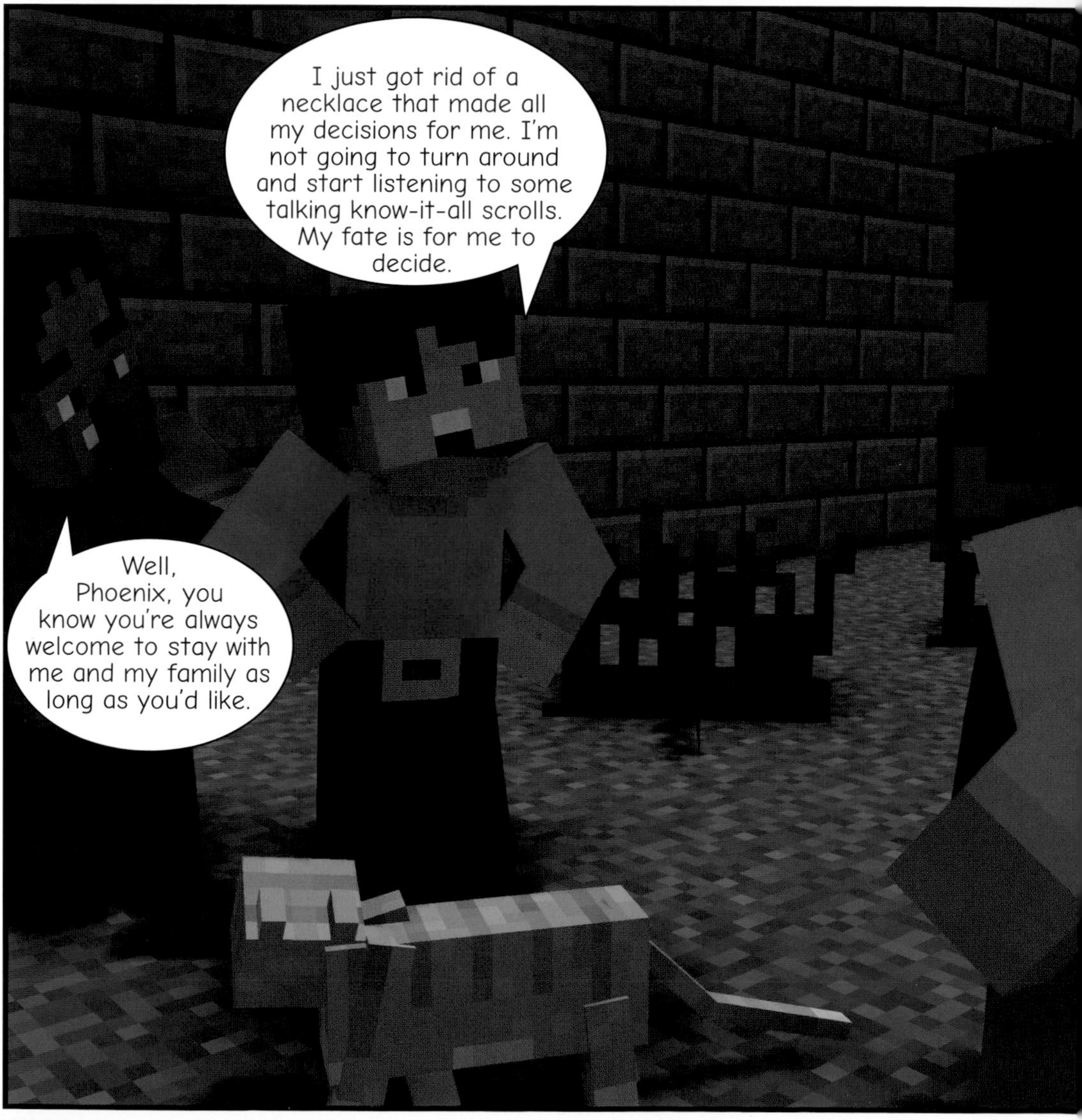
I just got rid of a necklace that made all my decisions for me. I'm not going to turn around and start listening to some talking know-it-all scrolls. My fate is for me to decide.
Well, Phoenix, you know you're always welcome to stay with me and my family as long as you'd like.

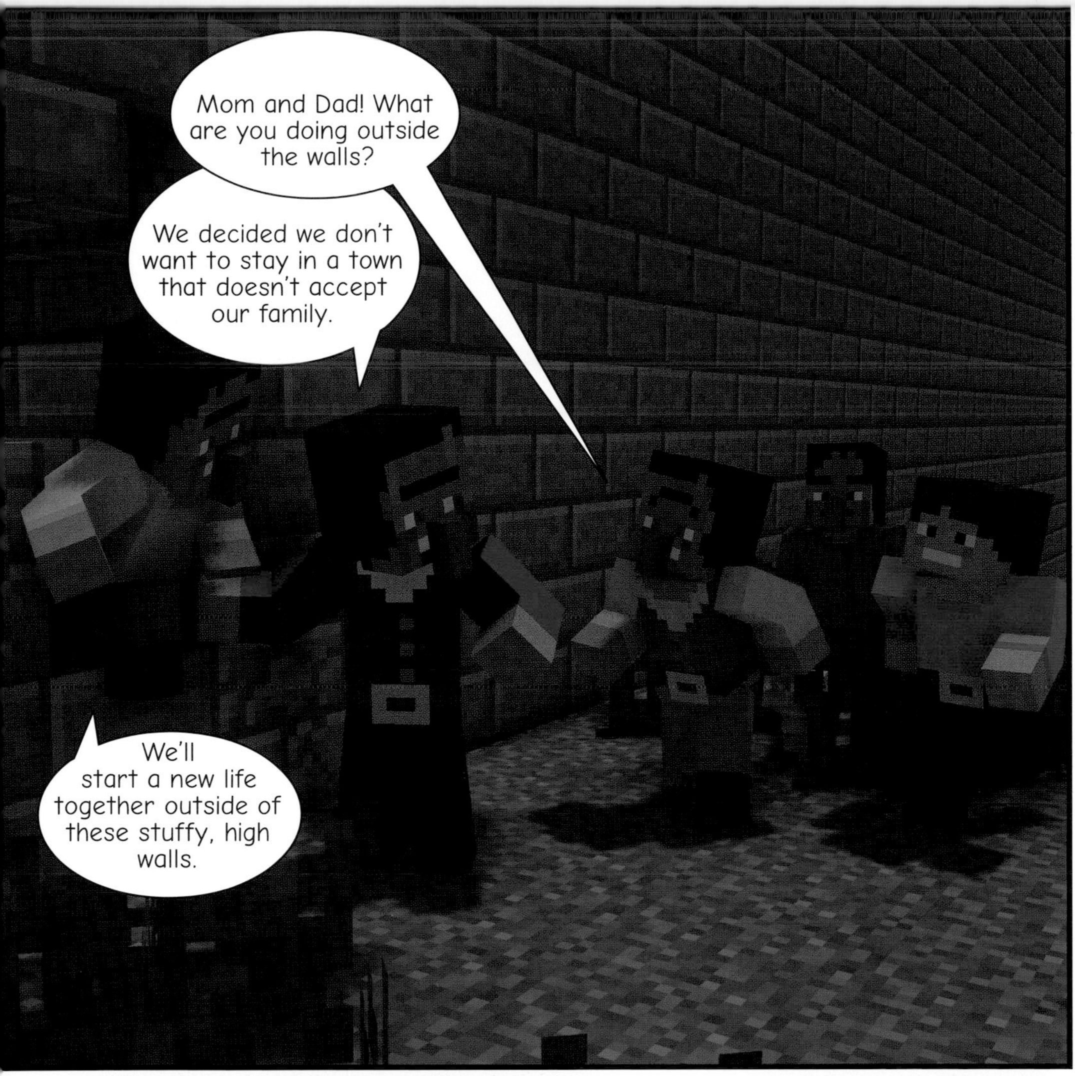
Mom and Dad! What are you doing outside the walls?
We decided we don't want to stay in a town that doesn't accept our family.
We'll start a new life together outside of these stuffy, high walls.

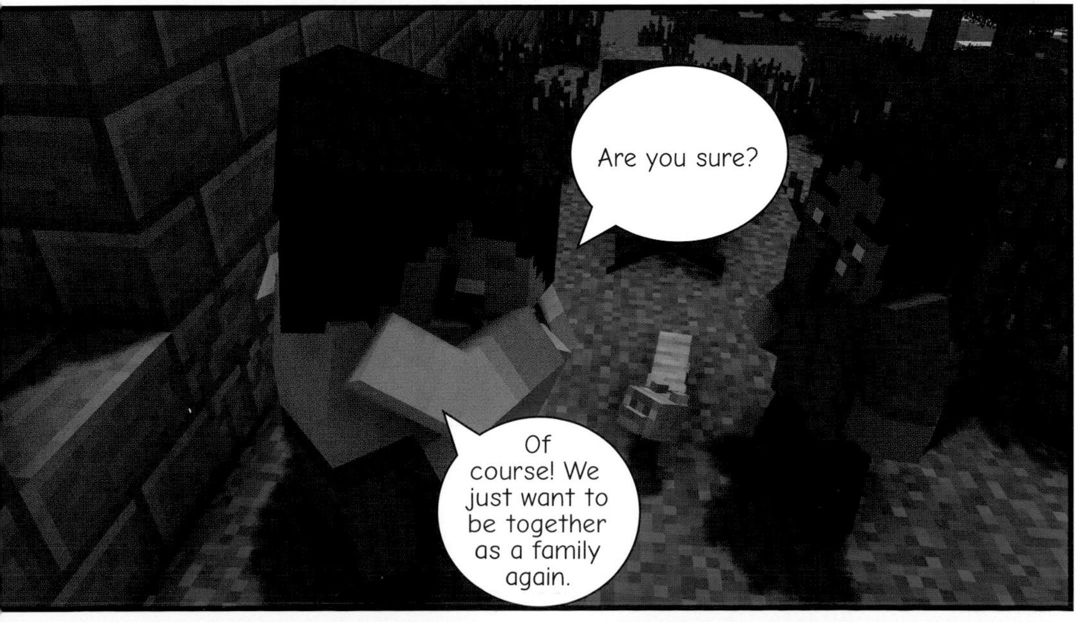
Are you sure?
Of course! We just want to be together as a family again.

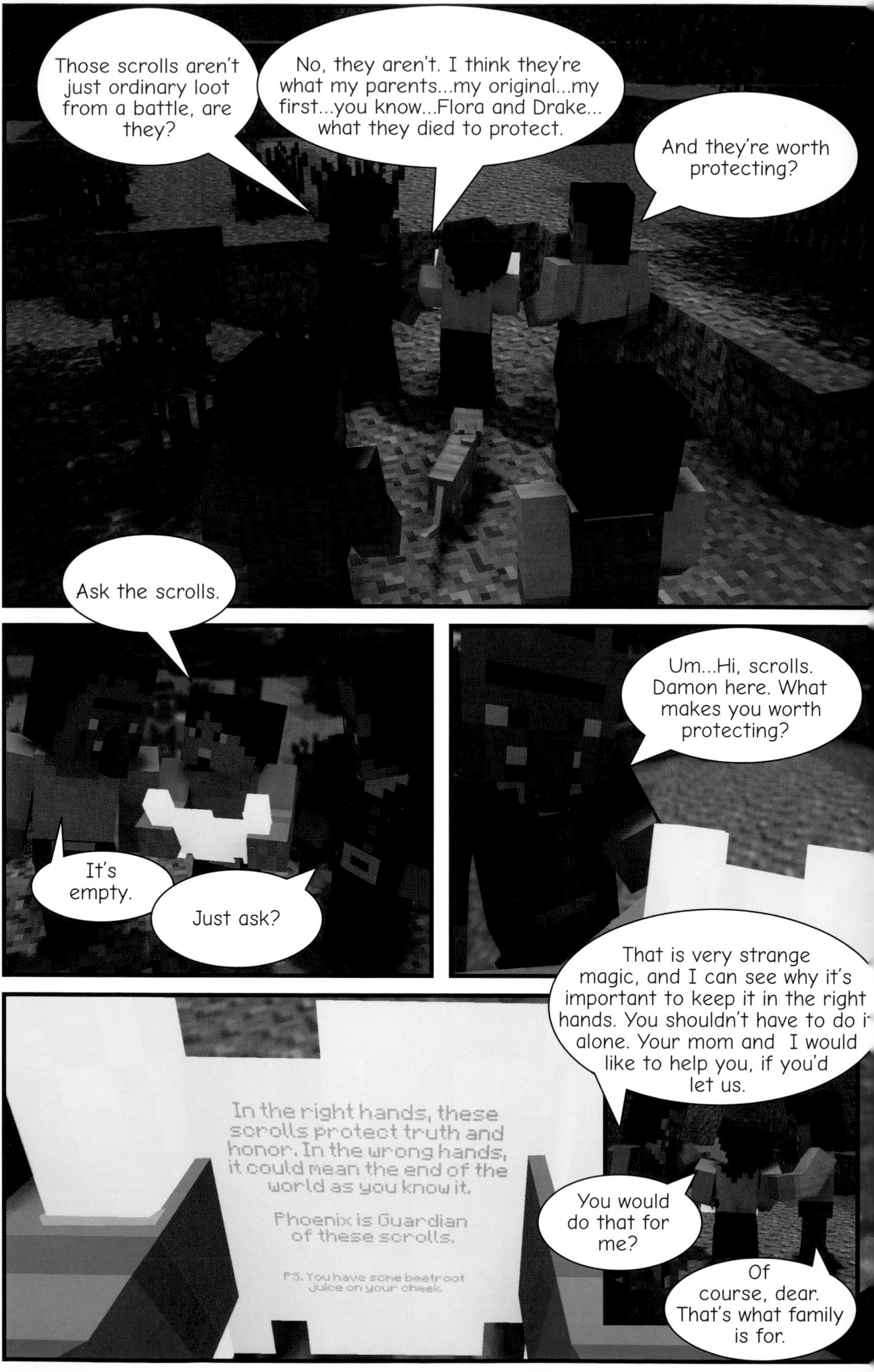
Those scrolls aren't just ordinary loot from a battle, are they?
No, they aren't. I think they're what my parents...my original...my first...you know...Flora and Drake... what they died to protect.
And they're worth protecting?
Ask the scrolls.
It's empty.
Just ask?
Um...Hi, scrolls. Damon here. What makes you worth protecting?
In the right hands, these scrolls protect truth and honor. In the wrong hands, it could mean the end of the world as you know it.
Phoenix is Guardian of these scrolls.
PS. You have some beetroot juice on your cheek.
That is very strange magic, and I can see why it's important to keep it in the right hands. You shouldn't have to do it alone. Your mom and I would like to help you, if you'd let us.
You would do that for me?
Of course, dear. That's what family is for.

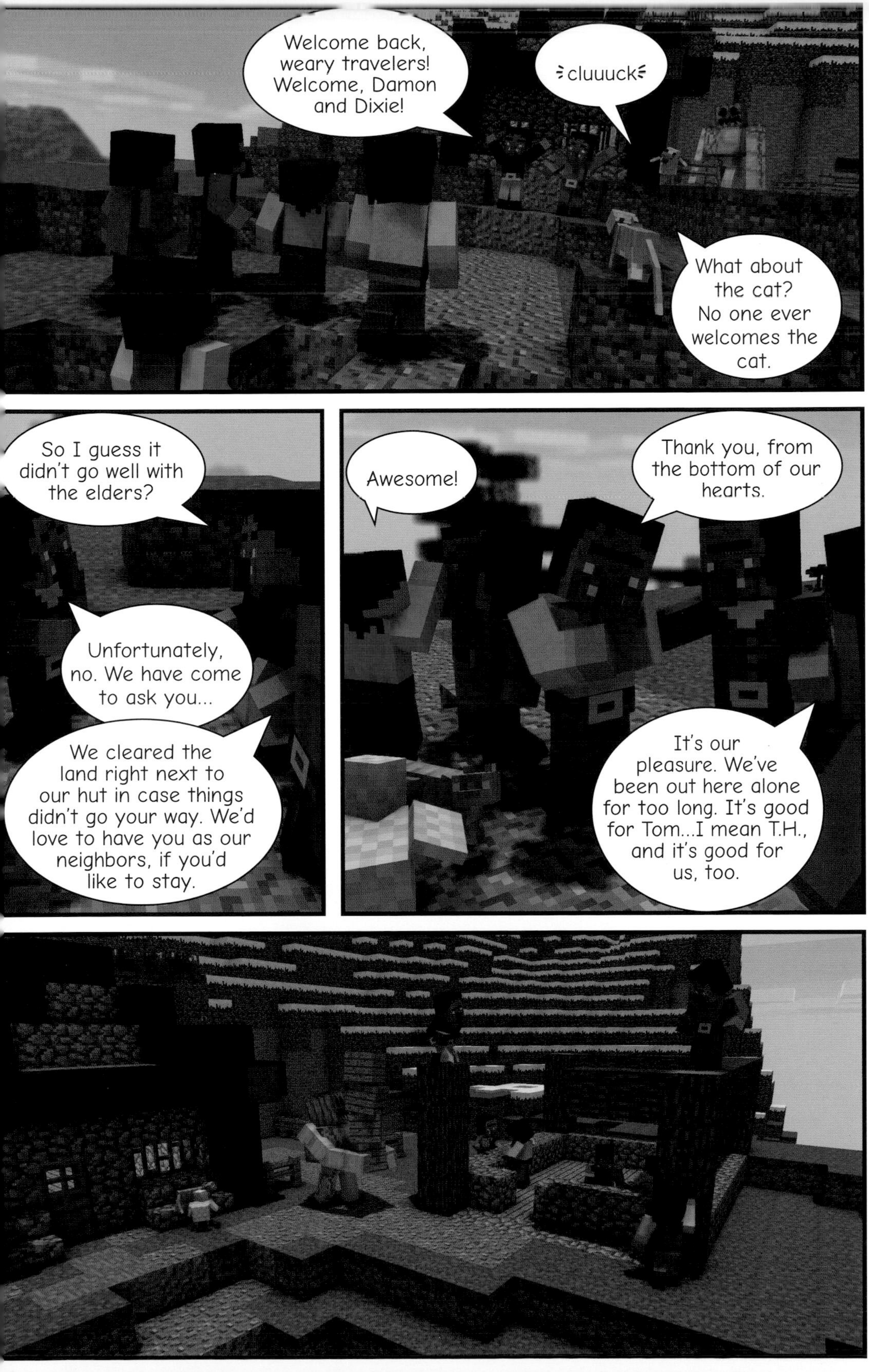

Welcome back, weary travelers! Welcome, Damon and Dixie!
cluuuck
What about the cat? No one ever welcomes the cat.
So I guess it didn't go well with the elders?
Unfortunately, no. We have come to ask you...
We cleared the land right next to our hut in case things didn't go your way. We'd love to have you as our neighbors, if you'd like to stay.
Awesome!
Thank you, from the bottom of our hearts.
It's our pleasure. We've been out here alone for too long. It's good for Tom...I mean T.H., and it's good for us, too.

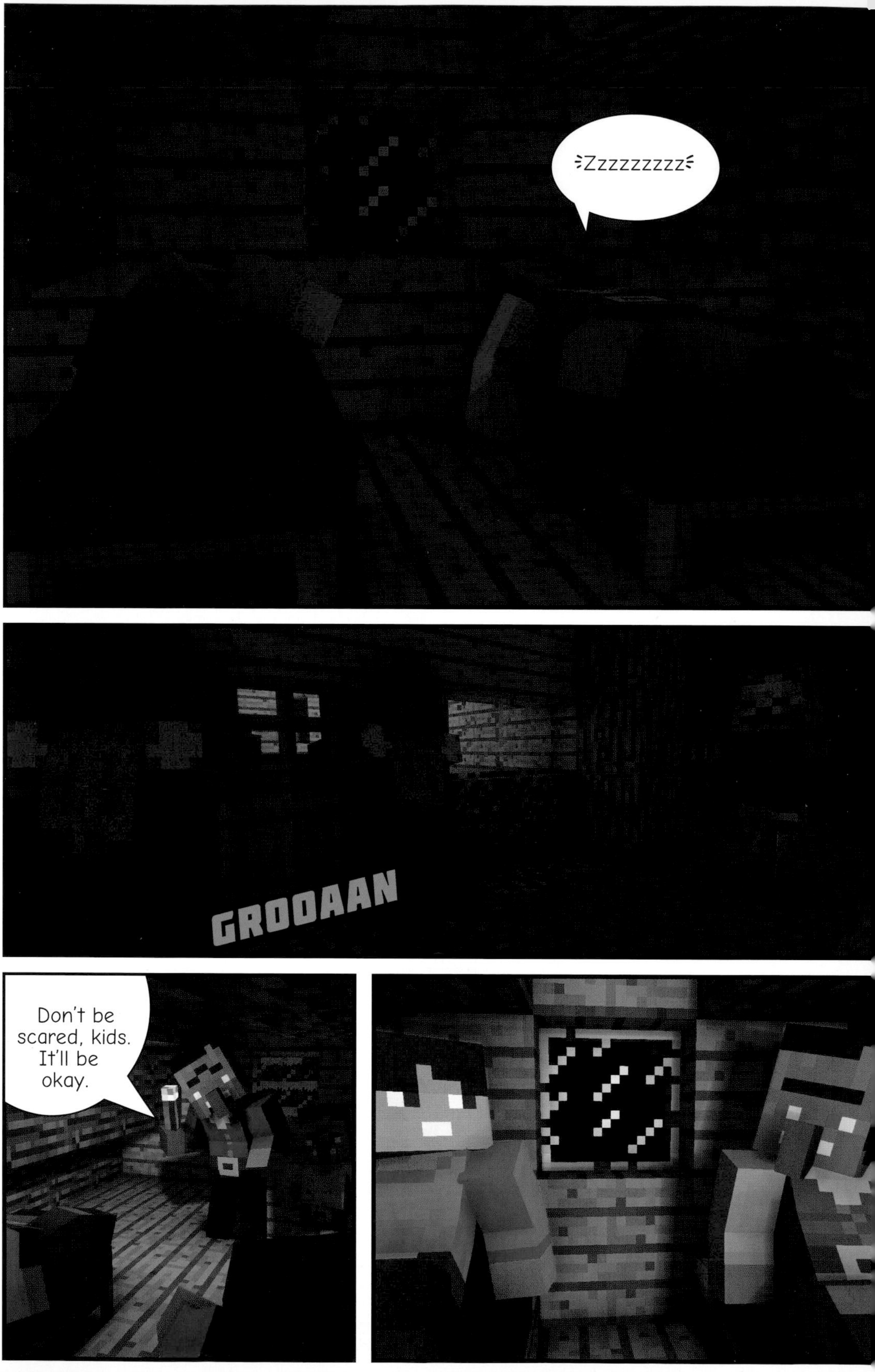
Zzzzzzzzz
GROOAAN
Don't be scared, kids. It'll be okay.

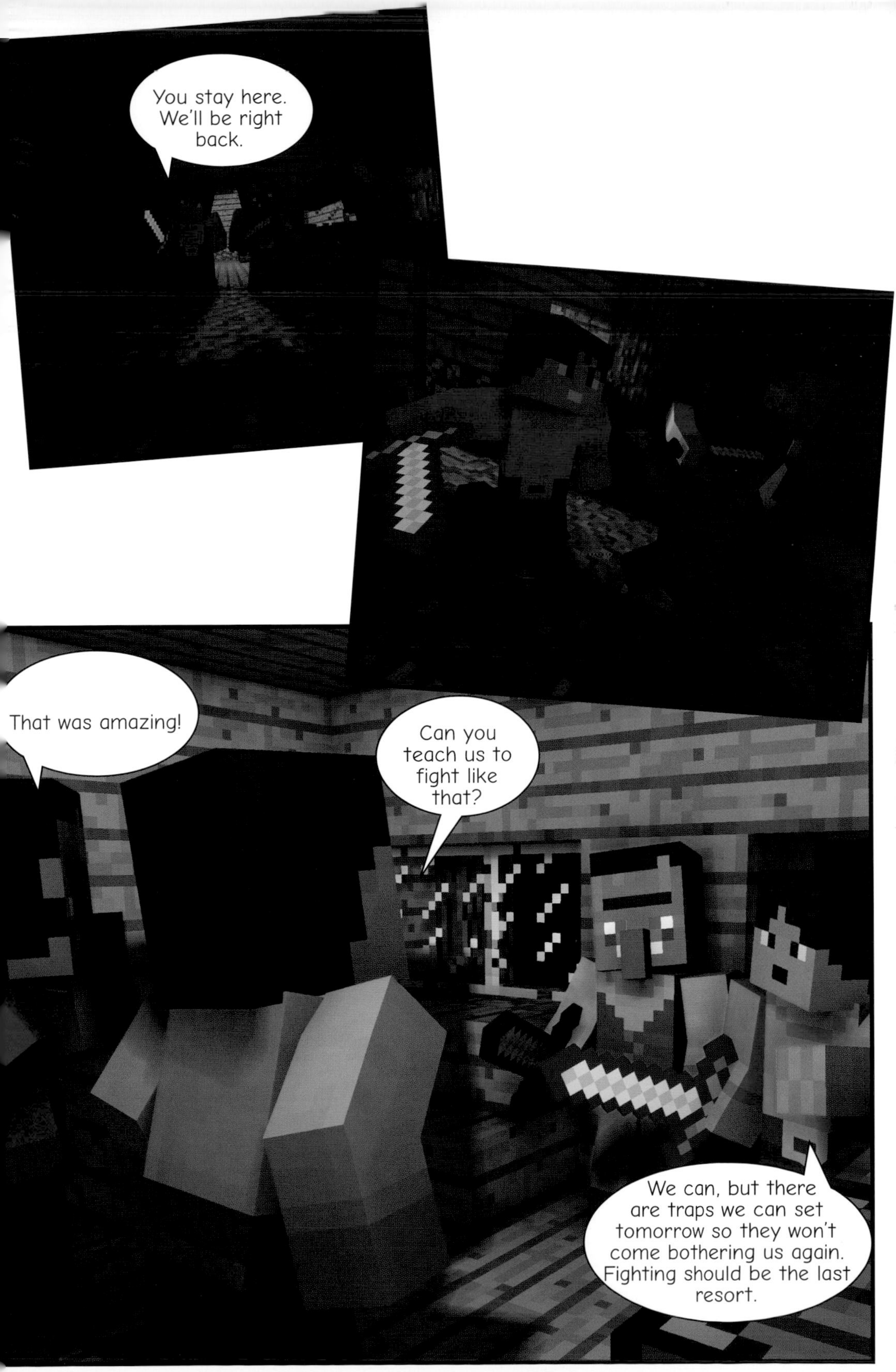
You stay here. We'll be right back.
That was amazing!
Can you teach us to fight like that?
We can, but there are traps we can set tomorrow so they won't come bothering us again. Fighting should be the last resort.

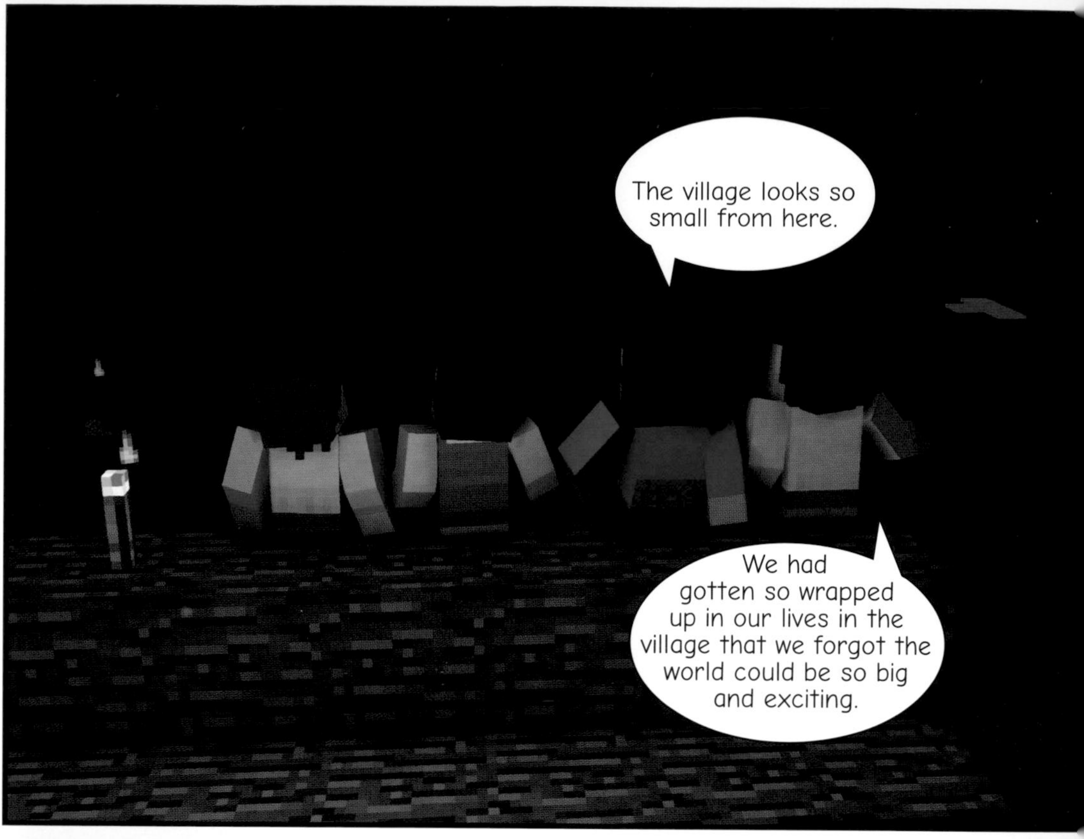
The village looks so small from here.
We had gotten so wrapped up in our lives in the village that we forgot the world could be so big and exciting.

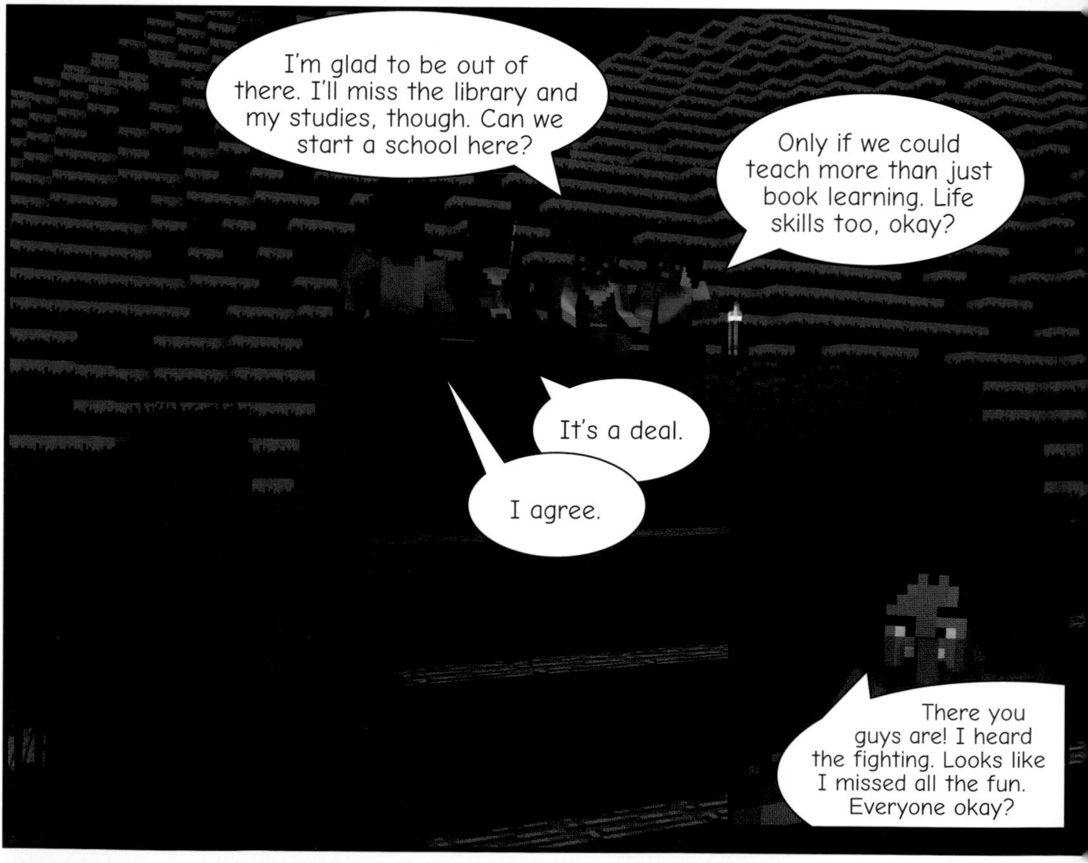
I'm glad to be out of there. I'll miss the library and my studies, though. Can we start a school here?
Only if we could teach more than just book learning. Life skills too, okay?
It's a deal.
I agree.
There you guys are! I heard the fighting. Looks like I missed all the fun. Everyone okay?

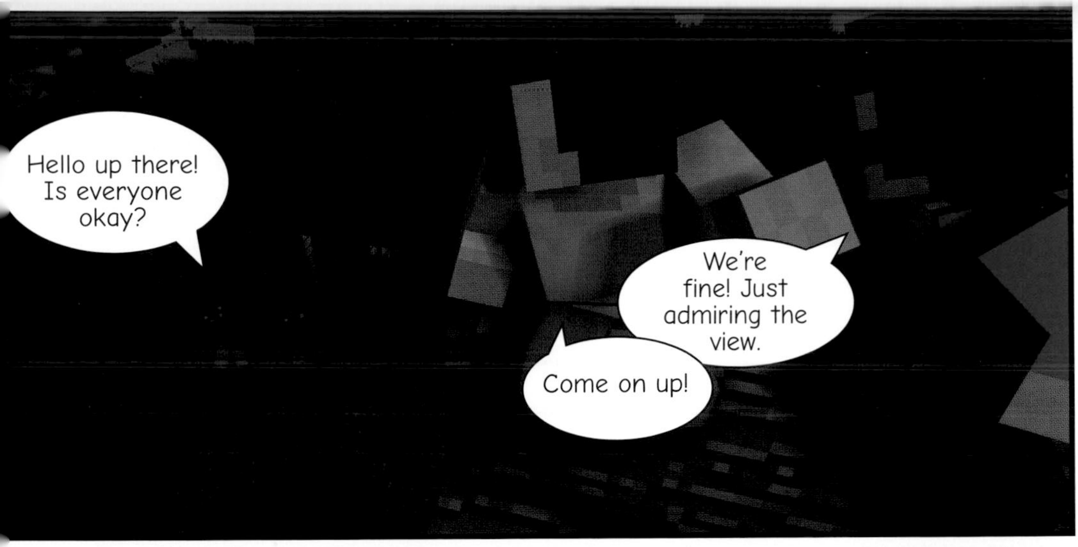
Hello up there! Is everyone okay?
We're fine! Just admiring the view.
Come on up!

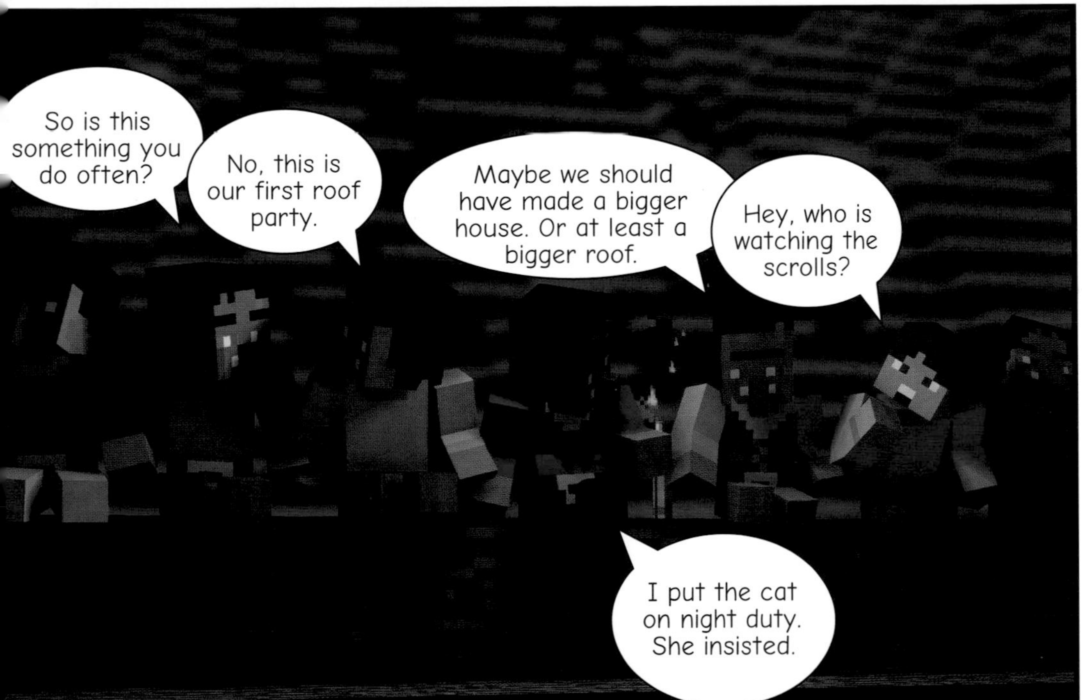
So is this something you do often?
No, this is our first roof party.
Maybe we should have made a bigger house. Or at least a bigger roof.
Hey, who is watching the scrolls?
I put the cat on night duty. She insisted.

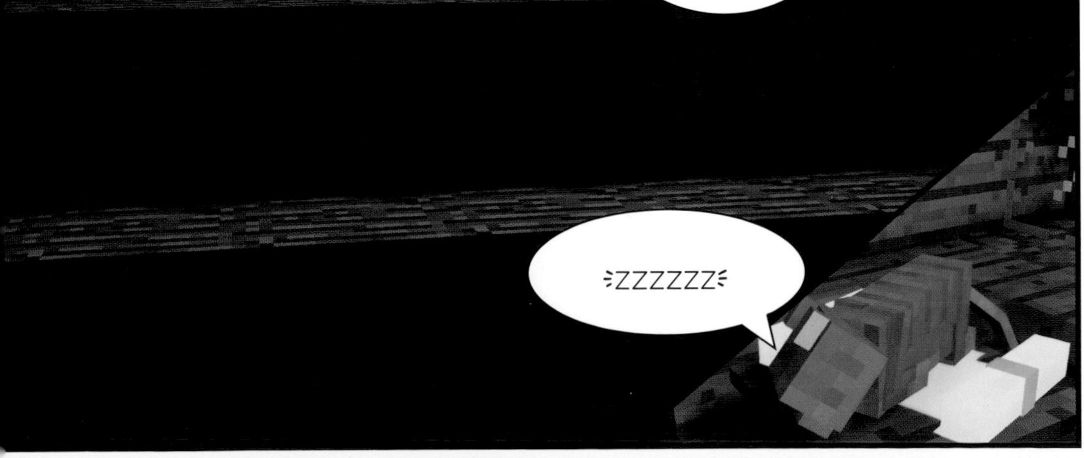
ZZZZZZ

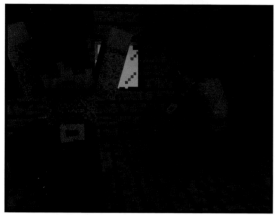

That house wasn't there when we went to bed last night.

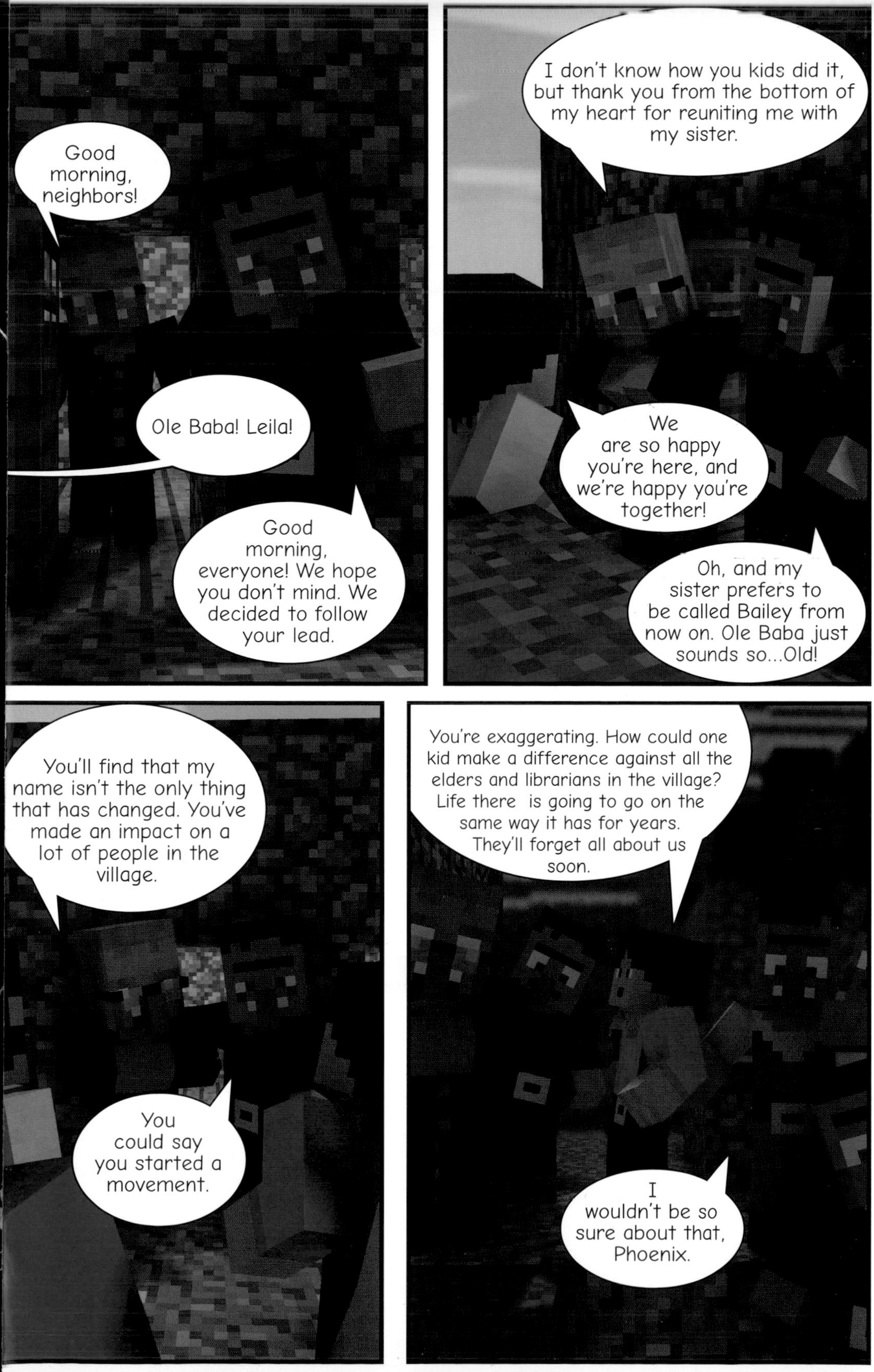
Good morning, neighbors!
Ole Baba! Leila!
Good morning, everyone! We hope you don't mind. We decided to follow your lead.
I don't know how you kids did it, but thank you from the bottom of my heart for reuniting me with my sister.
We are so happy you're here, and we're happy you're together!
Oh, and my sister prefers to be called Bailey from now on. Ole Baba just sounds so...Old!
You'll find that my name isn't the only thing that has changed. You've made an impact on a lot of people in the village.
You could say you started a movement.
You're exaggerating. How could one kid make a difference against all the elders and librarians in the village? Life there is going to go on the same way it has for years. They'll forget all about us soon.
I wouldn't be so sure about that, Phoenix.

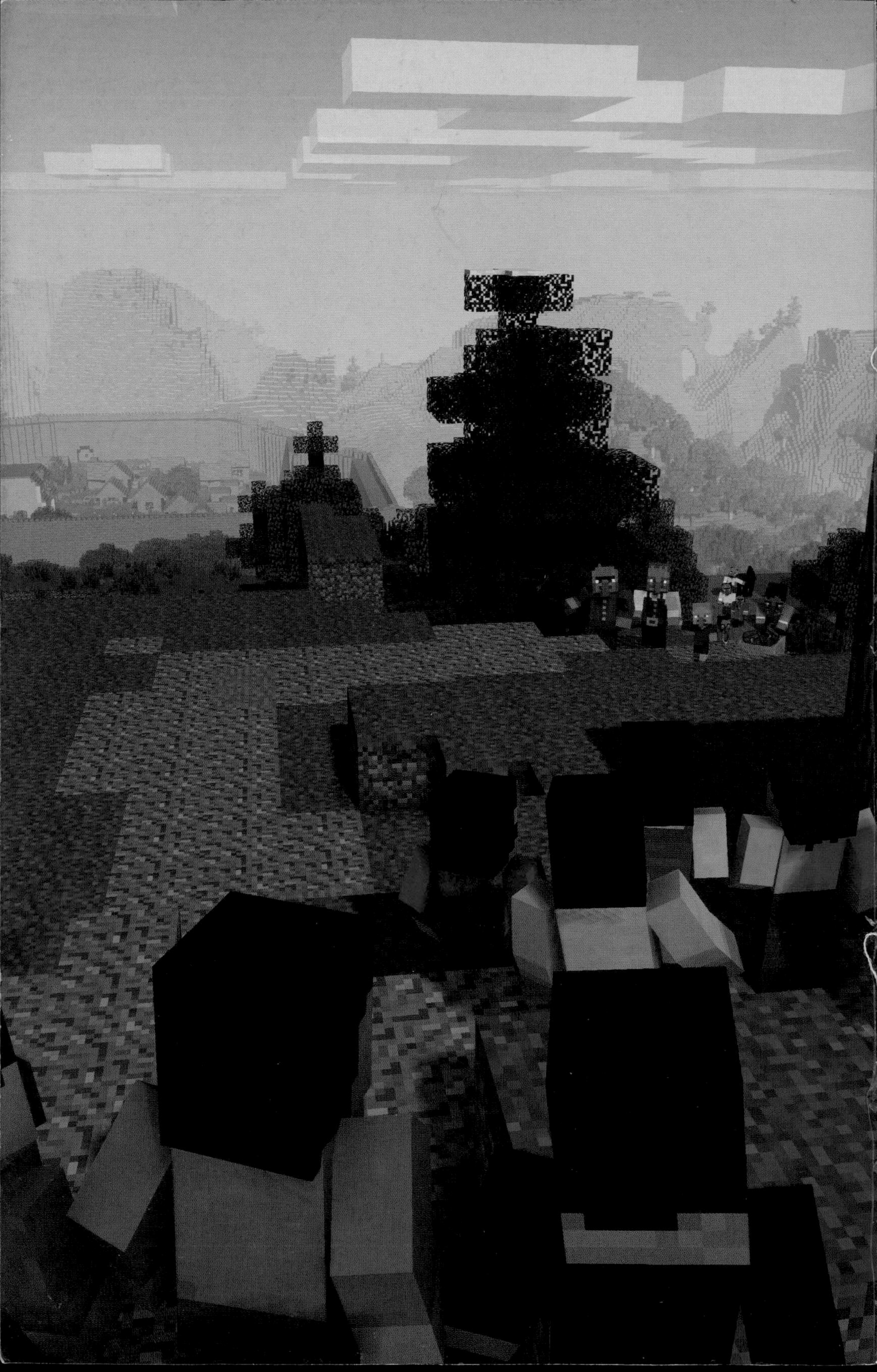